TOP SECRET

WITH BONUS EPILOGUES, TOO!

TOP SECRET

SARINA BOWEN
ELLE KENNEDY

CHAPTER 1
A STRANGER FOR THE WIN

KEATON

"Look," Annika whispers in my ear. Under the table, her small hand squeezes my thigh, while her cheek gently nudges my chin toward the doorway. "He's cute."

"Subtle," I tease before giving the object of her attention a cursory glance. He's just a tall guy with brown hair, nothing special as far as I can tell. "How about we save this conversation for later?"

She rolls her eyes. "We both know there won't be a conversation, Keaton. You like playing along, but you won't actually go through with it." This time she forgets to lower her voice.

"Go through with what?" one of my frat brothers asks from across the table. Tanner, Judd, and I had popped into the campus Starbucks for a caffeine fix after practice. Annika's next class is directly across the street, so she'd come to say hi before class.

"Nothing," I tell Tanner.

If you can call your girlfriend wanting a threesome with another dude "nothing."

Yup, my girlfriend wants a threesome. And here I'd thought

that, after six years together, Annika couldn't surprise me anymore.

She and I have been inseparable since junior year of high school. I know every last detail about her, from her food preferences to her pet peeves. I know she gets anxiety in long lines, that she sneezes any time she gets a whiff of cinnamon, that she loves the beach but hates skiing.

What I didn't know was that my girlfriend fantasizes about threesomes. The first time she brought it up, I thought she was kidding around. Annika Schiffer, heiress to a home-furnishings fortune, wants to bang two guys at the same time? *Yeah right.*

My girl is the president of her sorority, wears a pearl necklace (and not the fun kind) on a daily basis, and made me wait until we were eighteen to lose our virginities to each other. Don't get me wrong—she's not some uptight rich bitch with a stick up her butt. She's fun and warm and fierce when someone tries to mess with her or her loved ones.

But she's also... I'll just say it: vanilla.

I didn't think she was serious about the threesome thing until last week, when I'd asked her what she wanted for her birthday and she brought up the idea again.

I move my lips to her ear so Tanner and Judd can't overhear. "Don't you worry, babe, there'll be more than just a conversation," I rasp.

She shivers, and then flashes me a dazzling smile. Her face is flawless. Classic features, pouty lips, and smooth skin that's just the right amount of dewy. She works hard and spends a lot of money for that skin. I've been in her bathroom at the sorority house, so I've seen all the products she puts on her face to keep it looking so perfect. Not to mention the monthly facials, which require her to fly to New York every month because this little college town we live in doesn't have a "competent aesthetician"— her words, not mine.

It helps that her father owns a helicopter that can accommodate her monthly treks. I'm not one to judge, though. My dad has his own jet.

"I can't wait," she says before hopping off my lap. "Come over tonight after practice, okay, baby? I have to go to class now."

"I'll see you later."

"Bye, boys." Annika's hand flutters in a wave on her way to the door.

"Later!" Tanner calls after her. And if I'm not mistaken, he takes a longing look at her ass.

"Dude," I say. "If you're going to eye-fuck my girlfriend, you could at least be subtle about it."

"Why?" Tanner argues. "She'd be flattered. And you should know how good you've got it. Besides, I'm harmless." He flashes me a big smile. "What are we doing this weekend, anyway?" Tanner asks. "The Presidential Dance-off, right?"

I shake my head. "That's, like, in two weeks, man."

"Really? Why did I think it was sooner?"

"Because you're stupid," Judd offers helpfully.

Tanner gives him the finger, before turning back to me. "Do you know what you're doing for yours yet?"

I have no clue. And no, dancing isn't an actual requirement for our fraternity's presidential race. But it used to be. A few decades ago, the candidates running for frat president decided a dance-off was the *only* way to decide who was more fit to lead. Hence, the Presidential Dance-off was born. On our living room walls, there are old photos of well-dressed men with slicked-back hair and girls in poodle skirts on their arms.

My fraternity has long-held traditions that began well before the invention of the red Solo cup. But these days, Alpha Delta has evolved. Or devolved, depending who you ask. Instead of perfecting his twist and his mashed potato, the presidential candidate is expected to dazzle the other members by planning a kickass event. I'm talking epic. Monumental. The kind of party that will be remembered for years to come.

Although, like dance moves, I'm not entirely sure that party planning is a solid indicator of what makes a good president. Sure, frats throw a lot of parties, but there's a social committee for that.

The role of president is actually pretty lame, according to Reedsy, our current prez. He pulled me aside after I threw my name in the race and admitted that it's a boring gig and that I should reconsider. "So much fucking responsibility on your shoulders, dude," he'd bemoaned.

For a moment, I'd almost bailed. To be honest, I'm only running because my dad was president of Alpha Delt in his heyday, and my granddad before him. But that's also the reason I *couldn't* bail. My father would lose his shit if the Hayworth legacy ended with me.

So I have ten days to plan a legendary party.

"Maybe I can just hire an event planner?" I suggest.

"No way." Judd's response is immediate. "If that fuckhead Bailey finds out, he'll have you impeached."

"You can't impeach someone until he's elected," Tanner points out.

Still, I don't want to be accused of cheating. What a pain in the ass this whole thing is. "We can brainstorm about this on Sunday night. We have a game to win on Saturday."

"Oh, we're going to win," Tanner promises.

But I'm not so sure. Not only am I worried about the Northern Mass offense, I think my father is driving up for the game. So winning isn't even enough. If the Northern Mass players aren't crying into their helmets after the fourth quarter, my father will still give me hell at brunch the next day.

And here I thought weekends were meant to be relaxing.

"Fine," Judd says. "We'll talk about your campaign after the other meeting on Sunday night."

"What other meeting?" I search my brain and come up empty.

"Pledge Committee," he says, gulping the last of his coffee.

Oh, phew. "I don't have to go to that one. I'm not on PC this year."

"But I sent you that email?" Judd whines. "I told you I need you there. Initiation night is coming up and my committee is lame."

"Who's on it, anyway? What do you have planned?" *Note to self: be conveniently unavailable on Sunday night.* There is no way I'm sitting on the Pledge Committee again. Dealing with last year's pledge class was a total pain in the ass.

"There's Ahmad, who's smart but boring. Paul, who's just boring. Owen, who's fun but not exactly creative. And Paxton, who's just a tool." He sighs. "Whatever. At least Bailey isn't on it this time. Remember what a buzz kill he was last year? I fucking hate that guy."

No big secret there. Judd's had it in for Luke Bailey ever since the guy rushed Alpha Delt sophomore year. And say what you will about Judd, but he's not an asshole unless he feels you've given him a reason. He's a bro to the core—he believes in male bonding, high fives, and, in his mind, a friendship isn't official unless you've bled together, partied together, and nursed your twin hangovers the morning after.

Luke Bailey doesn't subscribe to this philosophy. The moment he scoffed at Judd's attempt at a fist bump, he earned himself an enemy in Judd Keller.

Since then, their tumultuous acquaintanceship has only gotten worse. Luke is a cocky ass when he wants to be, and Judd hates feeling like he's being mocked or judged.

Oh, and then Bailey banged Judd's ex. So there's that.

"You exert too much mental energy on that guy," Tanner informs Judd. Tanner's a psych major, so he's constantly dishing out (pretty good) advice that everyone mostly ignores. "Holding onto anger isn't conducive to robust mental health."

"First of all, say the word *robust* one more time and I'll clock you. You know how I feel about that, bro." Indignation flashes in Judd's eyes. "And second of all, Luke Bailey screwed my girl-friend! I'm never *not* gonna be angry at that prick."

"*Ex*-girlfriend," I hedge, but it earns me a deep scowl from

Judd. The two of us are teammates, and I do feel loyalty to him, but I'm also not afraid to call it like it is. "You and Therese were broken up for months."

"Me and Therese are *never* broken up. Sure, we take short breaks, a hiatus or two. But she's my girl," Judd says tightly. "Everybody knows that."

"Bailey says he didn't," Tanner says.

"That's bullshit. He's a liar. And now he's trying to screw K over!" Judd growls. "He joined the presidential race to get back at me. I just know it."

"You think?" Tanner looks skeptical. "Because that would be sociopathic lengths to go to just to spite you."

"Yeah," I agree with a chuckle. "Bailey's a prick, but I can't see him taking on the huge responsibility of running a fraternity just to flip you the metaphorical bird." Although if I'm being honest, I don't *know* why Luke Bailey is running for prez. The guy hasn't shown much interest in frat activities since he joined us.

"He totally would," Judd argues.

"Hey, we got class now," Tanner reminds our sulking buddy. "We should book it over there."

"Fine." Judd scrapes his chair back and gets to his feet. His cloudy gaze meets mine again. "I'm serious, man. Bailey is bad news, and we need to kick his ass in this campaign. There's no way I'm letting him be our president."

"Don't worry. He won't be."

Once my friends are gone, I let out a tired sigh. I don't particularly care about Judd's beef with Bailey at the moment. I have a football game to win, a campaign to plan, and a father to impress.

And a girlfriend to please.

I go up to the counter to get a refill, then settle in my cozy corner of the coffeehouse and open the app I downloaded last night. I hadn't lied to Annika earlier—her birthday request is in the forefront of my mind. I just need to do some investigating first.

Welcome to Kink!

Add a profile pic.

Add bio.

I'd wanted to fill all this out last night, but my frat brothers suckered me into an epic session of *Red Dead Redemption* that lasted till three a.m. Now I quickly scroll through the camera roll on my phone until I find a suitable one. It's of Annika and me, taken in Easthampton last summer. She looks smokin' hot in a teeny string bikini, and my abs are looking tight, if I do say so myself. I crop out our faces and load the photo.

I skip the bio for now, because I'm feeling impatient. I want to see what this app has to offer more than I want to break my brain thinking of one hundred and forty-five characters to describe how my girlfriend wants to bang two men at the same time.

Actually, that's pretty much the gist of it.

Still, I'm curious to check out the goods. *Kink* is more hookup app than dating app, and I'm pleased to discover it lets you search for users who've expressed interest in certain arrangements.

I click on the threesome box in the search section. There are an eye-opening number of options, combinations that hadn't even occurred to me. Annika wants another guy, though, so I ponder the easiest combos.

m/f/m

m/m/f

My finger hovers over the m/f/m button. The other option means the men are allowed to touch, I think. It's the moment of truth. Some guys would hate this idea. I don't, though. I'm a scientist. Experimenting is what I do.

I even dreamt about sex with men once. Or twice. I never mentioned that to Annika. But why would I? I've also dreamt of meeting a dragon who smoked clove cigarettes. The things my brain invents while I'm sleeping aren't newsworthy.

But I'd be lying if I said that Annika's shocking birthday request turns me off. I'll try anything once. And the app lets you click as many boxes as you want. So after looking over my shoulder once more just to make sure nobody I know is watching,

I tap both options and usher in the possibility of taking a walk on the wild side.

The threesome has to be with a stranger, though. I'm certain that any one of my frat brothers would be down to help me give my girl a night to remember. Well, except Dan, who's only down for dudes. And, well, Bailey, who thinks I'm an ass. I think he's an ass, too, so I guess we're even.

But I can't do this with someone I know. What if the whole night is awkward as fuck? If it's a brother, I'll still have to live with him. If it's a teammate, I'll still have to see him in the locker room.

And then there's the opposite scenario. What if it's not awkward as fuck? What if I like it a whole lot?

Yeah, I don't want my buddies judging me. A stranger for the win, then.

I lean back in my chair and start swiping.

CHAPTER 2
NOT STATISTICALLY UNLIKELY

LUKE

I'm questioning all my life choices tonight. And all because of a vending machine.

Here I stand, starving in the student center at eight o'clock on a Thursday. I don't work another shift at the club until tomorrow night, so cash is tight. So I put my last two singles in the snack machine and punch the button for the peanut butter pretzels. The metal coil turns, and the bag begins to move.

My stomach gurgles in anticipation. Skipping dinner to geek out in the statistics lab wasn't my smartest move, I suppose. But I'm trying to save both money and time—two things in short supply in my life.

I'm not a lucky guy, though. So before my meager dinner has a chance to fall into my hands, the coil stops turning. And my pretzels are caught there, drooping from the rack, hanging by a corner of the plastic bag. Stuck.

"Shit," I mumble. I give the vending machine one swift thunk with my fist. And nothing happens. *Figures.* "Fucking *shitty luck!*"

"It is unlucky…" a faint voice agrees with me. "…but not statistically unlikely."

I turn around to see a skinny girl in giant glasses waiting for her turn with the goddamn machine. "Any chance you were going to buy peanut butter pretzels, too?"

She shakes her head. "Peanuts put me into anaphylactic shock."

"Bummer. That's also bad luck, but not statistically unlikely."

She grins. "Want to borrow a couple dollars?"

"No thanks," I say quickly. I make it a point to never borrow anything from the rich kids I go to school with. That way, when I graduate summa cum laude and then snag the best possible job, nobody will be able to say that I won it because of their help.

I wish her luck and leave the library. My only choice is to go home to Alpha Delt and make myself yet another cheese sandwich. So I hike my backpack strap a little higher on my shoulder and head for the door.

Crossing the leafy campus always makes me feel like a guy on a movie set. The red bricks. The vintage gas lamps casting yellow circles of light on the pathways. The young Rockefellers and Carnegies, and whoever-the-fuck-else-is-worth-a-mint, crossing past me in their preppy dock shoes.

I love it and hate it at the same time. I've spent my whole life on the outskirts of this town. Nobody from the college ever leaves the campus unless they're headed for the airport. For them, it's like the town doesn't exist off the flagstone pathways.

It exists. And it ain't pretty. Darby is an old mill town that fell on hard times about a century after the college was founded. It used to be quaint and wholesome. Now it's a total shithole.

When I turned eighteen, though, I found a golden ticket in my chocolate bar. Seriously, it was almost that magical. The high school counselor told me to fill out a Darby College application. "The fee is waived by the school for locals. Just roll the dice, kid. You never know. With your test scores, we already know you'll get into State. This application is just for fun."

I'd submitted it and then forgotten about it. But that April, I got a fat envelope in the mail.

"Welcome to Darby College, founded 1804. Here is your scholarship award."

A free ride for the townie. I didn't even believe it when I read the letter. Apparently the state of Connecticut had put pressure on the college to improve their town/gown relationship. And scholarships for townies were the upshot.

Tuition is *free*. If I can just keep my life from crumbling for three more semesters, I'll have a degree from one of the most celebrated colleges in America.

Unfortunately, the scholarship doesn't cover room and board. It's assumed that locals wouldn't need a spot in the dorms. And up until last year, I was fine staying at my mom's place.

But living at home isn't an option for me anymore. So my sophomore and junior years at Darby have been all about fending off homelessness and starvation until I can graduate. Dorms and meal plans are expensive, so I rushed Alpha Delt and took the cheapest room. Problem solved.

Sort of.

Last year I worked two shitty jobs until I found a better gig at a club. The new job pays me more for twelve hours of work than I used to make in twice that much time. But the late hours are killing me.

Come senior year, my school workload will be even more brutal. So I've been brainstorming ways I could cut back on my work hours. Two weeks ago, during a drunken movie marathon with a couple frat brothers, one of them revealed something I hadn't known.

Fun fact: the president of the fraternity doesn't have to pay rent. He gets a free room.

A. Free. Room.

So guess who's running for president?

The Alpha Delta house is a big old Tudor mansion on the outskirts of campus. I strut into the front door like I own the place. Because I do—at least as much as anyone else. It doesn't matter that I'm not third generation Alpha Delt like some of the pretty boys who live here. My dues checks don't bounce, and that's really all that matters.

"Hey, boys," I greet four of my brothers. It's eight p.m. and since none of these guys have jobs, they're playing poker.

"Bailey," grunts Jako, my closest friend in the house. "How'm I doing?"

I move to stand behind him and consider his hand. He has a pair of queens, and there're two tens and an eight on the table thanks to the flop. Two-pair isn't a bad hand, but it wouldn't do to go crazy. Judd just needs one ten in his hand to have three-of-a-kind. As I watch, Judd raises and Jako calls.

I study Judd's face for a second and determine that he's not holding three tens. He's bluffing. But of course I'm not dumb enough to say anything. Judd hates me. So I just wait and watch. After the turn—the queen of hearts—Jako has a full house. He bets again, and everyone else folds.

"You called that mostly right," I say to Jako as he rakes in his winnings. "Probably coulda squeezed Judd for more cash if you'd bet that last round."

"No way," Judd argues, because that dude can't stand me. I unknowingly hooked up with his ex last year at a toga party, which is a serious violation of the bro code.

In my defense, it really wasn't malicious. Therese was cute, I was a bit buzzed, and not once did she mention Judd's name to me. Needless to say, that was the last Alpha Delt party I ever attended. Now I only go to the mandatory events.

According to Jako, the whole disaster could've been avoided if only I was more "engaging." Uh-huh, apparently I don't *engage*.

This is true, but it's not all my fault. I wish my life at Alpha Delt were more like a Hollywood comedy, where my besties and I crack jokes together into the wee hours and enjoy the camaraderie of our crazy college years. And maybe the other guys are living that dream. But I'm working like a dog and trying to keep all the proverbial balls in the air. The guys here have no idea what it's like to be me.

And I don't tell them, because that shit is both dark and boring.

So I haven't gone out of my way to get to know each and every brother, and I guess that's a huge crime. Jako says I would've known about Therese if I'd spent even thirty seconds conversing with Judd.

But why would I converse with Judd? He's been obnoxious to me since the first minute we met. In life, not everyone is going to become BFFs. Some personalities pull you in, others repel you. So I'm friends with the brothers I get along with, and I ignore the rest.

Or I used to, anyway.

Sadly, this perfectly reasonable strategy needs to change if I'm going to be elected president of the frat. I can't afford to have enemies. Which is why I swallow my pride and address Judd. "You played that really smart," I praise him. "Solid bluffing skills. Didn't reveal a tell at all."

There's an awkward silence while he eyes me, his brow furrowing suspiciously. "Thanks?"

I shrug and head for the stairs.

"Play a hand?" Jako calls after me.

"Can't. Got a paper to write." It's not a lie. Although a single compliment for Judd is all I'm able to muster. Besides, I'm starving.

I climb a flight of stairs, and then I climb another one. The third-floor suite consists of a big bathroom and two oddly shaped bedrooms—one giant, one tiny.

Mine is the closet-sized room, obviously. It's the cheapest room in the house, and the one that nobody ever picks. "It's, like, the servant's quarters," one guy had said during last year's rooming draw.

I'd pretended to do them all a favor by claiming the miniscule room, but I can barely afford even this. When I reach the top of the stairs, I pause on the landing, keys in hand. I don't hear any voices. Or any sex noises.

Sweet, sweet silence! Keaton must be at his girlfriend's place.

Yes, my neighbor's name is Keaton. It's worse than that. He's Keaton Hayworth III. And even worse than *that*?

He's my opponent in the race for frat president.

Most of the other guys think he's a shoo-in to win. And fine, he does tick off all the presidential boxes—*on paper*. He's well liked by almost everyone. His father runs a multinational pharmaceutical company, so he fits the wealth criteria. He's a football player, so he has the athlete thing going for him.

But like I said, it's all on paper. Off the page, he's a bit—fine, *a lot*—self-absorbed. The frat president has to put the needs of everyone else before his own. I don't think Keaton is capable of doing that, and the others are going to notice as the campaign unfolds.

"Dumb" and "selfish" will definitely be the descriptors I use if I decide to run a smear campaign against Mr. Jockface.

"Seriously hot" also works, although it kills me to admit that. Still, even though the guy's good-looking, he's not my type at all. I don't go for preppy jocks. When I'm in the mood for a guy, I like 'em a little rougher around the edges. But, hey, if you like handsome rich dudes, Keaton is your man.

I lock our door behind me. My stomach is growling like a beast.

You'd think that the kitchen would be a good place to keep my sandwich ingredients. But you'd be wrong. The guys I live with help themselves to whatever is in the refrigerator, because they have no shame. And they can't conceive of a world where those last four cheese slices are all I've got to eat.

I learned that lesson the hard way. Now I keep my food in my room. I have an ancient dorm fridge under my desk. The compressor is loud, but it keeps my cheese and mayo cool. And there's a loaf of bread on the desk.

Making my sandwich takes only a minute. I put it on a paper plate and sit back on the bed, my phone in one hand to entertain me while I eat.

I still have more studying to do. But I can burn a few minutes on a game. Or—and this can be even more fun—scrolling through the *Kink* app.

It's been a while since I had a hookup. There's been too much schoolwork and too many weekend hours at the club. Lately, I fall into bed in the wee hours of the morning and try to sleep a few hours until Mr. Jockface starts playing loud classic rock while he does sit-ups and pushups in his room. At home I'll bet he has an entire wing to himself. Keeping quiet for others has probably never occurred to him.

The app's home screen loads, offering me a tantalizing question.

What are you hungry for today?

As if sex is a handy buffet table I could sidle up to whenever I feel the urge.

Actually, it's a viewpoint that fits my sexual appetites pretty well. Some people use *Kink* to find partners who will fulfill a precise sexual fantasy. But I'm more of a variety seeker. Sometimes I'm in the mood to party with curves and the lighter touch of feminine hands. But guys are a whole lot of fun in bed, too.

Sometimes I don't have to choose at all. *Kink* also has a section for couples looking to add someone to their bed. That's what I tap on now. *Threesomes waiting to happen.*

It's not waiting for me tonight, of course. I have to finish homework for two classes before a weekend of late-night club shifts. But a guy can dream. Besides, it takes time to cultivate a threesome. You have to be sure that everyone is on the same page.

I flip past a couple of images that are familiar. One pic shows a hot couple that I've already partied with. They were fun, but the guy is too much of a Dom for my taste. He wanted me to kneel, and I let him know that wasn't an option. Then there's a gay couple. I'm not in the mood for two dudes, so I flip past it.

And, whoa! Fresh meat. There's a shot of a couple I've never seen before. They're on a beach somewhere. Her bikini leaves nothing to the imagination. Perfect tits and a stomach so flat that she might as well be on the cover of a magazine.

The guy has a well-muscled arm curled around her little waist. He's kind of beefy, but his proportions are nice. I'd like to slide my hands down those cut abs and into those swim trunks. They have little red lobsters on them, which makes me roll my eyes.

But all in all, they are a hot couple. Definitely appealing. The photo is cropped at their shoulders, so I can't see their faces. But that's just common sense. My photo is the same.

I swipe right.

The screen shimmies. *You're a match, hot stuff,* the app tells me.

"Aw, shucks," I say aloud, because I like my apps to flatter me. Then I get down to the serious business of inspecting the profile.

Male, 20s, in a relationship with female, 20s. She wants a m/f/m threesome for her birthday. I'm totally open to that. Looking for a one night thing in a few weeks.

That's all he gives me. Oh, and his handle is LobsterShorts, which makes me laugh. At least he can acknowledge the ridiculousness of that preppy bathing suit. Another vote in his favor.

My handle is SinnerThree. Because I acknowledge the truth, too.

I finish my sandwich and set the plate aside. The guy's profile has a glowing dot in the corner, which means he's active on the app. I'd lay all my money (which, fine, is none) on him having made this profile only hours ago. He seems kind of green. But that's not a turnoff. I'd bet the rest of my nonexistent fortune on the fact that he's never gotten off in front of another guy.

Blowing minds is at least half the fun, right?

As a rule, I keep the app's geolocation setting switched off. It's nobody's business where I am. But when I'm trying to decide whether to engage, I'll turn it on for a moment just to see if I can guess whether I'm looking at another Darby College student.

With those shorts? Probably. But I change the setting anyway.

Location: .9 miles away.

I turn it off again. Hmm. Less than a mile is pretty close. He could be a student, or an intern at the hospital. Or—and this is the worst-case scenario—a grad student who will show up to teach the next business course I take. Now that would be awkward.

My finger hovers over the message icon. There's no harm in chatting him up, right? I tap it, then send the standard greeting. **Yo**.

He doesn't keep me waiting. **Yo**.

Nice profile pic, I say. Because flattery works.

Thanks. Um… A laughing emoji pops up on the screen. **I never chatted up a dude before. But here goes: Likewise. I can see you're busy with the ab curls**.

You have no idea, I fire back. My tight abs are my bread and butter. **So you want a guy for a threesome but it weirds you out to chat me up on an app? How's that gonna play out for you on the gf's birthday? You could—gasp—see my actual dick**.

Might as well get the tricky questions over with immediately.

LobsterShorts: Simmer down. Just give me a minute to get used to the idea. You're the first one to DM.

SinnerThree: Aw, I popped your cherry? I'm so flattered. Was I gentle?

LobsterShorts: It was life-changing. I feel like a whole new person.

He adds an eye-roll emoji, and I snort with laughter. A sense of humor is a good sign. **Want to show me your pretty faces? If we end up making plans together, I'm gonna see 'em anyway**.

Can't, he replies immediately. **Not on an app. The gf and I haven't talked yet about when to reveal any personal information**.

SinnerThree: Aren't you worried that I'm ugly?

LobsterShorts: Are you?

SinnerThree: Fuck no. I was actually hired for my job because I please the ladies.

LobsterShorts: Well, my dentist used to put my face on the front of his brochure, until I asked him to stop. So that's settled.

I laugh again. **Can I give you a little piece of advice? If your** girl is worried about privacy, take the birthday thing out of your profile. Your neighborhood computer geek could cross reference that against social media pretty easily and find out who you are.

Fuuuuuck is his response. **BRB.**

Sure enough, his profile description has changed when I refresh the screen a minute later.

Thanks, he says a moment later. **You use the app a lot?**

SinnerThree: Define a lot. I log in constantly but don't have time for many meet-ups.

LobsterShorts: Student?

Part-time, I lie. Because you have to keep your distance. **You?**

LobsterShorts: Student. Full time.

Bummer. I'd rather hook up with people who aren't part of the Darby College community. These things are tricky.

Have you done threesomes with a couple before? is his next question.

Yeah, I reply, feeling like I'm on a job interview. **They're not as easy to set up as a plain old hookup. But when it works out, it's some of the most fun you can have.**

LobsterShorts: That sounds promising.

SinnerThree: You're a newb, right? Trust me that it's fun watching a couple push their own boundaries. It's like taking part in a porn shoot. Except it's real.

I get why that's hot, he replies.

And—I don't add this, but it's the best part—when it's done, it's *over*. Unlike actual dating, there's no expectations. We go our separate ways.

SinnerThree: Define the kind of hot you're looking for. What heat level are we talking here?

He takes a few seconds to respond. **I'm not sure what you're asking. Total newb, remember?**

I smile, because I appreciate his honesty. A lot. **Okay, you said this is your girl's idea. And you said you're open to it. But, open to what?** I decide to be blunt. **Watching me fuck her? Does she want to watch us? Do you want my hands on you or just on** her? Want to fuck me? Want to be fucked? Options are endless...

LobsterShorts: Whoa. OK. That's a lot to think about.

SinnerThree: No kidding. That's why this shit gets sorted out ahead of time. You can't just play it by ear.

LobsterShorts: You have to admit, tho, that there's benefits to making everything a game-time decision. How the fuck do I know what I want until I try it?

I let out a snort of laughter. **Do you ask waiters to bring you a taste of everything before you choose your food off the menu?**

LobsterShorts: What, like that's weird? Do you expect me to choose between the tavern burger and the fish and chips with no prior knowledge???

This guy. I hope I'm not being punked by some rando with no plans to go through with it, because I'm starting to like him.

SinnerThree: Okay, look. What kind of porn do you like?

LobsterShorts: The naked kind.

I tap out an eyeroll emoji. **Naked women?**

LobsterShorts: Yes.

SinnerThree: Naked men?

LobsterShorts: Sure, I guess? I watch a lot of gangbang porn, orgies, etc. Naked women with naked men, in all sorts of combinations. I dunno. My taste in porn is far-reaching. I'm more of a gourmand than a gourmet.

Like I even know what that means. I actually tap into the dictionary on my phone and type in gourmand. It bugs the shit out of me not to know what words mean. It's like my poverty is showing.

Gourmand: one who is heartily interested in good food and drink.

I knew I liked this guy. **You sound fun**, I admit. **If two dicks in a porno doesn't turn you off, that bodes well for you. But there's a difference between seeing it and doing it.**

LobsterShorts: True.

SinnerThree: Can I ask you something? Have you ever been with a guy before?

LobsterShorts: No. Why?

SinnerThree: Just wondering if you'd been tempted before.

LobsterShorts: I've been with my girl a long time, so it isn't something I think about.

Alone in my room, I shake my head. This is why I don't do relationships. When I have an itch, it needs to be scratched.

LobsterShorts: When my gf said "let's have a threesome with a dude", I almost swallowed my tongue. But I'm kind of a dare-devil. I like skydiving. I once ate an entire packet of crickets on a dare.

SinnerThree: Gross. I can promise that getting naked with me will be more fun than that.

LobsterShorts: Good to know. Although the crickets were seasoned with chili and lime, and had a nice crunch.

I let out a bark of laughter. **OMFG.**

LobsterShorts: :) Just letting you know that I don't scare easily.

SinnerThree: Good. But you still have to specify what you want to get out of this encounter. And how far you're willing to take it. Do some thinking, okay? Like I said—threesomes are fun, but only when the ground rules are clear. No disappointments, no regrets.

LobsterShorts: Roger.

How'd you guess my name? I joke.

Now I get an eyeroll emoji.

SinnerThree: I gotta sign off now. There's a paper to write so I can work all weekend.

LobsterShorts: What do you do?

Right. Like I'd ever tell him.

SinnerThree: All I'll say is, you'd laugh your ass off if you knew. And wait—I have a homework assignment for you.

LobsterShorts: Like I need more homework.

I wonder where he is right now. Library? Study session? It's kind of hot to think that he might be in public, discussing something so dirty.

SinnerThree: No, this is the fun kind of homework. I want you to imagine that I'm going to give you a blowjob. You let me unzip you. Then I reach inside your...briefs?

There's a short delay.

Boxers, he finally replies.

SinnerThree: Should I keep going?

Another delay.

LobsterShorts: Keep going.

SinnerThree: I reach inside your boxers, and you're already hard for me.

I stop typing and set my phone down on the bed. I wait.

And????? He types a minute later. **I'm waiting here with my dick out. Well, metaphorically,** he hastily adds.

I laugh so loudly it echoes against the walls of my tiny room. **That's all I'm saying. Your homework is to fill in the rest of this scenario. Report back tomorrow.**

LobsterShorts: What? You cliffhangered me?

SinnerThree: Night, Lobsterman.

I close the app. Leaving people hanging is kind of my specialty, anyway.

And I really do have to write that paper.

CHAPTER 3
OILED UP CO-WORKERS

LUKE

I spend most of Friday holed up in my room, racing to finish my Econ paper. Weekends are in no way conducive to home-work. My shifts start at nine p.m., and although the club has a one a.m. last call, I sometimes work a late bartending shift at the club next door, which closes later. I often don't get home till after five, depending on how long it takes to shower, change, and cash out.

Still, I'd rather spend the day sleeping so I can be well-rested for tonight. Or maybe sexting with LobsterShorts. Logging out of the app last night was painfully hard. So was the state of my dick. You have no idea how hot it is helping a guy explore his sexuality.

See, Lobster's girlfriend won't be getting anything shockingly new from the encounter. Instead of one dick, she'll get two. But for LobsterShorts—he's never had a dick in his mouth before. Or put his mouth and hands on another guy.

Goddammit. I might have to jerk off now. Studying with a hard-on is going to be impossible.

I'm just sliding my hand underneath the waistband of my sweatpants when my phone vibrates.

When I see the caller display, my dick breaks the world record for Fastest Erectile Deflation. And my teeth clench of their own volition.

I don't want to answer, but I also know my mother—she'll keep calling until I pick up. When it comes to her sons, her dedication is unparalleled. Oh, wait, did I say *sons*, plural? Silly me. There's only one male offspring Marlene Bailey gives a shit about, and it sure ain't me.

"Hey." I sound curt, but I can't help it. "What's up?"

"Hi, baby. It's Mom."

"I know who it is." Frowning, I sit up and rest my head against the wall. "What's up?" I repeat.

"I just…" Her tone takes on a desperate note. "You're still mad at me. Oh, Luke. It's been a year—you can't hate me forever!"

"I don't hate you."

"Then please don't be mad. What choice did I have?"

"I'm not mad," I lie. "What do you need, Ma? I'm a bit busy at the moment."

"I…" Her voice cracks and she sniffles.

I'm not buying it. My mother can cry on command. And trust me, she takes great advantage of this skill. My entire childhood, I watched her use tears to wrap her revolving door of boyfriends around her little finger. That shit works on my brother, too. But it's never worked on me. I've always seen right through her damsel-in-distress act.

"Mom, seriously," I say irritably. "Tell me why you called or I'm hanging up."

"I called to invite you to dinner on Sunday."

I nearly drop the phone. Um. What the fuck kind of game is she playing at now? "Dinner," I echo, unable to keep the suspicion from my voice.

"Yes, dinner." She pauses. "We have some news."

"What news? And who's 'we?'"

"You'll find out at dinner," she says stubbornly.

"Uh-huh. And will Joe be at this dinner?" Just uttering my older brother's name sends an eddy of sickness to my gut.

Joe is the reason I can't live at home. A year ago he was paroled from prison, where he served three years for felony burglary. Upon his release, he asked my mother if he could come back home. And naturally she said yes. "I can't wait to be a family again," were her exact words.

Unfortunately, *being a family* meant looking the other way while my brother resumed his illegal activities. And it's a two-bedroom house, so there was literally no way of escaping Joe and his lowlife friends.

The second month Joe was home, I found some empty tubes of a topical anesthetic in the kitchen trashcan. "No idea what that is," Joe had insisted. "Maybe Mom is having some kinda pain."

But I know a liar when I meet one. With a little help from Dr. Google I learned that lidocaine is frequently used to cut cocaine and convince buyers that the product is high quality. I confronted him. He started gaslighting me.

And then I found the gun under his mattress. Loaded. Not only is that dangerous, it's a blatant parole violation. "It's not mine," he'd said. "Bix left it there. I didn't know."

"He didn't know," my mother had echoed. She only believes what she wants.

"You can't stay here," I'd snapped. "Get your shit and go."

"Make me."

All Mom added to the situation was her tears.

So the person who eventually left was me. I wasn't going to share a room with someone who will undoubtedly be re-arrested and jailed again. In fact, I'm astonished he's lasted a year.

I haven't seen Joe since July, when Mom guilted me into coming to a "family barbecue" where her latest boyfriend made some hotdogs and then burned them. Oh, and I was asked to bring the beer. Of course I was.

"Please come to dinner," my mother begs me now. "You don't even have to bring anything."

Lucky me. "You still didn't say—will Joe be there?"

"Of course Joey will be there. It's his home."

I swallow a tired sigh. "Does he know you're inviting me?"

"It was his idea."

Where I was suspicious before, I'm now in full-blown distrust mode. It was Joe's idea to invite me over?

Yeah. I'd like to avoid a Red Wedding situation, thank you very much.

"Sorry, I'm busy on Sunday," I tell her. "If you want to share your big news now, I'm all ears, otherwise I need to get going."

"Luke," she whines.

"Okay, gotta go, Ma. Talk later."

We both know we won't be talking later.

As I drop my phone on the milk crate that doubles as a night-stand, my entire body feels weary. I know plenty of people have screwed-up families, but mine is something else. An older brother who will drag me down with him if I let him. A deadbeat dad I haven't seen since I was two. A drama-queen mom who would probably marry her eldest son if society didn't frown upon it. I'm not even joking here—Mom's love for Joey borders on…creepy.

I suppose I should consider myself lucky that her love for me is nonexistent?

Go me.

Footsteps sound beyond my door, and I stiffen instinctively. No matter how long I've lived at Alpha Delt, I still don't feel like I belong here.

Says the man running for president.

Fuck. What am I getting myself into?

A blast of music echoes through the little hallway between our rooms. Aerosmith's "Sweet Emotion." Wonderful. Mr. Jockface is home. And it's time for his pre-dinner workout.

I glance at the stack of textbooks on my desk, while Steven Tyler's shrill voice pours out of Keaton's room. If I had the money, I'd invest in an expensive pair of noise-cancelling headphones.

Unfortunately, I don't have the money.

———

I'm not in the best of moods when I arrive for my shift a few hours later. My paper isn't done, and I wasn't able to catch a minute of shut-eye thanks to Hayworth. I get that he's a football player, but Jesus fuck, how many hours of daily weightlifting do those meatheads require?

And just as I was drifting off, his girlfriend came over and spent a good hour bitching about one of her sorority sisters. The two of them didn't even have the decency to have sex. Listening to them fuck would've been way more interesting than hearing about how a chick named Lindy told Annika her highlights didn't look "natural." Lindy is clearly a goddamn monster.

Needless to say, I'm cranky tonight. And hungry. I salivate at the mere thought of all the tips I'll be getting tonight. I'll be able to feed myself, finally.

"You're late," my manager informs me.

I stride into the dressing area. "No, I'm not." I furrow my brow. "Am I?" There's no clock in the room, so I can't be sure. But I'm usually reliably punctual.

"Only by a minute," Heather says, breaking out in a grin. "I've just been waiting ages to chastise you for being late. It's such a drag what a good boy you are."

I grin back. "Well. That's the first time anyone's ever called me a good boy. Typically I'm told how bad I am." I wink at the older brunette, who rolls her eyes.

Heather runs one of two twin clubs—Jack's and Jill's. I've been working at Jill's for almost a year, but already Heather and I are great friends. She's a former stripper who married the owner of her previous club, and now the two of them run side-by-side locations.

Oh, did I mention I'm a stripper?

Some dudes prefer "male entertainer" or "exotic dancer," but I call a spade a spade. I spend two nights a week shaking my crotch in happy women's faces and stripping down to a G-string. Ergo, I'm a stripper.

"Well, you're on soon, bad boy, so you'd better get into costume." Heather pats my butt over my jeans and nudges me toward the long metal rack across the room.

"Hey, Heather?" I stop her before she turns away. "Is there any chance I can pick up a couple bartending shifts at Jack's this week? I'm short on cash."

"Well, sure, sugar!" She gives me a happy smile. "I'll put a note on the board and see if anybody needs a night off. But is everything okay?"

"Yeah, totally. There's a party I have to throw, if you can believe it." It's deeply ironic that the fraternity election calls this thing a "Dance-off." Because if I could become president by actually dancing, I'd win in a heartbeat. No contest.

But no. I have to dazzle my brothers with a good time. It's okay, though, because I have a plan.

"Glad to hear it," she says. "Now off you go to get pretty."

I roll my eyes and head for my cubby in the middle of the row.

"Bailey!" calls George, one of my "colleagues." He's sprawled on the comfy couch in the dressing room, bare-chested and wearing a stars-and-stripes spandex thong. He waves a handful of bills at me. "Guess how much bank I just made."

My gaze rests briefly on his lower body. "Hmmm. The Good American routine... Imma guess...a buck-fifty?"

America-themed acts are immensely popular. I guess patriotism makes chicks horny. And I'm not excluding gay or bi dudes on purpose here—Jill's doesn't draw a male crowd. Maybe it's the name. On a busy weekend, we might get two guys, *maaaybe* three. Most of them prefer the gay clubs, though.

Can't say I blame them. Jill's is campy. It's like the Disney version of stripping. We cater to girls'-night-out and bridal parties. The place is only open on the weekends, though, except for private parties. That's why I need to pick up extra shifts tending bar next door, which doesn't pay nearly as well.

"I made two-twenty!" George crows.

I raise my eyebrows. "Sweet." And from the first act of the night? This bodes well for me.

Contrary to what people believe, stripping is not easy money. Not for a male dancer, anyway. Women can start working and make a fortune on night one. Four, five hundred a night, easy. Men have a tougher time. We're contractors, which means we don't get an hourly wage (or a salary…cue my laughter at the notion of receiving a *salary*). We get paid in tips. Period. Nothing more.

I won't lie—that scared me when Heather and Louis first hired me. Quitting my two bartending jobs to roll the dice on *possibly* making bank as a dancer? Fucking terrifying. So instead, what I did was take two weekends off from my other jobs and give the dancing thing a trial run.

I made seven hundred the first weekend. Twelve hundred the second. I already knew I was a terrific dancer. Give me a hot, sultry beat and I'm good to go. But it turns out I'm even better naked.

So I gave my other bosses notice the day after, and now here we are.

"You're my new hero, G," I tell the big, beefy Italian.

"Yo," my buddy Xavier greets me.

"Yo." We tap fists, and he trails after me to the costume racks. "Nice," I say, noticing what he's wearing. "I love starting off with the fireman act." It's another crowd-pleaser.

"Luke. Bro. When are you gonna be done proofing my essay?" A fellow dancer—and fellow student—lumbers over. Brock attends a nearby community college and strips to pay for classes. He also waits tables, dabbles in landscaping, walks dogs, and works at a carwash. Poor kid is so busy, I offered to proofread all his papers this semester.

I'm a good friend. I'm also an idiot. Because holy shit, I barely have time to write my own papers, let alone proof someone else's.

"I'll have it back to you by Sunday," I promise. "You said it wasn't due till Monday."

"It's not. Just wanted to make sure you didn't forget." He slaps my shoulder and then calls out to another dancer. "Hey Lance, did you steal my suspenders? I can't put out fires without my suspenders, bro!"

"Luke," scolds Heather. "You're on in ten. Get naked. Now."

"Someone light a fire under this one's ass!" jokes Lance, who's already decked out in his firefighter gear and may or may not have stolen Brock's suspenders.

I strip out of my hoodie and undershirt, then unzip my pants. But I don't put the costume on yet. Instead, I dutifully wait for George to rub oil all over my bare chest.

"Best job in the world, eh?" His palms glide up and down my six-pack, and he's grinning as if someone just gave him a winning lottery ticket. The funny thing is, George isn't into men. He just honestly thinks rubbing oil on each other and shaking our asses on stage is the best job in the world.

"You're a strange guy, G."

"Oh come on, like you're not having a blast, Bailey! Good music, good company, good pay... Tell me this isn't fucking awesome."

I guess he's not entirely wrong.

"Shit, yes, *there* they are," Brock says happily. His blond head pops out of the props closet he was rummaging through, and he holds up a pair of red suspenders. "Found 'em!" And then he unzips his pants.

A lot of unzipping goes on in this room. And I ain't gonna lie —I work with some seriously hot specimens. But while I might be an idiot about some things, I'm wise when it comes to the work-place. As in, I never, ever shit where I eat. Most of the guys at Jill's know I swing both ways, and although one or two have not-so-casually insinuated they'd be down for...anything, I made it clear I'm not interested in going there.

I show up, I dance, I count my tips, I leave.

Oh, and sometimes I get to wave a big fireman's hose around and pretend I'm spraying my oiled-up coworkers.

But first I need my costume. I don a wifebeater; we use a special extra-cheap brand that I will literally tear off my body a little later. Cue the high-pitched female shrieks of joy.

Then I jump into the yellow fireman's pants with their attached red suspenders. There's a jacket with snaps that I can pluck open one by one when the cue comes. *We're here to put out the fire...in your panties!*

Yeah, it's no wonder why I don't tell anyone at Alpha Delt what I *really* do for a living. This job isn't subtle. Tomorrow I'll be a bleary mess. Sunday I'll be even worse. But I'll have money for groceries, rent, and gas. And I'll have part of the money I need for the fraternity event I'm throwing.

But right now it's time for a real-life Dance-off. He who gets the best tips, wins.

CHAPTER 4
MY OWN MENTAL SYRIA

KEATON

Sunday morning I wake up when my alarm goes off at ten. My father is in town. That's the only explanation for why I'd set an alarm on the Sunday following a football victory and a night of intense—and well-deserved—partying.

Annika is asleep beside me. We're both naked, but I'm pretty sure we were too drunk to fool around.

No time like the present, then.

I roll toward her and wrap an arm around her sleeping body. My eyes drift shut again. But I don't fall asleep. My mind goes back to the text convo I had. And the homework assignment SinnerThree asked me to do.

Fill in the rest, he'd said.

I've tried not to think about it these past two days. I mean, this threesome is supposed to be about Annika, not me. I'm not supposed to be intrigued by SinnerThree, or be wondering what it'd feel like to fool around with him.

But he's right. If we go through with this, I *should* have an idea of how far I want to take it.

So, fine. I'll do the homework. I mean, what's the worst thing that could happen? I'll have an orgasm? Jeez, the terror.

Okay...hmmm. What do I want SinnerThree to look like? Muscular. That goes without saying. I spend a lot of time working out, so fitness matters to me. A guy should take care of himself. Other than that, I don't know if I have a preference. Jock or fashion plate? Tattoos and piercings, or untouched? There's a hot version of everything, right?

A male hand. That's all I need for this fantasy. A big, rough hand wrapping around the base of my cock.

Said cock stirs.

Oh. All right, then. I guess we like the sound of that. I slip my hand down and run it along the underside of my thickening dick. Achievement unlocked.

The thing is, I usually avoid these thoughts. Group sex is hot as fuck to me, but I don't fantasize about guys. That's like a dangerous, war-torn country that I stay clear of. But SinnerThree told me I have to. So that makes it a little less weird.

I let myself picture a mouth. Lips tracing my shaft. And not just any lips—there's the scruff of someone's weekend whiskers, maybe. They're teasing my thighs...

And I'm hard now, pretty much instantly. Vacationing in my own mental Syria is surprisingly arousing.

I drop my hand, and kiss the back of Annika's shoulder. "Wake up, princess." I give her smooth ass a playful nudge with my erection.

"Sleepy," she grunts.

So that's how it is.

Only an asshole bugs his sleeping girlfriend for sex. So I give her a little squeeze, and then get out of bed for a shower and a shave.

She still hasn't moved when I'm almost done. "Annika!" I holler into the bedroom. "Come on, soldier. On your feet! Let's move."

A muffled groan is the only sound I hear from my room. My

girl likes to party, too. She's just not as skilled at it as I am. Annika is always a wreck the morning after.

As I rinse off my face, I realize I'm going to have to take drastic measures.

Stalking into the room, I pull my comforter down, exposing her naked back. And then I grab my phone off the dresser and find an up-tempo song that I know she likes. "Crazy In Love" by Beyoncé starts playing from my top-of-the-line Bluetooth speakers.

"I hate you," she says from my pillow.

Do I have a way with the ladies, or what?

A glance at the clock reveals that it's nearly eleven. "Up, princess. You know he gets all pissy when I'm late."

Annika turns her groggy face toward me and says the three words I've been dreading. "Go without me."

Fuck. "You said you'd come."

"It's early."

"It isn't." I turn up Beyoncé.

"Please?" I beg. "I really want you there."

Miraculously, the pillow slides off Annika's perfect face. "Okay. But only if you turn this song up so I can hear it in the shower."

"Sure, baby." It's an easy bargain. I crank it up louder.

Annika slides out of bed, grabs my towel off the hook, wraps it around her naked bod and stalks toward the shower.

Thank fuck.

I'm buttoning up a dress shirt when I hear a slam and a roar from across the hall. "...fucking bullshit is this? I'm gonna—" Whatever else my tool of a neighbor is saying gets drowned out by Beyoncé.

Luke Bailey's grumpy face appears at my open door. He's shirtless, and I wonder once again how he's so ripped for a guy who doesn't play a sport. His inky-dark hair is a mess, and there's a pillow crease down his cheek that makes him look more boyish than usual. But he ruins the effect by shouting at me. "Turn that shit off!"

"No can do," I yell over the dance beat.

His eyes bug out. Then he stomps over to my speaker and yanks the plug out of the wall.

Silence descends, and I have to admit that I don't mind. And yet...

"We had a deal!" Annika yells from the shower. "Where's Beyoncé?"

"Beyoncé," growls Luke, "is on a coffee break! It's fucking Sunday morning and I got home at four a.m.!"

"Easy," I say through a clenched jaw. "It's not Annika's fault you partied too hard."

"*Partied* too hard." His fists are clenched. "Yeah, I was out late having a *fine* old time."

Whatever, dude. "Maybe take it down a notch? We're on our way out, anyway."

His eyes scan me, and not in a nice way. He takes in my Zegna shirt and my Armani pants. "Tea with the queen?"

"Brunch with my dad."

"Nice," he says, but I don't miss his eye roll. "Stay out as long as you like." He turns on his heel, disappears into his room, and slams the door with a shutter-rattling bang.

Charming fellow. How startling that he isn't more widely liked. On the other hand, my presidential victory is totally in the bag.

Annika starts singing Beyoncé in the shower.

I roll my eyes at the whole fucking world.

———

Forty minutes later I'm apologizing to my father for our tardiness.

"It's all my fault," Annika admits. "I won't leave the house without makeup."

"You're worth the wait," my father assures her, kissing her on the cheek.

My father hates it when I'm late, but he loves the heck out of Annika. So I guess I'm getting a free pass on this one.

"Nice tackle during the second quarter yesterday," my dad says as I sit down. "Great game."

"Thank you!" I unfold my napkin in my lap, trying not to show how much the compliment means to me.

Pathetic, much? I'm twenty-one years old and still trying to please my daddy.

In fact, I just read a study, where a scientist did MRIs on some dogs. (I seriously can't imagine how. *Hold still... Good boy!*) And he found that their brains light up just as enthusiastically for praise as they do for food.

In other words, I'm as smart as a golden retriever.

My girlfriend opens her menu. "I always get the eggs Benedict. And Keaton always gets the waffles and bacon. But maybe it's time for a change..."

"You always say that." I drop my napkin in my lap. "And then you order the same thing, anyway. Maybe I'll get the eggs Benedict."

She arches one perfect eyebrow over her menu. "Don't you dare. I need a bite of the waffles with bacon."

My dad chuckles good-naturedly. "How's your father?" he asks her. "It's been a while since I brutalized him on the golf course."

"Has he brutalized you on the golf course in the meantime?" I ask.

Dad makes a show of kicking me under the table. This is why I wanted Annika here. It lightens our relationship to a bearable level for me. Dad is goofier when there's a girl present. Or anyone, really.

Annika has no idea how fraught our relationship is getting lately. Even though graduation is still a year and a half away, I feel it looming. Dad's interference in my life is only going to get worse, not better.

Luckily, the waiter is here again to take our order. My father orders the quiche and a mimosa.

"A glass for the lady, too?" our waiter asks. But then he frowns. "I'd need to see some ID, though."

My girl shakes her head. "January, then. I'll finally be legal. Just the eggs Benedict, please, and a glass of your fresh-squeezed juice."

After the guy walks away, my father asks a simple question. "Do you have any big plans for your birthday?"

Annika's eyes go wide, and when I try to swallow, my water goes down the wrong pipe.

Well, Dad, we're inviting a man to get naked with us and get us both off together. As one does.

I spend the next couple of seconds trying not to cough, but Annika covers for me by launching into a story about designing T-shirts for her sorority. I finally regain control of my esophagus just as she gets to the punch line.

Did I mention that I owe this girl big-time?

"How was your week, Mr. Hayworth?" Annika asks as our food arrives.

"I've known you since you were in pigtails and braces, Ani. How many times do I have to remind you to call me Keat?" Dad teases.

"I'll do my best, Mr. Hayworth." She winks, but despite the playful response I know she'll never, ever call him "Keat." Annika had already admitted to me that she feels awkward calling my father the same name as me. It confuses her.

Luckily, she's never had to be in the same room as me, Dad, *and* Grandpa Keaton. Her head would spin.

"My week was pretty ordinary," Dad says. "I spent it chatting up the administrators at Columbia Presbyterian about our clinical trial. But nobody wants to talk about me—tell me about the campaign, Keaton. Have you decided what you're doing for the Dance-off?"

I take another sip of my coffee, stalling. "Not yet," I admit when I can't drag out the sip any longer. "I want to plan something different, something that hasn't been done at the frat before, but I'm stumped."

"What event did you plan when you ran for president?" Annika asks curiously, the question directed at my father.

He breaks out in a grin. "Not to brag, but it was the best party I've ever thrown, or even been to in my life. The best night of my life, honestly." He chuckles. "I spent six months planning it."

Something twists in my gut. *Six months?* I've heard my dad talk about this party before, but it isn't until now that I'm realizing how much effort he put into it.

"The summer before, my sister Rosie and I went to a Cirque du Soleil show, and we had these VIP seats with a meet-the-performers party afterward."

Of course they had VIP seats. Dad buys the top-shelf version of everything.

"I was really impressed. I thought a circus was just trained dogs and clowns. But their show was so eerie and neat. And when I read the program during intermission, I got an idea. They were coming through New England during the school year. And I offered a dozen of them two free nights of lodging at Alpha Delt in exchange for a private performance."

"Cool!" Annika gushes. "A performance at the house?"

"In a tent on the lawn," Dad says, sipping his drink. "There weren't chairs, though. It was more like a rave where a dozen or so of the guests were contortionists, jugglers, and acrobats. I hired a DJ who really understood the vibe. And our guests wore only red and blue, like the performers. It was an experience just being there."

I know he's not lying. The photos are epic. I feel tired just thinking about it. How the hell am I going to come up with something unique? And now the pressure is twofold. Not only do I need to out-party-plan Luke Bailey, but I need to top my father's circus wonderland.

And I have only two weeks to achieve this.

Fucking hell.

I chug the rest of my water, wishing the waiter would hurry up and bring me the mimosa I caved in and ordered. Unlike Annika, I *am* twenty-one—and boy do I need a drink right now.

Dad's phone buzzes, and he peers down to read the incoming text. "Sorry. You know I don't typically condone phones at the table, but the docs at Columbia are giving me hourly updates on the trial."

"What trial is that?" Annika inquires.

"We have a Phase III trial going on right now for a diabetes medication. It works by tricking your metabolism into speeding up while you sleep."

She leans in. "That sounds fascinating."

"Really?" Dad laughs. "Well, I'm hiring. Keaton can't be bothered to take much interest in the family business. Maybe you can carry the flag instead."

And there it is—that little charge of hostility that's always between us. And even though I know better, I leap into the fray. "I never said I wasn't interested. I said I wanted to work for someone else first."

But he's actually right. I'm *not* interested. I'm getting the degree in biology that he wanted me to get. But I don't want to push pharmaceuticals into the world. I just don't. I want to get a graduate degree and do research, preferably in the marine biology field. Pure science is much more interesting to me than trying to push meds to baby boomers.

So I'm stalling. And we argue about it. A lot.

"Good," he says, oblivious to my pain. "I'm lining up a summer internship for you in the finance department. You'd be reporting to Bo, so there you go—you'll be working for someone else."

That's the biggest case of bullshit semantics I've ever heard. Bo works for Dad. Therefore, I'd be working for Dad, only I'll be in the— Wait. "The... What?" I demand. Did he just say *finance*?

"You heard me," he says. "I know you like science more. And there will be plenty of time for that. But to understand big pharma you have to see how the money end of things works, too."

"But...there will be other internships I'm applying for," I grumble.

"Such as...?" Dad asks.

Christ. I'm not ready to discuss the research expedition I'm applying for until I have a meeting with the grad student who's in charge. And it's only November. Who has his summer figured out in November?

"I didn't think so," Dad says at my silence. "We'll talk about it more later. Oh—HR needs your résumé, okay? That's part of the standard application. Send me one before the holidays."

"Sure," I grunt. But I'm not at all sure. There are only two ways this could end, either by me caving, or by me making him really angry when I sidestep his internship for the one I really want.

That's our relationship in a nutshell: me disappointing him, and then feeling bad about it. I'm a football player—it's his favorite sport. But the team's had two losing seasons since I started at Darby, and it's doubtful we'll see a championship this year. So I was only halfway successful in his eyes. He wanted me to be a scientist, so I majored in bio. But not biochemistry, which would have been his top pick.

A future job at his company might be our final showdown. And I really don't know who's going to win.

CHAPTER 5
YOUR MANLY LOBSTER TRUNKS

KEATON

I don't fully relax until that evening when I'm finally home alone.

Now that my study-group meeting is over, I should be working on my campaign speech and brainstorming Dance-off ideas, but I'm not in the mood to think about planning a party. Dad killed all my joy.

So I pick up my phone and open up the app that's been calling my name since I downloaded it. I have messages from a handful of guys. It's the usual *'sup* and *hey,* but I don't even bother with them. I go straight to SinnerThree's page.

He hasn't reached out to me again. Is it weird that I'm disappointed?

Pushing that thought aside, I tap out a greeting. **Hey man. Sunday night. I should be doing work but I was thinking about what you asked me**.

I send the message and lie back. It's been a frustrating day. I'm tense and in need of release.

SinnerThree asked me to consider how I felt about getting blown by a dude. It's still hypothetical at this point, but the hypothetical me doesn't hate the idea. I mean, at the end of a day, a blowjob feels great, right? Does it really matter who's blowing you? Won't it feel great regardless?

So many factors to this hypothesis... Good thing I'm a scientist. Because scientists aren't afraid to experiment, right?

So that's what I'm doing as I close my eyes now. I'm picturing a vaguely handsome guy leaning over me. And I'm imagining how good a guy could be at giving head. It takes a dick to know a dick, right?

Then I step on the third rail and let myself imagine a masculine face looking up at me as he deep-throats my cock with a dirty gleam in his eye.

And...hmmm. That image is more art than science. And I like the idea a whole lot.

My phone pings with an incoming message. I pick it up immediately. And I'm just a little too stoked that SinnerThree has messaged me back.

SinnerThree: Well? Did you ace my assignment?

LobsterShorts: I'm working on it right now.

SinnerThree: And?

Lobstershorts: I'm doing fine.

SinnerThree: Fine? Like B- work?

LobsterShorts: In my family a B- means a lecture and public shaming. I study to get an A.

SinnerThree: Bunch of nerds, are you?

LobsterShorts: Sure. But not the kind that gets shoved into lockers. I'm supposed to be the kind of son who dominates every competition just because I can.

Christ, I don't know why I shared that. We're getting off topic here. I signed in to talk about dicks, not my screwy family life.

SinnerThree: It could be worse. Smart assholes are more fun than dumb assholes. Trust me here.

LobsterShorts: Noted. You're surrounded by dumb assholes?

SinnerThree: Only when I go home. Which I never do unless I can help it.

Lobstershorts: Smart man.

SinnerThree: But enough about those losers. Let's get back to the fun stuff. Are you ready?

Lobstershorts: For?

SinnerThree: Me, dropping down on my knees in front of you. I tug on your manly lobster trunks and pull them off.

I sit up and fire back a message.

LobsterShorts: Wait. Are you hating on my favorite bathing suit?

SinnerThree: Are you stalling? I'm seconds away from touching your dick, and you want to talk about your preppy bathing suit?

The man has a point, I guess. But then again, he doesn't know me.

LobsterShorts: If you were seconds away from touching my actual dick, I don't think I'd stop for a convo. But just so you know, lobsters are cool. And they don't need an app to find sex.

SinnerThree: Okay, I'll bite. How do lobsters find their playmates?

LobsterShorts: The female pees into the male's shelter. And the dude is like OH BABY. Then they both pee on each other. She enters his den and molts. He kicks her clothes away like a prom dress. Then they do it missionary style.

SinnerThree: That's a lot of detail, dude. I don't know whether to be terrified or turned on.

Great. Now I've probably scared him off with my encyclopedic knowledge of crustacean sex.

LobsterShorts: Please carry on. My lobster shorts are discarded.

SinnerThree: Are you at home right now?

LobsterShorts: Now who's asking for too many details? Does it matter where this fictional dick-sucking happens?

SinnerThree: I meant are you ACTUALLY home. So you can shut the door and stroke yourself while I talk to you.

Whoa! My cock feels heavy by the time I finish reading the

sentence. But even as I roll off the bed and click the lock on my door, I'm not sure. There's a line between chatting and touching that he wants me to cross.

Am I really going there right now?

I unzip my jeans and kick them off. And—fuck it—I drop my boxers, too. I sit on the edge of the bed, naked from the waist down. Then I answer him.

LobsterShorts: Okay, door is locked. Shorts are history.

SinnerThree: Well, done, rookie. I wasn't sure you'd want to play along.

I'm not sure about anything, really. But I'm pretty curious about my response to his little homework project. And I suppose this is a harmless enough way of exploring the idea.

LobsterShorts: Let's do this. Talk to me.

SinnerThree: I think it should be the other way around. You tell me what you're doing, and what I should do to you.

Oh.

That's a different story, isn't it? This fantasy has to be in my own words? I set my phone to silent and wonder how to start. Jacking off in my room isn't exactly a new activity for me. But my pulse is elevated anyway. Because jacking off with help from a guy is.

And maybe I'm taking too long, because he nudges me.

SinnerThree: Am I naked too?

LobsterShorts: No. But now I ask you to take off your shirt. And you pull it over your head.

I hit send and look down at Sinner's profile picture and imagine that set of abs in front of me. And it's startling to realize that I *can* picture Sinner slowly removing his shirt, making sure to flex his chest to show me what he's got.

I blow out a breath, wondering how far I'm willing to take this. And why it's so easy to play the encounter like a movie in my head.

Then I keep typing.

LobsterShorts: I'm sitting on the edge of the bed. You kneel down in front of me.

SinnerThree: Yeah, okay. I'm down. So long as I don't have to call you "Master." I'm not into that.

LobsterShorts: Noted.

And now I'm picturing him down on the floor in front of me. Looking up at me, waiting for a cue.

Whew. Is it hot in here?

LobsterShorts: I have to spread my legs apart a little ways so you can get closer.

SinnerThree: Spread them wide, okay? I'm kneeling between your legs. I'm putting my hands on your inner thighs. And you're getting hard for me already.

Suddenly I find myself spreading my legs quicker than a cheerleader doing the splits. Because I really want those hands on me. But how, exactly?

It's dawning on me that having sex with the same person for three years leaves some gaps in my imagination. It's not that I don't find my sex life fulfilling. But I don't know how casual hookups work.

LobsterShorts: Just keep going.

SinnerThree: Okay. Maybe you wish I'd just deep-throat you immediately. To spare you the awkwardness. But I don't do that, because I'm kind of digging your nervousness. First I put one hand on your thigh, and you just kind of stare at it.

I suppose I would. And, hell. I can basically feel it there right now. I press my own hand to my bare flesh and it's not enough. I want more.

SinnerThree: Then—moving slowly—I use my other hand to stroke your balls, and cup them in my palm.

I swear I break out in a sweat as my hand reaches down to do just what he's described. My breathing quickens as my own palm slides under my sensitive sac.

SinnerThree: Are you with me? Touch them for me, okay? Then slide your thumb across your cock.

I let out a gasp as I touch myself. Then I type a response with one awkward thumb.

LobsterShorts: yup

My dick is standing at attention now. Not that it usually needs much encouragement.

SinnerThree: Now I lean down and take you in both hands. Are you cut?

LobsterShorts: yeah

SinnerThree: My thumb is teasing the underside of your shaft. And then the tip. Until I finally lean down and taste you.

Alone in my room I let out a groan, wishing that a real-life tongue was actually circling my cockhead. My own fingers are a poor substitute. I pick up my phone and text one-handed.

LobsterShorts: then what

SinnerThree: Are you still digging this?

LobsterShorts: I'd dig it more if you were really here on your knees with my dick in your mouth.

Shit, I can't believe I actually typed that. But…it's the truth. Figure that one out.

SinnerThree: Good. Stroke yourself a little faster. And I have a question for you.

With a groan, I pick up the pace.

SinnerThree: Riddle me this. Would you still be having fun when I look up at you? Because you aren't seeing just a talented mouth. You're looking at a guy who wants to fuck you if he ever gets the chance. Not like I'm going to ruin the mood and say so. I'm smarter than that. I'll suck you first. But when you're getting close I'll stroke your ass. And if it makes you moan, I press my luck and slide the tip of my finger inside.

My eyes slam shut, as if I'm afraid to read another word. Sinner's dirty talk has me hard and aching. I don't know what that means. But I even wish I could hear his voice. There's something base about his tone that I don't mind at all. It's honest. *Here's how I want you and here's how I'll get it.*

Apparently I have an honesty kink. Who knew?

When I open my eyes, there's a new message.

SinnerThree: Still with me?

It's not easy to reply one-handed.

LobsterShorts: Yeah. Are you jerking, too?

SinnerThree: I wish. But I'm not at home right now. I want you to finish yourself off now. Tell me if this helps...

A few beats go by, while I stroke myself slowly. But I can feel heat in my face, and my pulse is throbbing everywhere. I need release.

Then a photograph appears on my screen. I see jeans, and a black T-shirt that's pulled up to reveal a set of tight abs. The jeans are unzipped. And the guy is wearing gray underwear with a *prominent* bulge showing. His hand is spread out so only the thumb is touching the bulge. He's just lightly teasing himself through the cotton.

And it hits me—I made a guy hard. A guy who wants to blow me and play with my ass.

My phone slides off the bed and onto the floor with a clunk as I jack myself in earnest. He's kneeling in front of me, his hands on my thighs. His head bobs as he takes me deep. I put one hand on the back of his neck to hold him where I want him. There's muscle there, not softness...

That's when I come all over my hand, stroking myself through it, wishing SinnerThree was there to swallow everything I give him.

And then it's over. I'm sitting here alone with a sticky hand, my heart pounding. I get up and grab a paper towel off the roll I keep on my dresser.

I don't know what I just learned, except...not one of my thoughts these past ten minutes had anything to do with Annika or her birthday.

CHAPTER 6
THE COPS WILL LOVE THAT

LUKE

Three or four minutes pass, but LobsterShorts doesn't text me back. I've surreptitiously zipped up my jeans again under the library table. And I've put all my books away. Still. Blank screen.

I don't know why I should care. But I'm starting to like the guy. I mean—lobster sex! And here I thought nerds were boring. I'll admit it. I want to meet him.

My phone chimes, and I check it immediately. But it's only a reminder for the meeting I'm headed back to the frat house to attend.

As I leave the library and walk through the dark, I'm almost regretting my choice to run for president. Meetings are the worst, and I'm basically signing myself up for an endless number of them. Free rent for an entire year sounds like heaven, but is it worth the headache of running a fraternity?

Ugh. Yes. I think it is. Because if I'm not paying rent, I can cut my work hours down to one night a weekend. Or, if I save up enough during the summer? I might not even have to work *at all*. I could spend my senior year focusing only on school, graduation, and career plans.

And Alpha Delt. But I'm sure the prez duties won't be half as stressful as working vampire hours all weekend long.

When I get home, I find another meeting already in progress in our dining room. I guess tonight's the night for meetings. Jako, my campaign manager, hasn't arrived yet, so I kill time by eavesdropping on the Pledge Committee's discussion.

The head of the committee is Judd Keller. So I opted out this year.

"Who wants to go first?" Judd asks the guys around the table. "We'll brainstorm and then choose the best and craziest initiation ideas."

We tapped our pledges in September, and they've been probationary members since then. Now, we put them through hell for seven days before finally making them into full-fledged brothers. Last year, I sat on this committee because every member has to volunteer for something, and at least PC is a short-term commitment. But it was a nightmare, mostly because Judd is so fucking annoying.

"Maybe the pledges should do the paperclip challenge," a senior named Paul suggests.

"The what?" Judd asks. "Is that, like, a physical exercise?"

"No. We divide them into three teams of four. Each team gets a paperclip. And they have three days to trade it for something worthwhile. In this case it should be something they can donate to charity. They trade the paperclip for a pencil. They trade the pencil for a pen. They trade the pen for a stapler. And so on." Paul shrugs. "I learned about it in one of my management classes."

"What the hell for?" Judd asks.

"A couple things. It gets you comfortable asking for stuff, which is a life skill. You have to be willing to hear no if you're ever going to hear yes."

Judd begins to sneer. "I think I read that in a self-help book once."

"I don't know," says Ahmad Mithani. "I kind of like it. It's a nice break from the Haggar's Rules of Hazing."

I laugh, because I can't help myself. "Wait, there's a hazing canon?"

Judd's head swivels in my direction. "What the hell, Bailey. You're not even on this committee! Fuck off."

I stifle a grin. "Sorry. Just waiting for *my* committee to arrive. Is this house teeming with committees or what?"

Paul snickers softly.

"Don't mind me," I assure them. I make a zipping motion over my mouth. "I'll keep quiet."

Although Judd is red-faced, he doesn't argue. What's he going to do, kick me out of my own house? The dining room is off the living room, which is where I'm supposed to meet my campaign manager.

"I don't mind the paperclip challenge," Ahmad says with a shrug. "It's mildly humiliating, but with real purpose."

"They could just contribute money to a charity instead," Judd mumbles. "But, fine. Put it on the list of possibilities."

Ahmad hops up and goes to the whiteboard on the wall. He erases a giant drawing of a cock and balls, because what else do people put on a frat-house whiteboard? With the marker, he writes the heading IDEAS, and underneath it: *Paperclip Challenge.*

"Now, who else has an idea that won't bore me stupid?" Judd demands.

"I have a great one," Owen Rickman, one of Judd's football teammates, pipes up. "I call it Bloody Knuckles."

Judd nods in approval. "Sick name. Tell me more."

"Okay, so we haul those fuckers out of their beds at, like, two in the morning and take 'em outside. They line up in front of the back wall of the house and rub their knuckles against the bricks."

I won't lie—I'm fascinated.

By the sheer stupidity of this idea.

"What's the point of that?" asks Tim Hoffman, a senior.

"See how long they can last, how tough they are. Their

knuckles will be torn up, bloody as fuck. It'll be so gory, dude."

Judd is nodding again, his dark eyes gleaming. "And the guy who lasts the longest is rewarded with having to scrub all the blood off the wall and patio."

Tim snickers. "How is that a reward?"

"It's not," Judd says, rolling his eyes. "Because there's no such thing as *rewards* during Hell Week. These losers need to suffer."

Why? I almost blurt out. Why do they need to "suffer"?

To be honest, I've never understood the concept of hazing. It's supposed to be about bonding, right? Creating long-lasting friendships with your fellow brothers?

But we already live in a house together. We eat our meals together. We study together. We share bathrooms. We're each other's therapists. We hold our brother's metaphorical hair back (or literal hair, if we're talking about Jon Munsen's long surfer locks) when he's hugging the toilet after a kegger.

You're telling me all that doesn't generate a lifelong bond? We need to watch our brothers scrape their knuckles raw on a brick wall in the middle of the night in order to solidify these friendships?

"Yo."

I turn at the sound of Jako's low voice. He must have just come from the gym, because he's wearing a sweat-soaked tank top, track pants, and runners.

"Hey," I murmur back, so as to not disrupt Judd's meeting.

"You mind if I change quick-fast?" Jako asks. "I'll come back down in five."

"No prob," I tell him.

As Jako bounds off, I glance back at the dining area.

"Mithani, add Bloody Knuckles to the list," Judd is saying. "Next idea?"

Rounding out the group is Paxton Grier, the heir to a tech fortune. His dad is a Silicon Valley dude who invented an algorithm that compresses massive photo files, so it stands to reason his son is equally smart and innovative, right?

"My brother's frat does this thing called the Watermelon Sex Picnic."

I stifle a sigh.

Ahmad guffaws. "That sounds like the name of an emo band." They high-five each other.

Judd, of course, is hanging on Grier's every word. "Tell me more."

"We get a bunch of watermelons and take the pledges on a picnic, so, like, basically just setting up some blankets or tarps to contain the mess."

The *mess*? Oh boy, I already don't like the sound of this.

"We cut holes in the watermelons, strip the losers naked, and make them fuck the melons."

Owen hoots.

"And the guy that lasts the longest has to eat all the leftovers."

Ahmad starts gagging. "Oh shit. That is so gross."

"I love it," Judd declares. "Write that down on the board."

I genuinely feel queasy, and this is coming from a man who swallows when giving a blowjob. A man who was sexting with another dude right before this meeting. But the idea of forcing other guys, whether they're straight or gay, to eat a bunch of semen-covered watermelons is incredibly alarming to me.

Despite the fact that I'm not even on the committee, I step forward and clear my throat. "Don't write that down," I order Ahmad.

Judd directs a scowl at me. "You're not the president of this fraternity, Bailey."

"Yet," I mock.

"No, you'll never be," he growls. "And you're not the pledge-master either. *I* am. You don't call the shots here."

"No, but you know who does call the shots? The cops." I loosely cross my arms over my chest. "Forced sexual contact during hazing is against the law."

"They're drilling *watermelons*," Judd sputters. "Not each other."

"They're being forced to engage in a sexual activity, which most of them will do because they're eager to get into this frat. It's a power move for us and—" I stop, realizing I need a different tack with Judd. He *craves* the power. So I need to appeal to his... sense of self-preservation, I decide. "And if even one of those pledges talks about what happened or considers it sexual assault and tells the cops, you can say goodbye to Alpha Delt."

"Snitches get stitches," Owen says darkly.

"Yes, beat the shit out of them badly enough that they get stitches," I tell him, smiling politely. "The cops will love that, too."

Owen rolls his eyes at me.

To my surprise, Judd wavers, proving he's not a complete idiot. "No, Bailey's raised a good point. Whatever we make these fuckers do can't be overtly illegal."

Jako appears at the foot of the stairs, so I leave Judd and his cronies to brainstorm ideas that don't involve banging watermelons.

"That guy is a real piece of work," I mutter to Jako.

"Yup," he agrees. "But that piece of work is entitled to one vote in this election—and guess who needs to earn that vote, Luke? You."

I chuckle darkly. "Yeah, right. Even if I turned into a genie and granted him three wishes, he'd still never vote for me. He's ride-or-die with Keaton Hayworth."

Jako nods. "Maybe. But that doesn't mean you're not capable of changing his mind."

Ha. Getting Judd Keller to change his mind about me? I'd have a better chance trying to get cast on a season of *Dancing With the Stars*.

———

An hour later, I'm rummaging around in the kitchen for a snack. Now that I've got a wad of cash lining my wallet, I can afford to grab a bag of chips. We have a communal snack pantry that any of us can make use of, provided we contribute to the snack fund. Normally I abstain. Tonight, I toss a ten-dollar bill in the jar, and gorge.

Fuuuck. I forgot how good chips are. Maybe it's a good thing I'm usually too broke to snack on carbs. My livelihood depends on making sure my abs remain tight and lickable.

Nevertheless, I'm elbow deep in the bag and loving every second of it. As I munch, I check my phone. But no message from LobsterShorts. Did I scare him off? I reread our messages, but as far as I can tell, he was with me every step of the way. He was into it.

My last message to him was bold, though.

I want you to finish now. And tell me if this helps.

Maybe he wasn't into the pic I sent?

I think it over, then frown. Fuck that. My body is fucking awesome. Of course he was into it.

Granted, he admitted to never chatting up a guy, or being with one. Maybe the virtual blowjob didn't do it for him. He tried it out, couldn't get hard. Or maybe got so hard it freaked him out?

I can't deny I'm disappointed at the notion that he might be gone for good. He didn't unmatch me on *Kink*, so that's something. But he's also not messaging.

I skim the message thread again, but when footsteps near the doorway, I jam a finger on my phone to close the app.

"Hey," I grunt as Keaton Hayworth appears. But he doesn't even respond.

My gaze warily tracks Mr. Jockface as he ducks into the pantry. He's wearing sweatpants and a sleeveless red T-shirt, providing me with front-row seats to the gun show. Dude's got great arms. Too bad his personality is shit.

"Yo," he eventually grunts back, as I shove another chip into my mouth. I crunch loudly, continuing to watch Keaton.

He emerges from the pantry with a granola bar. One of those bland ones with nuts and stuff.

Neither of us speaks. Which is normal enough, I guess. Keaton and I have nothing in common, so conversations between the two of us are rare. We have no problem bitching at each other for playing our music too loud, but exchanging actual meaningful words? Not our style.

And yet I stop him before he can leave the kitchen. "Hey, wait."

When he turns, I notice his face is flushed, and he looks a little unsettled. "Need something, Bailey?" he snaps.

I set down the chip bag. "There was a meeting tonight. For the Pledge Committee?"

"Sure?" He frowns. "I'm not on that one. So?"

And here I tread carefully. "I know you're tight with Judd, and I thought I'd give you a heads-up. Maybe you can have a chat with him when the two of you are in the locker room, slapping each other's asses with towels."

One corner of Keaton's mouth quirks. "Is that what you think football players do in the locker room?"

The football players I've seen on PornHub do a lot more than smack asses. They fuck 'em. But I keep that to myself.

"Judging by the hard-on he got tonight at the thought of watching other guys fuck watermelons, I'd say, yes, it wouldn't surprise me if Judd was into locker room ass play."

Keaton's eyes widen. "Sorry, what?"

"Your bro has some messed-up ideas about how to haze our pledges. Figured you could try to nip that in the bud." I shrug. "Maybe remind him that consent and MeToo applies to men as well as women. I'd rather get through this year's initiation week without a lawsuit."

Seriously, if I wanted legal trouble, I could just live at home.

Keaton crosses those impressive arms and stares me down. "Are you pulling my chain right now?"

"What? No! Jesus. Ask him yourself. I've got better things to do than invent bad ideas, Hayworth. But we both know Judd listens to just one of us, and it ain't me."

He lifts a hand and runs it through his messy hair. He's edging toward the doorway, as if he's dying to leave.

"I'm serious, Hayworth."

"Okay, okay, I'll bring it up to him." He stops to glare at me. "But if you're just trying to make trouble between my teammate and me..."

"Oh, please," I sputter. "I'm trying to keep us *out* of trouble. I don't give two shits about Hell Week so long as nobody gets *sued* afterward."

"Simmer down," Hayworth grumbles. "Judd likes to talk. He's too smart to put us in any real jeopardy."

"Smart?" I spit before I can think better of it. "He drove a U-Haul truck into an underground parking garage, peeling the top off like a sardine can. And his ex-girlfriend had to get a new SIM card for her phone because he wouldn't stop calling her from alternate numbers."

My studly neighbor shakes his head. His whiskers are scruffy, which only draws more attention to his good looks. Some people have all the advantages in life.

Except common sense. "Judd cares about Alpha Delt," Hayworth says. "I'm sure he'll keep his head in the game."

"Well, I'm not sure," I say, just to make it clear. "If this turns into a shit show, I'm not taking the fall for it."

"It won't turn into a shit show." His lips tighten. "Are you done?"

"Jeez. Someone's feeling crabby tonight. What's wrong, Hayworth?" I crack. "You hard up? Your rich girlfriend isn't sucking your dick often enough?"

Keaton's face goes a bit pale, and for a second I feel bad about being such a smart-ass. But my remorse is short-lived, because Hayworth sneers at me and resorts to the most childish of comebacks.

"At least I have a girlfriend."

The smug bastard then wanders out of the room with his granola bar.

I check out his ass as he goes, just because I can.

CHAPTER 7
SEA SLUG SEX

KEATON

"**B**reakfast tomorrow?" Annika's voice chirps into my ear as I get ready for bed. It's just after eleven, but I've decided to call it a night. Today was a long-ass day and I barely got anything done.

"Can't," I answer, shifting the phone to my other ear so I can turn down the bedsheets. "I have a six a.m. practice, then a meeting with one of my TAs."

"Who cares about a meeting with a TA?" she grumbles. "It's not like he's your prof."

"No, but it's still important." More important than ever, actually. Charlie said he might have news for me tomorrow about an internship he's setting up.

Annika doesn't know about that, though, because I haven't told a soul. I doubt I'll get it, anyway. It's more of a guilty fantasy than a realistic option.

"Why's it so important?" she asks.

And yet despite her interest, which I appreciate, I don't offer any specifics. In fact, I flat out lie. "He's helping me with a paper that's worth fifty percent of the final grade."

"Fine. No breakfast, then. Let's do dinner with Lindy and Max."

"I thought we were mad at Lindy." I strip to my boxers and slide under the covers.

"We *were* mad, but now we're not."

I can practically *hear* her eyes rolling. "Okey dokey. Then I guess we're double-dating tomorrow night."

"I'll make reservations for eight?"

"Sounds good, baby."

We exchange good nights, and then I hang up and stare up at the ceiling for a moment. Why haven't I told Annika about the research trip to Chile yet? Initially, I told myself that it was pointless to mention the summer program to her unless it was a done deal, because it really does feel like a foolish dream more than anything.

But lately I've been toying with the idea of applying to graduate school next year. My dad would flip his shit. But it's my life, right? And my grandfather's trust fund would cover it, even if my dad cuts me off.

And he might very well take the nuclear option if I decide not to work for him. He's been grooming me to take over the family business since the moment I declared a bio major.

The thing is? I don't want his job. I don't want his life.

I want to spend three months sailing the coast of Chile, looking for an undocumented breed of orca. It's the kind of hands-on research program that makes budding marine biologists come in their pants.

Speaking of which… I never messaged SinnerThree after our little experiment earlier. I just didn't know what to say.

To him, or to myself, honestly. It shocked me how turned on I got talking to him. When Annika asked me to make her birthday exciting, I know she wasn't asking me to explore my sexuality with a stranger over an app.

So afterward, I needed a minute to cool off and get my head around the whole experience. Hell, I still do.

I grab my phone from the nightstand and open the app. Sure enough, there's a message waiting in my inbox. I don't get notifications from *Kink*—it'd be way too awkward for those to pop up when I'm with the guys—so I'm not sure how long the message has been sitting there.

A quick check of the timestamp brings some relief. He sent it only fifteen minutes ago.

SinnerThree: Please tell me the orgasm didn't kill ya. I mean, I've been told my mouth is dangerous, but never thought it was deadly.

I cringe. **Hey, sorry**, I type.

SinnerThree: He's alive!

LobsterShorts: I'm alive! Didn't mean to leave you hanging. Had to go for dinner, then I was dealing with a couple things, talking to GF, etc etc.

SinnerThree: I thought maybe I scared you off.

I hesitate. Do I tell him the truth? I suppose it's only fair.

LobsterShorts: I scared myself, maybe.

There's a brief delay, followed by: *B***ecause...you were bowled over by the power of my hotness? Did you come?**

Heat travels up my spine. Got right down to it, didn't he? Granted, why shouldn't he? We're conversing on an app called *Kink*, for Pete's sake.

LobsterShorts: What do you think? Of course I did.

SinnerThree: And?

LobsterShorts: And what?

SinnerThree: How was it? Life-changing?

How was it? I can't even begin to answer that. It was hot, definitely. I enjoyed it, obviously. But if you ask me how I *feel* about any of that...I'm still unsure. And even though he's joking, I don't want it to be life-changing. The point is to have some fun without changing my life.

LobsterShorts: It was hot.

SinnerThree: It would be even hotter in person.

I have a feeling he might be right. And I'm not sure how I feel about *that*, either. So I don't answer right away. And yet, some-how, this guy manages to read my mind, even via an app chat.

SinnerThree: You think so, too.

I take a breath, then carefully type, **Yeah, I think it could be hotter in person.**

SinnerThree: And? You think you want to go there?

I hesitate for a second. Fuck. I guess…here goes nothing.

LobsterShorts: I think…yeah. I do.

Before he can respond, I quickly add another sentence.

LobsterShorts: I think my gf will be really into watching.

Almost instantly, confusion ripples through me. I've confused *myself* by bringing up Annika. But the fact that I didn't think about her once during that sexting sesh still doesn't sit right with me.

SinnerThree: Tell me about her.

Now I'm wary. **What do you mean?** I ask. **What do you want to know exactly?**

SinnerThree: Relax, dude. I'm not asking for her name or social security number. Tell me what she likes in bed. How she likes to be touched, fucked… Or tell me more about lobster sex, if you want. I'm not picky about sex talk as long as someone's fucking.

I laugh softly. This guy's funny, I'll give him that.

LobsterShorts: I'm fresh out of lobster sex facts atm. BUT… lemme tell you about sea slugs.

SinnerThree: Omg yes. I can't wait for this. Hold on. Let me undo my pants.

This time I snort out loud. I know he's kidding, and I play along. **Actually, I'll do that, too. Having both our dicks out for this fun fact is so fitting.**

SinnerThree: Dick's out. All right. Slug sex. Now, baby.

LobsterShorts: OK—you ready for this?

SinnerThree: Hit me. Blow my mind.

LobsterShorts: Sea slugs have penis fights.

Dead air follows my revelation.

I see the three dots appear to indicate he's typing. Then they disappear. Reappear. Disappear.

Finally, a message pops up.

SinnerThree: I don't even know what to say to that. I guess... Why?? How?? Why???

I can't stop chuckling to myself as I type out a response. **It's exactly what it sounds like. Like two swords clanging against each other.**

SinnerThree: CLANGING? Are their penises made of metal??

LobsterShorts: No lmao. OK, bad analogy. Basically, they fence with their cocks. The contest determines who's the top and who's the bottom.

SinnerThree: OMFG. For real?

LobsterShorts: I swear. Look up "flatworm penis fencing." I'll wait.

And people wonder why I study animal behavior. It's endlessly fascinating.

There's another long delay before he says something. I hope he's staring at a photo of sea slug penises right now.

SinnerThree: You are a fun date, Lobsterman.

LobsterShorts: I don't like to brag, but...

SinnerThree: I was about to suggest we should do that when we finally meet. To decide which one of us gets fucked, but there's no point.

My pulse quickens immediately. This topic shouldn't be half as interesting to me as it is right now.

LobsterShorts: Why's that?

SinnerThree: Because my cock would be in your ass. The end.

I gulp, realizing I don't actually hate this idea. Try anything once, right? For science.

LobsterShorts: Uh-huh, is that how it is? You call all the shots?

SinnerThree: Most of the shots, yeah.

Lobster Shorts: And what if I'm not into that?

SinnerThree: Then we wouldn't be sexually compatible. But I have a feeling you might be. Into it, that is. Or at least you're more open to it than a birthday 3-way implies.

I look down at my crotch, where my boxers are already getting tight. And it's pretty hard to argue the point. It's pretty hard, period.

SinnerThree: Picture this: I'm behind you. My hand is wrapped around your rock-hard dick. And I'm jacking you while I'm drilling you.

I can't even swallow anymore—my mouth has gone from dry to completely arid. It feels like it's been stuffed full of cotton. Every word he'd just written sent a bolt of lust down my body. I can *picture* it. And he's right. I think...I think maybe I do want to know what that's like.

But that's not all I want, and although my fingers are trembling as I type, I manage to make my needs clear.

LobsterShorts: That does sound tempting. But so does the opposite—me drilling you while you come in my hand. So, naturally, my scientific brain kicks into gear and inquires: which option would feel better? My solution is, let's try both.

That's all a hundred percent bravado. I'm pretty far over my skis right now. I don't proposition men for sex. But I had to try it on. Typing it out makes it seem even more real. It takes me one step closer to the edge. And I wonder if I really have the balls to jump off. Or if I'm all talk.

God, I like the idea, though. I like it more than I ever let myself like it before. What would Annika think of me right now?

Annika! The reminder of her is once again jarring. What the hell is happening here? The conversation began with Sinner asking what Annika likes in bed, and somehow turned into the two of us discussing banging each other.

I draw a deep breath, trying to digest that, just as a response finally comes through.

SinnerThree: Since this is probably just a scientific hypothe-

sis, I'll agree to a deal. First time? I'd get your ass. If there's a second time? You'd get mine.

He's right. This is all just smack talk, anyway. If I ever meet SinnerThree, the night will be all about Annika.

So why is that so difficult to remember when I'm talking to him?

My cock is stone-hard in my shorts. I absently pass my hand over it, and my balls begin to throb.

GTG, I type. **It's getting late.**

SinnerThree: Uh huh. Feel free to review my pics while you're relieving some tension in a few minutes.

Christ.

LobsterShorts: Get out of my head.

SinnerThree: It's not your head that I want. Sleep tight and dream of me, baby. Or sea slugs.

The green dot beside his icon winks off.

I set down my phone. And then I slip my hand past the elastic of my boxers. And I do the thing that guys do when they need release. And I try not to think too much about why I need it so badly.

CHAPTER 8
IT GETS MESSY

LUKE

I t's another brutal week of school assignments and work. Those extra bartending sessions are killing me. But at least my Dance-off plans are shaping up nicely.

Unfortunately, the engine on my bike is making a rattling sound whenever I turn at an intersection. It might just be that the chain needs adjusting, but all my tools are in my mother's garage.

That's how I find myself stopping by there on Sunday, the way Mom asked me to. Besides, free food is free food.

Sitting at our small table beside my brother Joe isn't easy, though. Did it always feel this crowded in here? And the only one talking is Mom. Joe just shovels in the food and nods whenever he thinks he should.

It's not a bad strategy, really.

Joe leans back in his chair like a king as my mother scoops another portion of homemade mac and cheese onto his plate. "There's more deviled eggs," she clucks, offering him that dish, too.

Swear to God, the whole time Joe was in prison, my mother

paced our house, worrying. But she wasn't asking herself, "Why would my boy turn out to be a criminal?"

Not our mom. She was wondering if he was getting enough to eat.

She doesn't offer me seconds, and I have too much pride to reach for the dish. So I drain the water in my glass and ask to be excused. "I need to open up the garage and find a wrench, okay?" I push my chair back.

"Wait!" she says. "I didn't get a chance to tell you our news."

I pause, wary. "Okay. What's up?"

"We're starting a handyman business!" she announces, clapping her hands. "I'll do all the bookings. Joe will go out and do the repairs."

Holy shit. Because everyone wants to give a felon access to their homes?

It takes colossal willpower to avoid speaking my mind. "That's great, Ma. Could be good for both of you." And it's true that Joe can't easily find work. If you check that box on an employment application—convicted felon—nobody ever calls you back.

Then again, if he'd thought of that before breaking into homes to steal flat-screen TVs, maybe he wouldn't be that twenty-six-year-old loser who's still sponging off Mommy, would he?

I make my move to get up, but Mom puts a hand on my wrist. "Honey, I need a favor. Would you have five hundred dollars you could invest in our business?"

"Invest," I repeat stupidly. That's a word you'd use for a nice little mutual fund, maybe. Giving your money to Mom and Joe would be as productive as lighting it on fire.

No, *less* productive. At least you could roast a marshmallow over the fire.

"Just a loan," she says. "We have startup costs. We need an extension ladder, and we need to place an ad in the newspaper."

"Wouldn't an online ad be cheaper?" I ask before I can stop

myself. Business is interesting to me. But I can't offer to help this sad little venture. I will not be sucked into their issues.

There are so many of those.

"Maybe!" Mom says, gripping my wrist. It's probably obvious how badly I need to get away.

"I don't have any extra cash right now," I say, hopefully ending the conversation. "I'd love to help, but I can't."

She blinks at me. And then blinks some more. It's time for another performance of guilt and tears.

"I owe my fraternity seven hundred bucks on Friday," I tell her, which is the truth. "And I still need to eat and buy gas for my bike..." I sigh.

"Just this once," she begs. "Please think about it."

"Oh, I will." That comes out sounding darker than I meant it to. "I'll see what I can do."

The truth is that if I pick up more extra shifts behind the bar next week, I could loan her the money. But I've loaned her money before, and she never pays it back.

Why is that okay? Like, seriously. If she just said it had to be a gift, not a loan, I wouldn't feel so used when she asks me for money.

I escape to the garage in peace. If I have any luck at all, the rattle my bike is making is just a loose chain. I find my torque wrench and kneel down on the garage floor for a better look.

Sure enough, the tension is off a little. I can do this.

Or maybe I can't. You need someone's weight on the bike to get the tension right. Maybe there's a workaround? I pull out my phone to Google for a solution. Honestly, balancing some bricks on the bike would be easier than asking a family member.

There's a new message on *Kink*, so I open it up, because I have no self control. LobsterShorts and I continued to text each other this week. He's fun to talk to. Our chats always start off random before inevitably turning to sex.

It's a pattern, I think. Lobster is attracted to me, and probably men in general. But he feels guilty about it. Every time I get him riled up, he disappears for a day or so. Then he always comes back.

LobsterShorts: Today's animal behavior tidbit is about kangaroos.

There's a link, so I click it. The screen loads with a video of a kangaroo, all right. And he's...

Really?

SinnerThree: Is that kangaroo jacking off?

His response comes so quickly that I know he's been waiting there for me.

LobsterShorts: Of course he is. Did you really think that humans would be the only ones to discover that you can polish your own pole?

SinnerThree: I guess I've seen a dog lick his balls. But I thought you needed opposable thumbs to really get freaky.

LobsterShorts: Dolphins will hump an inanimate object. Or occasionally a diver.

SinnerThree: OMG. Humped by a dolphin? GTFO.

I'm sitting on the garage floor cracking up.

LobsterShorts: Lots of primates masturbate, including the females. Bats even jerk it while hanging upside down. And yes, it gets messy.

I'm dead.

"What's so funny?"

I look up fast as my brother comes around the corner. "Nothing," I say, hastily texting back. **GTG, asshole brother is in my face.** Shoving my phone into my pocket, I stand up.

"Look, about the money," Joe starts.

"That's what you want to talk to me about? *Quelle surprise.*" It makes him nutty whenever I remind him that I'm studying French. Or that I'm good at anything, really.

"Look," he says, not taking the bait. "I got a better idea."

I can't wait to hear this.

"You live in that fraternity house, with all those rich kids? All we need is one computer, Lukey. Just one will be worth more than the five hundred bucks that Ma wants."

My blood pressure quadruples in the span of two seconds. "That's the *worst* idea you've ever had. All laptops have that app now—*find my stuff*. The cops would pull up outside your door an hour later. Do you really want to go back to jail?"

"You don't like my idea?" he sneers. "Then give us the money, you little faggot. We both know you can."

I try to control my anger. Only my brother would use a hateful slur while trying to convince me to give him cash. "I'm thinking, okay? Do me the world's easiest favor and sit on the bike. I need to adjust the tension."

He waits a beat, and I think he's really so stubborn that he won't do this small thing for me. But then he throws a leg over and puts his weight on the bike.

Grateful, I sink down and quickly apply the torque wrench to the bolts. "Look, it's really not like I have five hundred extra dollars. I'd have to work some extra hours. And only if I can get the shifts."

"So how about you do that?" he says. "If you don't, I'll tell Ma what it is you really do for most of your cash, and it ain't tending bar."

It's a good thing he can't see my face, because I do a poor job of concealing my surprise. How the hell does he know about my job at the club?

I take a deep, slow breath and then call his bluff. "I don't care if you tell Mom. She doesn't give a fuck, just as long as she can treat me like an ATM."

But I'm bluffing, too. I care very much who knows about my job. If Joe told my fraternity brothers, that would be dangerous to my future. If they made a prank out of taking my photo or filming my ass on stage, that shit could wind up on the internet. And if it's attached to my real name…

I can't let that happen. Next year I'll be applying for jobs all over the country. And "male stripper" cannot be the first thing that comes up when someone searches my name.

There's nothing wrong with dancing. Stripping. Whatever. But I can't afford to be the punch line of a joke.

"Make it six hundred, then," Joey says as I fiddle with the bike chain. "One of those C-notes you pass to me privately."

Fuck you! I want to shout. *Fuck you, fuck Mom, fuck this entire fucking planet.*

But I don't.

"Okay," I say instead.

Like I even have a choice.

CHAPTER 9
REALLY, LOBSTERMAN?

LUKE

I nteracting with my family never fails to put me in the foulest of moods, which makes it difficult to concentrate on studying later that night. Eventually I give up. My paper on economic history can wait until tomorrow. Really, all that's left to do is tweak a few paragraphs, write the conclusion, and then proof-read. If I try doing any of that while my brain isn't sharp, I'll end up having to work on it tomorrow anyway.

So I flop down on my bed and open *Kink*. Chatting with LobsterShorts always boosts my spirits. I click my inbox and grin when I discover a message from him already waiting for me.

LobsterShorts: Woke up this morning and jerked off to a pic of your abs. And then I thought—I'm jerking off to abs? Why hasn't that bastard sent me a dick pic yet?

I snort out loud. Yup, in all of two seconds, this dude's managed to get a laugh out of me. In my regular life I'm hardly ever laughing, and if I am, it's usually sardonically. But Lobster evokes genuine amusement in me. He's goofy and sexy and this is exactly what I need tonight. Forget about my paper. This is way more fun.

SinnerThree: Um. Why haven't YOU sent ME a dick pic?

LobsterShorts: You never asked.

Yeah, I never asked because I thought it would send him back into hibernation. But if he's feeling frisky again, I'm totally here for that. Maybe he'll let me get him off again in real time.

SinnerThree: Tell you what. Quid pro quo. Dick pics will be exchanged. Also, if your girl's down for it, I wouldn't mind seeing some T&A from her.

Since his previous two messages popped up in seconds, the delay I encounter raises my guard a bit. Was my request out of line?

But no, it can't be. Lobster proposed a three-way, and all I've seen of his girl thus far is a photo of her in a bikini. If I'm going to be sleeping with both of them, it would be nice to see pics—of *both* of them.

And yet not once have you sexted about this supposed three-way...

I stiffen. And not in the southern region of my body. My shoulders draw up tight as I let the unsettling thought sink in.

LobsterShorts: Let me see what I can do.

The vague response brings a frown to my lips. Something's bugging me. Maybe my suspicions are completely ludicrous, but I can't stop myself from asking a blunt question.

SinnerThree: Is there really a gf, Lobsterman?

This time, the long delay doesn't surprise me. In fact, I'm convinced it might be more evidence to support my doubts. Lobster hardly ever mentions his girlfriend. Yes, his profile picture depicts two people, one of whom is clearly a hot chick. And I don't think it's a Photoshop job or anything—I'm sure he did have a girlfriend at one point. Or hell, maybe he still does and it's only the threesome that's bogus.

But I'm getting the sense that this guy doesn't want me to fuck him *and* his girl. He wants me to fuck him. Period.

LobsterShorts: Sorry. I'm confused. I do have a gf—I wouldn't lie about that. I don't understand why you think I would?

I decide to tread carefully. Because at the end of the day, I *like* chatting with him. I'm not ready to lose this connection yet. But I also don't have time for games.

SinnerThree: It's just that you never bring her up during our chats.

His response pops up as I'm still typing.

LobsterShorts: That's not true. One time I said she'd like watching us.

SinnerThree: Right. You did say that. But...you don't include her in these virtual fuck sessions. If there's a threesome in the cards for us, shouldn't we discuss how the third member of this endeavor fits in?

LobsterShorts: Of course you have a point. I thought we were still trying to figure out whether I can handle dude sex without screaming and running out the door.

SinnerThree: Babe. I think we established that after our first convo. You won't run out the door. Screaming...maybe ;) Actually, more like moaning. Loudly.

LobsterShorts: Someone's sure of themselves.

SinnerThree: Yes. I am. But anyway...yeah. I'm not worried about whether or not you'll enjoy my presence. Now I'm concerned about how you'll react to me being around your girl.

LobsterShorts: What do you mean?

SinnerThree: I mean, I'm going to touch her, you realize that, right?

LobsterShorts: Obvs.

Another frown reaches my lips. There's something very cavalier about how he responded to that. I can't figure out if he's putting on a front, acting like he's not bothered by the idea of his girlfriend sleeping with someone else. Or if he truly doesn't give a shit.

SinnerThree: I'm going to kiss her. I'm going to have my mouth on her tits, on her clit. My dick may be inside her.

LobsterShorts: Well aware of that.

Is he being snippy? That sounded defensive. Fuck, I really wish it were easier to read tone via text messages.

LobsterShorts: That's the whole point of a threeway, Sinner. You'll be touching her, I'll be touching her. You'll be touching me, she and I will be touching you.

SinnerThree: And you're perfectly okay with all of that?

LobsterShorts: Would I be on this app otherwise?

I try to figure out the best way to respond, but as I'm crafting the words, he pushes back again.

LobsterShorts: Why else would I be on this app?

SinnerThree: A lot of bi-curious guys, or closeted gay guys, use apps like Kink to act out the fantasies they can't act on in real life. Which is fine. Sexting is sexting. I don't care why someone is on here. I guess what I'm saying is—if you were one of those curious dudes and there was no girlfriend, I would be cool with that and there'd be no need for pretenses.

LobsterShorts: There's a girlfriend. I promise.

SinnerThree: K.

LobsterShorts: Are you disappointed by that? Lmao I honestly can't tell.

Am I? I can't fully decipher whatever's tugging on my stomach. I like talking to this guy. It's easy. And clearly we're sexually compatible, at least on paper. But I also swiped on his profile because at the time, I really *was* in the mood for a three-way. I enjoy fucking women. I enjoy it a lot. And I can't deny that his girl has a fire body that turns me on just as much as his does.

SinnerThree: No disappointment on my end. I'm dying to put my mouth on both of you.

LobsterShorts: That so?

SinnerThree: Yup. Your girl has phenomenal tits. Are they as sexy under that bikini top as they look in it?

LobsterShorts: Yup. Perky, a perfect handful. Dark pink nipples, and they get so hard when she's horny.

SinnerThree: How long have you been together? If you don't mind me asking.

In the back of my mind, it occurs to me that I'm shifting away from the topic of sex, but the question was biting at my tongue, and I had to type it. I wouldn't mind getting a sense of their relationship before I throw myself into the mix.

LobsterShorts: Years. Since high school.

SinnerThree: She the only girl you've ever slept with?

LobsterShorts: Yeah. And I assume you've slept with hundreds?

SinnerThree: Hundreds? Are you crazy?

SinnerThree: More like thousands… ;)

LobsterShorts: Eye roll.

SinnerThree: All seriousness, I've fucked a lot of women. More women than men, tbh.

LobsterShorts: Huh. I find that surprising.

SinnerThree: Why's that?

LobsterShorts: Because you sound so confident about this guy-on-guy action. You talk as if you've done it countless times.

SinnerThree: Well, I mean, I have. Just not as much as with chicks.

LobsterShorts: Which do you like better? Men or women?

SinnerThree: That's a loaded question. It's two very different kinds of experiences.

LobsterShorts: Have you been in any long-term relationships, guy or girl?

SinnerThree: Dated a girl in high school for one year. And a guy for two months freshman year of college.

LobsterShorts: Was there a preference there?

SinnerThree: Not really. Sometimes it's easier talking to a guy, though. I'm not saying men aren't as emotional as women—obviously we have emotions. But I feel like deep conversations with chicks are sometimes harder. Like, they expect me to read their minds, or to feel the same way they feel in reaction to certain situations.

LobsterShorts: Ikr? My gf expects me to know what she's thinking and feeling at all times. Granted, we've been together for so long that I pretty much do lmao

SinnerThree: Ha!

LobsterShorts: But it's true—she's not the easiest to talk to. Like, she thinks every problem has one solution, and that isn't always the case. Sometimes there are many solutions, and you need to analyze each one before deciding the course of action.

SinnerThree: I keep forgetting you're a boring scientist. Is your gf a science nerd too?

LobsterShorts: Nah. She's nowhere close to being as cool as I am.

SinnerThree: Eye roll times two.

LobsterShorts: She's very cool. She's smart, outspoken, feisty when you poke at her. You'll like her.

I hesitate only for a beat before typing, **And I assume, you love her?**

LobsterShorts: Yup.

No hesitation on his part. Except then he follows it up with, **She's my best friend. We've been together for ages.**

SinnerThree: How does she feel about this threeway thing?

LobsterShorts: It was her idea, remember? Her bday request.

SinnerThree: Right, I know. I mean, how does she feel about a threeway with ME. You've told her about me, right?

LobsterShorts: Um.

My eyebrows fly up. Is he joking? He hasn't told the third member of our threesome about the dude he's been sexting with for nearly two weeks now?

LobsterShorts: Before you jump to conclusions—it's not because of that thing you said before, about bi-curious guys and fake girlfriends. She's real. She's the best. And I haven't told her about you yet because up until now I was still sort of, I dunno, "vetting" you. She means a lot to me, and I don't want just any guy being intimate with her, you know?

Everything he says makes total sense.

And yet...I don't believe him.

I carefully ask, **Okay. When do you plan on telling her about me? When are the three of us doing this thing?**

LobsterShorts: I'll tell her this week, if that makes you feel better?

I'm not sure if it does or doesn't, so I don't answer. I just let him keep typing.

LobsterShorts: As for when... Her birthday is right after Christmas break. January fourth. It's even on the weekend. Does that work?

Weekends are tricky for me, because that's when I dance. But if this really happens, I'll make it work.

SinnerThree: Sure. I'll pencil you both in for mind-blowing sex on January 4.

LobsterShorts: Perfect. She and I will chat this week about everything.

SinnerThree: Don't forget to tell her about my massive cock.

LobsterShorts: Snort. It'll be the first item on the agenda. Now how bout you pull it out and send me that dick pic?

SinnerThree: Soon. Talk to your girl first.

LobsterShorts: Will do.

CHAPTER 10
A SUCCESS BY ANY MEASURE

KEATON

"Pledges!" I growl toward the bar that's set up in corner of the big tent. "You have ten minutes to tap those kegs."

"How many of 'em to start?" asks Jimmy in his southern drawl.

"Three. No—four. We'll get this party started right when the doors open in ten."

The last week has been sheer hell, between football practice, studying for finals, and planning this party. But I came through, damn it. It's going to be great.

"Keat?" Tanner calls from the entrance to the tent. "Are you expecting a florist?"

"Oh, shit. Yes. Will you handle it? You're getting a hundred leis."

Tanner's forehead wrinkles. "Like, the potato chips?"

"No! Jeez. It's like a flower necklace. In Hawaii."

"Uh, sure." He disappears.

"Flowers?" Luke Bailey says dryly. He's standing in the middle of the tent, surveying my work. "That couldn't have been cheap."

I ignore him, although he isn't wrong. The flowers did cost me a mint. I don't care, though. There's some kind of budget for the party, but I'm sure I overspent it. The only way to plan this thing quickly was to avoid looking at price tags. Besides, my father won't mind. Not if I'm spending it to secure the presidency.

"Keat!" Tanner returns, carrying a giant box of leis into the tent. "There's, like, a hundred and fifty sorority girls outside, waiting to get in." His grin is ear to ear.

"Only a hundred and fifty?" I tease. But if we're grading on attendance, this is a slam-dunk. "Keep those near the door. You're handing one to every girl who comes in. And don't forget the rule, okay? The dress code is bathing suits only. No—make that beachwear," I say, changing my mind. Not everybody wants to wear a bathing suit in public. "It just has to seem like they tried."

"We gonna freeze our asses off?" Jako complains. He's standing next to his buddy Luke, and they both look disgruntled.

"You think I haven't thought of everything? Well, I have." I snap my fingers at the pledges in the corner. "It's time, boys. Turn on the heat lamps."

Jimmy scrambles to do my bidding. A moment later, the warm orange glow of heat lamps illuminates our faces.

Both Luke and Jako tilt their chins upward, admiring my handiwork. Jako actually whistles.

"For fuck's sake," Bailey complains. "Try not to look so impressed."

His friend laughs. "Dude, we're at the beach. In December."

"How fucking original," Luke says with a smirk. "A beach party at a fraternity house. Who would have thought?" He rolls his obnoxious eyes.

He's half right. Lots of frats have beach parties—*in the spring*. Filling our yard with two dump truckloads of sand isn't a new idea. But doing it at this time of year? Super fun.

"Look, Bailey. Thanks for the helpful feedback. But this is going to be a rager, the only winter party on campus with half-naked guests dancing till dawn. And it won't even mess up our house, like most winter parties do. You're welcome."

Luke glances around, anger flickering in his expression. But I also glimpse a hint of envy.

And he should be envious. I've thought of everything. Besides the high-quality beer, there are punch drinks with little umbrellas in them. The steel drum band I hired is warming up, giving everything a tropical sound. When they finish their set, my DJ will step in and get the place rocking.

The brothers are already impressed. And because I know everyone so well, I chose my details carefully. Half those kegs are full of Paxton's favorite ale. And the other half are full of Reed's. The punch has rum in it, which Owen and Zimmer both love. And the DJ is Munsen's favorite. I even got a bunch of hula hoops for a contest later, because Mithani loves to shake his hips around.

The best part is that I put this whole thing together in three days. Once I stopped panicking about how to throw a ground-breakingly original fete, and began asking myself what my friends like, it got easy.

Who doesn't like the beach, right?

Everyone except Luke Bailey, apparently. But that dude doesn't like anything, and I knew better than to try to impress him.

"You better get ready," he threatens, "because you've got a hundred and fifty women outside."

"I know." I smirk.

"In their bathing suits," he adds. "In the *cold*."

Oh, fuck. I check my watch. "Tanner! Open those doors early. I can't keep my public waiting."

"Sure, dude," my friend agrees. "But, uh, you're not ready."

"What?" I look around again. I am ready. The sand is perfect. The heat is cranking. The drinks are ready, and the music has begun.

"You made a big fucking deal that we all had to wear our

bathing suits," Luke says, stripping off his T-shirt to reveal that eight-pack he's so fond of flashing around. "Where's yours?"

I look down. I'm wearing track pants and running shoes.

Fuck.

"Be right back," I say, and then jog toward the back of the tent.

I can hear that asshole Bailey laughing as I go. Whatever. This party is awesome, and he's just a sore loser.

"Bathing suit?" Annika asks as I trot past the spot where she and her friend Lindy are hanging the last strand of chili pepper lights around the perimeter.

"Yup!" I call. "Back in a jif!"

"Great party, baby!" she calls. "Save me the first dance?"

"You know it!" I rocket across the lawn and then vault up the stairs, two at a time.

It's like this for every big party I've planned at Alpha Delt— there's always one little detail that gets lost in the shuffle. Even as I'm hastily unlocking the door to my room, I wonder where my swim trunks are. I haven't worn them since the summer.

The moment I'm inside, I open the top drawer, pushing the boxers aside, looking for the red lobster print. But it's not there. I open the next drawer, frantic now. And the next.

Nothing. But then all of a sudden it hits me—I'm looking for the wrong thing. That suit is at our Hamptons house. I yank the top drawer open again and pull out my other favorite pair of trunks on the first try. They're blue, with yellow and white sailboats all over them.

I drop trou, yank on the blue suit, and heave a sigh of relief.

———

My party is a success by any measure. I come in fourth in the hula hoop contest, because the host has to make a good showing. The DJ is in a groove, and the pledges do a great job of serving everyone, and the compliments I've received tonight just keep piling up.

By one in the morning, I am cheerfully drunk, with sand between my toes. The punch is gone, but the beer is still flowing. The dance floor is packed, with Annika and me at the center.

"Look," she says, squeezing the arm that I have wrapped around her. "Tanner is having a good night."

After a quick look around, I spot him sprawled against an inflatable shark, making out with a cute, bikini-clad girl. *Go Tanner!* Sometimes he lacks confidence. But not tonight, apparently.

See? My beach party is good for the soul. I'm feeling very presidential.

The music slows down, and I pull Annika against my chest, one hand on her hip. I survey my domain, taking in all the happy partygoers.

"What do you see?" Annika asks over her shoulder. "Which animal are we behaving like tonight? None, right? Animals are too smart for *that*." She points at some drunk pledges trying to arm wrestle on the bar.

"Heck no, they're not." I kiss her temple. "There are these monkeys on St. Kitts that steal cocktails and get hammered. Their tolerance for alcohol is distributed among the community just like in humans. You have your social drinkers; they make up the bulk. And then you have a few who don't like alcohol, and a few wasted frat boys."

Annika turns around in my arms and smiles at me. "You are endlessly fascinating, Keaton Hayworth the third." She puts her body against mine, and dances closer. I rest my chin on her shoulder, and we rotate slowly, our bare feet in the sand.

She's soft and warm against me, her perky tits brushing my pecs. We haven't had sex in more than a week, as my libido tends to retreat underground like a frightened groundhog when I'm stressed out. I haven't sexted with SinnerThree, either. We've exchanged a few messages here and there, but it sounded like he was as busy as I was.

Annika was swamped, too, and since we've been together for

five years, one week without sex isn't something we really freak out about. We've gone through much longer dry spells, and neither of us ever complains.

The party rages on around us. My gaze snags on Dan Zimmer, the only Alpha Delt brother who's openly gay. I've never witnessed him on the prowl before. But—holy shit—he's got his tongue in some guy's mouth. As I watch, their heads tilt for a better angle.

The other guy, some blond dude in bright yellow board shorts, wraps a strong arm around Dan's bare waist. They're chest to chest as they devour each other's mouths, kiss after hungry kiss.

When Dan's conquest slips that hand onto Dan's ass and gives it a dirty squeeze, my cock begins to feel heavy and full. I know I should look away. I drop my lips to Annika's neck and kiss her warm skin.

But I can still see them. I'm openly staring as they make out, their bare chests bumping. And I wonder how that feels—hard pecs against your own. A happy trail, maybe.

Goddamn it. I force myself to close my eyes, but the image is still there, taunting me. This curiosity of mine is getting really inconvenient. And my exchanges with SinnerThree have only intensified it.

I'd promised him I'd tell Annika about him this week, but I've been putting it off. With arousal thrumming in my blood at the sight of Dan's PDA and the feel of Annika's full tits crushed against my chest, I decide now might be the time.

"I may have found us a candidate," I hear myself whisper in Annika's ear.

"What do you mean," she murmurs back, lazily stroking the nape of my neck with her interlaced hands.

"Your birthday present?" I prompt.

My girl leans back suddenly and looks up at me. "You mean…?" Her breath hitches, and I can't quite decode the look in her eyes. I think it's anticipation?

And yet the moment she asks, "Who?" I find myself clamming up.

For some messed-up reason, I don't want to tell her how awesome SinnerThree is. Annika and I have been a team since high school. We did—do—everything together. We share friends, food, experiences. This app connection I have with Sinner…right now, it's just *mine*. I know that soon it won't be. Soon I'll need to share him with Annika.

And I just… No. Not yet.

I'm not sure what I'm going to say when I open my mouth, but luckily I'm spared from speaking at all.

"Hayworth," comes Luke Bailey's grudging voice.

I was rocking a semi-erection, but it disappears the moment Bailey approaches. He probably has that effect on lots of people.

"Yeah?" I arch a brow. Is he going to tell me how much this party blows? That he's having a *terrible* time? Because last I saw, he was flirting with one of Annika's sorority sisters underneath a huge inflatable palm tree.

"You might suck, but this party doesn't," is what I get.

I can't help but snicker. From Bailey, that's high praise. "Does that mean you're conceding? If so, I humbly accept this presidency."

He snickers back. "Fuck off. Nobody's conceding here. A good politician is gracious to his opponents even when he's about to crush them."

I wave a hand at the elaborate party I expertly planned. "Crush me? Dude, look around. I *owned* you tonight."

Bailey smirks. "Keep telling yourself that."

He saunters off, and Annika and I stare at his retreating back for a moment. His sinewy muscles flex with each step he takes, and…fine, maybe his ass looks damn good in those snug blue trunks.

Beside me, Annika sighs softly. "That guy might be a prick, but he is *built*."

I tweak a strand of her hair. "Don't get any ideas. Neither one of us will be fucking him."

Her head tips in surprise, and it takes a moment for me to realize that she's startled by the smoothness of my words, how casually—and easily—I'd just spoken about sleeping with a dude.

One delicate eyebrow lifts up slowly. "Hmmm. You really *have* been thinking hard about this birthday request..." She hesitates. "Maybe we should go upstairs and do some warmups."

"Warmups?"

"Familiar drills," she says, pinching my ass. "Just to limber up before the big event. We can't go into the big game cold."

I kiss her neck. "I think I take your meaning. Okay, let's go. The coach needs you to blow his whistle."

Annika giggles against my chest, and then I turn her toward the exit and we head upstairs.

CHAPTER 11
ET TU, JUDD?

KEATON

Bailey's party is on Sunday night.

No, that's not the start of a bad joke—Luke Bailey *is* the joke. Because…

Who. The. Hell. Plans a party. On a Sunday night?

And I haven't even gotten to the punch line yet. Not only has Bailey scheduled his Dance-off event for Sunday (two nights after the dopest bash, courtesy of yours truly), it's not even a real party. It's a *dinner*. And he didn't let us invite guests.

Yeah… I've got the presidency in the bag.

Judd and I exchange an amused look as we take our seats. The dining room isn't big enough to seat all the brothers. So Bailey has set up long rented tables in the living room. And while there's enough seating for everyone, it's not exactly the roomiest of setups.

"Sweet sausage fest," Judd cracks to Bailey.

Luke just winks. He's clad in a dark-blue dress shirt, with a blazer over it, and crisp trousers. He requested that we all show up in semi-formal wear—suits, dinner jackets, the whole shebang.

So we're crammed like sardines at this dinner table, dressed like a group of young Republicans. Par-tay.

As Bailey settles at the head of the table, I notice a few other dudes sharing glances. Looks like my opponent isn't scoring any points with his constituents. I literally brought the beach to Darby in the middle of winter. He planned a dinner party.

Checkmate.

"Two-buck Chuck?" Owen gripes loudly, reaching for one of the wine bottles on the table. "You're seriously serving us this shit? You couldn't spring for something better?"

Once again, Luke appears unfazed by the criticism. "Best I could do on the budget we were given." He gives a small shrug. "And I'm not serving you anything. The catering staff's got that part handled."

As if on cue, the door separating the dining room from the living room swings open, and two pretty blondes saunter out. They're followed by two brunettes wielding trays of hors d'oeuvres.

"Oh," Owen blurts out.

I'm not sure if he's responding to Bailey or voicing his surprise, which only lingers in his expression for a nanosecond before his eyes darken with appreciation.

The four chicks are gorgeous, greeting everyone with dazzling smiles. Two of them begin pouring wine into each brother's glass. The other two—no, make that four. *Four* hot girls are now serving delicious-looking finger foods, while every dude in the room looks on in awe. Even Dan, who isn't into chicks, seems intrigued by our servers.

I furrow my brow, shooting Bailey a what-are-you-up-to look, but he offers another careless shrug. Then he flashes that arrogant grin at a dark-haired bombshell whose tits are so huge they're actually straining against the front of her white button-down.

All six—oh for fuck's sake, make that eight. *Eight* waitresses are now sashaying around the tables, smiling as they serve us. All of them wear identical uniforms: white shirts tucked into short, black skirts. And they're all in black heels, some of which seem way too high for caterers. But as Annika always tells me, high heels belong at *any* occasion.

My Alpha Delt brothers are digging into the appetizers. I slide a garlic shrimp off its little skewer and pop it into my mouth. Oh, that's good. Bailey might've sprung for cheap wine, but he did a decent job with the apps.

With that said, there's no way a *dinner party* is going to top my beach party. I don't care if this shrimp was flown in from the Gulf and prepared by Thomas Keller. Beach trumps dinner.

"Mmmmfhfhg," Judd mumbles as he stuffs a cheese ball in his mouth. He's trying to talk even as he keeps chomping.

"What was that?" I ask in amusement.

He swallows and becomes intelligible. "I said, 'try the cheese balls.' They're fucking excellent."

"Thank you!" comes a pleased female voice. One of the blondes touches Judd's shoulder. "I prepared these myself."

Judd peers up at her, grinning lewdly. "A woman who knows how to handle balls. I dig it."

I expect her to be horrified, but she just winks and moves down the line to take care of Ahmad. I guess this company has catered enough college events that they're used to horny frat boys saying inappropriate things.

Judd leans closer to me and murmurs, "You got this in the bag, bro. This dinner's lame."

And yet at the head of the table, Luke Bailey is completely unbothered, or maybe he's just oblivious to our reactions. Not just mine and Judd's, but *everyone's*. Even his own campaign manager, Jako, sports a look of bewilderment, as if he can't understand why Luke chose a fancy boys-only dinner for the Dance-off.

The hot waitresses clear away our apps, refill our wine glasses, and the next course comes out: a peach and avocado salad that is damn tasty. After that is the entrée, filet mignon au poivre, with scalloped potatoes and French beans. There's even a vegetable plate for Munsen, who doesn't eat meat. I don't miss the way the brothers devour everything.

For the first time all evening, a sliver of worry pierces my gut. *The way to a man's heart is through his stomach…* Fuck, that phrase is a phrase for a reason. Men like food. Men like being fed. Men *especially* like being fed by hot, big-breasted women.

There isn't a cup size lower than C in the room. And the servers seem to have no qualms about waving their boobs in our faces.

"Let me top that off for you," one of them coos as she practically drapes herself over Paxton Grier's broad shoulder.

Her left tit is legit pressing against his cheek as she pours the sparkling liquid into his wineglass. His tongue practically rolls out of his mouth and falls onto his half-eaten steak.

Narrowing my eyes, I glance at Luke again. He's deep in conversation with Tanner. Which isn't a sight I like to see. Tanner is solidly in *my* corner. He's my closest friend in the house after Judd. There's no way in hell he's allowed to vote for Bailey.

I mentally will their conversation to end, but I fail. Tanner throws his head back and laughs at something Luke just said. Goddammit. I'm losing Tanner. And then one of those hot temptresses rests a hand on Judd's shoulder and leans down to whisper something in his ear, and suddenly I fear for Judd's soul as well.

By the time our entrée dishes are carted off to the kitchen, the back of my neck feels real hot, and my dinner jacket feels too tight. I'm genuinely concerned that Bailey is winning everyone over. Dinner was amazing, I can't deny that. And I certainly can't deny that all the eye candy in the room is a stroke of genius.

I need this evening to be over before Bailey scores any more points. We just finished the main dish, so I'm assuming there'll be dessert now, and then I'll be done with this shit.

Except Luke Bailey has other ideas.

After the last dish is whisked away, he clears his throat to get everyone's attention.

"Gentlemen," he says when the room goes quiet. "If you'll please indulge me and pick up your glasses."

Judd rolls his eyes at me. I roll mine in return. Guess it's time for the big speech nobody gives a shit to hear?

But we humor the guy. Everyone takes a glass in hand, waiting.

The toast I'm expecting doesn't come.

"Um, you gonna say something?" Judd mocks.

"Nah," drawls Luke.

"You're not making a toast?" grumbles Owen.

"Nope."

"Then why the fuck are we all holding our glasses?" Tim demands.

"Oh, I wasn't clear about that, sorry. I just wanted you to pick up your wine glasses so there's room on the table." His gaze shifts briefly to a point behind Tim's head.

"Room for what?" Ahmad asks in confusion.

I glance over my shoulder to follow Luke's gaze. One of the waitresses, a tall redhead, is bending over a laptop near the entertainment center. Suspicion surges in my blood at the same moment a blast of music rocks the house.

"The entertainment," Luke shouts to Ahmad. His cocky gaze sweeps over the rest of us. "Time for the fun part, boys. You can look, but you can't touch."

That sneaky motherfucker—

Before I can blink, three of the women have hopped up onto the tables, strutting on the white tablecloth in their high heels. A sultry beat thumps in the room, shaking the walls, vibrating in the floor. When the song offers a sharp crash of cymbal, one of the chicks rips open her white dress shirt, revealing the sexy red bra underneath. It barely contains her tits, which are spilling over the lacy cups.

"Oh my God," Judd moans happily.

His reaction is shared by every other guy in the room, Dan included. Our only gay brother literally hops to his feet and starts bumping his hips against one of the girls who's still on land. Granted, he seems more into the song than the chick, but still. I feel betrayed, and Dan and I aren't even close.

Chaos erupts all around me. The seductive trio on the table shake their hips, dancing in sexy, sinuous moves that summon cheers and catcalls from the twenty-three other guys in the room. And—fuck me—they can really move. It's sexy, with hips swinging and asses shaking near my guys' overjoyed faces. But it's a real show, too.

Unfuckingbelievable.

I'm too stunned by this unexpected turn of events to fully appreciate the gorgeous, half-naked creatures dancing expertly for us.

I glower at Bailey, who just grins at me. "Who needs change for a twenty?" he calls as he circles the table. "It's polite to tip our entertainers." He's making the rounds, offering stacks of small bills to our frat brothers, who all dive for their wallets.

That fucking evil genius. Food and strippers. He really does know the way to a man's heart.

"Who's ready for strip poker?" Jako shouts from the kitchen doorway. He'd disappeared right after dinner ended, and now I know why—beyond his broad shoulders, I glimpse the three green-felt game tables he set up in our dining room.

So much for him being "confused" by Bailey. Obviously Jako was in on it the entire time.

"Fuck *yeah*!" Judd shouts back.

Ah hell. Everyone knows how much Judd loves poker. And now we're talking *naked* poker?

Evil fucking genius.

Judd lumbers forward, one beefy arm slung around the shoulders of a curvy dancer with big green eyes. On his way to the kitchen, my traitorous best friend stops to slap Luke Bailey's shoulder. "Epic," he tells Bailey. "This is fucking *epic*."

Et tu, Judd? Et fucking tu?

As I inwardly bristle, I feel someone's gaze on me. I stiffly turn my head and find Bailey grinning at me again. His big hand lifts, long fingers fluttering in a fuck-you wave. His brown eyes convey a very clear sentiment.

Game. Set. Match.

CHAPTER 12
TOO BAD I HATE SHARING

LUKE

On Monday, we have our chapter meeting, where we go over the calendar, the budget, and any issues that may arise. These are just as dreadfully boring as they sound, although I understand why they're necessary.

If you don't arrive early for these meetings, you don't get a seat, but even though I'm five minutes ahead of schedule, I'm still relegated to a standing spot against the wall.

Until Tanner, of all people, says, "Bailey, sit here. Anthony, move your ass."

I try not to raise my eyebrows. I've been receiving a helluva lot of praise from the guys since last night's home run, but Tanner is Team Keaton. Since when do Keaton's friends ask me to sit with them? And kicking Anthony off the couch, to boot? Is this an alternate dimension?

Still, I'm not about to look a gift frat horse in the mouth.

I settle on the sofa next to Tanner, while lowly sophomore Anthony scampers toward the wall.

"Yo," Tanner says. "Guess who texted me this morning."

"Who?"

"Cassidy," he answers, and there's a red tinge to his cheeks. "I'm taking her to dinner on Friday."

I nod in approval. "Well done. She's a sweet girl." In fact, Cassidy is of my favorite dancers at Jack's. I get along with all the women, but I have a soft spot for Cassidy. Not only because she's sweet as pie, but because we both grew up in Darby. The locals have to look out for each other.

"Can't believe you're friends with all those strippers," Paxton says from Tanner's other side. He sounds envious. "That's so fucking cool, bro."

I just shrug. But inside, I give a mental fist pump. I knocked my Dance-off party out of the park yesterday. Even Hayworth knows it—his face was darker than a thundercloud as he watched all his friends dance and flirt with my girls until the wee hours of the morning.

Cassidy and company aren't complaining, either. I paid them an hourly wage for serving the dinner, but then the brothers put a lot more cash in their hands. And nobody took things too far, thank God. I only had to remind one drunken sophomore that he wasn't allowed to touch the dancers.

"Are we starting or what?" Judd grumbles from the other couch. "I got shit to do."

Brad, our secretary, takes attendance on a clipboard. Along with sending out communications to our email list, this might be his only job. *No free room for you, sucker.*

"Okay, ladies," begins Reed, our president. "We have several items of importance to get through before we feast on hot dogs, beer, and the hockey game. Go Bruins. First up! An investigation into an item that's gone missing. Has anyone seen the toilet plunger that belongs in the second-floor bathroom? If this was some kind of prank, can it end now?"

I settle in as several theories are advanced and rejected. Someone makes a motion to buy a new toilet plunger and the motion is passed.

My mind wanders, as does my gaze. Keaton sits in one of the

armchairs across from the couch, dressed in a crisp button-down shirt, the sleeves rolled up a couple of times to expose his muscled forearms. I have to wonder if he wore that shirt to look more presidential. Or if sending shirts to the cleaner is just easier for him than doing laundry like a normal person. Maybe he just likes dressing like a Vineyard Vines model.

I fight off a yawn, but at least I'm not the only one. Last night was *lit*. I don't think anyone woke up before noon today. Except maybe Keaton, since he left my party early and went upstairs to sulk. Reed is now talking about the signup sheet for kitchen-cleaning duty. "This semester we went in alphabetical order. Next semester we're reversing it."

When I'm president, we're going to have to spice up these meetings. I take the lid off the cup of coffee I brought, and gulp the rest of it down just in time to hear Reed say, "And now, each of our presidential candidates will have ninety seconds to answer the following question. Why do you want to be president next year? We'll start with Keaton."

Reed taps the stopwatch on his phone, and the timer begins to race forward.

Still, Keaton takes a thoughtful moment before he opens his mouth. "It's funny, but I have two different answers to this question. The obvious one is that my father was president of Alpha Delta in 1988, and before that, my grandfather was president in 1962. So this is what my family does. And this gives me a nice perspective on what really matters here—not the missing toilet plunger in the green bathroom, but how to make sure that Alpha Delt is still here for the next hundred graduating classes."

There's no way I could ever compete with that kind of legacy. Which is why if he wins, the free room will go to the guy who needs it least.

"But, honestly, my history with this place isn't my real reason for running." Keaton's brow furrows. "Good thing, right? Because it's not reason enough. I'm really here because you are my people. When I come home every day, there's always someone to talk to.

There's always a game on TV, and someone to say, 'What's up? Grab a seat.' The real reason I want to be president is because I care about this place and I can't think of a better use of my..."

"Time," Reed says.

Keaton cocks a thumb toward Reed. "What he said." And everybody has a chuckle for our favorite muscled-up blue blood.

So now I'm supposed to top that? The whole "you are my people" thing would never play from me. So my gut suggests that some amount of honesty might be the best course of action.

Too bad I hate sharing.

All eyes are on me as Reed resets his timer. "Okay, Luke. How about you?"

Indeed. I wait for him to tap the timer. And then I give it my best shot.

"My history with this place could not be more different." Hello, honesty. "I have no family legacy here. I grew up in this town, in the shadow of the college. When I was a kid, I'd watch all the European cars line up outside freshman yard on move-in day. They had stickers on the back from schools that I'd never heard of. I'd ask, 'where the heck is Choate?'"

"It's nowhere interesting," a brother interjects, and wins himself a ripple of laughter.

I ignore the interruption. "They told me, never mind, kid, your school is this one with the bars on the windows and the metal detectors at the front door. But it turns out that if you have a lot of drive, you can still make it to Darby. And I rushed Alpha Delt when I got here, because I wanted the full college experience." Okay, not entirely honest here. But I can't exactly say, *I rushed the frat because my brother is a hooligan.* "I'm running for president today because I believe that this can be a place for everyone."

I check the faces around the room, and I'm getting some nods. So this is resonating with a few people, at least.

"In other words, let us carry the torch forward—so that wings night and poker and spring bash are the rule of the land!" As I raise an arm grandly, my cynicism is rewarded with laughter. But I barely have any time left on the clock.

"And by the way, I happen to be a finance major. So I like some of the jobs that other people don't. During my term as president I want to implement a new electronic bookkeeping system to make the house run more smoothly. So there's more time for everything fun. Thank you for your..." I break off and glance at Reed.

"Time!" he says, tapping his phone. Then he laughs. "See that? You flunkies are in good hands no matter how the vote goes in January. With that, I draw this meeting to a close. Hockey and dogs for all!"

A whoop goes up, and I rise from my chair.

"Nice job, man. Top shelf," Ahmad says as he slaps me on the back. "Great party, too."

"Dude, it was *sick*," enthuses Owen Rickman, another one of Hayworth's pals.

"That's high praise, my man." I manage to keep a straight face.

"Hey, Bailey? Hayworth? Wait up a second." Tim Hoffman is waving us over. "I need party receipts from you guys."

"Oh sure." I dive into my pocket, happy to be asked. I fronted the money for the party, and I'm counting on the reimbursement to make rent this month. Plus, I blew off Friday night's shifts, too, so I could witness Keaton's Dance-off. "Here's all my receipts, plus a spreadsheet printout with the totals."

"Thank you kindly," Hoffman says. "Keaton?"

"Oh, uh..." Keaton frowns. "I'll run upstairs and see what I can find. What was the budget? I'll just bring you receipts for that much."

"Twelve hundred," Hoffman says. "But dude, that was the *whole* budget. You weren't allowed to go over."

"I'm covering it," Keaton says.

"No." Hoffman shakes his head. "The point of the Dance-off is to throw a killer party inside that budget."

In the silence that follows, I realize what just happened.

Keaton broke the campaign rules. Badly, if the color of his face and neck are any indication.

And I might have just won the presidency.

"It's right there in the chapter handbook," I say slowly. But I'm suddenly cheering inside.

Our treasurer frowns. "Hey, Reed?" He beckons to our president. "We have ourselves a situation. Hayworth overspent the budget, which is against regulations."

"Really?" Reed's attention swings in our direction. "How much over was he?"

All eyes shift toward Hayworth.

Keaton hangs his head. "I easily spent triple that."

"It's a blatant violation of the rules," I say, just in case that's not clear.

"I didn't know!" he snaps. "Jesus. I was just trying to throw a good party."

"Uh-huh. Nice job." My laugh is merciless. "We definitely need to elect a president who doesn't bother to read the handbook."

His hazel eyes flash, and his big hands open and close again. The dude would like nothing better than to grab me and hurl me across the room.

So of course I smile at him. Because I never did know when to shut up.

"Guys?" Reed puts two fingers in his mouth and lets out a piercing whistle toward the TV room. "Come back here for a second! We're not done."

A collective groan rises up among the brothers. I can feel their frustration. *So close to freedom.*

After Reed explains the situation to the guys, it doesn't take long for most of them to draw their lines in the sand.

My buddy Jako leaps into the fray. "Obviously Keaton should bow out of the race."

"Says who?" Keaton demands

"Says common sense," Jako answers with a smile. "And honesty. Decency. Respectability…"

"Bow out?" Judd snaps, stepping in. "Nobody's bowing out."

"Keaton *cheated*," I growl.

"*Unknowingly*," Keaton says quickly. "You make it sound like a plot to overthrow the government. Chaos reigns! The plunger will never be found!" He rolls his eyes. But his neck is still the color of an embarrassed tomato.

"This is stupid," Judd declares. "K is as honest as they come."

"Damn straight," says someone else, and there are noises of agreement. I feel all my new allies slipping away like a wisp of smoke.

And I now realize this is not so simple. Keaton ought to bow out immediately. But if he doesn't, and I make a big stink over it, I'm going to look like a tight-ass for pushing him out on a technicality.

Goddamn it.

"I know," Owen says, brightening up. "Let's have another round of parties! It'll be a do-over."

"*No*," both Keaton and I snap in unison. Then we look at each other with identical frowns of irritation. But hey, at least we agree on something.

"There's no budget for two more parties," I point out. "And budgets matter. That's kind of the point."

Yup, I sound just like a tight-ass.

"Not to mention that winter break starts in four days," Judd says. "Are we done here yet? Keaton made a mistake. He's sorry. Would you really want to exclude the probable winner from the race on a technicality?"

As a matter of fact I would. But everyone is staring at me. They all want a hot dog and a view of the TV screen. I'm in the way of it.

"You know what?" I decide in a hurry. "Let's just say that candidate Keaton ought to go read the rules of the fraternity he's so keen to run. But it's true that the Dance-off isn't the most important measure of a man."

"Right." Owen nods. "We have dick measurements for that."

"So I'm going to let it slide," I say, as if the whole thing is up to me. "Keaton made an honest mistake."

Reed blinks. "Okay, man. That's the easiest solution."

I put my hands in my pockets and shrug. "Now let's watch some hockey."

Most of the brothers turn toward the TV room again, where it's going to be standing-room only until the grill is hot and the dogs are ready. I'm ready to follow them, when Keaton stops me.

"Bailey…" He clears his throat, like it might actually kill him to speak to me. "Look, I'm sorry."

"Uh-huh," I say, giving him nothing. "What's a few thousand dollars to you, right? Oops. Great party, though."

He flinches. "Yours was, uh, pretty great, too."

"Thanks, man. But I already knew that."

"You don't have to be a dick, Bailey, I'm trying to apologize."

"I'm not a dick if I let your sorry ass stay in the race," I hiss. "Let's not forget what really happened here. You fucked up and I let you off the hook. The end." At that, I push past him and go.

CHAPTER 13
SO GENEROUS

KEATON

It's Christmas day, and I am quite literally in paradise. I'm sitting on a lounge chair beside the private pool at the villa my parents rented for our vacation in Costa Rica. The sun's almost fully set, but the sky still has a pinkish, orangey tint to it, and the blue pool tiles seem to sparkle in the golden light. A balmy breeze ruffles my hair and warms my face, and the mango and pineapple cocktail I'm drinking is the perfect after-dinner treat.

So why do I feel so blue?

Oh, right. Because my family makes me want to tear out my hair. During dinner, my mom kept starting sentences with: "This summer, when you're living at home…"

But I won't be home if I can help it. And since I dread discussing this, I still haven't told them about my application for the trip to Chile. What's the point, unless I'm accepted?

But then my dad said, "Congratulations on your finance internship. You should get the paperwork just after vacation."

"I didn't even apply yet," I'd replied, like the dummy that I am.

And Dad just waved a hand, like it didn't matter.

"I didn't turn in the résumé."

"I turned it in for you," was his reply.

That's when I turned the same shade of red as my lobster shorts. "You...what? You *faked* my résumé?" My voice had gotten all high and crazy. It's a good thing I'm too young to have a spontaneous aneurysm.

"Nothing on it is fake," he'd said in a smug tone that made me want to slug him. "My assistant did a nice job of it. All facts, no filler. And it's just a formality, anyway. You think the HR department would ever turn you down?"

"I know they won't," I'd snapped. "But that isn't the point, and you know it! I don't want my daddy writing my résumé. Or his secretary."

"You watch your tone," my mother had chided. Because of course she would back him up. "Some people would kill for all the advantages you have."

That's when I had to leave the room. And I still haven't told that arrogant, meddling asshole about my summer plans. It's my big lie of omission that I want to do something to further science.

So I'm sitting out here alone. Seething. On Christmas. I need to talk to someone who understands me. And that person is Annika.

Besides, we need to plan her upcoming birthday celebration. That's my omission number two. In fact, I saw Annika at her parents' place right before we left to fly down here. The visit to the Hamptons wasn't just an excuse to collect my trusty lobster shorts. It's also when I'd planned to finally show her Sinner-Three's profile, and tell her that I'd found a potential partner. I thought we could take a photo together and send it to him.

Fun, right?

But at the last minute I realized I had a problem. That she might scroll through our app texts. Our very lengthy texts.

All my communication with Sinner was supposed to be groundwork. But as I scrolled (and scrolled, and scrolled) through hours of conversation and sexting, I saw it with new eyes.

What does cheating look like? Because I think it might look like this—sexy talk and shared confidences. Late-night chats and jokes.

I'm not a cheater. I sure don't want to be, anyway. And since her birthday is only a week and a half away, the point will soon be moot.

So I didn't show her the app. Instead, I waited until now. I open up *Kink* and take screenshots of Sinner's profile, and of our earliest conversations. Then I hit send.

Now I'm just sitting here, waiting for her to call or reply. I absently watch a tiny lizard scaling the wall toward the thatched roof of our villa. It disappears into a small crevice, and I'm jealous for a moment, because I'd love to disappear right now. Being in close quarters with my parents can be so suffocating. Sometimes I really wish I wasn't an only child. It'd be nice to have a sibling or two to act as a buffer whenever the folks get on my nerves.

My phone chimes, and I pick it up fast. But it's not Annika. It's my frat brother Munsen. **Dude, thanks. I will make good use of it**.

Hmm. The message doesn't make a lot of sense to me, but rando texts from my friends are pretty common.

But then I get *another* thank you, just a moment later. **Beer money! You guys are the best**.

Beer money?

My phone rings, and this time it is Annika. "Hey!" I say brightly.

"This is interesting, Keat," she says, but her tone is cautious. "What do you know about this guy, besides his abs?"

"He's a part-time Darby student. Undergrad, I think."

"There are part-time students at Darby?"

"Uh…" This detail had never jumped out at me before. But I don't think I can name another part-timer, come to think of it. "Apparently?"

She does not sound convinced. "What else do you know about him?"

"He's played with couples before. He likes the thrill."

"Do you know his real name?"

"Not yet. Because that stuff is quid pro quo, and I wasn't going to give your name to a stranger."

"Okay, good. But what if he's dangerous?"

"Annika." My tone is gentle. "I thought you wanted to do this."

"I do," she says quickly. "But I thought we would pick someone more… Verifiable. Apps make me nervous."

I chuckle uneasily, because it's not like her hesitation is crazy. "The whole thing is an adventure," I admit. "Do you really think I'd let anything happen to you?"

"No, of course not. But we could ask someone we know."

"Really? I'm not in the habit of asking my buddies to get naked with me. What if they're disgusted? Then I have to avoid them until graduation. No—longer. There we'll be at the ten-year reunion, drinking our first beer of the weekend, and I'll see him across the way. And his eyes will go all squinty. *There's the pervert who wanted to see my dick.*"

She bursts into nervous giggles. "Okay, point taken. But I could've done the asking. It's less weird coming from me."

I suppose that's true. "Did you ask anyone?"

"No," she admits. "I wasn't sure we'd go through with it."

"Really?" Annika doubts me? "But I said I would, and so I did. At least the set-up, anyway. It's been very educational. He asked me a lot of questions we haven't considered. Like who gets to touch who. He says we have to figure that stuff out ahead of time."

She gets very quiet for a minute. "How do we decide?"

"Well, that's kind of up to you. You never really articulated what you wanted out of this experience. And it's coming up soon. So tell me what you want to happen."

"Um, I guess…" She laughs nervously again. "I want the feeling of being overwhelmed with passion. Like, double the touching. Double the desire."

I can work with that. "So you're on board with letting him touch you?"

"Of course. But are you going to let him touch you, too?"

"Um." Again I kick myself for not having this conversation in person. I need to see her face. "I don't have a problem with it. Do you think he should?"

I don't know how much time it takes her to answer, but it feels like a year. "Yeah. I think he should. And I think you should touch him, too."

"Does that—" My voice actually cracks. "—turn you on?"

"Um. Yes. It does." She pauses. "But does it turn you on?"

You'd think I would have expected this question and prepared an answer. But honestly it stops me in my tracks. "I..." *Jesus.* "I guess we're going to find out."

Yep, I took the coward's way out.

She clears her throat. "So, you think this guy sounds normal? Like he's just some laidback student who sometimes likes to mash with two other people at once?"

"Yeah, I do. Exactly."

"Okay. But I don't want him to learn our names until we meet him. Just in case someone is catfishing you."

"Well..." I guess I'm not quite so paranoid. "What about photos of faces?"

"No," she says emphatically. "I think we set the whole thing up. And if he shows, great. And if not, we haven't lost anything."

I grin. "And if he shows and he's butt-ugly?"

"Then we have a drink out of politeness, and then pretend to chicken out, apologize profusely, and get the hell out of there."

A laugh slips out. "Out of where? Where should this happen?"

"We need a hotel room, of course."

"Of course," I agree, although she's way ahead of me as always. "I'll book a suite with a hot tub."

"And if the whole thing is a disaster, we'll get drunk on champagne and laugh about it in the hot tub."

"I knew you were special," I say, and she laughs.

So this could have gone worse.

After we hang up, I'm feeling pretty good about it for a couple of minutes. But then I check my texts, and there's a fresh pile of thank-you's there. One of them is from Tanner.

Dude, really? It's generous, but... Really?

My stomach drops. **Why am I getting all these thank you texts?** I have to ask.

When his answer arrives, it's even worse than I would have guessed.

Your dad sent everyone a $50 gift card for the Darby Brew Pub. Kinda glad you didn't know about it. Because it's kind of an asskisser thing to do.

What the fuck?

Please tell me you're joking. Are you sure it's from us?

A minute later I get a screenshot of Tanner's email. *Your gift card is waiting, courtesy of Keaton Hayworth Jr.*

I let out a loud groan. So much for paradise.

I jump off my lounger and stomp inside the villa, where my parents are side-by-side, drinking coffee and reading their respective books. "You sent everyone gift cards?" I accuse my father. "*Bribing* them? What were you thinking?"

"It wasn't a bribe," he replies, chuckling. "It was a holiday gift."

"Bullshit."

"Language," my mother chastises.

"Sorry, Mom. But that's total BS, Dad. You're seriously trying to *buy* a fraternity house election? Like it matters?"

"Keaton." He looks up at me over his reading glasses. "I did a generous thing, and you're bent out of shape over it? The presidency will look great on your résumé."

My goddamn fucking shittastic résumé! "It's disingenuous!" I shout. "It's probably against the rules! And I already broke the same damn rules accidentally."

He blinks. "You didn't mention that before."

"Yeah, because it's so much fun to look stupid in front of you!"

I thunder. "You're always so *generous* with your opinions when I make a mistake."

Dad makes a face like he's tasting something bitter. "Calm yourself. It's not against the rules if an alumni gives every active member the same gift. If you did the giving, then maybe I would understand the argument, but..."

Anger crackles through me like electricity snapping out of a damaged wire. "You should have *asked* me. This isn't your election. It doesn't have a thing to do with you." Except it does, and we both know it. I would never have run in the first place if he didn't want me to. "I look like an asshole now."

Dad shrugs. "So what? Assholes win. You know you're the best man for the job. Don't make this more complicated than it has to be."

I spin around and stalk back outside before I say something I'll regret. I'm stuck here with him for seven more days. And that's about six more than I can stand.

CHAPTER 14
UNFUCKINGBELIEVABLE

LUKE

Unfuckingbelievable. Fifty dollars at the Darby Brew Pub? If I received one of these, then so did every sitting member of Alpha Delt. Who does that?

Keaton is a giant, epic dickface.

I roll over on my bed and groan. I shouldn't spend it, right? If I spend it, that's taking money from the enemy. Well, not money. Thick, juicy burgers and the kind of beer I can't really afford.

"Fuck you, Keaton Hayworth the third!" I yell at the ceiling.

Luckily, nobody else is here to witness this moment of crazy. I'm the only member of Alpha Delt with no place better to be on Christmas.

Earlier I did swing by my former home, where I had the good fortune to find my mom home alone. I let her feed me a piece of pumpkin pie while I handed over the money she'd asked to "borrow."

"This is your Christmas gift," I said as I passed her the bills.

"Lukey! You know I'd pay you back!"

I know nothing of the sort. "Merry Christmas, Ma." Honestly

it's a gift to myself to avoid the disappointment when she *doesn't* pay me back.

Her Christmas gift to me is a winter hat with the Patriots logo on it. I've never been interested in football, but that's my mom for you.

Before I left, I'd put a sealed envelope on Joe's pillow with the hundred bucks he asked me for. Then I texted him a photo of it, because I don't really trust my mother not to take it.

Seriously, who needs family? They're exhausting.

The whole thing took maybe an hour, including travel time. Now I'm rattling around in my empty fraternity house, feeling like a lonely loser. Since all the stores are closed, I did some provisioning yesterday. I have food, and downstairs I get the seventy-inch TV all to myself.

When this place is full of frat boys, I usually wish they'd all shut up. But God it's so quiet right now that the silence is pressing in on my eardrums.

I pick up my phone and unlock it, wondering if LobsterShorts is around. What are the odds?

Good, as it turns out. There's a new message from him.

LobsterShorts: I fucking hate holidays and what is really the goddamn point?

I laugh out loud.

SinnerThree: Preach, brother! It took me way too long to realize that Christmas is a fucking crock. I finally got it when I was thirteen. Not only did I finally realize that nobody was ever going to surprise me with a decent present, togetherness makes people crazy. Mom and Grandma used to get drunk and scream at each other.

LobsterShorts: Ouch. I think I'm going to be the screaming drunk tonight. My family is really good at presents. But they suck at boundaries.

SinnerThree: But hey, presents!

LobsterShorts: Eh. I'm too old to be bought with the latest gaming console. The gift I want is respect. My father is such an

asshole. I thought we'd be fighting about my summer plans but I haven't even told him about those yet and we're already killing each other. What's your dream gift?

Now there's something I don't ever bother asking myself.

SinnerThree: A winning lottery ticket. I don't mean it in a flip way. I just want to stop stressing about money. Making rent every month is always a trial. I'm always down to ramen and cans of beans at some point during the month.

Then I read that over and wonder what the hell I'm doing.

SinnerThree: It's like woe is me day right now. Tell me something funny about animals.

LobsterShorts: Let's see. Rats laugh when you tickle them.

SinnerThree: No way!

LobsterShorts: Hummingbirds eat twice their weight in food every day. Although, so do I.

SinnerThree: Well, you are a growing boy.

LobsterShorts: In more ways than one ;)

He follows that up with, **As in, I'm growing right now...**

And then—oh *fuck* yeah—an image appears in the chat thread. He's growing, all right. The hard cock in the pic makes me salivate. It's been months since I've gotten laid. Not for lack of interest, but lack of time. Work, school, and the Dance-off have eaten into any time I might've spent finding sex. And teasing Lobster-Shorts over the app has only made it worse. I might explode from all my pent-up frustrations.

In the photo, his thumb rests right beneath the mushroom head of his cock, as if he'd snapped the photo while stroking that sensitive spot. My body responds to the erotic sight, cock rising beneath my sweatpants. Then I notice the waistband of the trunks he'd pushed down in order to expose himself, and I'm laughing even as I slide my hands beneath *my* waistband.

SinnerThree: Are you wearing the lobster shorts???

LobsterShorts: Of course. They're my fave.

He sends another pic, and I laugh harder. In this one, he's

zoomed in on one of the red lobsters, with his hand forming a thumbs-up beside it.

SinnerThree: Why are you in swim trunks, you asshole? Don't tell me you went somewhere warm for the holidays while I'm stuck here in blizzard land.

LobsterShorts: OK. I won't tell you that.

SinnerThree: So you're still in Connecticut?

LobsterShorts: No. I escaped to the beach. Sorry?

SinnerThree: You'd better be. I ain't lying about the blizzard. We got eight inches of snow last night.

LobsterShorts: I'll give you eight inches.

And then he does. Or at least I think so. I'll be better able to judge his dick size when I get my hands on it in person, but in the pics it looks nearly as big as mine. And I'm well-endowed, as the dollar-bill-waving women at Jill's can attest to.

SinnerThree: Yes. Please give it to me. I'm in a shit mood and it's the holidays. I require the gift of your cock.

LobsterShorts: Soon. First show me yours.

SinnerThree: I'll do you one better. Stand by.

I yank my sweats down and kick them away, making myself comfortable on my bed. I shove a couple of pillows beneath my head, grip my dick in one hand, and hold my phone in the other. A quick peek at the screen assures me that I'm not revealing any incriminating evidence about my identity. All he'll be able to see is my cock, my hand, and the patterned bedspread. I think I'm safe.

I rarely send videos because of this exact worry. Winding up in some jerkoff compilation on PornHub doesn't concern me so much as someone figuring out who I am. If I'm going to be a multi-millionaire by the time I'm thirty, I can't have dirty videos of me floating around the internet. Unless I make my millions building a Hugh Hefner-like empire… Maybe I'll put a pin in that one.

At the moment, I'm busy jerking off for Lobsterman.

Oh fuckkkkkk, is his immediate response after I send him a five-second vid of some lazy stroking.

Then he says: **MORE**.

Greedy fucker.

Grinning, I decide to tease it out. My fingers close in a fist, which I slowly slide down to the base, then equally slowly slide back up. When I reach the tip, I give a slight twist and squeeze. The camera perfectly captures the bead of pre-come that forms.

I hit Send.

LobsterShorts: You have such a hot dick.

My breathing quickens. I stroke a bit faster, groaning quietly, before realizing I'm no longer recording myself or responding to LobsterShorts. The heat in my blood and the ache in my balls distracted me.

LobsterShorts: What, can I not say that?

I swallow through my arid throat and still my hand.

SinnerThree: Sorry. Got caught up in the self-stroking. Can you not say what?

LobsterShorts: That you have a hot dick.

SinnerThree: God, no, definitely say it. That's what got me distracted ;)

LobsterShorts: Good. Send another vid. I wanna see more.

SinnerThree: Are you jacking yours right now?

LobsterShorts: Obvs.

I smile at the phone. He's gotten bolder and bolder with every chat, every naughty message. And it's been a while since he's disappeared on me. Lately, he's coming back for more almost instantly, instead of hiding because of his guilt. I…don't think he feels guilty about this anymore.

Since I can't record myself and read his messages at the same time, I rely on my brain to provide the stimulation I need. I picture Lobsterman kneeling between my legs, his head bobbing over me. His lips are wrapped tightly around my dick, tongue scraping the entire length each time he takes me deep. I picture my fingers tangling in his hair—*can* they tangle there? Is it long? Buzzed? I realize I've never thought to ask. And right now I don't care to. Fine. There's enough hair for my fingers to grasp, to tug on as I thrust my hips and fuck his mouth.

Hoarse breaths provide the soundtrack for my dirty video. A grunt. A torturous moan as my mind conjures up the image of me coming in Lobster's mouth and him greedily swallowing every drop.

I explode in real life, nearly dropping the phone as the climax rips through me. As it is, the camera work is severely lacking in skill, because I'm shuddering and groaning too hard to keep the phone steady. I guess that cameraman job on the set of Martin Scorsese's next film is out—and yet judging by Lobster's response to my masterpiece, I just created an Academy Award winner.

LobsterShorts: Fuuuuuuuuuuuuck.

LobsterShorts: Do you even realize how goddamn sexy that was?

I can't answer, because my body has sunk into the mattress. My limbs are jelly from the orgasm, and my abs are sticky from it.

I finally catch my breath just as a video message from him fills our chat. I find the strength to click on it, and in a heartbeat I'm back to being breathless. It's not even ten seconds long, but it's enough to make me semi-hard again, which I would've thought impossible.

Biting my lip, I watch as his strong fist works his dick. I listen to the husky moan he lets out as he comes.

My pulse is racing as I type a shaky message.

SinnerThree: Okay. Jesus. Enough is enough, dude. We need to fuck. In person. Like, ASAP.

LobsterShorts: January 4th, remember?

SinnerThree: Promise you won't bail on me? Because, fuck, I need this.

LobsterShorts: I won't bail. I need this, too.

It doesn't escape me that he wrote "I", and not "we." Which makes me wonder if his girlfriend is no longer part of this equation.

But he squashes that notion by adding, **My gf and I got a suite at the Grand Windsor. So. Saturday, around nine o'clock?**

Um. Yes, please. I just have to figure out how to make this happen without missing work. Saturday nights at Jill's are huge money. Maybe I can start at midnight instead of ten? But that's assuming three hours is enough time for all the fucking I have planned.

I'll figure something out, though. I always do.

SinnerThree: I'll be there.

CHAPTER 15
MAKE A WISH, HONEY

KEATON

Leaving paradise and returning to "blizzard land," as Sinner calls it, isn't something I'd normally be pumped about, but I'd rather sleep naked on a bed of snow than spend even five more seconds with my father.

He was insufferable this entire trip, constantly needling me about the finance internship at his company. And when he wasn't applying the job pressure, he was harassing me about the Alpha Delt presidency, offering "suggestions" about how to sway votes.

Needless to say, I'm happy to be home as I breathe in the frigid January air after stepping off the family jet. My folks are spending another week in Costa Rica, so I had the plane to myself on the flight back to Connecticut. Gave me plenty of time to think about tomorrow night.

D-Day. Or rather, T-Night. The threesome. The big ménage a trois.

Am I nervous? Yes. Excited? Also yes. Terrified?

Maybe a bit.

I have no idea what to expect. My girlfriend claimed that the idea of me touching a dude and vice versa turns her on, but what if it has the opposite effect in real life? What if she freaks out when faced with the reality of it? What if *I* freak out?

Even after a five-hour flight, during which I was alone with my thoughts, my mind is still racing as I go through customs and grab an Uber at the airport. And it's still racing when I wake up late the next morning. *Saturday* morning.

AKA T-Day.

It's Annika's birthday, you idiot. Don't forget that part.

Oh, right. I'm getting ahead of myself here.

I reach for my phone and call my girlfriend.

"Quick!" I shout when she answers. "Meet me at the liquor store, birthday girl! I need your ID."

Her soft laughter tickles my ear. "You're such a goofball."

"Is that a no? Because you're twenty-one now, which means there's no reason why you can't buy me booze."

"It's eleven thirty," she teases. "Do you really want a drink right now?"

"Nah." I chuckle, then sit up and rub my eyes with one hand. "We'll save the drinks for tonight."

There's a short pause.

"Babe?" I prompt.

"Sorry, yes, I'm here. And yes, I think there's going to be quite a lot of drinking tonight."

I can't tell if her tone is hesitant or distracted. The latter, I decide, when I hear a flurry of female voices on the other end of the line.

"What's going on in that sorority house?" I ask with a laugh.

"The girls are preparing a birthday brunch for me. Don't worry, I'll go easy on the mimosas. Hold on a sec, baby—" Annika's voice becomes muffled as she addresses someone else. "I'm coming down, I'm coming down! Keaton just called to wish me a happy birthday." There's a rustling sound. "Hey, I'm back. But I have to go. Lindy says my presence is required downstairs."

"Wait," I say before she can go. "There's one more thing."

"What's that?"

I put her on speaker, press play on the track I've cued up, and Beyoncé's "Crazy in Love" blares out of my phone. I let the song play for about ten seconds before shutting it off and saying, "Happy birthday, Ani."

"Oh, Keaton." Her voice trembles slightly. "I really do love you."

"Love you too."

We hang up, and I lumber naked toward the bathroom to empty my bladder and take a shower. I'm drying off my ass when the bathroom door opens suddenly.

I whirl around, and there's Luke Bailey in the doorway, a sour look on his face. "Do you mind? I'm almost done in here."

"Do you mind?" he echoes. "Or are you hell bent on bribing your way into the presidency?"

Fuck.

"It's not against the rules for my father to give out gifts," I say, tying the towel around my waist.

"It should be," he snaps.

The dude is right. Privately, I'm still mortified at my father's behavior. But I'm not a big fan of Luke's scowl, either. And I'm not going to hand him the presidency just because my father is a pushy son of a bitch. Bailey would make a terrible president.

"You don't think people can make up their own minds?" I ask, opening the medicine cabinet to look for my deodorant. But I haven't unpacked yet, so it's not there.

"I think you play the part of the laidback fun guy really well. But you're actually a conniving little bitch."

I laugh, because he's got it so wrong. I take two steps toward him, because he's blocking my way back to my suitcase in my room.

He holds his ground.

"Really?" I drawl. "You want to throw down right here in the bathroom over it?"

His scowl deepens as he steps aside. But then the bastard lingers in the doorway of my room, where I start to root through the suitcase on the bed. I pick up a double handful of bathing suits and beachwear, thinking to toss it onto the bed.

But, fuck. Bailey thinks I'm exactly the kind of spoiled rich guy who just came home from a tropical vacation. And I am, so it's not like I can argue the point.

I drop the clothes back into the bag and turn around, blocking his view of my stuff. "Do you have anything material to say? Or are you just here to whine at me."

"Just…" He sighs. "If you need to cheat to impress everybody, why even bother?"

"Why indeed," I say mildly. Not even Luke Bailey can dampen my spirits today. Even if he's right. I'm in far too good a mood. "Now if you'll excuse me, I have places to be."

———

The hotel suite I booked is killer. With a Jacuzzi tub, a giant king-sized bed, and a seventy-inch TV. Even the meal I ordered from room service is delicious.

But at some point between the crab fritters and the exquisite slices of chocolate cake, I realize that Annika is nervous.

She didn't eat very much, I realize. And now, as I light the candle I brought to top her slice of cake, I see uncertainty as well as candlelight flickering in her eyes.

"Happy birthday to you, happy birthday to *you*…" I do jazz hands, and really camp it up as I sing. "Happy birthday, dear sexy pants…"

She gives me a shy smile, but doesn't quite look me in the eye.

I finish the song with gusto. "Make a wish, honey. Feel free to make it a dirty one about me."

She inhales, looks me in the eye and…hesitates.

I wait impatiently, because everyone knows you can't sink your fork into the cake before the birthday girl is ready. And it looks like terrific cake. I can almost taste it now. Honestly, I'm like a giant ball of anticipation tonight. It's been a struggle not to keep checking the time.

Sinner is probably already on his way here. It's a quarter to nine.

Annika pushes her chair back from the table. "I don't know, Keaton. I don't think I can do this."

"It's just a wish, babe. And watch that wax—it's about to drip onto your ganache frosting."

She leans over and blows out the candle quickly. Then she sits back and sighs. "Keaton, is there really a guy on his way over here?"

I nod. "Why would I lie about that?"

Annika bites her lower lip. Then she throws me a curveball. "I think you should tell him not to come."

"Wait, what?" My fork hovers over my own slice of cake.

"I..." She visibly gulps. "I don't want to go through with it."

"Annika!" I set down my fork with a clatter. "This was your idea. We can't just text him to say never mind."

"Sure we can!" she squeaks, popping out of her chair and crossing the room to look out the window.

It's dark out there, so she can't really see much. When she turns to face me, I don't miss the misery swimming in her eyes.

"I was wrong," she moans, and her cheeks are slowly reddening, either from embarrassment or anger. The former, I suspect. "This isn't me. I thought I could be someone else for a night, and God knows our sex life needs a shakeup. But I can't get naked with a stranger. I can't."

"But..." I take a deep breath and realize that my heart is pounding. There's no way I can just bail on Sinner now. "This was supposed to be an adventure. You're just nervous, like that time we took that scuba class. That turned out fine."

"No." She shakes her head vehemently. "This is so not the same thing. I was trying to be fun and daring. And I was trying to give you some hints that we needed a mojo makeover."

"A... mojo makeover?" I'm so confused right now. "Is that a spa treatment?"

"No!" she shrieks. "I mean *sex*, Keaton. We're in a rut. I thought I would suggest a threesome, and you'd realize we needed to put some more effort into the bedroom. You could have just bought sexy handcuffs and edible massage oil."

It's suddenly very important that I make her understand. "You asked me for this," I say tightly. "And I delivered."

"I *can't*, Keaton. I'm sorry."

"You're just having cold feet because he's a faceless stranger," I try. "Let's just meet him and then decide."

Once again, she sounds miserable. "What will that accomplish? I'll just have to embarrass myself to someone in person. This way he'll never know which of us chickened out."

And that's exactly the problem. I consider Sinner a friend. And if I bail right now, he won't understand that it wasn't me who pulled the ripcord.

I don't know why that bothers me so much. But it really does.

"You're making me look like an asshole here," I mumble. I take my fork and plunge it into my untouched slice of cake. And then I take a big bite. The chocolate flavor explodes on my tongue, but it doesn't erase the flash of resentment that I'm experiencing.

I can't even look at Annika right now. If she'd never asked for a threesome, I wouldn't be in this position at all. I wouldn't have chatted with Sinner. And I wouldn't have wanted so badly to meet him.

"Keaton," she says in a low voice. "People probably bail on these hookups all the time. He has to know that."

"I'm sure he does. But they don't get bailed on by me."

I push the chocolate cake away. The force of my emotions is confusing to me. Annika is well within her rights to say no to a sexual encounter that she doesn't want. Only an asshole would get mad at his girlfriend for expressing her discomfort, for choosing to back out. But I *am* mad. I'm mad because—fuck. No.

Anger isn't what I'm feeling, I realize in dismay. That tightness in my throat, the shakiness of my pulse.

It's disappointment.

That's the real problem, right? I wanted this so much. She has no idea. Hell, *I* had no idea.

"Please, baby," she begs. "I'm so sorry. I know this is awkward. I guess I just didn't picture us actually going through with it."

Another rush of disbelief hits my veins. "I always keep my promises. Why would you think we wouldn't go through with it?"

"I'm sorry!" she hisses, her eyes glistening. "But you have to message him right now. He could show up at any moment. Or I could do it." She crosses the room to retrieve my phone off the bedside table.

Shit.

She unlocks the screen and scrolls through my apps. "What does it look like? I'll tell him I'm the one who bailed—"

There's a knock on the door. Three raps.

Our eyes meet from across the room. "Can I let him in?" I whisper.

Slowly, she shakes her head.

Fuck.

Crossing the rug to the door, I try to think of what I'll say when I step outside and apologize. That will be awkward, but at least I can say my piece. Maybe he's ugly, anyway. Maybe I'll laugh about this tomorrow.

Maybe this sick, sad feeling in my gut will go away.

Bracing myself, I open the door.

CHAPTER 16
SO MANY UGLIES

LUKE

After tapping on the door to room 409, I don't quite know what to do with my hands. This moment—when you're standing outside, waiting to meet your hookup for the first time…it's the most nerve-wracking part.

There are voices inside. A man's and a woman's. So I must be in the right place. But I've never been to this hotel. I never even gave it a sideways glance. It's the kind of place rich folks stay on parents' weekend.

Honestly, it would never occur to me to get a hotel room just for shiggles. Who does that?

I hear someone coming toward the door, and I suck in my stomach. Don't judge—it's a reflex for someone who's used to being on stage without a shirt. I'm just pasting a friendly smile on my face when the door opens, and—

What the…?

Are you fucking kidding me?

"Hayworth?" I bark. "What are you… I was just…" My brain is quickly backpedalling. I must be at the wrong door. My hand is already closing around my phone so I can check my facts.

But then I look at *his* face, and I know there hasn't been a mix-up. His ears are suddenly red, and his mouth is opening and closing like a fish's. Quickly, he steps out into the hall and closes the door behind him.

"You're *shitting* me," Keaton Hayworth III hisses. "Is this some kind of joke?"

"I don't know," I snarl. "Is it? You tell me."

"Did you catfish me, Bailey?" He looks suddenly furious.

"No!" I howl. "But now that you mention it, is that *your* game?"

"No!" he snaps. Then he looks up and down the hall. "And keep your voice down."

"Why? Are you slumming right now?" I'm too full of nervous energy to behave like a rational human. I take a step closer.

He looks down. Our chests are almost touching. "Back off, would you?"

"Why? Aren't you going to invite me in?" I don't really see this going anywhere, but I'm going to make him say it. "This was all your idea. Did you chicken out?"

His face goes a shade redder. "There's been a change of plans."

"I'll bet." I'm about three inches from his face, and I can see both anger and frustration rolling off him. "Good thing I canceled a shift at work for your little fantasy."

He blinks, and I see sweat beading at his hairline. It's just starting to actually sink in that Keaton is LobsterShorts. *He's* the guy who hates Christmas and knows which animals masturbate?

He made me laugh, and then I made him *come?* If heads blowing off were a real thing, mine would be detonating right now.

But then he opens up his big mouth and reminds me how it really is between us. "If you leave now, maybe you can get your shift back."

I roll my eyes, because that's such a Keaton Hayworth III thing to say. I'll bet he's never held down a job in his life. "Maybe. But the boss will still be annoyed. And I'll still be late..." I realize there's no point in explaining it.

"Sorry," he says stiffly.

I take a step back. And then another one. "Yeah? You're sorry that I'm someone you already dislike, huh? Better luck with your next match on the app, then."

Spinning around, I walk toward the elevators.

"That's not what happened!" he calls after me.

But I don't bother waiting to hear what excuses he'd give.

———

"I don't understand," Lance says several hours later. He shakes his blond head in confusion. "Why did you agree to bone your frat brother if you don't like him?"

"I didn't agree to bone my frat brother! I—" I drop my face in my hands and try to gather my composure.

You'd think that four hours after the big shock, I'd have found a way to compose myself, right? But nope. I'm still shook. The second the bouncers locked the club's doors, I collapsed on the nearest barstool and started pouring the tequila.

Most of the other staff left for the night, but a few of my fellow dancers stuck around to keep me company. Brock and George haven't stopped laughing since I told them what went down at the hotel earlier, but Lance still doesn't get it.

"It was an anonymous hookup, Lance," I grumble into my palms. "We've been chatting on *Kink* and we were meeting for the first time tonight."

"You and the frat guy and his girlfriend," Lance says.

"Yes." I raise my head and swipe the tequila bottle out of George's beefy hand. We stopped using shot glasses about an hour ago. It's almost three in the morning, we're half-naked, still covered in oil, and discussing the fact that I almost fucked my nemesis tonight—these are drink-straight-from-the-bottle times.

"So you went to meet them and it turned out you know them in real life."

"Yes."

He slants his head. "I don't understand."

"What don't you understand!" I sputter.

"Did y'all exchange pics?"

I nod. "No faces, though."

"No faces!" he cries in disbelief. "Why not?"

"I'm with Lance on this one," Brock pipes up from behind the counter. All the bartenders went home for the night, so he's usurped their domain. At the moment, he's twirling a stainless steel shaker as if he's Tom Cruise from *Cocktail*. His bare chest glistens in the neon lighting of the beer signs behind him. "Why on earth would you meet a potential hookup without seeing their faces? Did you *want* to get murdered tonight?"

"His girl didn't feel comfortable showing their faces," I mutter. And now I know why. Annika Schiffer is the heiress to a home-furnishings fortune that's worth *billions*—her father is like the American version of whoever owns IKEA. Of course she doesn't want her face plastered on some app dedicated to kinky sex.

Christ. Who would've thought. Annika Schiffer's into threesomes?

And so is Keaton.

I resist the urge to bury my head in my hands again. Keaton is LobsterShorts. This entire time, I've been sexting with my goddamn frat brother. Worse, the frat brother who's running against me in the presidential election. The frat brother I can't stand.

It's too hard to reconcile. Because I *can* stand LobsterShorts. I fucking *like* LobsterShorts. How the hell are they the same person?

"What if they were both ugly?" George demands. "Do you know how many ugly people are on those apps?"

"So many uglies," Lance says solemnly. "It's an epidemic."

I take another quick swig from the tequila bottle. "He assured me they weren't."

George blinks innocently. "Oh, what a relief! The random pervert on *Kink assured* you that he and his two-dick-craving old lady weren't ugly."

Brock snorts. "For real, bro. All ugly people are gonna claim they aren't ugly."

"I just had a feeling they were hot, okay?" I say irritably. Oh wow. I'm a grumpy drunk tonight. I don't think I've ever been cranky while drunk. Usually I'm a fucking blast.

That's probably my cue to leave.

I heave my drunken body off the barstool. "I'm gonna take off, boys. The room's starting to spin a little." When my feet meet the ground, my body sways slightly. "Thanks for keeping me company."

"Any time," George says, and even though my vision is slightly hazy, I don't miss the sympathy in his gaze. "I'm sorry you had a shit night, dude."

"What are you gonna do when you get home?" Lance asks curiously. "I mean, you gonna talk to him?"

"Tonight? No way, it's the middle of the fucking night." Though even if it was the middle of the day, I still can't envision myself talking to Keaton about this.

Nope. This shall not be discussed ever again. If he brings it up, I might just pretend I don't know what he's talking about. Fake some amnesia.

Outside the club, I heave myself into the backseat of an Uber. I hate spending the money, but I'm feeling too wobbly for the bus. I've never vomited while using public transportation before, and I don't intend to start now.

But by the time the driver pulls up in front of the Alpha Delt house, my stomach isn't lurching anymore. In fact, my composure finally seems to have returned, and I feel a lot more centered—and sober—as I drag my tired ass through the front door.

Upstairs, the first thing I do is take a quick shower. As my soapy hands scrub the lingering oil off my chest, I try to process what happened tonight, objectively. I mean...it's kinda funny if you think about it. What are the odds that the couple I wanted to hook up with was Keaton and Annika? So fucking random, right?

And is it really a big deal? Despite demanding to know if Hayworth was catfishing me, I don't actually believe he was doing that. I think this clusterfuck is just a huge coincidence.

We're in college. People experiment when they're in college. Keaton and Annika were looking to spice up their sex life with a third party, and I happened to be the third party they recruited. None of us knew each other's identities. It was just plain bad luck.

No, it's not a big deal unless we make it one, I decide as I step out of the shower. I snatch a towel from the rack and wrap it around my waist. Then I swipe my hand over the steam-covered mirror and study my blurry reflection. I look tired.

It's been a long night.

I pad barefoot back to my room. Just as I'm swinging the door closed, it pushes open, nearly knocking me on my ass.

My hand grabs for my towel before the terrycloth can slide off my hips. "What the fuck!" I growl as Keaton muscles his way into my room.

"You're asking *me* what the fuck?" he growls back. "Where the hell have you been? It's three in the morning! I've been waiting up for *hours*."

I stare at him. "You're mad that I'm home late? Who are you, my grandma?"

"Look," he snaps as he shuts the door. I notice he makes sure it's latched before raising his voice. "Why were you at the hotel tonight, Bailey? No bullshit. Why the hell were you there?"

"Because you *invited* me," I retort through clenched teeth.

"I didn't invite you. I invited SinnerThree." Anger ripples through his expression. "Why were you pretending to be someone else on the app?"

My jaw falls open. "Are you joking? I wasn't pretending shit, Hayworth. SinnerThree is my handle. I use *Kink* all the time."

He gives a stubborn shake of the head. "I don't believe you. I don't believe you fuck guys."

I can't help but laugh. "Why? Because I never sat you down and said, 'Hey Keaton, I'm bi'? Why would I ever do that? We're not friends."

"So you're saying you *are* bi."

I can't tell if it's an accusation. Either way, it makes me roll my eyes. "Yes, I am. Got a problem with that?" I answer my own question before he can. "Wait, of course you don't, because apparently you are too."

Keaton freezes.

Which makes me realize that he was swaying on his feet before. I study his handsome face, and notice his cheeks are flushed and his hazel eyes aren't entirely focused. He's been drinking, too.

"I'm not bisexual," he finally mutters.

"Pan? Gay?"

"Not that, either," he says stiffly.

I laugh again. Low, humorless. "Uh-huh. So why did you invite another dude into bed with you and Annika?"

"Don't say her name," he orders.

"Why not? Is she here?" I nod toward the door. "She hiding in your room?"

"I took her home."

"Shame. She must be bummed she didn't get her fantasy." I tip my head in challenge. "Or was it yours?"

His lips curl in anger. "Fuck you. I was being honest about everything. She wanted a threesome for her birthday. And then she backed out at the last minute. Which is a fucking godsend, because if she saw *you* walking into that hotel room, she would've freaked."

"Great. Awesome. So it worked out for everyone involved. Bullet fucking dodged." I'm still holding my towel to my side. "Can you please leave now?"

"No." He scrapes both hands over his dark-blond head. "Not until we straighten this out."

"Straighten what out?" I say wearily. "It was a dumb coincidence. I didn't set you up, you didn't set me up. I'm bisexual, you're bicurious. Whatever. It's done."

"Done?" he echoes, and there's a note of desperation in his voice now. "Do you realize how fucking embarrassed I am? To find out I've been talking to *you* this entire time?"

I'm not even insulted, because I feel the same way. "Join the club, asshole. I'm not thrilled, either." I told this guy shit I've never told anyone before. My relationship with my family? My money troubles? Yeah. Talk about embarrassing.

"If you even think about telling anyone about this, I will kick your fucking ass," Keaton warns. He takes a step forward, and although his legs appear steadier, his breathing is short, labored. "I mean it, Bailey. All the shit we talked about? All the stuff w-we...we did. Nobody ever finds out about that, you hear me?"

"What?" I say mockingly. "You're scared what Judd will think if he knows you fantasize about sucking cock?"

Keaton's jaw tightens.

"Scared Tanner might unfriend you if he knew how badly you want a dick in your ass?"

His eyes flash. "Careful, Bailey."

I just grin. "Hmmm. What do you think they'd say if they knew you've been sexting with one of your frat brothers for weeks?"

"Are you...*blackmailing* me?" he bites out.

"What?"

"You're threatening to tell my buddies about this if I don't, what, drop out of the race?"

I'm startled. "Of course not." Shit, but I can see why he thought I was. "I'm not blackmailing you, Hayworth. I was just teasing. Do you think *I* want anyone knowing about this? No way, man. My sex life is nobody's business but mine."

At the word "sex," Keaton's gaze flits from my bare chest to my towel, and then awkwardly lowers to his own feet.

It gets hard to breathe. I feel like Keaton is sucking up all the air in the room with the deep, ragged breaths he's taking.

"Look, this isn't a big deal," I say roughly. "It was just…bad luck."

"Not a big deal?" he roars. "Are you serious right now!" He draws another breath, then lowers his voice to a tortured pitch. "We watched videos of each other *jacking off*! You were going to fuck my girlfriend! We talked about having sex with *each other*."

He's panicking. I can see it on his face, in the way his chest heaves with each whispered word.

"And I can't even pretend that it didn't turn me on, that it was some kind of fucked-up prank I was playing on you, because you *saw* how hot it made me." His hands are clawing through his hair again. His broad chest trembles wildly. "You *saw* me come."

"So?" Despite my attempt to sound casual, my pulse has sped up. He's spitting out all these dirty, dirty things, and God help me, but it's turning me on.

"So that's not *right*," he shoots back. "I don't want you knowing this shit about me. I don't trust you not to use it against me. I don't trust you, and I don't like you, and if I'd known you were SinnerThree, I never would've—"

"Never would've told me what a hot dick I have?" I taunt.

"Fuck you—"

"Fuck me, yes," I interrupt, laughing darkly. "That's exactly what you wanted to do, remember, Keaton? You wanted to fuck me. You wanted me to fuck *you*. You *wanted* me. You wanted *this*—"

I grab him by the back of the neck and kiss him.

CHAPTER 17
ONE MORE THING

KEATON

A hot mouth suddenly latches onto mine.

Holy motherfucking shit.

He's kissing me. Luke Bailey is kissing me, and my brain can't make sense of it. Why is his tongue sliding inside my mouth like it belongs there?

Growling, I push at his chest. "What the *hell*—" But I stop talking, because his rock-hard body doesn't so much as budge thanks to my shove, and now my palms are pressed up against the tightest set of pecs I've ever felt.

Hell, the only set of pecs I've ever felt.

Bailey's body is unreal. And now the asshole's tongue is in my mouth again. I groan in surprise as pleasure jolts through me, and I swear I hear him chuckle, or maybe he's groaning too. I don't know. I'm too out of it. Too turned on, and too confused.

I'm gasping for air by the time I manage to wrench my mouth away. It's three in the morning and I'm drunk off my ass. That's the only reasonable explanation for what just happened here.

"Why'd you stop?" Bailey pants. "Go get your girl and let's go. You know you want to." His gaze is a lust-filled challenge.

"She dumped me," I blurt out. Or, rather, the vodka does.

His eyes widen. "Come again?"

"She dumped me. First she changed her mind about the three-some. And then after I sent you away, she said, 'Keaton, I was only trying to spice up our sex life because I think it's run its course. Let's just be *friends*.'"

I feel a stab right in my heart just saying it out loud. Annika thinks we're not hot together anymore.

"Jesus. I'm sorry, man." Weirdly, he sounds like he means it.

And I still can't shut up. "She said, 'you weren't supposed to get so excited about sex with other people. You were just supposed to get more excited about sex with me.'"

"That's bullshit," Bailey sputters. "Then why did she suggest it? I thought the whole thing was her idea."

"It was." I sit down on the edge of his bed, because standing up isn't working for me so well. And, fuck. The plaid bedspread —it's the one from the video he sent me. It was here all the time. I could have known it was him if I was a little more observant.

"That's cold," he remarks.

When I glance up at him again, he's pulling on a pair of sweat-pants. Which means I just missed a view of his bare ass.

Fuck me. I missed it.

"Maybe it's just a fight?" he asks, pulling a T-shirt over his muscular torso. "Maybe you two will kiss and make up in the morning."

"I don't know. She did that thing where she implied that if I was really paying attention, I would have understood that the threesome was a cry for help. 'I just wanted you to spice things up,' she said. 'I thought you would counter-offer the threesome.'"

"Counter-offer?" Luke repeats.

"Yeah, like bring in another girl instead. Or some role-play. I don't know." I stand up again because sitting on Bailey's bed is a bad idea. I've got to go sleep off this vodka. "All I know is I did love her. And it wasn't my idea to break up. But she says I don't thrill her anymore, and I don't know how you come back from that."

"Does she still thrill you?" Bailey asks.

I'm too drunk to keep the wince off my face. "Sometimes. Sure." But it's just dawning on me that sexting with SinnerThree was about the most exciting thing that happened to me in the bedroom.

Isn't that just sad?

"Well…" Bailey clears his throat. "Deep breaths."

"I should…" I make a vague motion toward my own room.

"Yeah," he agrees. "Hey, I meant it, Hayworth. I'd never say a word. About…you know." He lifts his phone off his desk to indicate what he means.

"Uh, thanks. I won't say anything, either." I measure the serious expression on his face, and I decide that he's telling the truth. And then it hits me that I had my tongue in his mouth a few minutes ago. Did that seriously happen?

And, Jesus, did I really like it so much? I did, damn it. And now I'm staring.

"You okay?" he says warily.

"How did you know?" I ask suddenly.

He rolls his eyes. "I told you, I *didn't* know."

"Not about that. That's not what I mean. How did you figure out that you, uh…" I can't finish the sentence. "Never mind." I take one step toward the door.

"Oh," he says slowly, my meaning dawning in his voice. "That I like guys?"

I stop and turn around. "Yeah. That."

"I started young, honestly. Noticing guys was a hobby of mine from ninth grade on. And one of the guys in my little circle at school turned out to be gay. And he noticed that I had a thing for the cross country team." His chuckle is strained. "So he made a point to invite me to stay at his house whenever his parents were out for the night. He wasn't really my type, but we were each other's handy training ground."

"And that was, like, okay with you?" I hear myself ask.

"Yeah." He toys with the edges of his phone. "See, I never felt like I fit in anywhere, ever. Not at home. Not at school. So I didn't let my sexuality freak me out. What's one more thing?"

"One more thing," I repeat slowly.

"Go to bed, Hayworth," he says, pointing at the door. "I think you need it."

"Yeah," I say, my voice thick. It's probably the best advice I've been given in a long time. "What a fucking awful day."

He makes a face. "We shall never speak of this again."

"Right. Night."

Then I get the hell out of there. I stumble into my own room and shut the door. My phone is on the bed, so I pick it up. And by sheer force of habit I touch the lock screen to see if there are any notifications from the *Kink* app.

There aren't, of course.

It occurs to me that I should delete the app.

But I don't. Not yet.

———

The next day I sleep past noon, only rolling out of bed when my need for painkillers becomes stronger than my need to disappear under the comforter.

Everything feels bleak. Usually on Sunday I'd meet Annika for brunch, or my dad if he's in town. But today I don't have plans, so I order a pizza from the only place that delivers. It's not even good pizza.

And then I run into Bailey when I'm collecting it from the pizza delivery guy. He's just back from the grocery store, apparently. I head upstairs, thinking to avoid him in the kitchen. But, damn it, he follows me up two flights of stairs, carrying his grocery bag with him.

"Why don't you keep that in the kitchen?" I mutter, which

really translates to, *why do I have to see you when I'm still embarrassed?*

"Because people take my food," he grumbles, giving his door a nudge with his hip. "Duh." It closes with a loud click.

That's when I remember what Bailey—SinnerThree—once wrote about money. That it was a constant worry for him. That he didn't always have enough money for groceries at the end of the month.

I attack my average-tasting pizza, feeling surly and hemmed in.

And what's that old saying? *There's no rest for the stupid.* Okay, that's not exactly it. But when I check my email, I learn that I have not one but two frat meetings today. There's a chapter meeting. And before that, a huddle with—wait for it—the officer candidates for the election.

So a few hours later I find myself face to face for the second time today with the one man I most want to avoid. Reed, our sitting president, has gathered Bailey, me, and the guys who are running unopposed for treasurer and for secretary.

"Okay, boys," Reed says after he closes the dining room door. "In a half hour the chapter decides who will be the cat-herder in chief. But before the vote happens, I just wanted to go over a few details. Because it sometimes feels like brothers sign up for these things out of optimism or loyalty or whatever, without knowing that there's work involved."

I bristle, feeling like this comment is directed at me. But I'm not at all confused about this. I already know that the presidency will make my senior year harder than ever.

"Here are job descriptions for all of you," Reed says. "You'll recognize the first part from the fraternity handbook. But below that I've added some notes about the practical considerations."

"Thank you, Reed," Bailey says quietly. "This is pretty great."

"Thanks, man," echo the others.

When Reed hands me his notes, I skim the lengthy paragraphs and try not to sigh. The details run to five pages.

"The president's description was the hardest to describe," he says. "I've used the word 'peacekeeper' a lot. The cats don't always listen. The buck has to stop with you, though. The bylaws are very clear about this. So if, say, your best friend has some stupid ideas about the initiation rituals, you have to shut that down." He gives me a pointed look.

Fuck. "Got it," I say stiffly.

"It's not a job that always makes you popular," Reed adds.

"I should be perfect, then," Bailey says, and the other guys chuckle.

"But, hey, at least you earn your free room," Reed says.

"Free room?" I ask, looking up.

Four curious stares look back at me. "You didn't know about the free room?" asks Jon Munsen, who's running for secretary. "Almost makes it worth it."

"Right." I feel like I'm ten steps behind everyone else. "Yeah, I remember," I lie.

"Okay, any more questions?" Reed asks. He waits, but nobody brings anything up. "All right. I'm going to go grab the ballot box out of the attic. And we'll get the chapter meeting started in fifteen minutes or so."

The room descends into a tense silence.

Well, *I'm* tense, anyway. Munsen and Edwards are noodling on their phones. Bailey also taps on his phone, looking carefree.

But I feel like I'm coming out of my skin. I can no longer remember why I was running for president of Alpha Delt. To please my father, I guess. I wonder what he'll say when I tell him that Annika dumped me. I can't even imagine the disappointed look on his face.

And why does that even matter? I'm twenty-one years old, almost twenty-two.

My phone buzzes with a notification. And I can't believe it, but it's from the *Kink* app. I open the phone under the table and find that SinnerThree has sent me a gif. It's of...a cowboy herding cats across the plain.

May the best asshole win, he writes.

I can't help myself. I glance up and find him looking at me. And that fucker *winks*.

Goddamn Bailey. I don't want to *like* the guy.

The room starts to fill with my fraternity brothers. They take up all the rest of the seats at the table, and then fill in the window seat and all the standing room along the walls.

"Here we go, guys." Reed puts a stack of ballots onto the table and then passes more of them around the room. "Oh, and here's some pencils," he says, placing a mug of them on the table.

Reed is great at this, I realize. He's a good president, and patient, too. A real cat-herder.

I glance across the table at Luke, whose chin is resting in his hand. I wonder if he knows he probably can't win. There are too many football players in the frat, and they'll vote for me just by default. And I'm friendlier, too. I've spent more time playing poker and watching sports in the living room.

Bailey doesn't. He works a lot, I think. I'm just realizing that he probably has to work all the time just to stay afloat. He told me as much when I was chatting with SinnerThree.

He's picking his cuticles right now. As if it doesn't matter whether he wins. But I'm suddenly realizing that it probably matters a great deal to him. The president gets a free room next year.

That part makes no difference to me whatsoever. The rent here isn't even very high...

"The meeting is called to order," Reed says calmly. "I thought we'd vote first, just to get the ballots squared away. Does anyone have any questions about the election? It's a straight majority setup. In the unlikely event of a tie, we revote once and then if that doesn't clear things up, the sitting officers will break the tie." He waits. "No questions?"

My heart rate accelerates, and I raise my hand. "Hey, Reed?" Everyone turns to look at me. "I changed my mind." The rest comes pouring out in a word-vomit of pure relief. "The presidency isn't really my thing, and I'm probably not the right personality for it. So I'm withdrawing my name from consideration. Still happy to do committee work, but, uh, cross my name off the ballots."

Judd groans loudly.

Reed only blinks. "You sure, man?"

"Totally," I say, feeling great for the first time all day. "I got enough on my plate." And my father can just shove it. If he wants a Hayworth to be president of Alpha Delt, he can re-enroll at Darby and run again.

Fuck his opinion. Fuck everything.

There is an uneasy murmur in the room. And then I make the mistake of glancing over at Luke Bailey. I guess I thought I'd see relief in his eyes. Now the free room is his.

Instead? He's glaring at me with murder in his eyes.

CHAPTER 18
MR. PRESIDENT

LUKE

There's no real vote. Nobody else steps up at the last minute to challenge me. After weeks of competing with Keaton for a position I only want because it saves me rent money, I'm dubbed president of Alpha Delta. By pure default.

Resentment roils in my stomach as I sit through the rest of the meeting. Somehow I manage not to vault over the coffee table and drive a fist into Keaton Hayworth's jaw.

What the fuck game is he playing now? My hands are trembling with anger, so I press them against my thighs and mentally urge Reed to quit babbling. I don't care that Hell Week starts tomorrow, or that we're running low on cleaning supplies. I need answers from Keaton Hayworth III.

But once Reed calls the meeting to a close, it's impossible to get Hayworth alone. Judd and his other football buddies drag him into the kitchen, and their hushed, angry voices tell me they're not thrilled by his sudden decision, either.

Jaw tight, I keep an eye on the kitchen doorway, but it doesn't look like they're wrapping up.

"Mr. President!" Jako comes over and slaps me on the shoulder. "We did it!"

"No, we didn't," I mutter. "I won by default."

"Who cares? We still got the end result we wanted. Come on, let's go out and celebrate. A bunch of us want to take you to Cinnibar—our treat."

I draw a steady breath. It's a nice gesture, and any other night I'd jump at the thought of free booze. But Keaton and I have unfinished business. I open my mouth to lie, then realize there's no reason to. "I'm waiting to talk to Hayworth," I tell Jako. "I want to know what the hell he did that for."

Jako purses his lips in thought. "Yeah, it was kinda weird. But…you won. Who cares why he dropped out?"

"I care." Beyond Jako's shoulders, I see several of our brothers milling about, waiting on us. "You guys go on ahead," I urge. "I'll meet you there after I talk to Hayworth."

"Fine." He claps my shoulder again. "But don't take too long." To everyone else, he shouts, "See you all at Cinnibar. Last one there buys the first round!"

I'm nearly killed in the resulting stampede. Despite the plethora of rich dudes in this frat, none of them want to part with their precious allowances. Meanwhile, Keaton and his pals are still arguing in the kitchen. When I creep closer, I hear Judd growl, "Not *my* president!"

I choke down a laugh. Oh for fuck's sake. I haven't even taken office yet and I'm already a hashtag.

They're taking forever. So long, in fact, that I pull my phone out of my pocket and open *Kink*.

SinnerThree: I need to talk to you. Now.

No response, obviously, but I'm gratified to hear the ding of a notification in the kitchen. Good. I hope someone asks Keaton who's messaging him. He'll be too embarrassed to admit to using *Kink*, and speed up his conversation.

But that doesn't happen. Instead, to my disbelief, Keaton,

Judd, and their friends exit the kitchen and brush right past me as they head toward the front door.

"Hayworth," I growl at his back. "A word?"

His broad shoulders stiffen. He glances over, his expression a bit sheepish. "Can't. We've got somewhere to be. Congrats on the presidency."

And then he's gone.

I stare at the door. Is he fucking kidding me? I deserve answers, damn it. He can't just drop out of the election at the last second without explanation. I furiously type on my phone again.

SinnerThree: You're such an asshole.

As expected, no response.

I shake my head a few times, standing there in the middle of the living room. The silence is slightly disconcerting. Every single frat brother has either gone off to Cinnibar with Jako, or has left with Keaton. And I can't even enjoy the solitude, because I'm still fuming over Keaton's actions.

He *handed* me the presidency. Why? Was it pity? I mean, it had to be. He'd looked genuinely surprised to find out the prez gets a free room, and he knows I don't have much money. Obviously he put two and two together. Before LobsterShorts, I would've assumed that adding two and two would be a difficult feat for Mr. Jockface. But I know better now. Keaton isn't a dumb jock. He's a biology major, and he's far more intelligent than he lets on.

I trudge upstairs, the resentment still churning in my gut. I text Jako to let him know I'm just changing out of my sweats and then meeting everyone at the bar.

I tackle the first part, throwing on a pair of ripped jeans and a black sweater, but my phone buzzes before I can leave the room. It's a *Kink* alert.

LobsterShorts: How am I an asshole? You wanted me to bow out.

SinnerThree: I wanted you to bow out when you broke the rules basically twice in ten days like an asshole. Not out of pity.

And that, right there, is what's really bugging me. Keaton was a lock for this gig. I would've received a fair amount of votes, sure, but we both know I still would've lost.

SinnerThree: I don't need your pity, dude.

LobsterShorts: It wasn't pity. I never wanted to be prez.

SinnerThree: Bull.

LobsterShorts: Truth. Look, can we talk about this later? I'm with the guys.

SinnerThree: Yeah, I know. I saw you flee, remember?

LobsterShorts: Wasn't fleeing. Judd wanted to go out. Pajama party thing at Beta Kappa.

SinnerThree: You're going to a sorority party? Seriously?

LobsterShorts: Sorry. I did suggest to them that we should stop at Cinnibar. Jako texted us to come. But Judd's...how do I say this tactfully...displeased by the election results.

Meaning, he refuses to support my reign by celebrating with me and the rest of the guys. Not that I'm celebrating. I'm sitting on the edge of my bed, sulking.

SinnerThree: I'm displeased too. That wasn't cool.

I don't get a reply this time, even after five minutes tick by. I imagine Keaton and his boys are surrounded by a slew of tipsy, PJs-clad sorority girls right now, so I force myself to jog over to the bar.

Cinnibar's is the most upscale bar on campus. The other two are primarily visited by the football crowd (hard pass) or the crew team (snoot alert), but Cinnibar offers a chill crowd and a laidback atmosphere. In fact, we're the only frat members in the place tonight.

For the next hour, I drink with my frat brothers, awkwardly accepting the praise, happily accepting the free drinks. Even some of the guys I'm not close with, like Paxton Grier and Edwards, are being nice to me, though in Paxton's case it's because he's trying to convince me to set him up with one of my "stripper friends." I'm trying to dodge his incessant pleading when I get a message from LobsterShorts.

"Hold that thought," I tell Paxton, all the while praying he just drops it. Which is looking likely, because I barely blink and he's lumbering off toward a trio of cute brunettes.

LobsterShorts: I'm sorry you're pissed, ok? But it wasn't pity, or some evil scheme on my part. I never wanted the job. My dad wanted it for me.

His confession chips away at some of my bitterness. Lobster-Shorts—I mean, Keaton—mentioned on numerous occasions that he has a difficult relationship with his father.

Maybe his dad *did* push him into running for president. I mean, that gift card stunt Mr. Hayworth pulled last week reeked of desperation.

LobsterShorts: And yes, the free room thing cemented my decision to bail, but trust me, bailing has been on my mind since the race started. If anything, knowing you're strapped for cash was the excuse I needed to back out.

Sighing, I type, **Fine. I believe you. But you could've warned me you were gonna do that.**

LobsterShorts: Didn't know I was going to do it until I did it. Anyway. Congrats.

SinnerThree: Thanks.

I put the phone away and accept the fresh pint glass Ahmad places in my hand. I'm on beer number three, but my tolerance is high so I barely feel buzzed.

Fuck. I won the election. It's finally sinking in now that my anger as dissolved. I don't have to pay rent next year, and the weight that suddenly lifts off my chest has me sagging forward in relief. Christ. This is going to help. A lot.

"Your first order of business is clear," Ahmad is saying. Unlike me, his tolerance is shit, and he's visibly inebriated. Bright red cheeks and extreme clumsiness.

"Is it?" I laugh.

"Yup! Another dinner party," he declares. "That food, dude! Soooooooo good!"

Jako snickers from the other side of the booth. "Wait, you want another dinner party for the *dinner*? Not the girls?"

"They can come too, I guess. But only if they bring the cheese balls."

We all howl in laughter. But my amusement is cut short when my phone buzzes again.

LobsterShorts: This party blows. How's the bar?

I frown at the screen. Why is he messaging? He's at a party. His hands should either be holding a drink or a hot chick, not his phone.

SinnerThree: It's awesome. Feeling nice and buzzed. And how could a sorority PJ party blow? Aren't they all in hot lingerie?

LobsterShorts: They are. But...I dunno. I can't hit on any of these women, Sinner. It feels wrong. Like I'm trying to replace Annika.

I find it interesting that he still calls me Sinner. I guess he's also having trouble merging my two identities. Sinner and Luke Bailey. LobsterShorts and Keaton Hayworth. There are four people in this equation when there should only be two.

SinnerThree: She dumped you, dude. You need to deal with that fact and move on.

LobsterShorts: I will. But who says I have to deal and move on tonight?

SinnerThree: Good point. With that said, a rebound never hurt anyone. I've heard it makes people feel better.

LobsterShorts: Nah. I told you, it feels wrong to hook up with one of these girls. Especially a sorority girl. I'd be thinking about Annika the whole time.

LobsterShorts: No women for me tonight.

SinnerThree: How about men?

Motherfucker.

Why did I send that? It sounds—no, it *is*—flirtatious. And I shouldn't be flirting with this guy. I'm still kicking myself for kissing him last night. That was a stupid move.

But the problem with hitting Send is, the other person still gets the message, because you fucking hit *Send*.

LobsterShorts: Is that a dare, Bailey?

Oooh boy. He used my name. Shit just got real.

SinnerThree: I'm just saying, if hooking up with a woman tonight is just going to remind you of Annika, maybe do it with someone who can't remind you of her.

LobsterShorts: Someone with a penis?

SinnerThree: Why not?

LobsterShorts: Someone like you?

I stare at the screen for so long that I draw the attention of my booth mates. "Bailey! Yo!" Hoffman calls. "Paxton paid good money for this round of beers. If you're not gonna drink yours, pass it over."

Paxton balks. "Hey! If he doesn't want it, why do *you* get it? I paid for the fucking thing!"

I absentmindedly slide my pint glass toward Paxton. "Have at it. I'll be right back."

Ignoring Jako's curious gaze, I hop out of the booth and amble toward a quiet spot at the end of the bar. My heart is beating faster than normal, and there's a stirring in my groin that's making it hard to concentrate. I reread Keaton's last message, mulling over how to answer.

A good minute passes before I force myself to admit the truth, but once I do…there's no debate about what to write back.

SinnerThree: The house is empty right now. I dare you to meet me there in 15.

I'm on pins and needles now. My pulse races, blood drums in my ears. My body feels hot and tight, and there's no way I can just go back to the table and drink another beer.

I power down my phone, so I won't be tempted to stare at the screen.

And I slip out and head home.

CHAPTER 19
GOLD

KEATON

I glance around the party and see all the usual mating rituals. Judd is refilling his red plastic cup while telling jokes to a sorority woman in a see-through nightgown. She laughs, and he reaches over to touch her elbow.

Seriously, the dung beetle mating ritual—where the male rolls a turd to impress his lady friends—is less predictable than this party.

I can't even carry on a conversation, because I just keep thinking about Luke-fucking-Bailey, and wondering if his dare was just bluster, or if he really went home like he said he did.

If I show up at the house right now, will he be waiting for me? Or did he pocket his phone and order another beer, saying to himself, *That will show the asshole.*

He logged off the app, too. There's no green dot by his name. He dared me and then disappeared before I could say anything. He got the last word. I hate that fucking guy.

I hate him, and I also want him to blow me.

On that thought, I set down my own red cup and break for the door. I don't even glance at Judd, because I sure as hell don't want him to ask me where I'm going.

It's about a three-minute walk to the Alpha Delt house, and I force myself to walk slowly. I'm not in a hurry to look like an ass if he's not really there.

What am I even after? I blow out a hot breath, and it appears before me like smoke in the cold January air. I'm unmoored tonight. I keep reaching for my phone to text Annika, and then realize we're not together anymore. And the text I got from my father is no consolation. He congratulated me on my presidency. He didn't even ask if I'd won. He'd just assumed.

The frat house is dark as I approach. I unlock the front door and step inside to dead quiet. When I close the door behind me, the sound echoes.

Shit.

I head for the stairs, because I have to know. There isn't a soul in evidence on the first or second floors.

But then I hear music.

My pulse jumps as I climb the last flight. And sure enough, Bailey is home. He's got some kind of house music coming out of his cheap speakers, a groove that's somewhere between R&B and electronica.

Whatever it is, it's just loud enough that he doesn't hear me approach. So I have a private view of him as he perches on the edge of the bed, raising and lowering his legs while balancing a dumbbell across his ankles to up the ante on the workout.

He's shirtless, and his cheeks are stained with the effort of using every core muscle he's got to lift that weight. His bare abs tremble as he does another rep while the music thumps sexily in the background.

For a long minute I just lurk there like a creeper and watch. And I like what I see, damn it. Maybe it's a side effect of the complete destruction of my life, but I am attracted to Luke-fuck-ing-Bailey.

Those abs, though. And that sinuous torso. Not an ounce of fat on him anywhere.

"Hey," I say finally, because I can't stand here forever and not get caught.

I've startled him. His chin whips toward me, those dark eyes locking onto me as he frowns. The motion destabilizes the exercise he's got going. In slow motion, the dumbbell tips and rolls off his feet. And the loss of the weight unbalances him.

Luke rolls off the foot of his bed and right onto the floor with a thump and an *oof.*

And I do what any red-blooded man would do at this moment. I laugh.

"Fuck," he grumbles from the floor.

"Don't get up," I say, trying not to bust a gut. And then I startle him all over again when I sit down beside him on the floor.

He turns to me with surprise on his face. "I didn't expect you to show."

"Yeah, I didn't expect me to show, either."

He doesn't say anything for a moment, and I'm way too aware of how close we're sitting, and of the sexy thump of the song keeping time with my heartbeat. "What is this music?"

"Chet Faker," he says with a sly smile. "The song is called 'Gold.' You like it?"

I forget to answer him, because his mouth is only a few inches from mine now. And I'm having a vague, drunken memory from last night. His tongue in my mouth.

Luke tips his head to the side, studying me. I'm probably about as subtle as a brick while I'm staring at his mouth, wondering if another kiss from him would taste as dirty and dangerous as the first one.

He moves in, and I sort of brace myself to taste him again. But at the last second he swerves, and his lips skim my neck instead. *Hello, goosebumps.* He palms my chin, shifting it out of the way, making space for a line of slow, dirty, open-mouthed kisses beneath my jaw.

I make an inarticulate noise of surprise. Suddenly, all the tension in my body is killing me. Needing to move, I lift both my hands to his hard chest. The heat and muscle against my palms is another shock to my system.

And his, too. He makes a soft sound of encouragement as my thumb grazes a flat nipple. When it pebbles under my touch, he whispers a curse against the corner of my mouth. Still, he makes me wait for the kiss. I'm vibrating with anticipation by the time he finally puts me out of my misery, rising up on his knees to claim my mouth.

Fuuuuuck. My body buzzes with expectation at the scrape of his stubble against my lips. I inhale the smoky scent of ale, and he deepens the kiss immediately. My mouth opens like a hungry bird's, and his tongue sweeps inside and clobbers me with sensation.

It's overwhelming. My head bumps against the mattress as he dives in for more, throwing a knee over my body, landing in my lap as he owns my mouth.

We're chest to chest, and my cock jumps at the proximity. Meanwhile, my hands give in to temptation, roaming his torso, wrapping around to explore the planes of his back.

All that muscle. And his rough mouth. It's so different than kissing a woman. I fucking love it. I drop my hands to his hard ass and squeeze.

He breaks the kiss, leaning back, staring down at me. "You're not afraid."

"What?" I rasp. "That's a requirement?"

He laughs suddenly, and the sound goes straight to my cock. "No. Whatever. Take your clothes off if you're so brave." He runs a hand down my chest, and my goosebumps redouble, as if nobody ever touched me before.

I fight off a horny shiver and then remove my football jacket. "Get off me if you want to get me off."

"Oh I do," he says, rising suddenly. His sweatpants have a very distinct bulge in front. And when he catches me staring, he reaches down and pumps his hand over the cotton. Then he steps away and kicks his door shut, clicking the doorknob lock into place.

I get up off the floor, and blood rushes to my face as I shrug off my T-shirt. This break in the action gives me a chance to think about what I'm doing. *Stripping down for Luke Bailey.*

Yup, thinking is overrated.

Luckily for me, he chooses that moment to slide his sweatpants off, bending over slightly, offering me a view of all his muscles from a brand new angle, and a seriously muscular ass straining the stretchy fabric of a pair of black boxer briefs.

I shuck off my shoes and jeans with shaking hands, still watching him. "You have, like, no body hair."

He snorts. "Professional upkeep."

"What do you mean—?" I don't get a chance to finish the question because he stalks into my personal space and kisses me again. He takes the back of my neck in one hand and devours my mouth with no preamble.

I feel my socks fall from my hands. He gives me a shove and I sit down hard on the bed. "That's right," he whispers against my mouth. "Lie back and take more of it."

Someone's feeling pushy tonight. It ought to annoy me, but it just doesn't. I'm too busy lying back on the same bedspread where he made a video of coming all over himself for me.

A moment later he lowers his body onto mine, and I gasp as all that smooth skin makes contact with mine. I receive a single, dirty kiss before he slides a hand right past the elastic of my boxers, palming my cock.

I gasp into the next kiss as my toes curl.

If letting your fraternity brother touch your cock is wrong, then I don't want to be right.

"You are seriously hot, for a muscle jock," he mutters, kissing his way down my throat. "Proof that nothing is fair."

I gulp as his mouth crosses my collarbone and then dips lower. He strokes my cock with a firm grasp, and I'm clenching every muscle in my body, wondering what he's going to do next.

Releasing me, he suddenly sits up and straddles my hips, his abs rippling. He's agile, I realize. Watching him move is almost as good as letting him kiss me. He reaches down and flicks both my nipples at once.

"Ah!" The twin sparks of pain only heighten my overeager senses. "Do that again."

He leans down and bites one instead, grinding his pelvis against mine. There're two layers of fabric between us, but I still feel the heat of his cock as it brushes against my shaft

"Mmm," he says, kissing his way down my chest, his fingers teasing my happy trail. "Do you want my mouth?"

"Yeah," I rasp.

"Really? Ask me nicely."

I groan as he tugs on my boxers. Lifting my hips, I let him slide them off me and toss them away. My leaking cock swings free and slaps me on the belly.

"Nice," he whispers, his hands coasting lightly up my thighs. He leans down and drags his lips across my hipbone, biting me lightly on the sensitive skin just to the side of my pubes. He lifts his head and I brace for his mouth, but it doesn't come. Only his breath grazes my cock as he teases my balls with one hand. "I didn't hear you ask, yet," he says sulkily. "How badly do you want this?"

Pretty badly, as it happens. "Please," I grunt. "Suck it."

"Concise." He snickers. "A man of few words. Okay, Keaton Hayworth the third. You win my mouth around your dick."

I raise my head as he takes me in hand. *Yes.* And I watch as that sulking mouth opens to engulf the head of my dick. At the first perfect pass of his expert tongue, I nearly shout with appreciation. But then he raises his dark eyes to mine, mouth stuffed full of me, and I have to lock the muscles in my thighs to keep from coming right then and there.

Jesus. I will not humiliate myself. Not *quite* yet anyway.

I sink back into the bed, willing myself to relax as he takes a deep pull of me. My hips roll because they just have to. And somehow my hand has found its way into his hair, as if having a hand on him might control the experience.

Which is ridiculous. I have never felt less in control than I do right now.

And I love that so much.

He groans and then swallows around me. I feel my cock bump the back of his throat, and my toes curl. The man is seriously good at this. My fingers tighten in his hair as he works me over with rhythmic sucks and licks.

I try to make it last, but it's too good. Too all-encompassing. "Gotta come," I whisper, pumping my hips again and again. "Look out."

He only moans and then gives me a good, hard suck.

And it's all over but the shouting. I arch my back and pour every ounce of my frustration into his willing mouth. I'm dizzy with relief as he swallows everything I give him. When I can't take it anymore, I collapse back onto the bed again.

Jesus Christ. Maybe Annika had a point about our sex life. The music still thumps through my veins, and I'm flushed and spent and more satisfied than I can ever remember being.

Luke isn't, though. He's stripped off his boxer briefs and straddled my hips again. "Touch me," he says, lifting my hand off the bed and wrapping it around his cock.

I'm barely functional, but it registers that I'm holding another man's dick for the first time. He puts his hands down on either side of me and thrusts into my hand. Those dark eyes drink me in as he strains above me. That hot gaze alone makes my skin heat even more than it already has.

"You like what you see?" I manage to mutter.

"I like it way too much," he pants. "Don't talk, though, unless it's to say you want my dick in your mouth. Nope, wait." His muscles tense. "Too late."

His cock jumps in my hand, and then he's coming in hot bursts that spill onto my stomach.

But the husky groan he lets out is drowned out by the sound of raucous laughter from downstairs. Oh *shit*. Somebody is home. A bunch of somebodies, from the sound of it. I'm not usually prone to panic, but the burst of anxiety that goes off inside me has me diving out from under him, and rolling off Bailey's bed.

The proof of his climax drips down my abdomen, but I'm so panicked about the possibility of getting caught that I ignore the mess. I just snatch my clothes off the floor and whip out the door, running for the shower.

CHAPTER 20
THE UNIVERSE DECIDED

LUKE

"I raise ya fifty," Judd announces, smirking at me.

I check my cards. We're playing five-card stud tonight and I've got two pair: tens and eights. It's the "dead man's hand," the same one Wild Bill Hickok was holding when he took a shot to the back of the head in some Wild West saloon. If I meet Judd's bet and lose fifty bucks, plus the ten we all threw in for the ante, I'll be the dead man. My year of free rent doesn't start until the fall, which means money remains tight.

But I suspect Judd's bluffing. And I'm feeling cocky tonight.

Nah, I've been feeling cocky ever since I fooled around with Keaton. He's been avoiding me for three days, and for some reason that makes me feel...victorious, maybe? Like I have the upper hand, which isn't a position I've ever felt like I had with Keaton Hayworth III.

"I call," I say carelessly, sliding my chips into the center of the table.

Judd's eyebrows soar. "For real?"

In the chair next to mine, Tanner starts cackling. "I think you just caught him in a bluff," he says, poking me in the arm.

I grin. "Let's see 'em," I tell Judd.

Jaw twitching unhappily, Judd lays down his cards. He has a pair of queens, and nothing else.

I flick my own cards on the table and drag the huge pile of chips toward me. Sweet. There's more than a hundred bucks here. I'm buying myself a steak dinner tomorrow.

"Dead man's hand," a familiar voice remarks as Judd flips over my cards.

I stiffen slightly. Keaton appears, peering at my winning hand.

"Yup," I say, sparing him a quick look. "Only this one doesn't come with a bullet."

"A bullet?" Ahmad asks blankly.

"It's the hand that a famous gunslinger was playing before he got shot to death," Keaton explains.

I notice he hasn't met my eyes once, not even when I looked at him. Pussy. I still remember the way he sprinted out of my bedroom on Sunday night, as if his ass was on fire. Hell, I hadn't even gotten my hands on his ass yet.

And judging by the way he's been keeping his distance, I never will.

But let's be honest, it's probably for the best. I can't deny I enjoyed blowing him, and I definitely wish I'd gotten the chance to fuck him, but the universe clearly decided it wasn't meant to be. And I'm okay with that. Screwing around with a frat brother is as terrible an idea as hooking up with one of my coworkers. Way too close to home.

Luckily, it seems like Keaton and I are on the same page about no repeats.

"You in for the next round?" Judd asks his best bud.

I fully expect Keaton to say no. And a beat of silence goes by as uncertainty plays across his features.

"Sure," he says suddenly. "Let me grab a beer. Anyone want a refill?"

Tanner and Jako take him up on the offer, and a moment later Keaton returns from the kitchen with two Sam Adams and a Dos

Equis for himself. *Huh*. He drinks Dos Equis? This is the first time I've paid attention to his beer of choice. And it's also the first time I have to forcibly stop myself from checking him out.

Before, a passing glance of admiration wasn't something I'd stressed about, but now I find myself going out of my way *not* to linger on his appearance. But he looks damn good in those expensive jeans and a snug gray sweater that stretches across his impossibly broad chest.

As Judd deals the cards for the new round, I sip my beer and chat with Jako and Ahmad about the new semester. Jako is an econ major, and he and I share a business class this term—a marketing seminar. Ahmad is majoring in biology, and I almost regret asking him about his schedule, because it ends up drawing Keaton into the conversation. Ack. I keep forgetting he's also a bio major.

"Marine Ecology is gonna be the shit," Keaton says as he sorts his cards.

"Excited to stock up on your animal mating rituals knowledge, huh?" I speak up without thinking, then curse myself for the foolish move.

Keaton looks startled, but recovers quickly. "Nah, I think it'll be more about environmental and population patterns, marine habitats, that kind of stuff."

"It's super-fascinating," Ahmad pipes up. "I took it last year."

I study my hand, trying to decide which cards to drop. Finally, I lay down two, tap two fingers on the table, and pick up the replacements that Judd slides over. I've got a pair of aces. Not bad. But not good enough to call Tanner's twenty-dollar bet. So I fold, all the while trying to ignore the fact that Keaton's gaze is on me.

The intensity of it bores a hole in the side of my head. Stupidly, I sneak a peek. A hot shiver rolls through me. The look he's giving me is loaded with heat.

But when our eyes lock, he breaks visual contact, lowering his gaze to his cards.

Judd bluffs again, but this time it works. Tanner, Keaton, and Jako all fold, and Judd wins the pile. As the next hand is being dealt, my phone buzzes. Before I even check it, I know exactly who the message is from.

LobsterShorts: Stop looking at me like that.

I have to fight hard not to laugh.

Surreptitiously, I type a quick note, keeping my phone under the table.

SinnerThree: You kidding me? You're the one undressing me with your eyes. I'm not a piece of meat, Hayworth.

Smirking, I raise my beer to my lips.

LobsterShorts: Then why do I want to eat you up right now?

I break out in a coughing fit. A loud, uncontrollable burst of coughs that actually spurs Tanner to lean over and slap my back several times. "You okay, man?" he asks, concerned.

"Fine," I wheeze out. Cheeks scorching, I glance at Hayworth, and he's the one smirking now. I can't believe he just said that. It's a bold statement from a man who Olympic-sprinted out of my room after we made each other come.

My phone vibrates again. I'm almost terrified to check it, but then I realize it's a call. Unease washes over me when I see my brother's name.

"Uh, I'm sitting this one out," I say when Judd starts to deal. "Important call."

Once again, I feel Keaton's eyes on me, but I ignore him and duck into the kitchen to answer Joe's call. "What's up?" I demand in a low voice.

"Yo, we need more cash for the biz," Joe says without preamble.

The fingers of my left hand curl over the edge of the kitchen counter. "You seem to be under the impression that I'm an ATM, big brother. Which I'm not." My tone is tighter than my muscles.

He sounds irritated. "What's the big deal? I know you have the cash."

"Actually, I don't. And in case you forgot, I just gave you and

Mom five hundred dollars." Plus an extra hundred to him as hush money. "You already spent it?"

"Yes, we already spent it." Sarcasm drips over the line. "That's what happens when you're running a business, moron. You spend money."

"Uh-huh, and you also *make* money. How's that part going for you?" I look down at my knuckles and notice they're pure white. I force myself to relax my grip on the counter.

"We're just getting shit off the ground," my brother retorts. "You can't expect us to turn a profit immediately."

"Sure, and you can't expect me to be the sole investor of this clown show you're running."

"Clown show?" Fury thunders in his voice. "You sanctimonious prick! Is that how you view our *mother*? She's a clown? She worked her goddamn ass off to make sure there was food on our table and—"

"I'm not calling Mom a clown," I interrupt. "*You're* the clown, Joey. You don't know the first thing about running a business, and I'm not giving you another dime unless you present me with a proper business plan for this handyman shit, along with a repayment schedule—that's the only way you're getting any more cash from me."

"You little faggot—"

I hang up. Then I sag forward and inhale a deep breath. It doesn't calm me. In fact, it simply makes me lightheaded and more anxious. The last time I put up a fight about money, Joe threatened to tell the people in my life that I strip for a living, and so I caved. But I'm not caving anymore. The thing about lowlifes like Joe is, if you give in once, they'll always come back for more.

It was a mistake to pay him. At this point, I'd rather risk being outed as a stripper than be trapped under my brother's greedy thumb.

"Everything okay?"

I turn toward the doorway. Keaton stands there with what appears to be genuine worry in his hazel eyes.

For some reason, the sight of him rubs me the wrong way. Maybe it's the designer jeans that probably cost more than I earned at work last weekend. Or his perfect, just-the-right-amount-of-tousled haircut by a barber I could never afford. I don't need his worry. Or his pity. Or anything from him, really.

"It's fine," I grunt.

He clearly doesn't believe me, because he saunters over. His strides are long, his expression unfazed. Anybody else would read my body language, the thundercloud darkening my face, and walk in the other direction. But not him.

"What's going on?" he says quietly.

"Nothing. It's all good, Hayworth." I take a step. "Let's play some more poker."

"Nah."

I roll my eyes, taking another step. "Suit yourself."

A hand curls over my biceps. "Come on, Bailey."

My gaze slides down to his fingers. His thumb lightly grazes my shoulder. I swallow. "Come on, what? I told you, everything's fine." Despite myself, a taunt rises in my throat. "Besides, suddenly we're talking again? You've been ignoring me for three days."

The moment the words pop out, I regret them. I don't want Keaton to know that I noticed, or that it bothers me.

"I wasn't ignoring you. I was working on a paper and didn't want any distractions."

"What paper? Nice try, but it's the beginning of the semester." And why am I acting like a little bitch all of a sudden? I should be *glad* he's been avoiding me. It means that I've been able to avoid the awkward morning-after chat in which I'd have to tell him I'm not interested.

"I got short-listed for this internship I applied for," Keaton says quietly. "The final applicants are required to send a two-thousand-word essay."

"Uh-huh." His eyes tell another story, though. And because I don't always do what's good for me, I won't let it go. "If you got freaked out, you could just say so. Wouldn't be the first guy who couldn't handle the truth."

His flinch is swift.

I sigh, because what I've said is true, even if it wasn't very sensitive. "Never mind. It's no big deal." I step around him and leave the kitchen, heading for the stairs.

By the time I've climbed a few steps, I hear footsteps behind me. He's on my heels on the second floor landing. And then he continues all the way up to the third floor, damn it.

"What?" I bark, turning around in front of our bathroom. "You have something to say?"

"Yeah." He drops his voice down low. "You're right. I did get freaked out. But not only because you're a dude."

"Really? Why, then? I've had enough of guys who want me to make them scream, only to turn around after and say it's *unnatural* or some shit."

Keaton actually snorts. "Anyone who uses the word unnatural to describe sex hasn't spent any time in nature. Nature is crude and coarse and up for anything. I'm too much of a scientist to ever say that."

"What is it, then?" If he's telling the truth, I'm probably about to become even more offended. If it's not that I'm a guy, then it's personal?

"It freaked me out that I wanted…" A burst of laughter comes from one of the closed doors on the second floor. It's just some brothers playing a video game or watching a movie.

Our eyes meet, and his look wary. Then he looks away. I watch him grab the whiteboard off of his own door. It's the board where you can leave messages for him. I guess I need one of those for next year when I'm president.

Keaton uncaps the pen with his teeth and writes on it.

My breath hitches when I read what he's said.

· · ·

It freaked me out that you're a guy. And that I let you take the lead. Part of me wants to forget it happened. Most of me wants you to do it again.

Ah fuck. Our eyes meet one more time, and there's heat in his gaze. He erases the board with his fist, caps the pen and hangs the thing back on the door. Then he turns around and trots back down the stairs and goes back, I assume, to the poker game.

All I can do is stare after him for a long moment. I'm stunned, although it does make sense. If Keaton has been screwing the same girl since they were both teenagers, I suppose my bossy ass would be kind of educational.

Ask me nicely, I'd demanded.

Please, suck it, he'd said.

An evil grin spreads across my face, right there in the hallway. As I unlock the door to my room, I like knowing that I blew his mind.

He enjoyed my bossy ass. He liked it so much that he couldn't even say it. He had to write it on a whiteboard instead.

I halt in the center of my room as the implication of that settles in. Keaton's confusion, his reluctance to voice his needs…it's a bad sign.

A very very very bad sign.

It's all well and good to have some casual fun with a friend who knows what he's getting into. And I sympathize with Keaton's sexual confusion, even if I don't share it.

But we're neighbors, and we're going to be frat brothers for another year and a half. It's a bad idea for me to blow his mind. Not if it puts him into a tailspin.

I take my phone out of my pocket and open the app. It only takes me a second to do the right thing.

Sorry, not interested. You and I are a bad idea.

CHAPTER 21
PUNCTUATION SAVES LIVES

KEATON

I put everything I've got into my internship essay. I mean, it's the only bright light in my shitty week. My girlfriend was spotted dining out with a lacrosse player. My ex-girlfriend, that is. When will I get used to saying that?

Meanwhile, my hot neighbor made it perfectly clear that I won't be broadening my horizons with him again anytime soon. And instead of feeling relieved, I wake up every morning picturing his lips wrapped around my dick. And hearing his voice tell me to lie there and take it.

I think I want to do it again. At least one more time. Or maybe ten. I don't know what that means exactly, but the thoughts, the fantasies, aren't going away.

And because life is cruel, I seem to run into him everywhere now. Our new semester schedules must be more closely aligned than before, because he's naked in the shower whenever I need the bathroom. Or he's chatting up the cute barista in my favorite coffee shop when I stop there between classes.

Fuck me. I'm single, I'm a little depressed, and I'm very horny, with a side of sexual confusion, too.

Then again, I'm a man who does *not* complain. So you won't hear any whining from me. But football season is over, and my single status leaves me with a lot of free time.

I'm at loose ends until Friday night, when I find out that it's Owen's birthday. "You have to come out with us, Keat!" he says. "It's gonna be epic."

"Where are we going?" I ask, trying to sound upbeat. Maybe a night of carousing will improve my mood.

"He's turning twenty-one," Tanner says. "Time to hit the titty bars!"

"You just want to see Cassidy dance again." He's taken out the dancer he met at Luke's Dance-off party twice already.

"Sue me!" My friend shrugs. "We're going to have a great time. Kinda pricey, but you only turn twenty-one once, right, Owen?" He slaps the guy on the back.

So that's how I find myself showering to go out.

Naturally, Luke is in our bathroom brushing his teeth when I walk in. I turn on the shower and then stand there in my towel while the water heats.

"Bunch of us are going out for Owen's birthday," I say awkwardly. "You should come."

"Gotta work," he replies. "Later!" He leaves without so much as a glance in my direction.

Right.

"Who's the designated driver?" Owen asks as we pile into two cars, including mine.

Silence.

I let out a groan. "Really? You brought me along so that I could Uber you around?"

"We could take an actual Uber," someone points out.

Grumbling, I start the car. The strip club my friends picked is not close by, and I guess I'd rather drive and drink only two beers than rely on ride-share apps.

They direct me inland, near the casinos, to a big parking lot in front of two clubs. One of them is called Jack's and the other one is Jill's.

We hop out of the car. I lock it and follow my brothers toward the buildings. They head left toward Jill's, instead of right.

"Um, guys?" I stop and study the buildings. There aren't any neon boobs or other tacky markings to distinguish the two. But I'm pretty sure that Jill's is meant to beckon to women. "Don't we want Jack's?"

"Well, Zimmer isn't here," Owen says. "And clearly the rest of us are into Jills."

As far as you know. But that's beside the point. "But there's an apostrophe. Jill's is *possessive...*"

"You mean Jill is a jealous bitch?" Tanner quips, and everyone laughs.

"No, I..." I sigh. "Go on. You'll see. It'll be tonight's fun little lesson in grammar. Who's getting the first lap dance?"

"Cassidy says they don't do lap dances here," Tanner says. "Sadly."

You won't be sorry about that in a second. If I'm right, this crew won't be wanting a lap dance at Jill's.

Tanner opens the door and gleefully waves everyone inside.

I'm the last to walk in. And I don't miss the frown of confusion on the female hostess's face. "Evening, boys," she says. "I think I should point out that—"

I put a finger to my lips. "This shouldn't take long, but it will amuse me."

She laughs and then shrugs. "No cover charge, then."

Sure enough, after three more paces, my boys get a glimpse of the stage, where four men wearing only G-strings and chaps are bucking across the stage to whoops of encouragement from the female audience.

Seven fraternity brothers go rigid with surprise.

"See? Punctuation saves lives," I call to them just as the song ends.

"Oh, shit," Tanner says.

"Are we in the wrong place?" Owen asks.

I really hope his tutors are on point this semester. We need him to keep his GPA up so we can advance in the postseason next year.

Seven guys hustle by me and out the door before two seconds pass.

Laughing, I pause in front of the hostess again. "That was totally worth it. Thank you for that."

"Happens at least once an hour," she says with a grin. "I suppose we could change the names to make things more obvious."

"But where's the fun in that?" I point out.

We high-five each other just as a new song starts up. It's that Sam Smith song, "Promises." I turn toward the stage instinctively. A very loud, very female shriek of joy rises over the music as a hot guy with dark hair saunters onto the stage in a crisp white shirt, skin-tight gray trousers, a matching suit jacket and a red tie. And then I do a vicious double-take.

Unless I'm losing my mind, it's Luke-fucking-Bailey.

I'm vaguely aware of my jaw hanging open as he saunters, barefoot, toward a desk and chair that have been rolled onto the stage. Sam Smith is already singing about all the things he wants to do for me as Luke begins to move his hips to the sensuous beat.

Jesus. The music runs through his body like a current. He's barely dancing, and yet the movements are somehow a hundred and ten percent sex as he sheds the suit coat and flings it over the chair. Then he loosens the tie. It's almost casual, as if he's alone with the music and the swing of his hips to the sexy beat.

The women shriek like they've all won a car from Oprah.

And I can't look away. I'm rooted to the floor as Luke slides the silk tie from his collar with a slow, sensual pull. A shiver runs up my spine, as if I can feel it myself—the slide of the silk over cotton.

On stage, his gaze is distant. There's no eye contact with the crowd. He doesn't pander, because he doesn't need to. Every eye in the room is already fixed on his fingers as they slowly unbutton that lucky shirt, while his hips circle and grind.

The effect is entirely voyeuristic, as if I'm watching his private thoughts as he prepares for sex.

Then he casts the shirt away and springs into action, hopping onto the desk with one gravity-defying leap. A spotlight illuminates those golden abs as they ripple and flex. And he slides a hand past his cock as if he can't quite stand how sexy he is.

I can't quite stand it, either.

The crowd loses its mind as he rotates, showing off those tight trousers as a hundred women sigh. It's fucking genius, because this is some serious wish fulfillment right here. Luke is playing the role of the hot CEO. He can provide for you, and then come home to make you scream.

Oh, and now we can also appreciate that he's well hung, because those skintight pants reveal every ridge and bulge of his gorgeous body.

Take them off, my libido begs. *And then take mine off, too.*

I told Luke that most of me wants to hook up with him again. That's not the case anymore. *All* of me wants it. Right here, right now—I've never wanted anything, or anyone, more.

Goodbye, sexual confusion. Because *confused* is the last thing I'm feeling at the moment. There's no other way around it—I like dudes. Especially that one onstage.

While I'm having this eureka moment, Luke takes a deep breath, and then turns in the direction of a metal pole that's maybe six feet from the desk. My poor little brain is just doing that math when Bailey leaps through the air like a sideways Superman, arms first, catching the pole in both hands.

And then he just sort of hangs there, legs out straight, body perpendicular to the pole. The maneuver requires either incredible core strength or a special insider's arrangement with gravity.

"Get the fuck out of here," I sputter, wondering how that's even physically possible.

A throat is cleared beside me.

I whirl around, but it's only the hostess watching me with an amused expression on her face. "Maybe you're in the right room after all?"

Shit. "Sorry." I feel blood rushing to my face as I try to recover myself. My frat brothers are long gone.

But I can't resist one more look at the stage. Bailey has a leg around the bar now. He's spinning slowly, almost casually, his muscles rippling while the women scream. Dollar bills are falling on stage like a blizzard.

I force myself to look away, leaving the club the way I came. The January cold smacks me as I step outside. I suck in the chilly air, trying to cool off my overheated body. It takes me a minute to put my game face back on.

Finally, I cross to Jack's and open the door, spotting Tanner striding toward me. "What happened to you, man? I was gonna send out a search party."

"Checking the car," I mutter. "Thought I forgot to lock it."

His arm lands on my shoulders. "Come in, already. I got you a beer. This place is sick."

I let him pull me toward a table where my brothers are all sitting, goggle-eyed at the women dancing in various places around the room. The women are all wearing G-strings and very little else. But I don't even see them. I'm stuck inside my head, which has become a very complicated place.

Luke Bailey is a stripper. Male entertainer. Whatever it's called. That's how he knew the women he recruited for his Dance-off dinner. They're his coworkers.

What's more shocking—the fact that Bailey takes off his clothes for money? Or that I want him to take off mine?

I settle in for a long evening of watching women shake their butts while I nurse two beers and a big secret. No, two secrets. One about Luke, and one about me.

CHAPTER 22
MUSIC. LOUD MUSIC.

LUKE

In the winter, I don't ride my motorcycle on the highway, which means I'm stuck using the bus to get to work. The worst part of my commute home from work is the last quarter mile. When I get off the bus near the student center, my muscles have already stiffened up, and the January wind bites my face.

I trudge through the two a.m. silence. When I unlock the door to the frat house, there's a blue glow coming from the TV room. I pass three guys playing a video game. But otherwise the house is quiet as I climb two flights of stairs to reach my door. I unlock it in the dark.

My bed beckons, but first I need a shower. Without ceremony, I drop all my clothes and head into the bathroom. The hot spray of water is like a lover's embrace. I pump a generous handful of shampoo and scrub off all the sweat and body oil until finally I feel human again.

When I turn off the shower, I hear music. Loud music.

Seriously? Keaton is blasting tunes this late at night? I'm going to choke him.

Hastily, I rub the towel all over my wet head, then tie it around my waist, ready to give him hell. But as I leave the bathroom, I freeze. That song. It's "Promises" by Sam Smith and Calvin Harris.

A chill snakes down my spine, because this can't be a coincidence. Mr. Classic Rock wouldn't develop a sudden affinity for my solo song two hours after I perform to it.

Would he?

As I stand there on the landing, trying to figure out what to do, I notice that Keaton has shut the door to the stairs, yet left the door to his room ajar. I take a step toward his door, nudging it open.

It's dark in Keaton's room, save for the glow of his stereo system and the streetlights outside. But it's enough to show me Keaton's very naked body lying among the tangled sheets.

"What the fuck are you playing at?" I hiss. "With this song. Are you threatening me right now?"

He sits up partway, leaning on one muscular arm. "Do I look like a fucking threat?" He drops a hand to his hard cock and strokes it. "Get over here."

Blood pounds in my...everything. But it's unclear whether I'm feeling more anger or arousal. Yeah, a naked Keaton is a beautiful thing. But you do not fuck with me over my job.

I cross the room to his expensive speakers and lower the volume. "Talk," I bark. "Why this song? Where were you tonight?"

"Where do you think? The guys walked into the wrong club for a second. And I've been hard ever since."

I look down again because it's late and I'm weak. His thick hand is wrapped around his girth. The memory of taking him in my mouth hits me like a blast of heat. I close my eyes and try to concentrate on what matters. "Who was with you?"

"Bunch of guys. They didn't see."

"Are you sure?"

"I'm sure. Jesus." Keaton flops onto the pillows. "Who cares, anyway? You're like sexy Spiderman, and all the ladies were screaming for you."

With a snort, I stalk toward the bed, looking down at him, letting my anger win. "As usual, Keaton Hayworth the third, you have no clue how the real world works. I can't become an internet joke right before I start applying for jobs."

Keaton sighs. "You're mad? Of course you are. It's your default reaction to everything." He tucks his hands behind his head, his beautiful body on display. "Fine. Get down here and punish me for daring to think you're hot when you dance. I guess the private performance I had planned is off?"

"Punish you?" My voice cracks on the words, because it's late and…

Fine, I like that idea a whole lot. Sue me. I close his bedroom door and lock it.

When I turn around, he's grinning at me, like he just won some kind of bet with himself.

"Smug is not a good look on you," I say, moving to stand over him. "Take off my towel."

"It is too a good look on me." He props himself up on an elbow in a big hurry. Then he reaches out and gives my towel a quick tug. "Aw, look who wants my body," he says as my semi bobs into view.

"Shut up." I put a knee on the bed. "I have something better you can do with your mouth." I palm the back of his neck and give him a destabilizing tug.

In a flash I've knelt in front of him at just the right height. "Oh, shit," he breathes as I wind my fingers into his hair, pulling him toward me.

Just the way he's looking at me—his eyelids heavy with both curiosity and lust—gets me to full mast by the time I feel his breath on my sensitive skin. "Let's have that smart mouth do something useful," I say as his tongue makes its first pass across my shaft.

And good God, the view! Keaton's aristocratic face descending toward my cock. He moans quietly as he opens his mouth and experiments with taking the head inside.

I break out in a sweat as his tongue tastes me. And I bite my lip as he hollows out his cheeks and sucks. My fingers tangle in his soft hair as he slowly bobs up and down, looking for a rhythm.

"Good…boy," I gasp. I thought I was tired. But hello, adrenaline. I catch myself moving slowly to the song. My song. Keaton's big hand finds my hip as he angles his face to take more of me.

This beats the snot out of my usual Friday-night routine.

He doesn't try to deep-throat me, but he doesn't hesitate to use one hand to play with my balls. He does this casually, like maybe he's spent a lot of time thinking about how much he wants to taste my cock.

I'm in awe that this is actually happening. A little too in awe, maybe. After just a couple of minutes of the star treatment, I feel my climax gathering like a storm. But I'm wide awake and feeling greedy now. I'm not ready for this to end. So I nudge him off me, and he looks up with wild, hungry eyes. "Not good?" he asks roughly.

"Too good," I assure him, running a hand through his unruly hair that I've already messed up. "What are you down for?"

"Honestly? Anything."

I lift his handsome chin. "Don't say that if you don't mean it."

"What if I do?" He rolls onto his back, his expression an odd mixture of shy and confident. "I have condoms and lube."

"Seriously?" A wave of heat rolls through my body. "You want me to top you?"

"Yeah, I do. And quickly." He bends one knee, the invitation unmistakable. "Before we both figure out how awkward this will get later."

He's not wrong. And maybe if it wasn't two in the morning, and I wasn't hard as a crowbar I would make a different call. The whole setup is irresistible. Hot frat brother who wants to be fucked? They make gay porn like this because real life doesn't actually work this way.

Except tonight it does.

Keaton reaches one of those muscular arms out to yank open the nightstand. And I'm already there, spreading my body out on top of his massive chest, reaching into the drawer. My hand closes around a bottle and a strip of condoms, and I drop them onto the bed beside our bodies.

His hands are busy doing other things, like coasting over my ass and pulling me closer. I lower my mouth to his in a blistering kiss. He grunts happily, and I take advantage of his parting lips, finding his tongue with mine. Christ, I like kissing him. Our cocks line up together. I love how hard he is for me.

I want to flip him over and drill him hard, but I don't do that. This is his first time, so I opt for a slow approach, stroking my hands over his body as we kiss. I lightly tease the crease of his ass. And although my fingers are gentle, my words are rough and dirty. "You ready for my dick to fill this sweet ass?"

"Yes," he chokes out.

"Are you gonna freak out tomorrow?"

"Dunno," he pants, kissing me again. "I'll just deal with that tomorrow."

Okay, then. His eagerness is such a turn-on. I grab the condom, prepping myself, but I don't fuck him yet. I get him ready, sliding a lube-covered finger into his tight passage. I tease and explore, and he's gasping for air by the time I add a second finger.

"Stop teasing," he mumbles. "Give it to me."

I lick my bottom lip, then bend over to suck on the head of his cock. His hips jerk off the mattress, but the moan he gives is laced with frustration. "Not your mouth. Give me your cock."

I lift my head and offer a lazy smile. "Why should I do that?"

"Because I want it." His cheeks are flushed with arousal, and he's beginning to squirm against my fingers. "More importantly, because *you* want it." His hazel eyes linger pointedly on my raging hard-on.

But then I remember what seems to turn him on even more. "I might give it to you if you ask me nicely."

He huffs out a breath. "Please."

"Please what?"

"Please fuck me," he groans.

I slap his ass just once, but hard. "Is this mine?"

He gasps. "Yes. Do it."

God, it's so gratifying to see how needy I've made him. I rise on my knees and guide my erection to where it's pleading to be. Keaton's eyelids grow heavy as he awaits my next move. He looks hot as fuck lying there beneath me. I'm tempted to reach over and flick on the bedside lamp, but the darkness also has its appeal. Fucking in the dark always makes everything so...dirty. Dangerous.

My pulse races as I slowly ease the tip of my dick inside the tightest ass I've ever encountered. Holy shit. I won't last long at all. This already feels impossibly good, and I've only begun.

"Ohhhh fuck," Keaton whispers as I slide in another inch. "That's...different."

I choke out a laugh. "Different bad, or different good?"

"Different. Awkward. But also amazing. Go deeper."

So I do. I lean forward on my elbows and give a slow thrust, and then another, until his body gives way and I'm buried all the way inside. *Oh boy oh boy.* Yup, this isn't going to take long.

I ease my body forward until I can brush a kiss over his lips before whispering, "Your ass is so goddamn tight. I'm about five strokes away from coming."

Keaton nips at the side of my throat. "That's no fun." And then he lifts his hips in a tentative thrust, and I see stars.

I dig my fingers into his waist to stop him from moving. "Tell you what's gonna happen," I say in a raspy voice. "You're gonna start jacking that big cock while I'm lodged inside you. You're gonna get yourself close, but you don't come until I tell you to, okay?"

He nods wordlessly, watching me with lust-glazed eyes. His breathing sounds labored as he lowers his hand to his groin.

Keaton starts stroking himself, and I swallow a groan. I'm aching to move, but I'm skirting too close to the edge right now. So I satisfy myself by watching him satisfy himself.

I don't know if I've ever seen anything so sexy.

Taking a slow breath, I sit back and begin to move. I wrap my arms around his thick thighs and pump my hips. And I know immediately when I've hit his prostate, because his hand falters and he lets out a helpless gasp.

"Right there," I whisper. "That's where you need me."

"Omifuckinggod," he rasps, shivering.

I knock his hand out of the way and reach for his cock. "You want to come?"

"Yes," he grits out, moving his hips. "So bad."

"Hold on." I bite my lip and look away from him as I thrust hard again. He's too hot for words—all blissed out and panting for me. Every slide of my cock threatens to undo me. I jack him and pound him at the same time.

I can't hang on. It's just too good. Tension coils in my balls and I feel the edge of pleasure slicing toward me.

"Come," I grunt through gritted teeth. "Now, Hayworth."

He lets out a strangled cry and then all his muscles tense at once.

And I'm done. My climax catches up to me and I lose my rhythm as I come helplessly, emptying my whole soul into his tight body and then landing awkwardly on his torso.

Two big hands yank me higher up his chest. His eager tongue invades my mouth just as hot semen erupts between us. I grind down on his trapped cock, and he groans loudly into the kiss.

"Christ," I slur against his lips a moment later, while my heart rate tries and fails to settle down.

Keaton nudges me off him, and I have to pull out to move. With clumsy hands I remove the condom and tie it off, barely opening my eyes.

He actually takes it from me and disappears. My head is heavy on his pillow. I need to get up but my limbs are too tired.

I'm contemplating moving when Keaton returns. He bends over me, and I wonder if he's about to suggest that I leave. But he kisses my neck instead. Then a warm washcloth makes a quick pass over my abs and chest.

"Thanks," I mumble, still needing to move.

But after a long day, followed by a long shift, topped off by mind-melting sex, exhaustion finally claims me, and I'm asleep before Keaton even replies.

CHAPTER 23
NOT SURE OF THE ETIQUETTE

KEATON

There's a naked man sprawled on my bed.

Cue: minor panic attack.

Only minor, though, because I locked the door after myself last night. So unless one of our frat brothers decides to kick down the door, the chances of anyone discovering Luke Bailey in my bed are slim.

I roll onto my side and prop an arm beneath my head. Luke's facedown on the mattress, bare-assed, one muscular arm curled over the pillow he stole from me at some point in the night.

My gaze skims over the sinewy lines of his ridiculous body. Now I understand why he's so ripped—he spends his weekends dancing, toning his tight body and working those muscles hard. I feel a throb down south, and it's more than just morning wood.

Heat tickles my chest as I remember what we did last night. Luke's powerful body crushing mine, his hips moving in the same sensual rhythm as when he danced for those screaming women. Only he wasn't dancing. He was fucking me senseless.

Okay.

So I'm bisexual. I try that out in my head. Scientists like to label things. I'm a scientist. But the idea of labeling myself isn't comfortable yet. Besides, the data set is still small. It was only last night. And that one other time. And the kiss.

Plus all those sexts over the app...

A sleepy groan interrupts my thoughts, and suddenly his eyes slit open. "Are you watching me sleep, Hayworth?" he mumbles. "Because that's creepy."

"I'd be sleeping myself if some jackass didn't lay claim to all the pillows." I give him a pointed look.

His expression grows more alert, and he looks at the pillow he's been cuddling with, as if just realizing it's there. "Ah. Sorry. Yeah, I'm a pillow thief. Blanket hog, too. Also..." He stops awkwardly, then sits up and rakes his fingers through his rumpled hair. "I don't usually sleep with people. Not sure of the etiquette."

I'm not surprised to hear it. Sharing a bed with someone requires a level of trust that Luke Bailey doesn't seem to feel toward many people. I'm pretty sure the only reason he crashed in my room was because he was dead-ass tired.

"Anyway." Before I can blink, he's sliding off the mattress. "I need to shower and work on my finance interview."

My eyes hungrily devour his body as he rummages around for the towel he was wearing last night. Oh, fuck me. I want to get off with him again. "Are you working again tonight?" I ask thickly.

"Yeah." He wraps the towel around his waist, offering a stern look. "And don't even think about showing up at the club."

"Why not? Can't perform if someone you know is in the audience?"

"Something like that." He heads for the door. "Later, Hayworth."

"Wait."

He stops, but doesn't turn around. I frown. He's clearly eager to bounce, and I don't like it. Is he freaked out about last night? Fuck, am I a bad lay? My list of sexual partners is a short one: Annika. And now Luke Bailey.

Insecurity creeps into me. "Are we cool?" I ask the back of his head.

He glances over his shoulder, nodding briskly. "Yeah. For sure."

I narrow my eyes at him. "Last night…it was good?"

There's a long pause. Luke's Adam's apple jumps as he swallows. When he speaks, his voice is slightly hoarse. "It was better than good," he says before sliding out the door.

———

I spend the rest of the morning alone in my room, trying to concentrate on the essay I'm writing for the Chile internship. It's due Monday, and I've been struggling with it all week. I'm supposed to write about the unique intellectual gifts I can offer the scientific team.

Like that's not an intimidating topic. And today I can't focus because my mind keeps drifting back to last night.

I had sex with a man. And I'm not freaking out about it. Not much anyway. And why is that?

Also, why do I care that Bailey skulked out of here within three seconds of waking up in my bed? It's not like I expected us to cuddle and act all lovey-dovey. We barely know each other. Hell, it wasn't long ago that I hated his guts.

But it bothers me that he left, because I don't know what it means. Are we one-and-done? He got my ass, and now he's off in search of a new man—or woman—to hook up with? I wish I could talk to someone, pick their brain about this, but who on earth would I tell? I'm not confiding in Judd or any of my other teammates. And no way I'm seeking the advice of a frat brother.

The one person I'd normally talk to is hooking up with some lacrosse player.

My throat squeezes at the thought of Annika. She and I have known each other forever. She's my best friend, and I can't believe I won't be able to talk to her anymore.

Why the hell can't you? a voice points out.

I shift my gaze from my laptop to the iPhone at the edge of the desk. After a moment of hesitation, I grab the phone and pull up a familiar name. I hesitate again, then shoot off a text.

Me: Hey. I know we're broken up, but I just wanted to see how you're doing. I hope that's okay. I'm not trying to get back together. I just...miss my best friend.

Not even thirty seconds pass before my phone rings. I can't help but smile when I see Annika's name.

"Hey," I say softly.

"Hi," comes her familiar voice. "I'm doing okay, and...I miss you too."

A wave of emotion flutters through me. "I hate not talking to you."

"I hate it too. I keep wanting to call or text you, but I've been trying to keep my distance, give you your space, you know?" She pauses. "I still think breaking up was the best decision for us, Keaton. But maybe I didn't handle it in the most tactful way. I..." She sounds uncomfortable. "I wasn't trying to imply that you're bad in bed."

"I know you weren't."

"But the spark was just...gone. For me, at least."

I swallow. I love Annika. I really do love her. But as much as I hate to admit it, the spark was gone for me too. Look at how hot Luke got me last night. Look at how desperate he made me feel. I don't remember the last time that sex with Annika was that explosive.

Possibly never. And what does *that* mean?

"I understand," I say gruffly. "And I meant what I wrote in that text. I'm not asking you to be my girlfriend again, but I do want us to be friends."

"I would love that," Annika says. Her voice catches, and I know her well enough to recognize the sound of her fighting tears. "I'm always going to love you, Keaton."

"Right back atcha. I—" I stop when I hear a muffled voice

beyond my door. I think it's Bailey's, and I swear there was a note of anger in his tone. "I have to go, actually," I tell my ex-girlfriend. "But maybe we can meet for coffee or lunch sometime this week?"

"That sounds perfect," she says happily. "I'll text you my availability."

"Awesome. Later, babe." I'm already walking out into the hall, toward Luke's closed door. His voice is louder now, and he's definitely pissed about something.

"—sure he'll turn up… No way… Come on, Mom. He's a grown man, and he's *not* my responsibility." There's a long pause. Then Luke releases a growl that has me taking a step back. "For fuck's sake!"

I probably shouldn't be eavesdropping. He's talking to his mother, and clearly there's some animosity there. It's none of my business.

And yet I don't leave.

"Fine, okay? Fine," Luke snaps. I hear him start stomping around in his room. "I'll see if I can borrow a car…" Stomp stomp. "No, I can't take my bike. The roads are covered in ice." Stomp stomp. "I'll see you soon. Just relax. Please. You're stressing me out."

His footsteps thud toward the door, which flies open so fast I don't have time to retreat to my room. Luke's eyes widen at the sight of me, before narrowing with displeasure.

Busted. I shrug sheepishly. "Sorry for eavesdropping," I tell him. "I heard yelling and wanted to make sure everything's okay."

"Well, it's not," he spits out, his movements jerky as he zips up his black hoodie. "Sorry, but I don't have time for this. My asshole brother is AWOL and I was just guilt-tripped into tracking him down."

He stalks toward the door at the end of the hall, but I stop him before he reaches the stairs.

"Bailey."

"I told you, Hayworth, I don't have time—"

"I heard you need a car," I interrupt.

He halts, throwing a wary look over his shoulder. "Yeah. I do."

I nod slowly. "All right. Let me grab my keys."

———

"Take a left here, if you wouldn't mind," Luke says from the passenger seat where he's staring at his phone. "It's just up here. If he's not at Bix's house, then I give up. We'll just go back."

"Why is your mom so worried about your brother staying out all night?" I have to ask. "Is he underage?"

Luke snorts. "He's twenty-four. But the last time he didn't come home, he was in jail. She worries about him being rearrested, I guess."

"Oh shit." That was so not what I expected him to say.

"Yeah, my brother is bad news. He and his friends are the reason I don't live at home. Pull over there. This will just take a second."

Before I've even put the car in park, he's jumped out. He crosses to a beat-up little green house with a sagging stoop.

Luke knocks several times before someone finally opens the door. A bulky guy with a shaved head steps outside and gives Luke a shove.

And I'm out of my car and walking toward them one second later.

"Easy," Luke says casually. He gives me a warning glance. *Be cool.* "Bix was just expressing his appreciation for getting dragged out of bed at two p.m. on a Saturday."

"Seriously," the guy rasps.

"He needs his beauty sleep," Luke adds. The big dude lunges for him again, but Luke hops off the porch with a teasing smile.

"You're still a little punk, Baby Bailey."

"You know it. Can you tell Joe to call Mom, so I can get on with my fucking day?"

"Sure, dude." They high five, and I relax.

But even as he disappears into the house, another man fills the doorway. He looks like an older, doughier Luke. "What the fuck do you want?"

"Nothing from you. Just call Mom so she'll stop blowing up my phone."

"She's a controlling bitch."

Luke throws up his hands. "She worries. You're obviously fine. Just text the lady. It will take you two seconds." He turns to leave the little porch.

But his brother moves faster, grabbing Luke by the jacket. "I need four hundred bucks."

Luke laughs, but I can hear the tightness in it. "Yeah, me too."

"Did you work last night?" the goon asks.

"Of course. And it's all going to rent and buying the textbooks I couldn't afford when the term started. You know how much those things cost? No wait, I guess you wouldn't."

Luke's brother literally throws him off the porch step. And I'm closing the distance between them a second later.

"Oh look here!" The asshole brother finally notices me. "You must be the new boyfriend."

"Right," Luke snaps. "Because every guy in my fraternity is my boy toy? I thought I was the only Bailey who watches gay porn. What's your favorite channel on Hamster, bro?"

Oh, hell. I brace myself.

Sure enough, Joe pounces. But nimble Luke is already side-stepping him. "You little faggot," Joe snarls, his hands in fists.

"Hey!" I roar. "Fuck off already."

Joe turns on me, and I do the math on which punch to block. But he seems to think better of it, which means he has at least a small brain in that head. He's a big guy, but so am I. And guess who's in better shape?

I'd flatten him in seconds.

"Let's go," Luke says in a low voice. "This is stupid. Text Mom," he says over his shoulder as he walks toward my car.

"Bite me," is his brother's response.

We get back in the car. Luke slumps in the seat and closes his eyes. "Sorry," he mutters. "Can't believe I took his bait."

I say nothing. Luke's brother is clearly a turd with anger issues. I can't even think of a funny animal comparison to cheer Luke up. There's no animal kingdom model for self-destructive behavior.

Sometimes animals are a whole lot smarter than humans.

Luke's phone rings, and he answers it immediately. "Ma, he's fine. Just his usual asshole self. He crashed at Bix's place. I saw him just now with my own eyes."

"Did he say..." I don't quite catch the rest of his mother's question.

"He didn't tell me anything. He asked me for money and threatened me and my friend. Fun times with Joe."

He shifts the phone and I hear her response. "Lukey, thank you! I'm so relieved."

"The point, Mom, is that I'm not doing this anymore. If Joe doesn't come home, you call someone else to hunt him down."

He moves the phone away from his ear to hang up, but she's still talking. "Luke, honey, Joe did our second job yesterday, hanging some vertical blinds."

"Okay?" he says, bringing it to his ear again. "That's nice? What does that have to do with me?" He listens to more yapping with a pained expression on his face.

I pause at a stop sign, because I'm turned around, and I need him to tell me how to get back to campus.

"He didn't say anything about the cash from the job." Luke's sigh is weary. "And if I had to guess, he drank it all. But you can take that up with Joe."

The next thing I hear from his phone is loud weeping. "They won't deliver heating oil until I pay up, honey! The house is so cold!"

"What?"

"I owe the oil company and the money we made yesterday was supposed to pay them off."

Luke groans. "How much?"

"I owe four fifty."

"I only have two hundred."

There's more mom babble after that. I catch "good boy." And "I love you."

He hangs up and then speaks in a flat voice without looking at me. "Can you turn right on Calhoun and then pull over? Last stop, I swear."

"Sure," I say, trying to keep my voice neutral. But I don't feel calm. My dad is an asshole, but he's trying to *give* me shit. Luke's family are assholes who only want to bleed him dry.

He pulls out his wallet, removing some cash. Then he leaps from the car the minute I stop.

I watch him run up the steps of a squat little brick house. A woman comes to the door in a ratty bathrobe, a cigarette clamped between two fingers. She tries to wave him inside, but he shakes her off, thrusts the money into her hands and then closes the door.

He's back in the car a moment later. "Thanks," he grunts.

I wait.

"Can we go now? This is already embarrassing enough."

"Any time. You just have to tell me how to get back to campus."

He turns to me quickly. "We're, like, two miles away." He points to a traffic light in the distance. "That's College Street."

"Sorry, I never leave campus." I pull away.

"Why would you?" He sighs. "I wish I didn't, either. And I'm never answering the phone again. Never."

Then he turns his head toward the window and doesn't speak to me for the rest of the car ride.

CHAPTER 24
EMBARRASSED, I GUESS

KEATON

Judd is in the living room when Bailey and I stride through the front door. His head jerks up, eyes widening and then narrowing at the sight of us. "Yo," he says warily.

"Yo," I echo, kicking off my boots. "Where is everyone?" It's Saturday afternoon, and the NFL playoffs are underway on the weekends now. The house should be packed.

"At the bar," Judd answers. "Everyone went out to watch the Patriots play the Chiefs."

"Why didn't you go?"

My buddy raises his beer can. "Dude. Why the fuck would I spend money on booze in a packed room where I can't even hear the game, when I could drink here for free and actually get to pay attention to what's happening?"

Good point.

My peripheral vision catches a flicker of movement, and next thing I know, Luke is heading up the stairs. "Gonna take a nap," he mumbles without looking back.

I'm tempted to hurry after him, but Judd is watching me. So I wander over to the couch instead, flopping down on the other end of it. I gesture to the six-pack on the coffee table. "You mind if I have one?"

"Go ahead."

I grab a can and pop the tab. It's only when the cool liquid slides down my throat that I realize I hadn't eaten breakfast or lunch, and so my first meal of the day is *beer*. As if on cue, my stomach rumbles angrily, prompting me to get up. "I'm hungry," I announce. "Want anything from the kitchen?"

"Nah. I'm good." Judd's gaze is fixed on the TV.

After making two peanut butter and jam sandwiches, I'm back on the couch to scarf them down. But to be honest, I'm not too focused on the football game. The urge to sneak up to Luke Bailey's room only grows stronger. I want to understand what the hell happened in town today. His brother's clearly a little punk, and, from the sounds of it, a criminal. And his mom hitting him up for money like that? Savage.

It makes sense that he joined this frat to escape his family. But I want to know more. I can't believe I've shared a floor with the guy for more than a year, and I only just found out that he has an older brother. That he strips for a living. Hell, that he's a business major. I'm a bit ashamed that I didn't make a lick of effort to get to know the guy.

Though in my defense, Bailey's been an asshole to me since the day we met.

"Okay. Really?"

Judd's incredulous voice slices through my thoughts. I look over. "What?" I ask between bites of my sandwich.

"We're really going to pretend you didn't come home with Bailey just now?" he demands. "What the hell were you doing with that loser?"

I delay answering by taking another huge bite. "Needed a ride," I say with my mouth full.

"Huh?"

"He needed a ride into town."

"And you gave him one?"

"Yeah. What's the big deal?"

"Are you seriously asking me that?" Judd is eyeing me as if I've personally betrayed him. "Bailey's such a prick, dude. And he pretty much stole the presidency from you!"

"First of all, he's not *always* a prick." The half-assed defense of Bailey just pops out of my mouth that way, because it's accurate. The dude is as prickly as a porcupine, but he seems to have his reasons.

Judd snorts.

"And he didn't steal the presidency. I dropped out."

"Yeah, and you still haven't even told me why!" Judd slams his beer can on the table. "You just said you changed your mind—"

"I did change my mind," I protest.

"And now you're acting like you're all cool with Asshole Bailey being in *charge* of our frat, which is fucking unacceptable, and that's not even the biggest slap in the face, Keaton—the *real* slap in the face is that I have to hear from Therese that you and Annika broke up. What the fuck?" Judd's anger sputters out like a dying car engine. He goes quiet. Defeated.

Shock silences me for a moment. Judd is upset with me? I honestly had no idea. "Oh." I clear my throat. "Oh. I...ah, I'm sorry, man. I..."

"Forget about it," he mutters, reaching for his drink again.

"No, I'm not going to forget about it. I really am sorry," I say roughly. "I should've told you about Annika, but...I was embarrassed, I guess. You were all happy about getting back together with Therese, and I didn't want to admit that I got dumped."

He raises an eyebrow. "*She* did the dumping?"

I nod.

"Fuck. I didn't know that. Therese just said you guys broke up." Judd lets out a heavy sigh. "I'm sorry, too. I mean, I figured you'd tell me about Annika eventually, but you weren't saying anything, and you've been acting all weird lately—"

"Weird?" I cut in. Shit. Does he know something?

"Like, distant," he clarifies. His jaw tightens. "And then this morning I see you leave here with Luke-fucking-Bailey—"

"He needed a ride," I repeat. "We're not best friends or anything." The denial burns my throat. Except we're really not friends. I merely let him fuck me last night.

But that's top secret. Judd can never know.

A flutter of panic fills my throat. Christ, what have I gotten myself into? I wasn't panicking this morning when I woke up next to Bailey. And when I remember the sex, it doesn't evoke much anxiety, either.

But *this*—the notion of telling my friends that I...like dudes. Or, oh God, telling my parents? How the hell are they going to react? Look at Luke's family, for fuck's sake. I've never met anybody who seems more secure about their sexuality, and yet Luke's own brother calls him a faggot.

No. I'm definitely not ready to share this with anybody.

"I'm sorry if I've been distant," I add. "I was caught up in finals, and the holidays, and this Annika mess. Not to mention that our season ended so poorly after that winning streak..." Bad as I feel about it, bringing up football is a calculated move on my part. It's a tried and true method to distract Judd Keller.

"I know, right?" he laments. "I can't believe New Hampshire made it so far in the off-season. We're like a million times better than those fuckheads."

"Right?"

"Next season, I'm taking charge of the defense," Judd says firmly. "Dano was such a shit captain. He was so bad for morale, and you know how important morale is when it comes to..."

I tune him out. Again, I feel bad doing it, but my mind is elsewhere. This thing with Luke is confusing. I'm wildly attracted to him and I want to have more sex—that much I know. But anything else, whether it's friendship or something more...I have no fucking clue about.

———

Luke sleeps until dinnertime. I know this, because I'm studying in my bedroom and I don't hear a peep from *his* room until six o'clock rolls around. Then he's a symphony of noise—footsteps in the hall, the shower cranking on, water running. After his shower, I hear him in his bedroom again. Music comes on, and my cheeks heat up at the sound of the sultry beat. It's not the same track he danced to last night, but very similar.

I wonder if he's warming up for his shift at Jill's tonight.

And look at that, my dick is hard.

I rake both hands through my hair, the bio textbook in my lap all but forgotten. Luke Bailey is definitely messing with my head. Not only is this newfound attraction to him making me act "weird" in front of my friends, but apparently now I can't even think about the guy without developing a full-blown erection.

Screw it. I drop my book on the bed and head for the door. For *his* door. I don't even knock, I simply walk into Luke's room unannounced. Because, hey, if he's jerking off, even better. I'll just go over there and finish him off.

But he's not jerking. He's sitting cross-legged on the patterned bedspread, staring at his laptop screen. His teeth dig into his bottom lip in frustration.

"Hey," I say over the music.

He glances up. Instantly, suspicion fills his expression, and I wonder if there'll ever be a time where he sees me and his default emotion *isn't* mistrust. I hope so.

"What's up?" he asks, his gaze returning to the screen.

I close the door and move deeper into the room. As I pass his wireless speaker, I turn down the volume. "I wanted to see if you, ah, wanted pizza for dinner," I lie, because he's plainly busy and I'm certain he'll reject me if I suggest fooling around. "We're all pitching in."

He flicks me a knowing look. "Is that so."

"Yeah." I shove my hands in the pockets of my sweats. "Well. No."

Luke grins. "You wanted to hook up, eh?"

I blow out a breath. "Yes."

Husky laughter tickles my ears. "I created a monster." He laughs again, and then gestures to his laptop. "As much I'd love to fuck your brains out right now, I'm a tad occupied. And before you ask, no, it's not going well. This entire day has been one big clusterfuck."

"When it rains, it pours."

That gets me the finger. "Thanks for that, oh wise one."

Grinning, I sit at the foot of his bed. "What's wrong now? You forgot to do a homework assignment or something?"

"I never forget an assignment." His hard voice tells me he's speaking the absolute truth. I doubt this guy has ever slacked off in his life. He clearly works like a dog.

"So what is it?"

"Minor hiccup," he says, but the frustration returns to his gaze again, belying his casual words. "For my finance class, a major component of the final grade is an interview with a finance executive who's raised money in the capital markets. I had an interview lined up this week with the CFO of a Stamford venture capital firm, but the fucker's secretary just emailed to say he's heading out of town early. And won't be back for three weeks."

"Shit."

"Yeah." He types something on his laptop. "I had all my interview questions prepped already. But now I'm sending out emails to every CFO in Connecticut requesting an interview. And on Monday I'll have to make some cold calls."

"What happens if you don't find anyone?"

"I don't have any idea." His tone becomes glum. "I'll have to ask my professor for help, which will reflect poorly on me. And he'll probably send me to some young alumni who's willing to do me a favor."

An idea tugs at my brain. "You should come to brunch tomorrow."

Luke stares at me. "Um. Yeah. I don't see how that solves my problem in any way, but, thank you, I guess? I'm going to pass, though."

I smirk at him. "Oh really? You're going to pass on brunch with the CEO of a pharmaceutical company? They just issued convertible stock last week. It's all my father could talk about over the holidays."

There's a pause. "Wait... Really?"

"Why not? My dad drives up from Long Island most Sundays to have brunch with me." To keep tabs on me, really. "I'm inviting you to join us, moron. In fact, let me check something..." I hop off the bed and duck into my room to grab my phone.

I try not to think about it too hard as I compose a message to my father. Because didn't I *just* freak out downstairs about revealing that I'm attracted to men? What if Dad sees me and Luke together and somehow *knows* we hooked up?

Bringing Luke to brunch has the potential to create chaos I don't want to deal with, and yet when I return to Bailey's room, I can't stop myself from hitting Send.

"Who did you text?" Once again, Luke's entire face is stiff with distrust.

"My dad. I asked him if he'd be willing to sit for an interview with you tomorrow."

Luke's jaw falls open. Then it snaps shut. "Hayworth." The two syllables wield a sharp edge.

I look up from my phone. "What?"

"What the hell is this? Some kind of charity bullshit?" His cheeks flush. "I told you, I don't need your pity."

"It's not pity." I offer a shrug, my brain working to phrase everything in a way that won't raise Luke Bailey's hackles. I'm discovering that he's mighty sensitive when it comes to receiving assistance. "This is an entirely selfish move on my part. I fucking hate sitting through these Sunday brunches. Usually I have Annika there as a buffer, but, well, you know what happened with that. Plus, I haven't told Dad that I lost the election. This way I can leave that honor for you."

It's Luke's turn to smirk. "Making me do your dirty work, huh? Pussy."

My phone buzzes with a text.

Dad: Your fraternity brother is more than welcome, son. I must say, I am overjoyed that you're finally taking an interest in the business. Looking forward to discussing the ins and outs of convertibles with you boys.

"Dad says he's happy to talk to you," I tell Luke. "So what do you say? Let me use you shamelessly so I don't have to engage one-on-one with my father?"

"Sure. I'm in."

And although I'm pleased that Bailey accepted my help, I find it incredibly telling that he only agreed to it when he thought I was using *him*. Someone helping him from the goodness of their heart is completely inconceivable to him, and damned if that isn't one of the saddest things I've ever encountered.

CHAPTER 25
PRESENTABLE

LUKE

When my alarm goes off on Sunday morning at nine thirty, I throw my legs over the side of the bed, and force myself to wake up. I had another long shift at the club last night, followed by a long bus ride home. But now I need to look sharp and charm Mr. Keaton Hayworth Jr. into giving me enough detail about his capital structure to write a paper.

My problem can't possibly be this easy to solve, could it? I don't trust it.

I drag myself into the shower and then shave carefully. My eyes look bloodshot from lack of sleep, but there's nothing I can do about that. In my room, I stare into my closet. Next year I have to interview for jobs. I'm going to have to buy at least two suits, some nicer shirts, and shoes.

So just add that to the lengthy list of things I'll need to save up for.

Now, though, I put on my best oxford shirt and my only pair of khaki pants. Then I study myself in the mirror.

The dude staring back at me looks presentable. There's

nothing about my reflection that says: *stripper with a fucked-up family, from the wrong part of town.* Although nobody would mistake me for Keaton or one of his rich friends. Someday they will, though. I won't stop until I have everything I want.

And wherever that is, it won't be anywhere near Darby, Connecticut. I can't wait to leave this place behind.

I'm ready to go by the time I hear Keaton step into the shower. I wait at my desk, reading everything I can find about convertible stock and about Hayworth Harper Pharmaceuticals.

"Knock knock," the company's young heir says from my doorway. "I was gonna ask if you were ready, but I can see that you are."

"Yep." I grab a notebook off my desk. "Let's do this. You really think he'll answer my questions?"

"Sure he will. Talking about himself and his business is Dad's favorite thing in the world."

I grab a jacket and follow him downstairs. The house is quiet, because most everyone sleeps late on Sundays. We climb into Keaton's BMW for the second time in two days. And both times I've managed not to comment on his choice of vehicle.

Go me.

"So," I say as we roll toward the waterfront, where all the expensive restaurants in the county are. My credit card will hate me for this. "What is my role here, besides interviewing your dad?"

"Ah," Keaton says. "Your role is to be someone he doesn't know well enough to criticize me in front of. That's all you have to do. Oh, and run up his credit card."

"I can't let him pay," I say. "Not if he's doing me a favor."

"Pfft," Keaton says. "Of course you can. That's what parents are for."

"Really? I wouldn't know." I regret the comment as soon as it leaves my mouth.

Keaton turns to me immediately with an apologetic glance. "Shit, I'm sorry. That's what parents *should* be for, anyway."

A wave of embarrassment washes over me. I can't believe Keaton witnessed the shit show that is my family yesterday. "Moving on."

"It's just up ahead," he says. "And we're on time, for once. Dad will be astonished."

"You're usually late?"

"Annika," he mutters, and then sighs.

"Still feel bad about that?" I'm genuinely curious. I mean, he didn't seem all that broken up about her on Friday night...

"Kind of," he grumbles. "We spent a lot of time together. It will take a while to get used to not having her around. And Dad will be bummed." He shakes his head. "He loves Annika. And he'll ask me what the hell I did wrong."

And sure enough, the first thing Keaton's dad says as the host of this slightly fusty wood-paneled restaurant leads us to his table is, "Keaton! And Luke? Great to see you both. But where is Annika?"

Keaton waits until I've shaken hands with his dad and we're both seated and holding oversized menus printed on parchment. Then he says, "About Annika. She dumped me."

His dad sits back in his chair suddenly, like a man slapped. As if he's astonished that a woman would ever reject a Hayworth man. "What ever for?"

"No particular reason," Keaton says carefully. "She just wants to widen her horizons. Or something." He tugs at his shirt collar, looking uncomfortable.

"What's good here?" I ask, changing the subject.

"Everything," Mr. Hayworth says. "When I'm really hungry, I go for the steak and eggs. The quiche is also excellent."

The waiter pours coffee all around. Mr. Hayworth orders a mimosa, but I ask for plain orange juice.

"I'll have the pancakes and bacon," Keaton says.

"I'd love the eggs Benedict," I say, passing over my menu.

Mr. Hayworth laughs, and I have no idea why. "That's what Annika gets," he says.

My gaze collides with Keaton's, and then we both look away quickly.

"I'll have the quiche Lorraine," Mr. Hayworth says, noticing nothing.

But I still feel a frisson of discomfort. If it weren't for this interview I so desperately need to ace, I would never have come. My sex life until now has been set up to avoid meeting the parents of the people I'm screwing. And it's not like I'd start now.

Here we are, though. I feel like a fraud, as usual. I'm playing the role of someone who fits in at Darby College. I'll keep playing it until someday, hopefully before I die, it feels like I really do belong.

"What's your major, son?" Mr. Hayworth asks.

"Business, with a finance concentration, sir." I break a roll in half, and move a pat of butter from the butter dish to my bread plate on the left. These are things I learned three years ago on YouTube when I was trying to get a waiter's job in a decent restaurant. But they're things that Keaton was taught from birth.

"I've set up a finance internship for Keaton over the summer," he says. "But it would be great if he could take finance courses next year, too."

"Wow, sounds like a great summer opportunity."

I glance up at Keaton, who suddenly gives a lot of attention to buttering his roll. And didn't he tell me he was applying to some kind of research internship for the summer?

Hmm. If his father doesn't know that, I'm not going to be the one to break the news. At least now I know Keaton wasn't fibbing when he said he disliked brunches with his dad.

I clear my throat. "I was really hoping you could tell me about that convertible bonds deal you just did. Specifically, why convertibles?"

"Ah, of course!" Mr. Hayworth says. He's actually beaming. As if I was asking about his favorite child. And maybe I am. "Pharmaceutical companies love convertibles. The debt comes at a reasonable interest rate, because the buyers are hoping our development products will get FDA approval, which will lead to an equity upside."

I flip open my notebook and click my pen. "How reasonable is the interest rate?"

"Well, if you take a look at LIBOR spreads in the pharmaceutical industry…"

I start scribbling. And I write down everything he says.

CHAPTER 26
IT'S ALWAYS MY TREAT

KEATON

I stop listening about two seconds after my father starts talking. There is nothing less interesting than (the ironically named) interest rates.

But Luke takes to this shit like a duck to water. He's taking notes and asking follow-up questions using terms I don't understand and never will.

My father eats it up, too. All he ever wanted was for me to take an interest. But I really don't understand why. The man is hardly starved for attention. He runs a business where literally hundreds of people hang on everything he says.

He isn't terribly interested in me, either, unless I'm talking about one of his favorite topics. Those are, roughly in order: business, football, and Alpha Delt. That's the part that makes me feel stabby. It's fine to be jazzed up on your own interests. But to assume that your favorite things should be important to everyone else? It's both self-centered and ridiculous.

The waiter sets a plate down in front of me, and my mood lifts a little. I tuck in to my plate of pancakes and bacon. Carbs, salt, and fat are utterly restorative.

For a while, Luke is too busy taking notes to eat. But then he and my father eventually dig in, still talking about "equity upside" and "implied volatility," whatever that is.

I'm irrelevant to this meal, and it's glorious.

"Thank you so much," Luke says when they finally run out of nerdy little details to discuss. "I am so getting an A on this paper."

"As well you should," my father says, draining his mimosa. "You've got the analytical part down. Keaton is going to learn all about it this summer, too."

Fuck.

"Excuse me one moment," Luke says, pushing back his chair. "The men's is…?"

I point toward the back corner of the room, and then that fucker abandons me here with Dad. He struts away from the table, and my eyes follow him, because I feel reckless and it's just dawning on me that I have a confidence fetish.

"Great kid," my dad says after Luke has disappeared into the bathroom. He gestures to the waiter for more coffee. "He's Alpha Delt too, right?"

"Yup," I say with a sigh. "Actually, he's our president elect." I might as well come clean about that.

Dad blinks. "No, you are."

"Not true." I shake my head. "I dropped out on election day, because I don't actually want to be president, and he does."

"Why?" Dad gasps.

"Why would anyone want to be president? Good question."

His face reddens. "Don't be flip, Keaton. Why did you drop out?"

"I'm a loyal member of the frat, Dad. I love Alpha Delt. But I was only running because you wanted me to. And that wasn't a good enough reason."

"But why wouldn't you want to be in charge? That makes no sense."

"Because I'm *not you*. And that would make plenty of sense if you could ever figure out that I have interests, too. They're every bit as valid as yours."

"Watch your tone," he hisses.

"I watch it all the time," I whisper. "But then you don't hear me."

Luke is approaching the table now, so Dad clamps his jaw shut. He won't make a scene. It's not his style.

Instead, he signals for the check. "I hear congratulations are in order," he says to Luke. "You're the next president of Alpha Delt."

"Thank you, sir," Luke says carefully. "My first order of business will be to move the finances into Quickbooks. Right now they're using the receipts-in-a-shoebox method of accounting."

"Ouch." My father chuckles. "It's good of you to bring us out of the stone age."

"I'll try." He lifts his hand just as the waiter approaches, and so the guy passes the check to Luke.

"Oh no," Dad says. "It's always my treat."

"It's already taken care of," Luke says, flipping open the wallet to add a tip to the receipt and sign the bill. "You saved my finance grade, and I'm grateful."

He must have slipped a credit card to the waiter when he went to the men's room. Sneaky.

Dad beams at this bit of trickery. He doesn't care about the money, but I can tell that Luke has impressed him.

Isn't that hilarious? We're both a little obsessed.

Luke thanks him profusely before we go.

Dad wishes him the best of luck. And then he slips a business card from his pocket. "Call this number on Monday. Ask my secretary to give you the email address for Chad Christy, the guy who runs our summer internship program. And when you write to Chad, you make sure to tell him that I sent you."

Luke blinks. "Thank you, sir. I appreciate it."

"My pleasure. Great meeting you. And call me tonight, Keaton. We have a conversation to finish." He doesn't even look me in the eye when he says this.

Oh joy.

We get back into my car, and I let the engine warm up. "You can't just accept a favor without picking up the check, can you?"

"Nope," he says. He's staring at the business card in his hand.

"You might as well call about that internship, though. I'm seventy-five percent sure there's going to be an unexpected opening in the finance department."

Luke looks up. "He doesn't even know you're applying for that thing on the boat?"

"Nope. Didn't want to have that fight until I got the acceptance letter." It's going to be so much worse than the fight we just had.

"I can't take the internship."

"Surely you don't consider *that* to be charity?" I snort. "Every company has cushy internships."

"No, I mean I can't swing it. It will pay a stipend, but it won't be enough to live in New York for three months. And we're not exactly commuting distance here. Does your dad drive over two hours for brunch every week?"

"Not really. He takes the car ferry from Port Jefferson on Long Island. He does it to avoid going to church."

I pull out of the parking lot and head back toward campus, feeling disgusted by life. Luke wants the internship but can't afford it. I don't want it at all and shouldn't have to do it.

"What will he say when you bail on your internship?" Luke asks.

"That I'm lazy and ungrateful. That I refuse to work up to my full potential."

"But none of that is true."

"Luke Bailey!" I hoot. "I believe you just paid me a compliment. I promise not to let it go to my head."

"Why did you invite me today, anyway?" he asks. "He's pissed about the presidency."

"We went over this. He can't rip me a new one in front of you. Besides, I knew he could fix your problem with that paper."

"Yeah. I thought maybe you did it to claim sexual favors."

"It's possible to do a favor just because, you know."

"Possible, but rare," he says.

"You are a piece of work. I might claim sexual favors just to put your mind at ease."

He gives me a hot look that I can feel even without taking my eyes off the road. "Maybe it won't be only my mind that's eased."

"Now you're talking." I reach a hand across the console and brush my fingers across his crotch. My increasing boldness surprises me. "When? Now?"

"I should write this paper first."

I groan.

He laughs. "You're probably sore anyway."

"So?" Athletes don't complain about pain.

"So that's off the table."

I can't quite grasp the disappointment that fills my chest. "Forever?" I find myself asking. The look he gives me says he knows exactly what I'm thinking.

"For today."

That tight feeling in my chest eases. My voice sounds too husky, and far too needy, as I say, "But...it's going to happen again?"

His low chuckle heats the air between us. "Yeah," he finally drawls. "It's going to happen again."

CHAPTER 27
TURKEY SANDWICH DAYS

April

KEATON

Routines are a funny thing. They sneak up on you. Like, one day you wake up and eat a turkey sandwich, and then two months go by and you've eaten a turkey sandwich every single day, and you think, *Huh. I guess I eat daily turkey sandwiches now.*

Although in this case, turkey sandwich is a euphemism for hot sex with a dude.

Days have turned into weeks. The snow has melted and spring is in the air. And so is my dick. Luke's warm fingers encircle the base of my shaft. He gives a lazy stroke, and I groan softly.

It's nine thirty-ish in the morning, and we're in my bed, naked and horny. The first couple of times he crashed in my room, I worried that one of our frat brothers might catch us, but eventually my anxiety tapered off. Bailey and I are the only ones up here on the third floor, my door has a lock on it, and the only guys who *might* barge in are Judd and Tanner, who're both out of the house by six a.m. on weekdays for baseball practice.

Luke's free hand strokes the cleft of my ass. We probably don't have time to fuck right now, but just the suggestion makes me harder. There's no denying how much I like it. My prostate is my new best friend. And when we're in a hurry, there's a dozen other fun ways we get each other off. Bailey gives the best blowjobs on the planet.

What he doesn't give me a lot of is words. He's a tight-lipped bastard and nearly impossible to read, so sometimes it's a challenge being around him. For example, this morning I asked him if I could come to the club tonight to watch his set, and instead of answering he just kissed me and started rubbing my dick.

It worked, too. That's why I've forgotten to complain these last few minutes. His kiss is deep and hungry. My hands explore the muscles of his back, and his narrow waist. Only when we're making out does he let me touch him anywhere I want.

He sighs happily, stroking me. It's almost enough to make me forget the question I'd asked.

"You didn't answer," I mumble against his lips. "Maybe I'll just show up tonight, either way."

I immediately regret saying that, because his hand leaves my cock.

A pair of stern eyes bore into my face. "Don't." His sharp tone invites no argument. "My work is off-limits. I already told you that."

"What's the big deal?" I protest, all the while wishing he'd touch me again. "You're hot when you strip. I'm talking Magic Mike-level heat."

"I know I'm hot when I strip—it's my *job* to be hot." To my disappointment, he climbs out of bed. His massive hard-on swings up and smacks his tight abs. "I need to focus when I'm at work. You showing up would be a distraction."

"Fine. I won't," I promise. "Now will you come back here and finish what you started?" I fling the sheet off my lower body, and my erection bobs up to say hello.

"Nah."

"Why not?" I demand.

He sweeps his tongue over his bottom lip. "Because you displeased me."

I sputter with laughter. "Are you serious right now? I *displeased* you?"

"Yeah, by bringing up the work shit. Your big mouth cost yourself *my* mouth." Luke's eyes gleam dangerously. "Bad boys get punished, Hayworth."

Ohhh. I see where this is going and I ain't gonna lie—I'm fully on board. So is my dick, judging by the way it grows impossibly harder.

Luke doesn't miss my body's response. But when I slide my hand down my stomach toward my groin, he stops me with a swift, "Hands at your sides."

"But I'm horny," I whine.

"Don't care. Hands at your sides." When I hesitate again, he mocks, "Don't make me ask you a third time."

My mouth goes dry. I slowly press my palms to the mattress on either side of me.

"Good. Now lie there and let me eye-fuck you." He grabs hold of himself with one fist.

Oh Christ. Is that how it's going to be? He's going to torture me by getting himself off and forcing me to watch? *Just* watch.

He pumps his shaft, and, yup, apparently that's precisely how it's going to be.

Bailey's eyes greedily roam my naked body as he strokes himself. I want to mimic what he's doing, but I've been ordered not to move. So I simply lie there, harder than a post and aching for release. When his fist moves faster, my breathing becomes labored.

"You're wishing you could jack yourself right now, aren't you?" Luke taunts.

My gaze is glued to his. "Yes," I croak.

"Don't look at my face. Look at my cock. Look how hard I am."

I dip my gaze. Oh Jesus. He's the sexiest thing in the world. "Iwantit," I mumble through my arid throat.

"What was that?" he teases.

"I want it," I repeat, clearer this time.

Luke slants his head in thought. Down south, he's jerking himself off, slowly but deliberately. "What do you want?"

"Your cock."

"Nah," he says again. "You're going to watch me come. And you're not going to say another word, make another sound, until I do. And then, *maybe*, I'll let you come too. But only if you show me you can follow the rules."

His rules. The rules I've been following for more than two months now. Don't get me wrong, I love it when he bosses me around in bed. It turns me on something fierce. But his *my-way-or-no-way* temperament extends beyond the bedroom, and for some reason I'm beginning to resent that.

Right now, though, I only resent not being able to give myself any relief.

"So," Luke drawls. "Are you going to follow the rules?"

I nod wordlessly.

With a sultry smile, he gives himself another stroke. "Fuck," he grinds out. "You look so hot lying there. You get me so hard, every time."

I bite my lip to stop a moan. If I make a sound, he'll stop. We've been together enough times for me to know that Bailey doesn't make idle threats.

He lets out a hot gasp, and I think he's getting close.

And while I enjoy watching, I also want to touch him. So I beg him with eyes. *Come here.* I lick my lips. *Taste me. Own me.*

He avoids my eyes, setting that laser gaze on my quads and then lifting it to my straining cock. But maybe the mind-meld thing I'm trying to do is working. Because he lifts his chin and shows me those dark eyes.

And just for a second I see something there that I like a whole lot. It's ownership, with a side of need.

Come here, I inwardly beg. *Right where I need you.*

He moves fast, spreading his body over mine, nipping my shoulder. "Jack me," he whispers. "Quick."

I don't need to be asked twice. I shove a hand between our bodies and take both of us in hand.

"Fuck," he whispers, before kissing me harshly.

I fucking love it. I open for him, inviting him in. He moans into my mouth as I stroke him fast and dirty, the way he likes it.

He makes a broken noise, and I open my eyes to watch him tip over the edge. He's so beautiful when he comes—all flashing eyes and desperate groans. His cheeks flush darkly.

For once, our gazes lock as he shudders and pulses in my hand. "Ah!" he gasps, losing himself in the moment. I crane my neck and kiss him again, needing to be there as he comes.

My hand is drenched, and he bears down on me, scraping his cock against my oversensitive skin. "Now you," he breathes. "Go."

I love it when he tells me to come, and my body is triggered and ready. Three or four strokes are all it takes until I'm sucking on his tongue and moaning against his mouth, spending into my hand.

He collapses onto me with a sweaty sigh, and I hear nothing else over the heartbeat pounding in my ears.

I grin up at the ceiling. *Hi, endorphins. Thanks for stopping by.*

Luke kisses my neck slowly. I like it a whole lot. And I rub my clean hand slowly along the curve of his ass.

This part lasts all of five seconds, though. And then Luke hauls himself into a vertical position and grabs the paper towels.

He does that every time—either gets up or rolls over. Like staying in my space would break one of his many rules.

"I gotta hit the shower before finance," he says now.

"Bailey," I call before he can leave.

He makes a rumbling sound as he turns to face me. "Swear to God, Hayworth, if you bring up the visiting-me-at-work thing again—"

"No, not that," I assure him. "I was just going to invite you to Sunday brunch again."

He visibly swallows.

Ha. I knew that would get his attention. And I don't miss the indecision that crosses his expression as he mulls over the invitation. We've gone through this several times before: I invite Luke to brunch with my dad, Luke hesitates, and then he either rejects the offer or caves in. For five out of eight invites, it's been the latter, resulting in him once again serving as my Dad buffer.

Initially I was a bit dismayed that Luke and my father get along like rabbits in heat. But every time I bring Luke to brunch, he's an incredible buffer. Hell, he's even better than Annika when it comes to placating my father. They talk business the entire time, and I get to play Candy Crush on my phone.

He never orders the eggs Benedict anymore, though.

"Nah," he says now. "I can't make it this weekend. But thanks for the invite."

Frustration fills my belly as I watch him slide out of my room. I swear, this guy is so difficult. It's like he's determined to keep everyone at arm's length.

And I still have to show up at brunch, damn it.

I lie here feeling sorry for myself for a moment. And then the perfect solution presents itself to me. I grab my phone off the bedside table and open up my favorites. I touch a number that I don't dial very often anymore.

"Hey, Annika!" I say when she answers. "Want to come out for brunch on Sunday? For old time's sake?"

I'm probably just imagining it, but I swear Luke growls a little in the next room.

———

And clearly I'm a genius, because brunch with Dad is totally fine. Annika orders the eggs Benedict and makes lots of small talk. Plus it's great to catch up with her. So I'm winning at life.

Now we're in my room, listening to music and theoretically studying for an economics test that bores us both silly. I can't even blame my father for making me take this class. It's a Darby requirement.

"What do you think he'll ask about international trade?" I ask my ex, hoping she has a better handle on this material than I do.

"Keaton, I'm seeing someone," Annika says suddenly.

It takes me a second to realize that we've shifted topics. "I thought you were already dating a lacrosse player?" I ask carefully. Annika and I are still friends, but we don't talk about our sex lives. Obviously I can't discuss mine. And I'd assumed she keeps me in the dark about hers out of respect for having dumped me.

"Oh, I wasn't dating him," she says. "I just needed a date for a couple of parties. We both know lacrosse is a stupid sport. I could never get past that on a long-term basis."

I burst out laughing, because Annika always could make me smile.

She pulls out her makeup kit and starts messing around with the various tubes and bottles she keeps in there. It's a tell that she's nervous. I still know her so well.

"The thing is," she says, inspecting an eyeliner pencil. "I'm super-obsessed with this guy I'm seeing. And I know that obsession isn't often a healthy emotion, but this is so different for me. It's exciting."

"And you're telling me this because..." I really can't figure that out. "You need me to say it's okay?"

"I guess so." She raises her eyes from her compact mirror. "I really don't know if he's my forever guy. In fact, he's probably not. But I feel like this is something I needed to do."

"You mean *he* is something you needed to do." It comes out sounding a little bitchy.

She makes a sympathetic face.

"Look, I'm sure you were right," I say quietly. "I get it now." She was obviously right that we weren't sexually compatible.

Hell, I'm still coming to terms with my sexual stuff. "I'm not even angry about it anymore."

"Really?" She sits up straight and sets her makeup bag aside. "I'm pretty relieved to hear you say that. I never wanted to hurt you. In fact, it would be great if you could get a little dose of what I'm getting."

I bite my tongue. Because if she's banging a dude, I *am* getting that.

Not that I'm allowed to say so.

My glance drifts toward my stereo, which is actually playing a Sam Smith song right now. I wouldn't listen to this guy at all if it weren't for a certain obsession of mine. But I can't explain that, either. And honestly it pisses me off. Lying gets old pretty fast. And I'm not used to bottling up my feelings.

"There is someone," I admit. "I'm not comfortable discussing it with you. But I want you to know that I understand. We both needed to make some changes and try a few things out."

Annika gasps like she's just heard there's a sale at Bergdorf's. "Really? Who? And I already regret bringing it up."

"Wait, why?"

"Well, duh!" She sits up straight in the middle of my bed. "Because now I'm *desperately* curious and you said you won't tell me."

I snort.

"Just share a *crumb*, Keaton." She blinks at me with pretty eyes.

"No. And stop asking." I take a sip of my coffee and hide behind the cup.

"Is she a dominatrix?"

I promptly choke on my coffee.

"Omigod, she is!" Annika squeals. "I knew it. I called it!"

"You…what?" I sputter.

"I guessed it, Keaton. You're a submissive. That's what was missing. Do you prefer being lashed, or being tied up?"

"No! You're not even…" I swallow my denial. I can't argue

with her because I don't want her to keep making guesses.

"Where'd you meet her?" Annika demands. "Is there, like, a sex dungeon around here? I read *Fifty Shades of Grey.*"

Just kill me already.

"I know you think I'm sheltered." She swallows hard. "But I have intuition. I knew you needed something I couldn't give you. And I know it's private but..." She sighs. "I hated feeling like I was always disappointing to you."

"Annika! Jesus. You were *never* disappointing to me. It's just that we got together when we were super young."

"I get that. And I also know that breaking up with you was a big risk. There are days when I wonder if I'll look back someday and think—Keaton was the best man ever in my life, and I was too young to realize it."

"Aw, that won't happen." But is she a great girl, or what? I put down my coffee cup and pounce on her, wrapping my arms around her, but then putting one finger under her ribs where I know she's ticklish.

"Oh my God! Get off of me, you beast."

But I don't relent and she howls with laughter.

"Everything okay in here?" Luke's face appears in the doorway. I've grown to look past that scowl he wears, but right now he looks extra grumpy.

"Well, Mr. President," Annika says, "I would like to lodge a formal complaint about your roommate, here. It's rude to tickle people that you outweigh." She takes a better look at Luke's expression. "Are we being too loud?"

He shrugs. "I've got work to do, but maybe I'll just shut your door."

"Actually, I'd better go, anyway," Annika says, untangling herself from me. "We aren't good study partners for this econ test because we both hate it. Do you have it this term, too?" she asks Luke.

He shakes his head. "Took it freshman year for funzies."

"Ugh." She shudders. "What else do you do for fun? Income

taxes? Oral surgery?"

"Riiiight," he says slowly. "Oral surgery. How'd you guess?"

I can't help it. A smile takes over my face, and I bite the inside of my cheek to avoid laughing. When I glance at Luke, he's got a tight lid on his own humor, of course. Nobody has a poker face like Luke Bailey. But I know him well enough to see the nanosecond of humor in his eyes.

"You're a fun guy, Bailey. No matter what they say." Annika shoves a bunch of cosmetics into her bag and hops off my bed. "You, too. Keaton. Thanks for the eggs Benedict."

"Anytime!"

She blows me a kiss on her way out the door. The smile I give her is a little bigger than necessary, maybe. But if that's the most petty thing I do all week, then I guess it isn't too bad.

"Fun brunch?" Luke asks, still lurking in my doorway.

"Sure. Dad only made two cracks about maybe getting us back together. So there's that." I roll my eyes just thinking about it.

"Does she want to?" Luke asks, heaving himself across my bed, face down.

"Nope. She's seeing someone new, and she's obsessed with him. Her words." I sit down on the edge of the bed, one hand on Luke's back. "Why?"

He shrugs without turning to look at me.

"You're jealous. Knowing you, it's only a little. But you still won't to say so."

"I don't have any reason to be jealous," he says. "We're not a couple."

"But we are exclusive," I point out. That was my one big demand. I don't feel comfortable with the idea of him sleeping around, especially while I'm still wrapping my head around the fact that we're sleeping with *each other*. And since Luke's a fan of easy, convenient sex, he was fine with it.

"Yeah. We are."

"So why wouldn't you call us a couple?" I ask. "Isn't that the definition?"

He rolls over, breaking contact with my hand. "Because what's the point? Any second now you'll get sick of this arrangement. And you'll go back to dating people you can bring home to Daddy."

"Because my father's opinion is so fucking important to me," I scoff.

"Oh, please." He sits up. "It obviously is, or you would've already told him that you don't plan to ever work for his company."

"That's just avoidance of the inevitable. Which is exactly what you're doing. I think you're really happy dating me, as long as you don't have to call it what it is."

"But why does it matter?" he asks me. He shifts his weight and frowns at something he finds in the pillows—it's Annika's eyeliner and mirror. He opens the mirror and inspects it. "What would change if we called it dating? It's not like you really feel like letting anyone in on the secret."

I bite down hard on my lip. Because he's mostly right. *Mostly.* I don't look forward to awkward conversations with my friends and teammates. And the idea of people making fun of me behind my back gives me the cold sweats.

On the other hand, acknowledging my sexuality is starting to feel inevitable. My attraction to Luke isn't just a one-off thing. My attraction to men is here to stay and keeping that bottled up feels wrong now. It makes the secret feel enormous.

"Look," I challenge. "You say you don't lie about your sexuality. Why should I, then? Right now I lie all the time, and it's a drag." It makes the secret feel dark, when I need to feel okay about it, instead.

He just stares at me for a minute. "I can't be president of this fraternity and also bang one of the brothers. Can you even *imagine* what people would say?"

"We have a gay brother already," I point out. "And since when do you care about what people think of you?" He's just dodging me because he thinks I'm needy.

"I don't, but…" Luke scrubs his chin with his hand. "I'm not you. I'm not well-liked. The guys downstairs would say some seriously ugly shit if you stood up at a chapter meeting some night and said, 'Oh, by the way, if you hear moaning on the third floor it's because I've discovered I'm bisexual and now I'm Bailey's new boy toy.' Your buddy Judd would flip his shit."

He would. It's the truth. "Not everybody is Judd."

"Good thing." Luke snorts.

We lapse into silence, just eyeing each other warily. My fingers itch to touch him. I want to use my thumb to smooth out the furrow between his eyebrows. I like Luke Bailey. A lot. That's my other secret. And forget about my frat brothers—it's Luke who can't handle that one.

"You know what I think?" he says suddenly. "I think you need to justify us. Like you're not a hundred percent okay with getting it on with a guy. And if I tell you we're more than sex, you'll feel better."

"That's not true," I protest. *And get out of my brain.*

"I'm sort of scary to you, and you need to shape it into something that's more familiar. But it won't ever work."

"And why's that?"

He flops down on my bed with a sigh. "I'm going to put this into terms that you can understand."

"This better be good."

"You're a yellow lab."

"I'm…*what?*"

"A dog. A big, happy dog chasing Frisbees on the beach with his pals. You're a pack animal."

I snort. "And you're…a pit bull?"

"Not even. I'm a tomcat in the alley," he says. "Just passing through. No collar. Not very friendly. No good at catching Frisbees…"

"I get it. Jesus." It's not the worst analogy. Although I think Luke secretly wants to be a dog and join the pack. He won't admit it. But the guy rushed a fraternity, for fuck's sake. He claims it was the cheapest way to find a place to live. But I call bullshit. Luke won't admit all the things that he wants.

Who am I to criticize, though? A guy who willfully ignored his attraction to men for many years can't go around pointing out other people's ignorance.

Instead, I lay down on the bed beside him and run a thumb across his forehead, smoothing out his brow. He closes his eyes.

Tomcat my ass.

I wrap an arm around him, and he allows this, too. But even as he begins to weave his fingers through my hair, he says, "You need to think of us like a vacation, Hayworth. Vacations feel real enough. But they always end. Like everything good."

"Okay, that's exceptionally cynical. Even for you. What is *up* with you today?" I reach over and tickle his ribs, too. "So surly."

He swats my hand away like a fly. "Work problems. Last night there was a funky smell in the bathrooms. We all noticed it. Well, Heather emailed me just now to say that it's a major problem with the plumbing. And so the club will be closed next weekend. And maybe even the weekend after that."

"Oh, shit." I put a palm on his arm and give it a squeeze. I can't stop touching him. I'd do it all the time if he'd let me. "I'm really sorry. Can you bartend next door instead?"

"Probably not, since there will be so many volunteers. And the bartenders don't ask for coverage on the weekend very often."

"That sucks," I say.

What I don't say is that I can lend him money. Or give him money. Both of these things are true, but he doesn't want me to offer.

"Anything I can do?" I ask instead.

He rolls over. "Maybe that thing you do to my shoulders? Please? I think I strained something last night."

I get up off the bed, closing and locking the door. Then I get back onto the bed, straddling Luke's waist, placing my hands on his shoulders. I grip them hard, digging in with my thumbs, massaging the tight muscles I find under my hands.

He groans happily. "You are my favorite person in the whole fucking world."

It might even be true. I just hope it's enough for my greedy little heart. I press my luck. "You want to watch that French movie together tonight? The one for your class?"

"Maybe," he mumbles. "We'll see."

I roll my eyes. Mr. Elusive. My hands bear down on his traps and he groans with happiness. The sound does nice things to my insides. So I can't help but lean down and kiss the back of his neck.

Affection comes easily to me, damn it. I am a yellow lab. Sue me. I give Bailey a terrific massage, interspersed with kisses. And when I've turned him into a relaxed puddle of a man, I spread my body out on his back and sigh. "Now I'm horny."

"Of course you are," he slurs. "I'm irresistible. That's why we can't watch that movie together later. I'm supposed to take notes. I'll end up fucking you instead."

"Or vice versa," I tease, pushing my hips against his ass. "You know I'm going to have this sooner or later."

He says nothing.

"It's a good thing you're not really a tomcat."

"I so am."

"Nope. I'd know."

He turns his head to the side. "Am I going to learn something weird about cat sex right now?"

I grin, and graze his cheek with my lips. "A male cat has barbs on the back half of his penis."

"Shut the front door."

"It's true. I'll send you a photo later." I kiss his neck.

"Of course you will." With a ninja-like motion, he slides out from under me. But then he pulls me into his arms. "Thanks for making me feel better."

"Any time." *If only you'd let me do it more often.*

I kiss him instead of saying it aloud.

CHAPTER 28
A BROTHER NAMED JOE

LUKE

My phone vibrates with a notification as I'm changing into my running shorts. When I check, it's a message from LobsterShorts. **Sea salt & vinegar or BBQ?**

Craving chips? I don't like taking things from him. He knows that.

You said you'd go for a drive with me, he writes. **I was gonna bring snacks.**

Nothing for me. I'm heading out for a run.

After I hit send, I regret my answer. Chips sound pretty good right now, and lord knows I'm hungry. Dinner will almost certainly be another can of soup, and a few slices of cheese. I'm putting off my grocery store run, because only have $100 to get me through the next week. Or more, depending on the plumbing issues at Jill's.

But my regret is bigger than that. I know it wouldn't kill me to accept a bag of chips from Keaton. It wouldn't kill me to spend more time with him, or to tell him more often how much I like his company.

I don't, though. Affection doesn't come naturally to me, to put it mildly. And I've been on edge since Keaton brought up the "C" and "D" words. And no, I don't mean *cock* and *dick*. I love those words. I'm talking about him asking if we're a *couple*, pointing out that we're *dating*.

Fuck. How did we get here? I've had friends-with-benefits arrangements before, but none that have lasted more than three months. And clearly Hayworth is catching feelings.

I see the way he looks at me. It's an unsettling combination of fascination, tenderness, and frustration. I see him biting his tongue a lot, as if he wants to dig deeper into my psyche, peel back my layers like I'm an onion.

I like Keaton a lot. But nobody gets to do that.

Usually I'm good at keeping my armor on. I don't let anyone see what I don't want them to see. But it's getting harder to do that with Keaton. I really do like the guy. He makes me laugh. Makes me come. But this *couple* and *dating* talk makes my skin prickle with discomfort. Makes me want to flee.

Luckily, now that spring is here, I'm able to get back into my running routine. So I lace up my shoes and park my phone on the desk along with everything but my keys.

And then I jump down the stairs and head straight outside. I love feeling the wind slapping my face as my sneakers tear across the pavement. I find my rhythm and head for the end of the street.

There's a great trail near campus, and today I run it twice, hoping the three miles of solitude might help to clear my muddled mind.

But the unease I'm feeling about my arrangement with Hayworth sticks to me like glue and follows me right back home. I'm sweating through my hoodie by the time I jog up the walk of the Alpha Delt house. When I open the door, Jako is lurking in a chair that nobody uses at the bottom of the stairs, looking troubled.

"Something wrong?" I pant.

"Maybe?" he says. "You tell me."

Instantly, I'm on guard. The wariness in his eyes triggers my internal alarm. Why is he looking at me like that? Is this about Hayworth?

Oh shit. What if Jako came upstairs last night to find me, or something, and heard Keaton's strangled moans as I fucked him senseless in the shower?

My brain goes into damage-control mode. Just because he heard two dudes banging doesn't mean those dudes *had* to be me and Keaton. Maybe I can pretend I had some random guy over? Maybe—

"You have a brother named Joe, right?"

I blink.

I did not expect him to say *that*. And once he does, my next thought is, *Holy shit*.

"Yeah," I say slowly. "Why?"

"He was just here."

My spine straightens. "Here?" I echo.

"Yeah." Jako stands up and jams his hands in his pockets. "He said he needed to talk to you. I told him you were out for a run, and he said he needed to leave a note for you in your room."

"Did you let him?" I can hear the panic in my voice. "Please say no."

"Well, I asked him to show me some ID. And he did. So I told him where your room was and he went upstairs."

Without another word, I run past Jako and take the stairs two at a time. *What did you steal, Joe?*

Jako is right behind me. "Dude, I'm so sorry. It seemed a little off, but he's your brother. He looks a lot like you. But I didn't even know you had a brother."

My tone is stiffer than my spine. "Yeah, there's a reason for that."

At the top of the stairs, I see that my door is standing open. That's not surprising, since Joe learned to pick a lock before he learned to shave, and the locks on our rooms aren't exactly deadbolts.

I reach over and try Keaton's door. It's locked, and I heave my first sigh of relief.

If Joe steals from me, it's not the end of the world. Besides, I'm so broke there's barely any money in my room.

Or *was*. Sure enough, the bottom drawer of my desk is ajar. That's where I keep my coffee can. When I yank open the drawer, the can is empty.

"Shit," Jako says. "I'm so sorry."

But seriously, I'm mostly relieved. "Dude, this isn't on you. And it doesn't matter so much anyway. I only had a hundred bucks in there. How long was he out of your sight?"

"Three minutes, tops."

"All right," I say, giving him a smile. "Coulda been worse. Let's not worry about it."

"Maybe we should tell the other guys not to let him in?" Jako suggests, worrying his hair with his fingertips.

"I guess we'd better do that. Next meeting," I agree. I can't *wait* to hear what Judd has to say about that. The only saving grace is that Keaton wasn't home when Joe showed up. I don't want my felon brother anywhere near my fuck buddy.

Come on now.

The disapproving voice brings a sliver of guilt. Okay, that was harsh. Keaton is more than a fuck buddy. We're friends.

Come on now, the voice chides again.

Fuck off, I tell it.

"Thanks for the heads up, man." I clap Jako on the shoulder.

"Of course. Poker later?"

"Maybe. I need to shower and proofread an assignment, but I'll be free later tonight."

It's really weird to have no plans. For the first time in forever, I actually have the entire weekend off. It's a much-needed break. And with finals coming up, I can get ahead of my coursework so I'm not racing to write papers at the last minute.

"Cool," Jako says. Then he disappears down the stairs, and I disappear into the shower. The sweat from my run slides down the drain, but no amount of scalding-hot water can wash away the layer of grimy disgust evoked by my brother's visit.

No, not a "visit." A theft.

I close my eyes under the harsh spray. My disgust dissolves into shame. Can't scour that off my skin, either. Is it any wonder I don't trust anybody? My own brother just stole from me. My mother is a leech.

Why the fuck does Keaton want to date me, anyway? What's wrong with him?

Speaking of the devil, he's sitting on my bed when I walk in after my shower. "Hey," he says.

"Hey." I head for the dresser and fish out a pair of briefs. "What's up?"

"Everything okay? You look tense."

"Nah, I'm good." I don't mention Joe. I know I shouldn't wait until the next frat meeting to tell Keaton about it, but... A sigh lodges in my chest. I don't want to see Keaton's eyes soften with sympathy. I don't want him to try to *talk* to me about it.

"Great," he says. "Now get dressed. Let's take that drive."

I'm really not in the mood. "Can it wait? I need to proof my paper."

He tips his head. "The one that isn't due for two weeks?"

"Yeah, but—"

"But nothing." With a cocky grin, he gets to his feet. "Let's go. You promised."

I stare at his muscular back as he saunters out of the room. I swear, nothing fazes this man. I can glower and glare at him all day long, and he won't bat an eye. My brooding doesn't bother him. My refusal to talk about my feelings doesn't test his patience. He's rock steady, and I don't get it.

Doesn't he realize he's wasting his time?

And yet, despite my reluctance to lower my guard around

him, I find myself sliding into the passenger seat of Keaton's BMW twenty minutes later. Nobody ever said I was smart.

"We're going out to dinner," he says as he pulls away from the curb. "I'm kidnapping you, because I want a steak."

A knee-jerk spike of anger makes me lean back against the leather upholstery and close my eyes. Miraculously, I don't say anything rude. In fact, I don't say anything at all. I take a deep breath. "You're a good friend, Keaton." He knows I'm having a financial crisis. He's managed not to offer me money, either. Which I really appreciate.

He's smart enough not to say anything more.

I take another deep breath. "So where are we going—Outback? Longhorn?" I ask, naming the only two steakhouses near Darby.

"Yeah," is his response, which tells me nothing. Hopefully we're going to Longhorn. The prime rib there is to die for.

A light drizzle falls onto the windshield as Keaton leaves campus and steers onto the highway. The Bluetooth kicks in, and a moment later, a familiar voice blasts out of the car speakers.

I look over with a wry grin. "Are we seriously listening to Beyoncé right now?"

He grins back, turning the volume down. "Annika shared a playlist with me on Spotify. Queen B is her number one."

My stomach does a hot twist. For fuck's sake. The tug of jealousy is completely unwelcome. What do I care if Keaton is still best buds with his ex-girlfriend?

I shift my gaze from his face to his hands, watching as he taps his long fingers on the steering wheel. He's got such sexy hands. And a sexy face. Sexy body.

I'm so busy checking him out that it takes several minutes before I realize we're still on the highway. Getting from campus to either restaurant doesn't require this much travel.

My forehead creases. "Where are we going?"

He winks. "Wouldn't you like to know."

"Yes," I say irritably. "I would like to know. Are we heading to Hartford?"

"Nope."

My annoyance increases. Something about his satisfied expression is rubbing me the wrong way. "Then, where?" I demand.

Keaton casts a devious grin in my direction. "That's for me to know, and for you to find out."

CHAPTER 29
CARRIED AWAY

KEATON

This might have been a bad idea, I decide an hour later. Luke's expression as he studies our hotel suite in Stonington isn't as…encouraging as I'd hoped. A muscle ticks in his jaw when his gaze settles on the massive four-poster bed in the center of the room. Then he turns to me and sighs.

"How much is this costing you?"

I know I've overstepped a boundary by surprising him with a weekend away. But it seems he's not worried about the intimacy of taking a trip so much as the cost of it. So that's good news.

"Honestly, not much," I assure him. "It's nowhere near high season yet."

"Fine, then let me pay for half," he says immediately.

"No way. This is my birthday gift to you."

Silence ensues.

Luke stares at me for so long I start to feel uncomfortable. I shove my hands in the pockets of my jeans and bite my lip uneasily. "Jako and Ahmad talked to the party-planning committee about organizing something for next weekend," I say when Luke doesn't speak. "So I asked what was going on next weekend, and Jako said it was your birthday."

Luke still doesn't answer.

"So I thought, hey, he's got this weekend off, so maybe I'll surprise him with an early birthday thing," I finish lamely.

The discomfort I'm feeling is nothing compared to the intensified version of it I see in Luke Bailey's eyes.

Hoo boy, this was a bad idea, all right. I didn't expect him to jump up and down with joy, but I didn't think he'd be this put off by my efforts.

"You planned a weekend away to celebrate my birthday," he murmurs.

I gulp. "Yeah."

"What else did you plan? What exactly are we doing this weekend, along with boning on that huge bed." He gestures vaguely to the California king.

I meet his eyes. "Tonight we're having steaks at the hotel restaurant. Tomorrow afternoon we're going to a craft beer festival in Mystic."

He nods slowly. "Okay. And?"

He knows me well. "Uh, Sam Smith is playing at Mohegan Sun. I got us tickets," I mumble. The seats are front row, center. But I don't mention that. He'd probably do the math, figure out the ticket prices, and have a nervous breakdown.

Luke lets out an uneven breath. "Hayworth," he says roughly. "I…"

I swallow again. "You what?"

He hesitates. "I…" He's visibly swallowing now, too. "I got to hit the head. I'll be right back."

To my dismay, he makes a beeline for the private bath and firmly shuts the door. I sit down at the edge of the bed and run a hand through my hair. Shit. I feel like such an idiot. As Annika can attest, I tend to get carried away when it comes to special occasions. I mean, I arranged a *threesome* for her birthday, for fuck's sake. And for her birthday last year, I took her to Paris.

Money has never been a factor for me. My trust fund is enormous. I don't dip into it often, but when I do, I don't hold back.

But Bailey isn't Annika. Annika grew up as wealthy as I did. Bailey did not.

I'm such a fool. Of course he's freaked out by all this.

When the bathroom door opens, I half expect an outraged Luke to stomp toward me and demand to be taken back to Darby.

Instead, I find myself gazing at a stricken Luke whose dark eyes are slightly rimmed with red.

"Hayworth," he starts. Then he stops. "Keaton."

I remain seated. "You okay?" I ask cautiously.

He gives a slow shake of his head.

Fuck. I open my mouth, armed with an apology, but he cuts me off with a strangled groan.

"I want to be pissed off at you. I really do. Because this is so fucking *extra*. One dinner would've been a sufficient birthday present. Actually, way more than sufficient. But dinner *and* two nights at this fancy hotel *and* a beer festival *and* a concert? Are you out of your mind?"

Once again, I open my mouth to tell him that all Hayworths like to party. It's just in our blood. Our annual beach barbecue is legendary.

But once again, he speaks first. "I'm not pissed," he says helplessly. "I'm not pissed, because do you realize that the last time anybody *remembered* my birthday, let alone celebrated it, was back in high school?"

I frown. "Not even your family?"

Luke laughs bitterly. "Especially them. The last time my mother wished me a happy birthday was when I turned sixteen." He shakes his head a few times. "I can't believe you did this."

"But you're *not* pissed," I hedge.

"Not much. I'm fucking touched, okay? Even if I want to punch you for making me feel this way—hey! Wipe that grin off your face! This isn't funny."

I press my lips together to fight my amusement. "No, it's kinda funny."

Bailey's trademark scowl twists his sexy mouth. I notice his fists are clenched to his sides, and more laughter bubbles in my throat. I want to tease him about this, or maybe just assure him that it's okay to feel moved, that he's allowed to accept this gift, but I don't want to push him any more than I already have.

So I hop off the mattress and give his ass a little smack. "All right, you done bitching? Because I'm hungry for steak."

———

Dinner is great. The company is even better. Bailey and I somehow down two bottles of wine, so we're tipsy for most of our meals. The waitress knows it, and teases us about our growing intoxication. And by the time I sign the receipt slip with our room number, I'm rocking a semi, because for me, drunk = horny.

Ergo, I have my tongue in Luke's mouth before he can even close the door to the suite.

"You are the most sex-starved person I've ever met," he mutters against my greedy mouth.

"You love it," I mumble back. I'm already clawing at his clothes.

He squeezes my ass and guides me backward toward the bed. Then I'm flat on my back and he's on top of me, and we're making out hardcore. His fingers fumble with my zipper, yanking it down as his tongue fills my mouth and robs me of sanity.

But through the haze of lust, I register the persistent chime of my cell phone. I'd left it in the room when we were at dinner, and it isn't on silent or vibrate.

"Ugh, let me shut that off," I groan against Luke's lips. "It's gonna annoy me."

"Hurry," he growls, then rolls onto his back and rubs his erection through his pants.

Grinning, I dive off the bed toward the desk. I plan on

switching the phone to silent mode, but the notifications on the lock screen catch my eye. Two missed calls from my father. Which normally I'd just ignore. But he also sent a text after his calls weren't answered, and what I read before the notification cuts off is enough to trigger my internal alarm.

Dad: I assume congratulations are in order! I just saw the hotel charges on your...[read more]

I glance at the bed, where Luke is totally eye-fucking me. "Hey, sorry, I need to read this message."

Luke flicks up an eyebrow. "Something important?"

"I'm not sure. Right now it's just confusing." I unlock the home screen to scan the rest of Dad's text.

When I'm done, I'm fuming so hard I wouldn't be surprised if Luke commented on the steam rolling out of my ears.

Dad: I assume congratulations are in order! I just saw the hotel charges on your credit statement, and your mother points out that it must mean you and Annika are back on track. We are both thrilled to hear it, son!

No need to phone me back tonight. I assume you and Annika are busy enjoying your weekend away. But we have to speak when you return. There's also a credit card charge for an application fee for a summer program? That had better not interfere with the finance internship you promised to do. Call me tomorrow.

"Everything okay?" Luke calls.

I realize I've just been standing here like a marble statue, glowering at my phone.

"No," I retort. "It's not." I turn and march to the bed, where I drop the iPhone in Luke's hand. "Can you believe this man?"

Luke skims the message. His eyebrows shoot up again, and he gives me an incredulous look. "He checks your credit card statements?"

"Yup." I can barely get that one syllable out, my throat is so tight with anger. "The card is connected to my trust account, and Dad has access to that. I'm used to him checking up on what I'm spending money on, but this…this is *bullshit*." I blow out a harsh breath. "What the fuck is wrong with him? He's breathing down my neck, for one. And I *never* promised to do that internship. So he's just perusing my credit card on a Friday night, connecting the dots on my *life?*"

"It's certainly intrusive," Luke agrees.

"Shit, and knowing him he'll reach out to Annika, too. And she's dating somebody else. She'll probably be humiliated."

"Oh come on, he wouldn't really do that, would he?"

I drop my ass back on the bed. I scrub my face with my hands, moaning in aggravation. "That is absolutely something he would do, and has done. I mean, we're talking about the man who sent gift cards to every single member of his son's fraternity to win votes. I can't deal with this anymore, Bailey. He's my father, and I love him, but holy fuck do I need him to just leave me alone."

"Then tell him."

With a wry smile, I lift my head. "Really. You want me to tell my father to leave me alone. Solid plan."

Luke sits up too, coming up behind me on his knees. To my shock, he curls his fingers over my shoulders and begins kneading my tense flesh. "Christ, you're stiff as a board. Breathe, Hayworth."

I breathe, but it does nothing to diffuse the hostility I'm feeling. "I can't stand it anymore," I repeat.

"Then tell him," Luke repeats.

Laughter sputters out. "Stop saying that."

"No." He massages a knot of tension between my shoulder blades. His hands are strong, rough. They feel like heaven. "Because that's exactly what you need to do—tell him how you feel."

"I have," I protest. "He doesn't listen."

"Then make him listen." Luke's thumbs continue working on that stubborn knot. "As someone who's quite skilled at dealing with toxic parents, I promise you, the only way to save your sanity is to set clear boundaries. I could've continued living at home after Joe got out of prison—it would've been hella cheaper and saved me so much stress. But my mental wellbeing was more important. I made it clear to my mother that I wasn't going to be dragged down by her or Joe any longer. Yeah, I throw money her way sometimes, but that's only because I wouldn't be able to sleep at night knowing her heat is shut off. But I'm trying hard not to enable her bad behavior anymore, and I definitely don't tolerate the narcissistic bullshit she tries to manipulate me with."

I stay quiet, because I'm terrified he'll stop talking if I say something. This is the first time he's spoken at length about his family. No, about his *feelings*. Luke Bailey doesn't share.

"But I get that it's hard. When I give her an inch, Mom still uses me shamelessly," he says gruffly. "She always has. Joe was her favorite, but we all knew that kid was going nowhere. Me, on the other hand—I was smart, ambitious, motivated. I was working two jobs by the time I was fifteen. She knew which son was going to be her meal ticket, and she used every trick in the book to guilt me into giving her whatever she wanted."

I raise a hand to cover his on my shoulder. I caress his hand, and he traps mine there with his thumb.

"So yeah," he finishes. "It's not easy. But I'm really trying not to enable her anymore. And that's what you're doing with your dad—you let him get away with his bad behavior, and as long as you keep letting shit slide, he'll keep doing it."

I gulp down the lump in my throat. "So what do you suggest I say? Because I've tried asking him to back off, and it hasn't worked."

Luke kisses the back of my neck. "Yeah, you've *asked*. And what I'm telling you to do is *tell* him. This is your life, not his. He doesn't get a say in what you choose to do with it. That means you can't let him bully you into stuff anymore—running for frat president, this finance internship that—no offense—you are going to suck at."

"No offense taken," I mutter. "I hate business, and I particularly hate finance."

"Exactly, and you need to be firm about that. Draw your line in the sand, babe. When we get back to school, you need to phone him up and say, 'Dad, this is how it is. I'm not interning at your company this summer. I'm going to Chile to play with Shamu—'"

I snicker. And I wonder if he realizes he just called me *babe*. But I don't mention it, because it'd probably send him into a panic again.

"'Furthermore, if you keep snooping around in my bank accounts and making judgments about my purchases, I'm going to apply for another credit card that you don't have access to. Also, I am not back together with Annika. I'm bisexual and I'm spending the weekend with a guy. In fact, I'm about to suck him off.'"

I curl over in a wave of laughter. "Oh, is that so?" I demand between chuckles. "You're about to get sucked off?"

Abandoning the massage, Luke twists me around so we're facing each other. The combination of heat and tenderness on his face makes me shiver. "Come here, Keaton."

Keaton. He usually calls me Hayworth, and it always sounds like he's keeping his distance. But not today.

"I'm waiting." He crooks his finger.

So I move, pushing him down on the bed like an overeager puppy. "You got something you need to say?"

"Yeah." His voice is husky. "You're pretty great. That's all. Now forget about your pushy old man and kiss me."

CHAPTER 30
MY BEST IDEA EVER

KEATON

"Fourth gear is huge, did you notice that?" I ask, leaning back in the passenger's seat. Luke asked if he could drive home, and I was all too happy to say yes.

I'm just plain happy. Last night was everything.

The concert was a good time. We'd stood there at the foot of the stage, dancing, Luke's hands on my hips. And naturally when we got back to the hotel, I was ready to give the king-sized bed another workout.

"Are you sore?" Luke had asked me between kisses.

"Kind of," I'd admitted. We'd been crazy men the night before. "But athletes don't complain about pain."

"Sure, but…" He'd popped the button on his own jeans. "Maybe you'd better fuck me, then."

He'd said it just like that. Like we were deciding between the stuffed mushrooms and the chicken wings on the appetizers menu. But I didn't question it. I'm not a stupid man. A half hour later I'd had him gripping the headboard and moaning my name.

Getting out of town was my best idea since throwing a winter beach party. My best idea *ever*.

"Yeah, fourth gear has lots of torque," Luke agrees, down-shifting to make a lane change just for fun. "And it feels like fifth is just for cruising."

"Uh-huh." The sun is warm on my face, so I close my eyes. "I've never dated anyone who wanted to discuss my manual transmission before."

I realize my mistake the second I make it. "You know what I mean," I mumble.

He's quiet for a second. "No, I do. We are heading in that direction, Keaton. I get it now."

I'm so surprised that I actually stop breathing.

"No sense in me arguing the point. I just hope you know you've got an amateur on your hands, here. I'll probably do everything wrong."

"I'm not worried," I say quickly.

"Really? You should be. People are going to notice how much time we spend together. What are we going to say?"

"I haven't figured that out yet," I admit. "I'm an amateur, too. At this. Can't we sort that part out on our own time?"

"Maybe," he concedes. "As long as there aren't any leaks on our top-secret security team. Like Tanner grabbing your phone and opening up the wrong app…"

I snort. "I have that sucker well hidden. But there will probably be a point in the future when you feel less like it matters, right? This semester ends in just a few weeks. Next year you'll already be president…"

Now I've done it again. I've assumed that we'll be together next year.

"Suppose it won't be as big a deal," Luke concedes. "Eventually."

We lapse into silence again, but my whole outlook has changed this weekend. All my patience has paid off.

Luke Bailey acknowledges that we're a couple? Pinch me.

When I woke up this morning, Luke was sleeping curled up against my back, his arm wrapped around me. It was so peaceful that I held still as long as I could, just to make it last. And when he finally woke up, he didn't untangle himself right away. He kissed me between the shoulder blades instead.

I want that again. And I like it a whole lot. I've always known that coupledom felt right to me. The part I didn't understand is that it works even better for me when that other half is a man.

Here's the part I haven't told anyone—even Luke. I'm starting to wonder if bisexual is even the right label for me. Lately my sexuality is tilted further toward men than women. Lately I notice men *everywhere*. It's as if I took my blinders off and started seeing everyone differently. The shapely biceps, quads, and glutes of the men of Darby, Connecticut are everywhere suddenly. Which is weird, because I've been surrounded by athletes my whole life.

Before, though, I might be admiring a guy at the squat rack thinking, *nice form*. These days I just think...*nice*.

"You're thinking pretty hard over there," Luke says as he passes a Toyota.

"It's all good. I'm well-fed. The sun is out."

"You're feeling the warm glow of sexual satisfaction," he says and then snickers. "But all vacations end, Hayworth. The minute we pull into town, you'll have to pull a poker face when everyone asks where you've been."

"So what if I do? I just wanted to spend some time with you. And I'm going to keep on doing that. It's nobody's business but ours."

"Yeah, okay." He clears his throat. "Sounds good to me."

I chuckle, because the discomfort in his voice is so hard to miss.

"Go ahead and laugh," he says. "But I am trying."

"I know you are." I reach over the console and squeeze his hand.

He squeezes mine back.

———

It's all fun and games until we get back to town. There's no parking on College Street as we approach the Alpha Delt house. "Sometimes I find a spot over on Elm," I suggest.

He's coasting down the street at maybe fifteen miles an hour. But even if Luke were driving faster, there'd be no way we'd miss all our housemates in the front yard, or the cop car double parked out front with its lights on.

"Holy shit," Luke says. "What do you think happened?"

"I have no idea. There's no ambulance, at least. Pull up behind the cops."

He does. And I open the door and step out.

"Hayworth!" Judd calls. He comes walking toward me. "Have you seen Bailey?"

Instinct makes me turn to look at the car. Luke is already standing, his gaze taking everything in.

"Why?" I croak. Because I sure have seen Bailey. All weekend. Everyone is staring at us now.

Did I fuck this up already?

Two cops come walking toward us. "One of you Luke Bailey?"

"I am," Luke says, his voice wary. "Why?"

"Step away from the car."

Luke closes my car door and tosses me the keys. His face is already white.

"Whose vehicle is this?"

"Mine," I say immediately.

But they aren't even glancing in my direction. "Luke Bailey, please put your hands on the hood of the car. You have the right to remain silent. Anything you say can and will be used against you in a court of law. You have the right—"

"What is this about?" Luke growls.

"Hands on the car!"

His hands land on the hood immediately.

"You have the right to an attorney. If you cannot afford an attorney, one will be provided for you. Do you understand the rights I have just read to you?"

"Yes," Luke says. "But…"

The next sound I hear is the click of handcuffs on my boyfriend's wrists.

"Holy shit," Judd says. "They're throwing Bailey in the pokey."

CHAPTER 31
I'M PANICKING

LUKE

I'm in the back of a cop car, and I'm panicking.

Keaton just watched the cops handcuff me. My entire fraternity just watched them push me into the car. There's a fucking cage between me and the guy in the front seat. I don't even know where they're taking me.

All I know is I have never been afraid like I am right now.

My breath is coming too fast, in rapid puffs. But I still can't get enough air. Like I'm drowning back here. "Can you... open the window?" I gasp. "I can't get enough air."

"You're doing just fine," says the cop in the passenger seat.

"No I..." Alarm races through me. "I feel dizzy."

"You're just hyperventilating," says the driver. "Breathe through your nose."

Hyperventilating? I thought that was a joke for TV sitcoms. I clamp my lips together and breathe through my nose. But it feels horrible. Like I'm suffocating. And my arms are trapped behind me, awkward and useless.

What the hell is happening?

———

Forty minutes later, my breathing is back to normal. But everything else is still chaos. The police take my wallet out of my pocket and use my ID to enter me into their systems. "What's the charge?" I ask.

"Burglary."

"What? Of what?"

"Where's your school ID?" one of the cops asks.

"On a lanyard... In my room?" I guess. "It's not a law that I have to carry it." My bravado is thin. "I didn't steal anything. Why am I here?"

They don't answer. And then I'm walked through the humiliating procedure of being fingerprinted. At least the handcuffs are off.

They take a mug shot. I stand in front of that thing that shows your height. And I turn to the side when they ask me to.

I want to die the whole time.

"Why am I even here?" I keep asking. But nobody will explain. My mind whirls through the possibilities. There aren't many.

This has to do with Joe. I'm sure of it, even if I can't guess how.

Finally someone shows me into an interview room. It's barely larger than a closet.

"Now will you tell me why I'm here?" I ask.

"You're going to do the telling, and I'm going to do the asking," the cop says. He has a salt-and-pepper flat top and no neck.

"Okay, ask me questions," I grunt. Maybe I'll learn something.

"Which campus buildings does your student ID open?"

His first query startles me and tells me nothing. "Well, lots of them. The gym. The library. Classroom buildings. Just like anyone's ID." My mind races. What could he be getting at?

"And where is your ID right now?"

"It's... I have no idea. Probably on my desk? I haven't needed it since Friday."

"Uh-huh." His tone is disbelieving. "Do you have a Red Sox cap?"

"Sure. Like half the people in New England."

"What color?"

"Uh, black with a red logo on the front. I don't wear it often, though. Only on a really bad hair day."

"Was yesterday a really bad hair day?"

"Not at all."

He opens a folder and pulls out a single sheet of paper. It's a poorly rendered photo of a guy holding something in front of his body. You can't even see his face, but he's wearing a Sox cap that looks a lot like mine.

"Who is this?"

"That's you, wise guy. This shot is from yesterday. They have security cameras in the computer lab. Sorry if you didn't notice that before."

I blink at the picture. It might be my brother? This picture sucks. "I was nowhere near here yesterday," I say, unwilling to guess at why they think this is me.

"Yeah? Your ID logged into the system three times. Once in the Vanderbilt Library and twice in the business school."

"Oh Jesus." Now I understand. "Look, my brother broke into my room on Friday. I thought he only took cash. He obviously has my ID. I'd bet money on it."

"Your brother?"

"Yeah. Joe Bailey. I only have one brother." I'm rambling now, but my brain is busy piecing it all together. He took my ID, and he used it to wander around campus looking for computers. He went to the library first, but that space was too public.

The business school would have been quieter on the weekend.

"You say he broke into your room? At the frat house?"

"Yeah, he picked the lock on my bedroom door. I thought he only cleaned out my cash. I didn't notice the ID. Or the hat. Actually, I think he has the same hat."

The cop scowls. "You were stolen from, and you didn't report it?"

My heart sinks. "It was just some cash. And he thinks he has a right to my stuff. I was relieved he didn't pick off anything that belonged to someone else. And what would even be the point of reporting him? My mother takes cash off me every chance she gets." I hate everything I'm saying. It sounds awful. Who would believe me if I come from a family like that?

"But this is you," the cop says, sliding the photo toward me.

"No it isn't." I jab a finger at the photo. "And I didn't take whatever he's holding. It was the computer lab, you say?"

"Did I? I don't remember."

"Oh, please." His tone is infuriating. "I'm not taking the blame for this. Joe isn't the sharpest guy. If you pick him up he'll still have whatever he took. He's the reason I don't live at home anymore."

"You're throwing your own brother under the bus for this?"

"Yes!" Although it sounds awful. Like we're all a bunch of crooks. "Yes," I say anyway. "Because he clearly intended to do the same to me."

The cop scratches his head. "So, someone steals your cash and your ID. And you don't worry about why, huh? Oops!" He throws up his hands. "Seems kind of convenient, that's all."

"No! I didn't realize the ID was even gone. I was headed out of town."

"Where?"

"Um…" Fuck. What the hell can I even say to that?

"You're the smart brother, right? The college student? You tell your brother that you're headed out of town. You also tell him where to find your ID."

"No! It's not like that."

"Where'd you go out of town, anyway?"

"I…" I am so fucked.

"Did you go with anyone else? Did you stay in a hotel? Did you use a credit card, or your EZPass?"

If only I had used a credit card. But of course Keaton paid for everything. And there's no way I can drag Keaton Hayworth III into this.

It turns out I'm not the smart brother at all.

"I need a lawyer," I say slowly. I should have said that right away.

"Are you sure? That just looks guilty. If you were out of town, that's easy to prove, right? We can sort this out like men."

"Like men." I sigh. Yeah, I'm never telling him how I spent my weekend. "No, I need a lawyer to untangle this bullshit theory of yours."

"You got someone to call?"

And that's the big question in my life, right? I don't know any lawyers or how to find one in a hurry. Calling home is out of the question. Mom is no help and Joe wants me to go to jail for him.

Keaton, though. He'd know exactly who to call. But I won't drag him into this.

"How do you get a public defender?" I ask the cop.

"Be prepared to wait," he says. "I'll let 'em know."

He heaves himself out of his chair and stomps out of the room.

I hear the lock click into place as he leaves me behind.

CHAPTER 32
MY BRAIN IS FULL OF STATIC

KEATON

I always thought of myself as the kind of guy who keeps his head and who knows what to do in an emergency. Once, I rescued a drowning couple from the ocean, and everyone praised my cool demeanor and quick thinking.

Well, that's gone now. My brain is full of static. My ability to think has fled the room. And it's all because of the look on Luke's face as the cop pushed him into the back of the patrol car.

It was panic. Sheer terror.

"Where were you guys, anyway?" Tanner asks me. We're in the living room of the frat. I'm sitting on a sofa, my phone in my hand. But I can't think what to do.

"Out of town," I say.

"What for?"

"Just to get out of town," I snap. "Since when do I need to explain?"

"He's got a good reason to be curious," Judd argues. "The cops searched Bailey's room. They had a warrant. Reed had to open it up for them, and they spent like forty minutes in there."

"Looking for what?" I croak. I've been in Luke's room dozens of times. It's not very big, and there's nothing to hide. The only thing that surprised me about Luke's room is the tiny refrigerator under his desk where he keeps cheese and apples.

"No idea," Judd says. "But it can't be good."

"This will have something to do with his brother," Jako says. "That guy is a creep, and he broke into Luke's room on Friday."

"Wait. He did?" I ask. "Bailey didn't tell me that."

Everyone just stares at me.

I don't know what to do. Luke doesn't like anyone to know about his life. He definitely doesn't want anyone to know about us. On the other hand, the cops just took his ass away in a patrol car. I can't just pretend I don't care what happens now.

"Reed?" I ask, looking around for our president.

"Yeah?" He's right beside me.

"What do you do if somebody is arrested. I can't think straight right now."

"Well, you need a lawyer if they're pressing charges. Someone to speak for you at your arraignment."

Right, okay. "How can we tell if someone will be arraigned?"

"They read him his rights," Tanner says. "They don't do that if they're just taking you in for questioning, right?"

"I don't know." And I feel so ignorant right now. Watching cop shows on TV doesn't give me much to go on. "If you were dragged off to the police station, what would you want your frat brothers to do?"

There's another silence, and I look up into the faces of my friends. They're all looking back at me with expressions ranging from clueless to skeptical.

"I don't see how this is our problem," Judd says.

And that pisses me right off. "Seriously? If it was you, I'm supposed to just go upstairs and finish my bio lab?"

"But the cops don't show up for me," Judd says. "So it's just not relevant. What's your deal with Luke Bailey, anyway?"

I ignore him. I pick up my phone and tap my father's number. Luckily, he answers right away.

"Keaton! Let's talk about this application fee—"

"Dad," I break in. "Forget that right now. I need help. Luke Bailey is in trouble."

It takes him a beat to answer. "What's the problem, Keat?"

"He and I just drove back into town—"

"I thought you went away to a hotel with Annika?"

"Just because you thought it doesn't make it true," I growl. "I did spend the weekend at a hotel. But not with Annika."

There's another silence, and I wonder if I'm going to have to spell it out for him.

"Oh." I don't miss the weight of understanding that he puts into the word.

"Yeah."

"Oh," he says again.

I sigh. "You can wrap your mind around that later. Right now I need you to focus on this—Luke was arrested the second we got back. What do you do if someone is arrested?"

"Any guess at the charges?"

"I have no idea. And from what I can gather, neither does he. But his brother is a real piece of work, and no stranger to illegal activity."

"You need a defense attorney," Dad says immediately.

"Know any?"

"Has to be someone who practices in Connecticut. Give me twenty minutes."

The line goes dead. My brain is just catching up, though, so I sit there with the phone to my ear for a long beat before I finally look up.

A dozen of my frat brothers are staring at me, their mouths open.

"What?" I snap.

"You and Bailey…?" Tanner can't bring himself to finish the sentence.

"Went away for the weekend?" I challenge him. "Yes."

"Uh…" He just looks perplexed.

And I can't do this right now. "Whatever you're thinking, go ahead and think it. I have to park my car before it gets towed. And I have to get a lawyer for Bailey." I stand up.

"I'll park your car," Tanner says. He holds out a hand for the keys. "I got this. You can just take care of business."

"Oh." I take a deep breath. "Thank you."

I hand over the keys.

Nobody else moves.

"Please tell me you and Luke Bailey aren't..." Judd looks ill.

Apparently everyone forgot how to finish their sentences while I was away. "So what if we are? It's none of your business."

"Jesus," he hisses. "That explains so much."

"About what?" I snarl.

"He *turned* you," Judd says. "So he could take the frat presidency. He flipped the straight guy. You're a big notch in his belt, right? Did he ask you for money, too?"

"FUCK you!" I shout, getting to my feet.

"Nah, I don't swing that way," Judd snaps. "No matter how good the blowjobs are. Did he teach you that, too?"

And that's when I lunge for him.

CHAPTER 33
OPEN TO A PLEA DEAL

LUKE

I'm shown into a holding cell with five other guys. There are benches along the walls, but no other furniture. Nobody even looks up at me as I enter, and that's just fine. I sink down on a bench and try not to think. Because every thought I have is a horrible one.

Even if I somehow manage to walk out of here tomorrow with the charges dismissed, will Darby College keep me? Can they revoke my scholarship for having a brother who steals?

And then there's the frat. There's some line about lawfulness in the members' handbook somewhere. If you're convicted of a crime, I think they can toss you out.

I *cannot* get convicted. Of anything. Even if I got a fine instead of jail time, it would ruin my life. I'm thirteen months from getting a degree. If I get a criminal record instead?

Shit jobs for the rest of my life.

At some point my name is called again. I'm shown into another interview room, where a public defender in a too-tight suit asks me all the relevant questions.

"I know my brother did this," I tell him as loudly as I can. "Did they investigate him? I can give you the address."

He scribbles it on maybe the twentieth page of his legal pad, under the pile of other cases that are already there.

"I will argue for bail to be set at your arraignment," he says.

"How does that work?

"If they set it for five thousand dollars, you'd pay seven hundred and fifty to a bail bondsman, who posts the rest."

Seven hundred and fifty dollars. I don't have that money. My family sure as hell won't, either. Holy shit. I'm trapped in here, unless I ask Heather or the guys at Jill's to get me out.

Keaton would pay it, of course. But I'd rather owe *everyone* else on the planet than ask him.

My lawyer gets ready to leave only a few minutes later. It's obvious to me that his one goal is getting me out on bail tomorrow. "We'll work on the case when we get a trial date," he says. "Are you open to a plea deal?"

"No!" *Jesus.* "I didn't do it. And I have an alibi. Can you call the hotel and ask them if there are security cameras?"

"Uh-huh," he says, clicking his pen again. "When we get a court date. Sure."

I have never felt as hopeless as I do right now.

They take me back to the holding cell, where I sink down on a bench and put my head in my hands. I would do anything to rewind this weekend to a point where I might have done something differently. Like call the cops on Joe after he broke into my room.

If only.

————

"Bailey! Bailey. Bailey?"

I jerk awake, bouncing my head off the concrete wall. "Right here," I gasp.

"Your lawyer is here to prepare for your arraignment."

I stand up, and my back complains. I spent the night hunched over, trying to sleep without having a place to lie down. My mouth feels disgusting, and my T-shirt probably smells like this hellhole.

This is how I have to face a judge?

Numb, I follow the uniformed officer back toward the little interview room. We've just reached the doorway when I hear my name again, from further down the hall.

"Luke Bailey? Where can I find Luke Bailey?"

"Right here," I say, confused, as the man with the salt-and-pepper beard in the impeccable pinstripe suit barrels towards me. He's carrying a satchel with brass clasps.

"Good, good. How much time do we have?" he asks the bailiff.

"About twenty minutes."

The man pushes past us into the little room and his satchel lands on the table with a thump. "You're dismissed," he tells my public defender. "Leave the case file."

My lawyer gets up with a squeak of his chair against the linoleum.

"Wait!" I say, panicking. "You can't send the lawyer away."

"I'm your new lawyer," Mr. Pinstripes says, opening his satchel. "Robert Grant, attorney at law. Sit down, we're wasting time."

The other lawyer slips out of the room without so much as a word.

"But…" I snap my jaw closed, because this man is opening up a laptop already, and on its screen I see a photo of the hotel where I spent the weekend.

So I shut up and sit down across from him.

"Checkout time from the hotel is eleven a.m. on Sunday. Do you remember when you two drove away?"

"Uh, not until after eleven thirty at the earliest, because we ate lunch at the hotel restaurant." I say, still groggy from a night of dozing on a bench. "Who gave you that information?"

He looks up. "Keaton Hayworth. Junior, or the third, whatever. The Hayworth kid. The hotel is pulling security footage from the elevators, too. Your name wasn't on the reservation, which is a shame, but it isn't the most important thing. My investigator will find someone behind the desk who remembers you."

I am speechless for a second. "Who hired you?"

"The Hayworths. Now talk to me about your brother. Does he still reside at this address on Calhoun Street?" He swings the computer screen to face me, and it's a Google Earth shot of my mom's house.

"Yes," I say slowly. "I know he took my ID and used it to take whatever is missing."

"Uh-huh," the lawyer says, typing like crazy. "Totally plausible. But we don't have to solve this case for the lazy assholes who arrested you. We're going to show you weren't anywhere near Darby on Saturday. They know when the place was robbed, they have the shitty footage to prove it." He glances at me over his screen. "That still shot they showed you was straight-up bullshit. There is other footage that shows your brother's face. I'd bet money on it."

"Okay." I clear my throat. "How much do you cost?"

"Not relevant to the next sixteen minutes. Hey, put this on." He reaches into his satchel and pulls out an oxford shirt, still wrapped in plastic. "And these." He's got a pair of khaki pants with the tags still on them. "Keaton guessed the sizes. Hurry up. Oh, and…" He also sets a can of deodorant on the table.

I rise and strip off my T-shirt, tossing it right into the garbage can in the corner. I'd strip off my skin, too, if I could. I never want to see this place again, and I don't need any reminders that I was ever here.

Pulling on the shirt that Keaton bought for me is only slightly more comfortable, however. I can't believe he had to do this for me.

I feel nothing but shame.

———

When I'm halfway presentable and Mr. Grant has asked me fifty questions in fifteen minutes, I'm marched by a bailiff to a busy courtroom, where the judge is seated on the dais, several people convened in front of him.

I take a seat on yet another bench.

My fancy lawyer—my new favorite person—is hissing at another man at the side of the room. "This is an ACD," Grant says. "Looks bad if you lock up a college kid before exams, whose only crime is sharing DNA with a turd you already convicted."

The other man makes a face.

"The college looks bad if this is on the news," Grant says, and it sounds like a threat. "And when the college looks bad, your boss gets a call."

My lawyer is a scary dude. And I don't even understand the things he's saying.

"Case 418636!" calls a bailiff in front.

"That's us," Grant says, snapping his fingers. I rise and move toward him like a well-trained dog. "I speak for you," he says under his breath. "Just answer 'Yes, your honor,' when the judge confirms your name."

And so I do.

Two minutes later the district attorney—that's the guy my lawyer was talking to—says "We've reached an agreement of ACD."

I don't know what that means, but the judge grunts. He hands a sheet of paper to the DA. "ROR for ACD." Then he taps his gavel and picks up some other papers on his desk.

"Thank you," murmurs Grant to the DA. "Wise decision. My client will make himself available to you whenever necessary." Then Grant takes my elbow in his hand and drags me up the aisle and out the door.

"What just happened?" I ask when we've reached the lobby.

"ACD means Adjournment in Contemplation of Dismissal."

"But what about bail?" I ask as he lets go of my arm.

"No bail. You're just free to go. I'll supply them with hard evidence of your alibi. Meanwhile, the DA's office will try to find the *actual* burglar and then they'll dismiss your case for good. So don't get arrested for anything else, kid. Don't drink and drive. Don't trespass. Don't even run a stop sign."

"Okay?" My head is spinning.

"And if they come by to interview you about your brother, call me right as you sit down with them. You do not have to go near the police station. But you do need to be as helpful as possible. Call me for anything."

"I will."

"Now let's get your personal effects so you can go home."

And so we do.

CHAPTER 34
EBOLA

LUKE

Apparently I contracted Ebola in jail.

Well, not actually. But based on the silence and the stares that greet me when I walk into the Alpha Delt house, you'd sure as shit think I was a carrier for a deadly disease.

Wary eyes track my movements as I enter the living room. Keaton is nowhere to be seen, but Judd, Tanner, and a few others sit on the couch, dropping their video game controllers to their laps at my entrance. In the dining room, Jako and Zimmer are bent over a stack of textbooks. Their heads snap up when they spot me, and Jako is immediately on his feet.

"Bailey!" he calls out in relief, and he's the only person in the room who looks happy to see me. Once again, I wonder where Keaton is. I've been trying hard not to think about him. But now I have to.

He watched the cops push me into a cruiser. I feel nauseated every time I remember that.

"Hey," I greet everyone, awkwardly shoving my hands in my back pockets.

"How was prison?" cracks Judd.

I give him a look that would make most people quail. But not Judd. I knew my housemates would ask questions, but it grates that Judd is the one to lead off the Inquisition. He's sporting a black eye, too, which just makes him look more like the surly hooligan that he is.

"I wasn't in prison," I reply as evenly as I can manage. "I spent the night in holding."

"Same diff."

"No, not the same at all." My stiff legs carry me to the center of the living room. I sweep my gaze over the guys on the couch and then the rest of the bodies that are slowly filling the room. "I've got an announcement to make," I tell everyone.

"Oh, there is absolutely no need," Judd taunts. He stands up and moves toward me so that we're facing off in front of the coffee table. "We know far too much about you already." He glances around. "There's no way you're going to be president."

Our current president appears at my side, rolling his eyes. "Keller," Reed chastises. "Enough."

Judd's lip curls. "Are you serious? Your replacement just got *arrested*, Reedsy!"

"And released," I interject. "The charges will be dismissed. I didn't steal anything."

"You stole *plenty*," Judd drawls. "You're disgusting."

"And you don't know what the hell you're saying," I growl. "On Friday when I got back from a run, Jako let me know that my older brother Joe came by."

Jako steps forward with a nod. "Right, but—"

"I was worried," I press on, "because Joe did time for breaking and entering a while back. So I went upstairs to investigate and discovered he stole some cash from my room. At the time I thought it was *just* the cash. But as it turns out, he…" I draw another breath. "He also stole my Darby ID." Shame and disgust twist my stomach into knots. "And then he used that ID to steal some computers from the school."

"Shit," Jako says quietly.

"Seriously?" Judd is having none of it. "That's supposed to make us feel better?" He turns to Reed. "He just admitted to letting a convicted felon roam around unaccompanied in our house!"

Jako speaks up again, his tone hard. "No, *I* did that. *I* let Luke's brother into the house, so anything he took from us is on me."

"No, it's not," I say firmly. "It's on *me*."

"Damn right," Judd says viciously. "I am fucking done with this. I vote to impeach the cocksucker in chief—"

"*Judd*," Reed snaps.

"Again with this shit?" Zimmer says from right behind me. "How many chances does he get, Reed? Muzzle his bullshit or I am fucking done, too."

My poor, tired brain is trying to keep up. Although "cocksucker" is one of Judd's favorite words. It sounds like he knows…

"Hey," a stiff voice says from the stairs.

I turn my head, and Keaton is right there, walking toward me. His hazel eyes conduct a quick head-to-toe tour of me, as if he's assessing me for damage.

But, Christ, all the damage is his. Keaton's lip is split. There are deep circles under his eyes, and there's a tightness in his expression that I have never seen before.

"Shut it, Judd," Keaton says now. "If anyone is getting tossed out of Alpha Delt, it's you."

"Yeah?" The asshole takes a step toward Keaton. "Let's have that vote. It might not turn out the way you think. Are you even gonna show up and participate? Or will you pussy out again and let Bailey call the shots?"

Keaton pales, and everyone else seems to brace himself. Until Tanner steps between Judd and Keaton, keeping the two of them apart. "Back to your corners."

I suck in a breath. What is happening right now?

"Un-fucking-called for," Keaton growls.

"I gotta go upstairs," I mutter. Not only do I need to wash the smell of loser off my body, but I'm too tired to think. If Judd mouths off one more time I'm gonna punch him for sure. And then I really will get thrown out of Alpha Delt. Just like he hopes. I turn toward the stairs, maneuvering past Reed and Zimmer.

"Your fuck buddy will be right up, I'm sure," Judd chirps.

I freeze as silence descends on us. But then I have to turn around. And sure enough, everyone is watching me, wondering what I'll say.

I'm too shocked to speak. Because...everyone knows? Jesus Christ. When did that happen? And *why*? Keaton could've come up with a million excuses as to why we were together when we pulled up in that car. I mean, obviously he revealed the truth about our weekend to the lawyer, because he went on the record as my official alibi.

But he told the *fraternity*?

Keaton's is the last face I check. He's pale, his mouth a hard line. When he catches me look at him, he closes his eyes.

Oh my fucking god.

"I'm sorry," he grinds out.

"Yeah, I'm sure you are," I mumble. I'm sure he's sorry he ever met me at all.

Keaton flinches, but I don't know if it's because of my words, or because there's someone pounding on the front door right now.

"Luke Bailey!" shrieks a voice from the other side of the six-panel oak door. "Someone help me!"

I'm across the foyer and yanking open the door in a huge hurry. "Mom," I say gruffly as soon as I see her tear-stained face. "Calm down."

She tries to push past me into the house, but I tighten my grip on the door, keeping her outside. "Aren't you going to let me in?" she sobs.

"Not necessary," I say in a low voice. "Why are you here?"

"Lukey! You need to come home *right now*! They took Joey!"

"When?"

"Just now! Those pigs showed up and accused him of stealing

computers or something," she sobs. "They arrested him and took him away! We need to go and get him out. You have to post bail—"

"No," I ease the door closed behind me so that we're alone on the stoop.

"W-what?" Her voice trembles, and she's sniffling repeatedly. "W-what do you mean, no? He's your *brother*. He needs help."

"Yes, he needs help," I agree. "But it's not going to come from me, Mom. Those computers he stole? He tried to blame the theft on *me*."

As always, my mother passionately comes to Joe's defense. "You're wrong. Joey would never do that!"

"He would, and he did." Bitterness coats my throat. "He stole my ID and broke into my school, Mom. And then he let me take the rap for it." Her voice isn't the only voice that's shaking. "I-I spent the night in lock-up. Do you...Christ...do you know how demoralizing that was?"

"We need to post Joey's bail," she says without acknowledging a word I've said. "It's only seven hundred and fifty dollars! And then we have to work on the lawyer..."

"*No*," I repeat, angrily this time. "I won't be posting his bail. In fact, if for some reason the justice system fails and he isn't thrown back in prison for this, I'll be filing a restraining order against him." I take a breath. "I never want to lay eyes on Joe Bailey again."

There's a short, shocked silence.

When she speaks again, I don't expect what comes out.

"You ungrateful little shit," my mother growls. "Do you realize how much he's done for you! How much we've both done for you! I gave you *life*—"

My jaw drops. "Really? You're going there, are you?"

"And now you have the chance to save your *brother's* life and you're deserting him? You're just going to let him rot in jail?" Her sobs grow louder. "Who *are* you! You're not my son! My son would never do something like this! I swear to God, Luke, if you do this you're not my son anymore!"

I feel perfectly hollow inside as she says this. She's never gone with the nuclear option before, but I feel strangely calm, anyway. Because we were always going to end up here.

"Okay," I finally whisper.

Mom's sobs literally cut off mid-wail. "Okay?" she says, standing up straighter. "You'll post bail?"

"No." I try to swallow the enormous lump in my throat. I fail. "Okay, then I guess you and I are done. Write me out of the will, Ma." My laugh is brittle.

"You little shit," she hisses. "No loyalty. Just like your father."

"Ma," I gasp, the insult catching me completely off guard. It's the deepest cut she's ever given me. My whole life she's referred to him as "that cruel man who did us a favor when he left."

"It's true," she says. "I'm sure you'll wind up as lonely as he is."

That's not a thing that mothers are supposed to wish for their sons. Then again, when has this woman ever been a *mother* to me? But even knowing that, a wave of sorrow crests over me just the same. This is really it, then. The last conversation we'll share. I ought to feel relieved, but I'm gutted instead.

Sucking in a breath, I take a step back toward the door. As I turn around, I don't miss the sight of faces in the window. People are watching my mother cast me out of her life, like they'd watch a fight at the hockey game.

I open the door and step inside. Without another word to the woman who gave birth to me, I close the door again and lock it. Then I bolt up the stairs—all of them—and escape to my room.

The shower waits for me. I turn the taps to a scalding temperature and shed my clothes.

Too bad shame doesn't wash off.

———

"Bailey."

Keaton's gruff voice reaches me as I pull on a clean T-shirt. He's in the doorway, concern written all over his handsome face.

"Are you okay?" he asks.

"I don't know. Does it matter?" The whole frat just witnessed my twenty-four-hour lifesplosion. I'm basically numb by now.

He steps forward, as if to hug me. But I just can't right now. I take an awkward step to the side and bend over my desk, rifling through my papers. "How much did the lawyer cost? I need to set up a payment plan with your dad."

"There won't be any payment plan," he says, letting his irritation out.

"Yeah, there will be. I don't want your dad rescuing me. I don't want anyone rescuing me."

"Even me?"

"Especially you. It wasn't even twenty-four hours ago when I pointed out to you that Alpha Delt would hate this." I make a motion between his body and mine. "I guess I called that one."

"They don't matter," he says quickly.

"At all?"

He swallows hard. "Whatever. I don't care."

"But maybe I do."

"You do *not*," he spits. "That's a cop-out. You're just looking for an excuse not to step out of your comfort zone! Shit got ugly and you bailed on me again."

"How is this a surprise to you? I don't like to owe people. You know this. I hate feeling like an ungrateful little bitch."

"So don't be one!" he roars. "And I'm not talking about money. That's beyond your control. When it comes to love, you're a fucking miser. Like it would kill you to admit that you care."

It *would* kill me, though. Because when I look at Keaton Hayworth III, I see the kind of man who can never be mine. Whatever he thinks he sees in me will eventually get old. One day soon he'll wake up and wonder what the hell he's doing with a punk who nobody else ever bothered to love. His obsession will fade.

Maybe it's because he gets sick of my bullshit. Or maybe another, badder bad boy catches his eye.

Either way, we were never going to last. I've never been more sure of anything in my life.

"It was just a hookup, Keaton," I say quietly.

"It wasn't."

"Yeah? When did you change the rules? Is this like the election all over again? You bend the regulations, and I fall in line?"

His neck gets instantly red. "You don't get to keep throwing that mistake in my face!"

"You make a lot of mistakes, apparently. I was the biggest one. Ask anyone downstairs. Go on."

He blinks, his eyes red. Then he lifts his aristocratic chin a couple of degrees. And he leaves my room.

CHAPTER 35
AS THICK AS YOUR HAND

KEATON

Another Sunday. Another brunch with Dad.

Except nothing at all is the same. I've just had the loneliest two weeks of my life, and I don't know where I'll find the energy to make nice with my dad.

This time I've changed the venue. I had to get out of the Alpha Delt house. So when classes ended on Friday, I got into my car and drove down to New York for the weekend.

But, shit, even driving down 95 made me think of my outing with Luke. The last weekend I got away from school was so amazing.

This time there's no sexfest and no drunken kisses. I crash at my father's tiny midtown condo for the weekend. It's where he sleeps when he doesn't want to go back to Long Island after late nights at work.

On Sunday morning I walk all the way from Midtown to the Upper West Side. Our plan is to have Sunday brunch at Good Enough to Eat. The Hayworths know how to party. And this place has slices of bacon as thick as your hand. It's almost good enough to cure my heartache.

Almost.

Two long weeks have passed since Luke's arrest, and he's still not really talking to me. Or sleeping with me. Or even looking me in the eye.

In fact, he's avoiding the house altogether.

And so am I, if I'm honest. I catch my friends giving me the side-eye sometimes. It's not like I think they're worried about catching gay cooties or anything. It's more like they can't figure out what to say. Anyone with eyes can see that Luke and I are on the outs. But I guess they think you can't use the same back slaps and tequila challenges to sweep away a breakup with a dude.

Although Tanner offered to take me out and get me drunk. And Dan Zimmer quite awkwardly offered his ear if I had any questions for him. "I could teach you the secret handshake," he'd joked.

But I turned them down. I'm not in the mood for anyone to make me feel better, I guess. So my gloomy face continues to discourage questions. And I'm still getting glances that range from curious to worried.

And sometimes it's Luke who is sneaking looks at me. On those rare occasions when we're both around, I see the regret in his eyes. He's not very good at hiding it.

I know he still wants me. I know he never stopped. But you can't make someone get over their issues and love you. I know that he's never had anyone trustworthy in his life, and I really want to be that person. But what if he's just too broken to let me?

Luke is much like an abused stray. Okay, now I'm comparing the guy I like to a dog. But animals are my jam, so that's actually a compliment from me. Anyway, you see these heart-wrenching videos of abused dogs who thrive with the right kind of attention. They gain weight, and their coats become glossy. If you believe YouTube, they're the most loyal animals in the world.

But if you read enough animal-behavior literature, you know it doesn't always end that way. Some dogs never get past their terror.

When I reach the corner of Columbus Avenue and West 85th, I'm already depressed. But I plaster on a pleasant face and cross the street to meet my dad.

Today's the day when I will finally tell him how to steer himself off the exit ramp of my life. So at least I have a plan.

It's a warm day in early May, so I scan the outdoor tables first. And—shit! My mother is the first person I spot. She's sitting there next to Dad.

I'm being tag-teamed. Awesome.

"Hey guys," I say, straightening my spine. Whatever I can say to one parent, I suppose I can say to two.

"Keaton!" My mother pops out of her chair. "Hi, baby!"

I kiss her on the cheek and force myself to smile.

The tables are tight, and my dad is trapped beside her, so he offers his hand to shake. Like real men do.

To be fair, he hasn't said a word about my little revelation. I honestly don't know what he thinks about me right now. But it doesn't change my message.

I take a seat, and the waiter swoops in. He has an Aussie accent and hipster glasses. He's pretty cute. Stuff like that just pops into my head all the time now, and I don't try to chase it out like I used to. So at least I have that going for me.

"I'll have the Lumberjack," I say before he can even offer me a menu. "And coffee. Thanks."

My parents order, and then we all just stare at each other for a second.

"How've you been?" Dad asks finally.

"All right. The end of the term is always hard."

"I hope you're getting enough sleep," Mom says.

"Plenty, actually." I clear my throat. Sleep isn't really an issue now that I'm alone in my bed every night.

"Also…" I decide to get it all out in the open before we eat. "I got this last week." I pull a piece of paper out of my pocket and unfold it. I hand it to my father and watch as he scans it.

Welcome to the Orca Expedition, it says. *Departing from Valparaíso, Chile, on May 19th*.

"I got in, and I want to go," I say. "It doesn't cost anything…"

"That was never the issue," Dad points out.

"Just saying." I sigh. "You wanted me to get a degree in biology."

"Or chemistry. Or finance," Dad adds.

"Finance was never happening," I tell him. "It's not the least bit interesting to me. And I'd be terrible at it. I really like biology, though. And I want to study animal behavior in graduate school after I leave Darby."

His shoulders sag. "But why? A PhD will take five years if you're fast and seven if you're slow. That's pushing back your employment at Hayworth Harper for years."

"That's just it, Dad. I don't want to work for you. I love research. I'm going to be an academic."

He groans. "Swear to God, can't you just be gay? Do you have to be an *academic,* too? It's like a dagger through the heart."

My jaw opens as wide as a python's before a meal.

The silence at the table drags on for several seconds, until Mom finally speaks. "Honey, is it serious with that boy?" she asks.

"No," I mumble. "But I wish it was."

Mom blinks.

Dad visibly swallows.

I search for the right words, but luckily the cute waiter returns. He puts a mug of coffee down in front of me. "Thank you," I say with genuine gratitude. Because I really need something to do with my hands.

"Keat," my mother says, covering his hand. "Talk to us."

"What do you want me to say?" I awkwardly wrap my hands around the mug. "That I'm gay? Because…yeah. I think I am."

Dad pounces on the *I think* part. "So you're not sure?"

I take a breath. Then I release it in a fast burst. "No, I am sure," I admit. "I guess I was trying to soften it up for you guys. But I'm certain about this. My relationship with—" I stop, rephrasing.

"Being in a relationship with a guy gave me all the answers I didn't even know I was searching for."

Mom nods slowly. "Annika…?" She lets the question hang, but I'm not entirely sure what she's asking.

"Annika didn't know," I say with a shrug. "I actually haven't even told her yet. But if you're worried that I was, I dunno, using her, or leading her on…I wasn't." My tone is firm, because it's the total truth. "I loved her, and our relationship was real to me. But there was always something…missing, I guess. Something that didn't feel entirely right."

This time Dad is the one nodding. "It always felt very platonic to us," he says grudgingly.

I eye him in surprise. "Seriously? All you did was talk about how much you wanted us to get married."

He shrugs. "Because she's a wonderful girl, and she'll make a wonderful wife to some lucky man. But if we're all being honest right now, your mother and I did notice that your relationship seemed to lack passion."

Mom sighs. "We did notice."

I have to smile. "And you couldn't have filled me in on that?"

They both break into nervous laughter.

I take a gulp of coffee, then set down the mug again. "I can't believe how cool you're being about all this."

Dad arches a brow. "Did you think we'd disown you?" he says dryly. "Who do I look like, your uncle Chris?"

Mom is quick to come to her brother's defense. "Christopher didn't disown Madeline! He just froze her trust fund until she completed her rehab program."

My cousin Maddie broke her back a few years ago and got hooked on painkillers. Uncle Chris wasn't thrilled. Fortunately, she's clean now.

I guess I won't point out that my father just compared my sexuality to a drug addiction. You have to pick your battles. "So you're *not* disowning me," I tease.

Dad rolls his eyes. "For your sexual orientation, no, Keaton. For your betrayal? I'm still considering it."

"Keat!" Mom chides, lightly swatting his shoulder.

"What if you came to work for the finance department after this expedition docks?" he suggests hopefully.

Somehow I knew he'd ask this. "I'm back in mid-July," I admit. "But I don't want the internship. I just don't want it. And we both know I don't deserve it. But I know someone who does."

"You want me to hire Bailey?" He hands the page back to me. "I am pretty sure they already made him an offer."

"Really?" This is a detail I hadn't heard. "He turned it down?"

"I'll ask Bo." Dad pulls his phone out of his pocket and taps the screen.

"Is this trip dangerous?" Mom asks. She's taking a turn with my Chile letter now.

"Not really," I hedge. "It's on a research boat in the ocean. But we're not diving with sharks, Mom. We'd be looking for a new species of whale."

"A new species?" She makes a skeptical face.

"I know, right? There's a strange kind of killer whale that people have reported once in a while over fifty years. But it's never been filmed or tagged. This expedition aims to prove that it exists."

"How is that more important than curing diabetes?" my father asks.

"I never said it was. But my interests are *my* interests. And nobody ever told you what to study."

"The hell they didn't." He snorts. "You think your grandfather was an easy man? He used to dig through my school bag for corrected tests and berate me for each missed math problem."

"And you think that's horrible?" I challenge him. "Because when you parse through my credit card charges to comment on my life, it's kind of the same."

He flinches. "You're an adult, Keaton. I'm sorry if I ever made you feel like I was checking up on you."

You were. I bite this criticism back, though, because it won't help me get what I want. "I'm going to Chile. And then graduate school. I'm sorry if you wanted me to take over the company someday. That's a nice idea, but I don't think it's in anyone's best interest."

He sighs. Then his phone chimes, and he picks it up. "Bo seems to think that Luke wanted the internship but didn't think he could make it work. Bo offered him an unpaid position."

"Oh." I feel a pain right between my ribs for Luke. A job he wants but can't afford? That's just cruel. "Luke can't work an unpaid internship. He barely has enough money right now to eat. He works late-night hours every weekend just to make the rent."

"Isn't there financial aid for that?" my mother asks.

"He has a full academic scholarship. But it only covers tuition. And his mother calls every couple of weeks asking him for money."

My father sits back in his chair, a disgusted look on his face. "What kind of mother asks her kid for money?"

"His kind."

Dad picks up his phone and starts tapping again.

"Honey, at the table?" my mother complains.

"Just a sec," he says. "I'm telling Bo to offer that kid an actual summer job and one of our corporate studios in Hoboken."

I wonder if Luke will kill me for interfering? Then again, what difference does it make? He's not currently talking to me. If he gets this job, he'll be better off and still not talking to me.

Yup. Worth it.

The waiter puts a plate down in front of me, overflowing with scrambled eggs, two big pancakes with strawberry butter and two thick slices of bacon.

Things are looking up. And let's face it, everything wrong in my life falls into the category of First World problems.

So I pick up my fork and tuck in.

———

As we're finishing breakfast, my mom talks me into visiting the Vermeer exhibit at the Metropolitan Museum of Art with her. "Come on, any good gay son would look at art with his mother."

I practically spray my coffee on the table. But since my parents are taking my career change—not to mention my sexuality— much better than I thought they would, I agree to go with her anyway.

By the time I get back to Darby, it's evening already. I climb the stairs to the third floor with the usual amount of trepidation. Lately, I'm always listening for Luke's key in the lock, so I can accidentally appear on the landing at the same moment.

Subtle of me, I know.

Tonight, though, I hit it just right. Luke is walking out of our bathroom and unable to reach the safety of his closed bedroom door before I arrive. "Hi," I say quietly.

"Hi." He jams his hands in his pockets. "If you had anything to do with the job offer I just got, I appreciate it."

"What job offer?" I say stiffly.

He rolls his amazing dark eyes.

"Fine. Go ahead and yell at me some more. I may have nudged my father into checking into your summer application. But it's only because I care about you."

Luke's gaze drops to the floor. "Thank you," he says so quietly that I almost can't hear. "I'm sure I don't really deserve it."

And before I can argue, he goes into his room and closes the door.

———

Two more torturous weeks pass. I'm not someone who gives up easily, but it's starting to look like this time I don't have a choice. Luke is still keeping me at arm's length, and I leave for Chile tomorrow.

It might be time to call it.

"No way," Annika's outraged voice exclaims out of the speakerphone. She's keeping me "company" while I pack for my expedition, and clearly she's not happy with the conclusions I've reached. "You're not calling it, Keaton. You care about this guy."

"Yeah, but he doesn't care about me," I protest.

She snorts loudly. "Ha! Of course he cares about you. Why else is he avoiding you this hard? He's running from his feelings."

I can't believe we're even having this conversation, but I can't deny that it feels nice to talk to someone about it. Judd and I are barely speaking, and while I'm on good terms with Tanner and the others, it's not like we sit around talking about my newfound gayness.

I'd been nervous as hell the day I told Annika, but she was so immediately supportive that I almost feel stupid for thinking she might *not* be. She's my best friend, and her warm response to my news only proves that she'll always be that.

"Maybe. But it doesn't change the fact that we're not together." I've been trying to chip away at Luke's defenses ever since his arrest, to no avail. He's a stubborn man, and it's obvious the events of the last month not only embarrassed him, but sent him right back to his default state of pure distrust.

"I'm leaving tomorrow morning," I say glumly. "And he hasn't even said goodbye yet."

"*Yet,*" she echoes. "I'm sure he will."

I'm not sure at all. These days, Luke's either holed up in the library or working at Jill's. He's so determined to keep his distance from me, I wouldn't be surprised if he didn't come home tonight at all.

"It's over, Ani. I don't know what else to do to get through to him. He's never going to fully open up to me. Or anyone, for that matter."

She gives a soft sigh. "Oh babe. I'm sorry. But I still don't think you should give up. Before he got arrested, he *was* opening up to you. Right? He was talking about himself, his feelings, that kind of stuff?"

"Yes, but feelings is a bit of a stretch. The only time I think he was truly transparent with me was when we were chatting on the —" I stop suddenly. The app.

That's *it*, the answer. Luke has never been great with face-to-face interactions, outside the sexual variety. But when we were getting to know each other on *Kink*, he was so candid, so beautifully honest, it was one of the reasons I wanted to meet him.

"I have to go," I tell my ex-girlfriend. "Just thought of something."

"Oooh! What's the plan?"

"Not a plan, really. I'll fill you in later."

After we hang up, I tear off a sheet of notebook paper and start scribbling. My final message to him, this man I never expected to fall for, is short and sweet.

> *L—I'm leaving tomorrow and so I just wanted to say goodbye. I'm hoping this isn't a forever goodbye. Really hoping that. For now, I'm giving you the space you so obviously need. But I have one request. Just one, and I promise it's not insanely unreasonable.*
>
> *Don't unmatch me on Kink.*
> *Love,*
> *KHIII*

Then I slide it under his door and hope for the best.

CHAPTER 36
WHO AM I KIDDING?

LUKE

It's nine o'clock on a July morning, and I've been at my desk for an hour and a half. I'm hopped up on free office coffee and I've already finished the project Bo gave me last night on his way out the door.

This desk is mine for only six more weeks. But I'm going to make every one of them count.

Bo—my boss and the CFO—finally saunters in, phone pressed to his ear. "Uh-huh. And why do we care if our options are bid up? Right. Gotcha. But can't we hedge out that interest rate risk?" He sits down in his chair and nudges his computer mouse to wake the system up.

I love working here, and I wish I could hear the other side of that call.

Instead, I tidy up the printouts I've prepared and staple the pages together. And when Bo hangs up, I pounce before someone else can steal his attention. "Hey! Morning. Here's the rates you asked me for." I drop the papers on his desk.

He blinks. "The convertible comps?"

"Yeah, see?" I flip past the cover page to show him all the data

I assembled from his Bloomberg terminal. "I know you said you only wanted drug companies, but I threw in a couple of medical equipment manufacturers because the data set was pretty small."

"I just asked you for this at eight last night."

"Sure. But your terminal has the data I needed, so I sat down after you left and knocked it out. So what's next?"

"Breakfast," he says. "And reading your report. Then I'll ask you to start looking at senior debt because our bankers want to talk about a long-term debenture."

"Sweet!" I say with undisguised enthusiasm.

He laughs. "Get a life, kid. I can't keep up with you."

"You are my life this summer." I'm not even joking. They're putting me up and paying me a terrific wage. I'm spending all my time here, learning the ropes. What else am I going to do, anyway? I have to save every penny I can. My textbooks for next term aren't going to buy themselves.

"And I appreciate that," Bo says. "But I'm old and I need caffeine and carbs. The hospital directors I entertained last night can sure hold their liquor." He digs his wallet out of his suit coat pocket. "I'll buy, you fly. Scrambled eggs with bacon and cheddar on a roll. And—"

"—double cappuccino with skim milk and cinnamon."

"Good man." He hands me a twenty. "I'll read your report while you're gone."

On my way toward the elevator, I stop by his administrative assistant's desk. "Marcy, I'm going down to Lenny's for breakfast. Anything I can bring you?"

"Luke Bailey, you are *dreamy*," she says, handing me a five-dollar bill. "I don't know what I'll do when you go back to school. Feed myself, I suppose. Please bring me a muffin. Corn or blueberry. I can't decide. And my usual tea."

"Yes, ma'am."

Five minutes later I'm rattling off our order and then stepping aside to wait for it.

Honestly, pleasing people at Hayworth Harper has been easier than I ever thought. All you have to do is pay attention and ask questions. I'm having a great time. And I feel calmer, somehow. Like it's all going to work out for me eventually.

I *really* needed to get out of Darby-fucking-Connecticut.

The deli is full of people dressed like I am—pressed shirts and trousers, in spite of the summer heat. Leather shoes, and corporate ID's on clips or lanyards. I don't mind being a worker drone. It's going to get me out of Darby for good.

Someone's order is called, and the line shuffles forward. My phone buzzes in my pocket with a notification. I'm not going to check it. The line is not that long.

Okay, who am I kidding? I'm totally going to check it.

At first, I didn't think it was a good idea to let Keaton text me this summer. I knew I'd hurt him. And while I'm not proud of it, it's hard to express how deeply freaked out I was by a one-night trip to jail. For weeks afterward I couldn't sleep. My brother had almost managed to blow up my entire life in a single weekend.

I felt stained, if not toxic. And I didn't want to take anyone else down with me.

When my terror eventually began to wear off, it was too late. Keaton had stopped giving me the kicked-puppy face, and he was all jazzed up for his trip to Chile. I didn't want to complicate his life, so I let him go.

Now I miss him terribly.

The phone in my pocket is yelling my name. Keaton is my big weakness, so I pull it out and open our favorite app. One of the first things I did after he left for Chile was to Google the places he was headed. And I learned that the waters where his expedition would travel have, according to National Geographic, "the worst weather in the world."

Honestly, that scared me almost as much as a night in jail.

So in spite of the fact that each new message from Keaton is— obviously—proof of life and doesn't really need to be speed-opened, I do it anyway. Because a message from him is still the highlight of my day.

Today I open up the app to find a photo of a calm sea and a purple sunrise. And, incredibly, a pod of dolphins variously breaching the surface of the water.

Day 47: We have calm seas, which is nice, but still no orcas. Last night at dinner I was thinking about you. Lots of things make me think of you, but this time it was lobsters. Remember that early text when I told you how lobsters have sex? I was sure you were going to block me just for being weird.

But since you're still reading these messages, here's something you probably don't know about lobsters in Chile. They don't have big claws! The claws are just not there where they should be. You see the legs, and then the antennae. And...no big hooked claws. Which means 1) they look more like bugs and 2) the lobster emoji is ALL WRONG down here.

I mean, my world is rocked.

Also, I still miss you. And I wonder what you're doing right now.

Until the next update. --K

"Bailey? Bailey?"

My chin snaps up as I realize the guy behind the counter has been calling my name. "Thank you," I say quickly, taking the bag and the molded paper tray with the drinks on it. I head back out the door and down the block to the office.

I haven't been chatting up Keaton, because I promised myself I wouldn't play with his emotions. But I feel the tug. It would be so easy to slide back into our familiar conversation. And into bed, of course. Some nights I miss him so badly that my chest aches. He's my only regret.

The rest of my life feels so optimistic now. Like maybe I can have some of the things I never thought I deserved.

The lobby of Hayworth Harper is teeming. I wave my ID past the sensor, and the turnstile gate slides open. Every time it does that I feel irrationally happy. *You belong here*, it says.

There's an elevator that's just about to leave, so I hop inside as the doors begin to close. Everyone else on the elevator looks a little stiff, and I don't realize why until a voice says, "Luke Bailey."

I look up into Keaton Hayworth Jr.'s face, and realize that I've lunged into the elevator with the CEO. "Hello, sir. Good morning."

"Isn't it?" He chuckles. "I see you've made a run to the deli for Bo. After last night, he needed an egg sandwich, didn't he?"

"There may be some truth to that, sir."

He snickers. "Keaton likes those egg sandwiches, too. I think they might be the only thing he ever liked about Take Your Kid to Work Day. Have you heard from my son lately? I shouldn't have Googled his expedition. It says that part of the Pacific has, and I quote…"

"The worst weather in the world?"

"You read that page too, huh?"

We both step aside to let a few people off the elevator. I pull my phone out of my pocket and open the app, blowing up the photo to cover the whole screen. "See? Smooth sailing today."

He gazes at the photo. "That is just incredible. I'm happy to see that." He hands back my phone with sigh. "If I wasn't so pushy last year I might be getting those photos, too."

Okay, *awkward*. I keep my mouth shut, because I refuse to weigh in on the boss man's parenting in an elevator full of coworkers.

"At least he's coming home soon," he says. "Just two and a half weeks more."

My stomach lurches, and it isn't because of the elevator. I knew Keaton's summer excursion was shorter than my internship. But I can't believe it's only two and a half weeks. How do I become a completely new man in two and a half weeks?

I can't, obviously.

The elevator reaches the executive floor, and the doors part, and we both step out. "Better give that sandwich to Bo before he expires at his desk." Mr. Hayworth puts a hand on my shoulder. "Thanks for showing me the photo."

"Anytime, sir." *Depending on the photo.*

Honestly, texting Keaton was some of the most fun I had all year. And then I let my fucked-up life ruin it.

I deliver food and drink to my grateful colleagues and take care to give them their change.

Then I go back to my desk with the sandwich I bought for myself. I set the bag on the desk. I take a photo of the bag and open up the app on my phone.

I'm going to text him back. He deserves that, and so much more. I'm still a wreck. And we're still complicated. But at least I can reply to a fucking message.

He said I was stingy with love, and he was right. I am really not sure that will ever change. But if there's anyone in the world I could change for, it's certainly him.

Dear Lobstershorts, I saw your dad today. He asked me if I'd heard from you. I hope you don't mind that I showed him the photo you sent me. He was really happy to see it, and honestly a little mopey that you haven't been in contact.

He also told me that you like Lenny's sandwiches. I'm definitely a fan.

TL;DR: My pics aren't half as cool as yours, but I want you to know that I'm pulling myself together. Mostly. Well, I'm probably still the same disaster you always knew. I know you deserve better than what I gave you. I don't know if I'll ever be boyfriend material. But I'm working on my outlook.

I'm going to eat this sandwich now and then compile a report on interest rates of senior debt across the yield curve. Which is fun, I promise.

You take care. Keep the photos coming. Even if I'm hopeless at relationships I still look forward to every one of them.

I hit Send, and then eat my sandwich.

———

An hour later I'm composing a beast of a spreadsheet when my phone buzzes with a new message. My greedy heart immediately thinks: Keaton!

Hi there, tortured psyche. It's me again.

It's not him, though. But it's almost as good. Mr. Grant, my lawyer, has sent me an email exactly one line long. ***Charges officially dismissed today. It's over. Take care!***

He doesn't say whether Joe was convicted or not. Before leaving Darby, I was interviewed by a detective, who took notes about my brother's visit to the frat and about my stolen ID. And Jako had to do the same.

I don't know if my brother is behind bars or not right now, because I blocked both his and my mom's phone number. That feels...shitty, honestly. But I have to stay strong. If I let them into my life, they'll bleed me dry—emotionally and financially.

And if I don't cut them out completely, I'll spend the next twenty-one years waiting for some kind of epiphany that never comes. *We're sorry. We love you.*

It's embarrassing how much I want to hear that. And never will.

But I have interest rates to console me. I make a few more entries on my spreadsheet, and then I get stuck and have to pop into Bo's colleague's cubicle and ask a question. "Hey, Jim? Do I put the double-A and the double-A-minus on the same column?"

"Yup," he says. "Sure."

"Thanks."

"Hey, Bailey?" the younger man calls as I am about to leave.

"Yeah?"

"You're gonna apply to come back after graduation, right?"

"I really don't know." I'd need a job opening, for starters.

"You're gonna get a lot of offers," Jim says, tugging on his necktie. "Just don't forget our number, okay?"

"Don't worry, I won't." *A lot of offers.* That's such a foreign concept to me. "How does the recruitment program work, anyway?"

"I'll check," he says. "I think there's some kind of signing bonus for guys who lock us in before New Year's."

"Really," I say slowly. I could have a job *five months* before graduation? And a signing bonus? "That could knock some serious hours off my work schedule second semester."

"What do you do during the school year?" he asks.

Oh, shit. "I work in a club."

"Bartender? Bouncer?"

He's just making conversation, and I should never have mentioned a job at school. But it's not a good idea to lie to my future employer. Jim might even be my boss if I show up here next year. "I'm a male entertainer," I tell him with a smile that's more confident than I feel. "You might call it a stripper."

"Ha!" He slaps the desk. "Good one, kid. Now how long until you finish that report?"

"Half hour?" I squeak.

"Cool. I'll be waiting."

Relieved, I walk away.

A lot of offers. That sentence sort of echoes through my head as I go back to my desk. And as I sit down in my ergonomic chair, something unfamiliar unfurls in my chest.

I think it might be optimism.

CHAPTER 37
BEEF JERKY

KEATON

"Ahoy matey! Beef jerky?"

I glance up from my book as Mateo bounds into the minuscule cabin we've been sharing for the past five weeks. He thrusts out his hand, offering me a stick of dried jerky.

I almost gag. "Seriously? Do you *want* me to keep you up all night as I'm hurling my guts out into poor Lucy?" I nod ruefully toward the bright red bucket underneath the small desk that's bolted to the cabin floor.

Nothing in this room is unsecured. The way the *Esmeralda* rocks and pitches and lurches and dips, no item is safe. Even Lucy, my puke bucket, is secured with a bungee cord to one desk leg.

I'm not going to lie—the sea and I aren't the best of friends. I'm not a novice to sailboats, and normally I love being out on the open water, but this stretch of ocean near Cape Horn is brutal. The waves are choppy and the wind is constantly gusting. After five weeks, my stomach has settled for the most part, but when it's storming outside like it is tonight, I try not to eat.

My roommate, on the other hand, is addicted to eating. You'll never see Mateo without food in his hands. Beef jerky, fruit, granola bars, those sunflower seeds he munches on and spits over the deck every morning. It's a wonder he's as thin as he is, considering how much stuff he shovels into his mouth.

"*Dios mio!*" he says, blanching. "No, please don't bring out Lucy. I can't suffer through that again."

I grin at him. Honestly, I lucked out having such a cool roomie. Mateo is a grad student at the University of Miami, and this is his third summer on an expedition like this. He's also fluent in four languages, and he's been teaching me the dirtiest phrases. Luke would love him.

Ugh. I was hoping not to think about Luke today. But who I am kidding, I think of him *every* day. I've messaged him non-stop since I left Darby, but aside from that one message about deli sandwiches and my dad, he's been disappointingly quiet.

"Doc VanBoerk is setting up a poker game in the galley," Mateo says as he munches on his beef jerky. He chews loudly before speaking again. "I told him we'd be there soon."

I groan, my gaze darting toward the tiny porthole. It's way past sunset, so I can't actually see anything, but the incessant rocking of the boat tells me the waves are probably pretty huge. The last time we tried playing poker during a storm, the chips kept rolling off the galley table and bouncing onto the ground.

"C'mon, what else are you gonna do?" Mateo coaxes. "Read? You read too much, Keaton! Come experience life!"

I hide a smile. I guess "experiencing life" means playing cards with a bunch of science geeks, including our Dutch captain whose best friend is a dolphin named Pippy. Dr. VanBoerk runs a marine-life sanctuary in Florida, where he and his staff rescue animals affected by oil spills and rehabilitate them. He's a pretty awesome dude.

So I haul myself off the bottom bunk and join Mateo and the others in the galley. We play poker as the *Esmeralda* bobs in the angry waves like a cork in a wine bottle. Afterward, Mateo and I head back to our bunk. He passes out almost instantly. Me, I make use of the very shitty Wi-Fi signal to send a quick message.

LobsterShorts: Stormy again tonight. I swear, I'm popping anti-nausea tablets like candy!

To my shock, Luke replies within seconds.

SinnerThree: Still seasick??

LobsterShorts: Only when the water's rough. Which here, apparently, is all the time.

SinnerThree: What are you doing up so late?

It's past midnight in Chile, so just after eleven in Connecticut.

LobsterShorts: Playing poker with the crew. I lost 50 bucks.

SinnerThree: Of course you did. You suck at poker.

I smile at the screen. Fuck, I've missed him. Missed the easy flow of conversation between us. Which is why it kills me to have to sign off.

LobsterShorts: I should go. I need to be up at six tomorrow. Just wanted to say a quick good night.

SinnerThree: Big day planned?

LobsterShorts: I hope so! We dropped anchor four days ago and still no Big Willy sighting. Tomorrow will be the day!

SinnerThree: God. You are such a dork. Good luck!

I power off my phone and tuck it inside the desk drawer, then burrow my body under the thin covers and fall asleep with a smile on my face.

————

The next morning, everyone is back in expedition mode. According to reports, the mysterious orca species we're hunting was spotted at these coordinates less than a week ago. Several accounts describe seeing a small pod of killer whales. One actually swam close to the fishing vessels, and two fishermen reported that the whale looked smaller than usual, with a narrow, pointy dorsal fin not normally seen on your typical orca.

I've been calling our elusive friend Big Willy. But once again, Willy and his crew are determined to remain hidden.

I can't complain, though. I'm standing on the bow of a 155-foot research vessel, with the sun shining down on my face. Sure, it's windy out, but today it's more of a warm breeze as opposed to a cool gust. Next to me, Mateo is using a sharp switchblade to peel off pieces of a mango.

"Are you excited to go home and see your friend?" he asks as he pops a piece of fruit into his mouth.

He always refers to Luke as my "friend." I don't think he's homophobic, nor does he seem uncomfortable with the idea that I was dating a man before we embarked on this voyage. So I always let it slide.

"I don't know if I will," I admit. "It's the summer, and usually I stay at our house in Easthampton. Luke is somewhere in Hoboken."

"Then you should go to Hoboken and shack up." The breeze snakes under Mateo's shoulder-length brown hair, rustling the long strands.

I snort. "My dad will kill me if I miss the annual Hayworth barbecue."

"Then go after that. You want to see him, don't you?"

"Of course." So much that my heart hurts. But since I left, Luke hasn't once mentioned us seeing each other again.

"Then go." Mateo gobbles down another piece of mango. "Make the first move."

I mull over the advice for the rest of the morning, but reach no conclusions. If I'm being honest, I don't *want* to make the first move. I already made it before I left. I tried talking to him, connecting with him, reaching out to him. He pushed me away.

And since I've been gone, I've messaged him every single day. I've made it more than clear that I'm thinking about him and that I miss him. That I want us to be a couple, a real committed couple, when I return.

And he's distant.

So why should I be the one to fight for us? And is there even a point in fighting for someone who doesn't want to love you?

———

The following morning is more of the same. No Big Willy sightings, so Doc VanBoerk organizes a dive to observe a school of Patagonian toothfish. Which is so fucking fascinating that I'm grinning from ear to ear by the time I'm hauling off my SCUBA gear.

I can't believe I almost got pressured into a *finance* internship at Hayworth Harper Pharmaceuticals. To think, I would have missed seeing the Patagonian toothfish!

I'm so pumped that I message Luke via *Kink* the second I'm back in my bunk. Although it's the middle of a workday, he responds swiftly. In fact, the last few days his replies have been quick and reliable. It's almost enough to get my hopes up. Almost.

SinnerThree: I have so many geek jokes I could make right now. But...I'm just going to say, congratulations on catching a toothfish?

I'm aghast as I type, **Catching?? Are you insane, Bailey? We were just observing. No fish were harmed in the making of this expedition.**

SinnerThree: LOLOL I guess it's probably not a good idea to catch a toothfish. They have teeth, I assume?

LobsterShorts: Pointy ones.

SinnerThree: Christ. Yeah. Stay away from that nightmare. I would never, ever eat something called a toothfish.

LobsterShorts: I hate to break it to you, but... You already have.

SinnerThree: What! Explain yourself!

I'm shaking with laughter as I compose a response. Fuck, I've missed this so much.

LobsterShorts: The Patagonian toothfish has an alias. Also goes by the name Chilean seabass. Which is what I believe you ordered at the restaurant in Stonington?

I immediately regret bringing up our weekend at the hotel.

That's when Luke got arrested and everything fell apart for us. Shit. He's definitely going to bail now.

To my surprise, he doesn't.

SinnerThree: Seriously? That was the best fish I ever had! Why does it have two names?

LobsterShorts: Because some fisherman back in the day decided the toothfish needed a name that sounded more enticing to the American fish market. He went with Chilean seabass.

SinnerThree: Good call.

LobsterShorts: But enough about me. How's work going?

SinnerThree: It's awesome.

I wait for more details, but they don't come. I stifle a sigh.

LobsterShorts: Glad to hear it.

SinnerThree: Speaking of work, I should get back to it. Keep me posted on the Big Willy hunt.

He signs off, and I'm left feeling equal parts encouraged and *dis*couraged. Once again, he pulled back. But he did request I keep him posted. So…that's progress.

Right?

———

LobsterShorts: GUESS WHO I SAW TODAY!!!

SinnerThree: Do I dare? Could it be…?

LobsterShorts: Big Willy! And not just him. There were about twenty of 'em in the pod. And holy shit, babe, they were spectacular. I can't even describe the experience. It was…beautiful. Like, witnessing these creatures that nobody knew existed just swim up to the boat. They circled us for hours, almost like they were as curious about us as we were about them. It left me breathless.

I wait for Luke to come back with something witty. Maybe tease me, or, if he's feeling edgy, mock me about my sheer joy over seeing some whales.

He does none of those things.

SinnerThree: I've missed you.

My breath catches. Did I misread that? I blink a few times, but those three words remain the same. He's missed me.

I'm shaking as I sit up on my bed. As much as I want to babble on and on about the whales, this is way more monumental.

LobsterShorts: I've missed you too.

No answer.

LobsterShorts: Can I see you when I get back?

SinnerThree: We're in the same frat. You'll see me all the time.

LobsterShorts: That's not what I mean and you know it.

No answer.

LobsterShorts: Bailey?

No answer.

Frustration tightens my throat. Damn it. It's always one step forward, two steps back with this man.

LobsterShorts: I know you're still there. I know you're reading this, and I know you'll just run away again if I try to push the issue. So this is what's going to happen, Luke Bailey. I get home in two weeks. I'll be landing at JFK and heading straight for my folks' place in Easthampton.

I draw a deep breath and ask myself if I'm an idiot. Is there a point to this, or am I chasing after someone who just isn't into me? I desperately want to believe Luke feels the same way, but he refuses to communicate with me, so I can't be certain about his feelings. I can't be certain about anything.

LobsterShorts: Our annual Hayworth barbecue is the day after I return. July 22. This is your official invitation.

Still no answer, but I wasn't expecting one. I can almost picture Luke at this moment, sitting at his desk at work, or maybe having lunch alone somewhere. His gorgeous features creased with anxiety, his teeth digging hard into his bottom lip as he contemplates every word I'm saying.

LobsterShorts: I miss you and I want to be with you. I want a relationship with you. And I'm no longer interested in hearing

excuses. **My family doesn't care. The frat will get over them-selves. Your hesitation has nothing to do with any of the excuses you gave me last month. It has everything to do with you being afraid. Of me, of trusting someone. Of loving someone. And I'm telling you, here and now, you don't have to be afraid. But what you do need to do is decide. Decide if we're worth the risk.**

Although it kills me to type my next message, it needs to be said.

LobsterShorts: I'm going to give it until midnight. If you show, then that means you're ready to give our relationship a chance. If you don't, then...I'll have no choice but to move on. I can't pine over you forever.

I'm breathing hard as I finish my epic speech.

LobsterShorts: Come to Easthampton, Luke. Take the risk.

CHAPTER 38
OUR SUPERPOWER

KEATON

Like I've said before, the Hayworths know how to throw a party. It's our super power. There's a giant smoker on the beach. Caterers in paper hats hand out brisket sandwiches and spicy chicken legs. There's rum punch and beer and music for our two hundred guests.

The annual barbecue is my favorite Hayworth party. *Was* my favorite one. I've ruined it for myself this year. I've spent the last hour standing here looking down the beach like an idiot, wondering if a certain dark-haired hottie is going to step off the tram my father hired to ferry people from the train station to our fete.

Luke isn't here, though. I watch the tram drive away again, empty. It's after eight o'clock already.

"Keaton," Annika chides. "Stop it."

I turn back to her with a sigh. "Sorry."

"Eat one of these." She thrusts a plate in my face filled with finger sandwiches. "They're cucumber and crab salad."

That does sound good. I shove one into my mouth and chew. It's good to be back on land. It's good to be on a pristine beach in the sunshine, surrounded by people who like me and aren't afraid to say so.

So why do I feel so crummy?

"Now taste this." Annika offers me her cup of punch. It's sweeter than I like, but I take a sip anyway. "Now come this way," my bossy ex-girlfriend insists, clamping her manicured hand over my wrist. "We're going to play badminton."

I laugh, because Annika isn't a fan of sports. "You don't have to do this."

"Yeah, I do. I'm tired of seeing that mopey look on your face. Just be gentle." She disposes of our food and drinks, and then hands me a racquet.

I duck under the net to take up a position.

"Oh no, you don't. Your spot is over *here*." She points at the opposite side of the net, the one where I won't be able to watch for the tram.

Yup, she's got my number.

"Besides, if I let you take that side, you'll play distracted. You'll get whacked in the forehead with a birdie, and the guys will call you Cyclops."

I laugh again, and it's not hard to figure out why I spent so much time with Annika. Maybe she and I aren't sexually compatible anymore, but she's a great friend.

"Heads up, Hayworth," she says as she serves.

I return the birdie, nice and easy, and soon we have a nice volley going. I play each return trying not to get her out, but rather to keep the birdie in play. I'm sure she can tell that I'm taking it easy on her. But she tries to ace me anyway.

And then she succeeds. I hear the sound of the tram approaching, and I miss the next shot.

Annika falls to her knees in the sand, like Serena declaring a Wimbledon victory. I move to turn around and she barks at me, "No, Hayworth! Stay with me! Don't go toward the light!" She stands up and peers toward the tram herself. She gives a single shake of her head that dashes my hopes.

I'm just a guy, standing on a beach in nothing but his favorite pair of lobster shorts, waiting for the right man to love me.

"Your serve," Annika says cheerfully.

We go back to our game, and I allow myself to be distracted. "I get next game!" calls Henry, Annika's younger brother.

"Sure, pal." I bounce the birdie back to Annika, enjoying the sun on my face. It's winter in Chile, so the summer temperatures are a balm on my soul.

When I hear the tram again, I don't turn around. I hit the birdie over the net.

Annika makes a little squeak of surprise, though, and returns it to me sloppily. I miss my next shot because I'm already turning around.

A guy has just stepped off the tram. His dark hair shines in the sun. Wearing mirrored sunglasses, a polo shirt and khaki trunks, he surveys the crowd a little uncertainly.

"Luke!" Annika yells.

He turns his handsome face in our direction.

That's when Jim, a dude from the finance division, steps up to him, slapping him on the back, then shaking his hand.

I see Luke's eyes dart toward me, then back to Jim. Luke can't be rude. He probably reports to Jim at work. He's drawn into a conversation.

"Oh, crap," Annika says. "We could rescue him."

"No, it's okay," I say, tossing my racquet to Henry. "I'm patient. And I don't want to make a scene."

Luke doesn't need that, either. He's surrounded by guys from Hayworth Pharma now. And even though I'm impatient, it's cool to see how many people he knows. Someone hands him a beer. Bo, the CFO, steps in and introduces him to several more people.

I wait.

"This is so romantic," Annika whispers beside me. "He's almost free. Except...darn it!"

Now Luke is captured by Marcy, Bo's secretary. She is clearly smitten. She pats his arm and pinches his cheek. When she hugs him, Luke looks right over her shoulder at me. *Oh my God*, he mouths.

I let out a bark of laughter, and Annika covers her mouth as she giggles.

"Who is that guy?" Annika's brother asks, twirling his racquet in his hands.

"He's my..." I swallow hard. "Boyfriend," I say carefully, hoping its true.

"*Reallllly*," Henry says, drawing the word out, sounding stunned.

I hope it's true, anyway. Would he come to this party after that ultimatum I gave him and then reject me?

Either way, I'm about to find out. He disentangles himself from Marcy and begins crossing the sand. I tense as he waves to a couple more guys, but he manages not to get drawn in.

My God, he's handsome. I'm rooted in the sand, just dazzled all over again by his square-shouldered swagger. I don't come unstuck until he reaches up and pulls those sunglasses off, revealing a vulnerable expression. "Hi, Lobsterman," he says quietly. "Somebody told me that missing this party would be a huge mistake."

"It's true," I say, my throat constricting. "It would be a damned shame."

And I don't even know who moves first. But he's in my arms a heartbeat later. Our hug happens so fast that it sloshes his beer. He holds it out to the side and laughs as his free hand wraps around my lower back.

I put my lips on his neck and inhale. "God, I missed you."

"Same," he says in a low voice. "I'm sorry I've been such a dick."

"You're not so bad," I stammer as my throat tightens again. "Better late than never." I take one more deep breath of his scent —sunshine and spicy aftershave. Then I make myself take a step back.

Luke gives me a shameless full-body onceover. "You're right. This is a beautiful beach."

"Isn't it?" Annika giggles, reminding me that we aren't alone.

Although alone sounds really good right now.

"Why don't you give Luke a tour?" she chirps.

The girl is a genius. "Can I show you around?"

"I'm all yours," he says. And then he does something I've never seen Luke Bailey do before. He blushes. It's adorable.

"Go on, you two. I have some badminton to win here."

"As if," her brother snarks.

I clear my throat. "Want the tour?"

CHAPTER 39
IT'S A SUN SHELF

LUKE

"Sure," I say in a hoarse voice. This is obviously a great party but I feel so raw right now. Showing people that I care doesn't come easily to me. I feel like my skin is peeled back, exposing things that have never seen the light of day.

Besides, it's been way too long since I was alone with Keaton.

"Then right this way," he says, gesturing inland, where I assume the house awaits.

I follow him up the path from the beach, and discover that the party is twice as large as I'd assumed. The beach path gives way to a manicured lawn and then a palatial pool area.

"Are those chairs *in* the pool?" I ask, trying to make sense of the layout.

Keaton chuckles. "That part of the pool is just four inches deep. The realtor called it a 'sun shelf,' whatever the fuck that is. But on a hot day it's totally the place to be."

Honestly, it looks like heaven. Barefoot guests are draped all over the six cushioned chaise lounges in the water. Drinks in hand, they are living the dream.

But it's crowded here. Various partygoers stop Keaton and slap him on the back. "K3!" an older man says. "How's college?"

"Great, Mr. Brown," he says, giving the man the politest of brushoffs. He keeps moving. "I'd introduce you to everyone here," he says quickly. "But I kind of want you to myself."

"Noted," I say. "Can't say I'm in the mood to schmooze when I can get the private tour with you."

This wins me a lingering glance from the shirtless hottie in the lobster shorts.

My impatience, coupled with the scope of the Hayworth's spread, make the trip toward the house seem long. We pass a pool house, a covered pavilion with a bar area, a tent sheltering a DJ, and a hundred more people sipping tropical drinks.

"We used to have a little beach house, like normal rich people," Keaton says as we skirt the edge of the crowd. "But then Dad traded up to this place when I was in high school." He rolls his beautiful eyes. "This crazy pool. The private beach. Clay tennis courts." He points toward the fenced-in courts. "Do you play?"

"Tennis? What do you think, Hayworth?"

He gives me a sly smile. "I think I like it when you surprise me, that's all. And tennis would suit you, 'cause you're quick on your feet."

"Aw shucks," I say in my usual cool manner. But the flattery hits me square in the chest. "Maybe you can teach me."

"Yeah?" He lights up. "That would be so fun. The tennis pro that Mom has on call is good eye candy too, just saying."

I laugh out loud. "Male or female?"

"Oh, it's a dude. A dude in tight white shorts."

"Does your mom know you think he's hot?" I'm still trying to figure out Keaton's family.

"Of course. We've had long discussions about his hotness, and how we don't like to serve the ball into the net when he's watching." He leads me around to the front of the house.

And then finally we reach the house itself—a low-slung

modern structure that looks like something you'd see on the cover of an architecture magazine. There's a living room that can't decide if it's indoors or outdoors—it's completely open on one side. But Keaton bypasses that to lead me around to the side, where there's an ordinary screen door into the kitchen.

He holds the door open and I step into a ridiculously large kitchen that's teeming with caterers. "Oh for fuck's sake," Keaton hisses, taking my elbow and steering me through the madness. "It's Grand Central Station in here."

We exit the kitchen on the other side, stepping into a quiet space. It's a grand hallway with art on the walls and a thick carpet underfoot.

We're the only ones here. Finally. So I do what needs doing. I grab Keaton with two hands and back him up against the modern stone tiles on the wall. Then I lift a hand to his perfect scruffy chin and kiss him. Hard.

"Oflug," he says against my lips. It takes him maybe three seconds to get over his surprise. And then two hands yank me closer.

Like I said, I'm not used to laying myself bare. But right this second I don't have a choice. Keaton parts my lips with his tongue, and I moan the second I taste him. What was I ever thinking? I need this man. And even if being half a couple doesn't come easily to me, I have to try. Nobody has ever gotten under my skin the way he does. Nobody has ever needed me the way he does.

Not one person.

It's terrifying.

Still. I don't pull away yet, because the things I want are bigger than my fear. I want the slide of his mouth against mine, and I want the hum of pleasure he makes when I kiss him back. And I want the happy sigh I make when he holds me closer.

Yeah, I've got it bad.

I don't pull back until we both need air. And even then, I tip my forehead against his and stare into his eyes. "I really missed you." Four little words. So hard to say, but his quick smile makes it worth it.

"Missed you, too," he says quietly.

I ease back to stand up straight again and look around. This place is like a museum. Art everywhere. "So this is the Hayworth beach mansion, eh? This is where the magic happens."

"Isn't it obnoxious?" Keaton spreads his arms wide. "You are probably disgusted."

I turn around, where there's another vast living room and more windows that open onto the ocean. Even in here you can hear the low roar of the surf. "That's not what I think at all. I think it's an amazing house. And honestly someday I hope I can figure out how to own one just like it."

"Huh. Maybe we can go halfsies," Keaton suggests. "Hey, you brought a bag?"

I look down at the rug, where my gym bag fell sometime right after I got a taste of Keaton's kiss. "Yeah, just in case I had somewhere I needed to stay. There's a train back to Penn Station at eleven, though. And another one just before two a.m."

Keaton bends over and grabs my bag off the floor. "Come on," he says.

"Where are we headed?" I follow him down the hallway.

"My room. Duh." He leads me toward a big wooden door. Its surface is roughly hewn, like beach wood. Yet it opens neatly to reveal a killer bedroom. The big windows are open, and the DJ's music floats past tasteful white curtains and a surf board suspended on wall brackets.

There's also a king-sized bed, which I try not to stare at.

"You surf?" I ask, because that sounds like fun.

"A little. The Hamptons doesn't always have great waves. The guys who are really into it spend a lot of time driving around looking for action."

"Like me on the apps in the olden days," I joke.

Keaton turns around with a serious expression on his face. "But not lately?"

"No," I say quietly. "I met this great guy and kind of lost my taste for hookups." I look away then, because old habits die hard.

Keaton's room might be fancy, but it's lived-in. There's a stack of paperback thrillers on the dresser beside a sandy Frisbee. (See, he is a yellow lab!) And also…a black silk top hat?

"Stay here with me tonight," he says. "I really want you to."

"Yeah, I want that, too." I make myself look right at him again, and I know he can see how much I really do want it. "But only…" I cross the room and grab the top hat. "Only if you can tell me why you have this in your room. Did you mug an eighty-year-old?"

He laughs. "No, but I wore it in a wedding."

"Is there photographic evidence?" I ask.

"Probably. Besides, that hat is sexy," he insists. "When I wear it, the babes are drawn to me like moths to a flame."

"Uh-huh. Let's see." I flip it around in my hand and then drop it on my head. Then I move my body in a wave motion to the beat of the music, just to make Keaton laugh.

He doesn't, though. "I rest my case. You look hot when you do that."

"Yeah?" I flip the hat off my head and slide to the right, flipping it on again. "Hmm. See, if I were still dancing, I'd try to make something out of this. Props are fun." I turn around, toss it in the air, and then somehow slide into just the right spot to let it land on my head.

"Keep going," Keaton says, sprawling out on the foot of his bed to watch me. "Do you miss dancing?"

"No," I say, and then think for a moment. "Not really. I didn't like having to be 'on' when I wasn't feeling it. But it had its moments. That pole kept me in terrific shape. And sometimes…" I slap my own ass and slide toward the bed with a dirty grind. "… sometimes all those eyes on me were fun. When the whole crowd is screaming for you, that's a great moment."

"So how would you make a new routine?" he asks, sitting up. "Break it down for me."

"Hmm. Okay." I know Keaton has always wanted to watch me, and I never gave in. Tonight's the night, then. I came all this way to give the man what he wants. "This song works pretty well, honestly. It has a nice steady riff."

The track is "Girls Like You" by Maroon Five. I swing my hips and let Adam Levine's voice slide down my soul. With a flick of my wrist, I remove the hat and hold it between my hands.

A quick drop into a faux split makes Keaton's eyes widen. "Oh, hell yes," he says, laughing. "Keep going."

Popping up again, I circle my hips in time with the beat. Keaton's hot gaze is pasted on me, and I love his attention. Without dropping the rhythm, I toe off my shoes and kick them out of the way. I don the hat, and ease my way across the room in a sensuous roll of torso and shoulders. Then I start in on the buttons of my shirt, teasing them open one by one.

When I run my hands down my bare chest, Keaton flops back onto the bed with a groan. "I'm dead," he says. "Three months without you and now this. It's the best kind of torture."

"Then it's working," I say, adding some footwork while he watches with wide eyes. "Stripping is all about the tease."

"You're great at teasing," he grumbles. "Get over here already."

"Oh, I'd like to. But I can't fuck you during a party at your parents' house." Anyone could look through the window, or walk in here looking for the john.

He sighs. "I suppose not. Want to go swimming? Maybe that will cool the fire in my trunks."

"Sure, LobsterShorts. Take me swimming."

He sits up and smiles at me, and that smile makes me stupid.

How did it take me so long to trust this man? "Keaton?"

"Yeah?"

"I love you. And I'm sorry I couldn't figure out how to get over my own bullshit before and just be your guy."

He swallows. "Can you be now?"

"I want to. If you'll let me try."

He gets off the bed. "Come here." He pulls me into a hug. "We have to go swimming now, otherwise I'm going to maul you."

"Okay," I whisper in his ear.

"I love you, too. I know it's easier for me to get there than it was for you. I don't blame you for your scars."

"Thank you," I mumble. I wrap my arms around his wide body and sigh. "Are we really going to go outside and pretend we're not just counting the minutes until we can take each other's swimsuits off?"

"I have an idea," he says. "Follow me."

He walks out of the room, and I hurry after him down another hall I didn't notice before. He grabs two striped beach towels off a stack and keeps going.

We leave the house again. But we don't go back to the party. We cross the darkening side lawn and then a driveway paved with white stones. "Is this all your property?" I ask.

"Nope." He leads me farther, until I spot another house and another pool. "We're going to the neighbor's."

"Why? Where's the neighbor?"

He hooks a thumb back toward his place. "Enjoying the free food and booze, courtesy of my parents. Mrs. Pennyworth won't be home for hours. She closed down the party last year."

Sure enough, the neighbor's house is dark. The sky is a deep blue now, heading towards black. The only lights on here are in the pool itself, underwater.

Keaton tosses the towels onto a chair. And then? He tugs the lobster shorts off his trim hips and drops them, too. Naked, he walks to the edge of the pool and dives in.

Hayworths really do know how to party. He wasn't wrong about that.

I quickly shed my own suit, looking over both shoulders, hoping nobody is watching. But nobody is. I follow him into the water, which is a surprisingly comfortable temperature.

This is the Hamptons. It's heated, of course.

"Wow," I say when I come up for air again. "I like the way you think." I swim over to Keaton, who's sitting on what turns out to be an underwater bench. "This pool is nice."

"But they don't have a sun shelf," Keaton says, teasingly.

"You're right. Piece of trash, then. I'll renovate after I buy the place from Mrs. Pennysworth."

Keaton doesn't laugh, though. He wraps an arm around my shoulders and kisses my neck.

I let out a hot breath. And as his mouth makes a slow journey across my skin, I close my eyes and let the sensation push every thought from my mind. In just seconds, I have goosebumps and a hard cock. The warm water laps against my body, and I groan.

"Yeah," he whispers. "Come here."

Tonight it doesn't seem weird at all letting Keaton boss me around. I climb into his lap willingly, straddling his big thighs. "I love the Hamptons," I say as I lean in and kiss him.

He laughs against my mouth, and then I lose myself in his kiss.

———

Two hours later we're seated in Keaton's kitchen. The last few caterers are packing up around us, and Keaton and I are splitting a platter of food. An actual platter. We're like Vikings at a banquet.

If Vikings ate brisket sliders and crab salad.

The first of what promises to be many more sexual adventures has left us hungry. So I have messy hands and a mouth full of food when a well-dressed woman with Keaton's coloring strides into the kitchen.

"There you are!" she says brightly.

Oh shit. I'm scrambling for a napkin and trying to chew faster. I can feel my face getting red. And it's not just the mess. It's the knowledge of what her son and I were doing only a little while ago...

"Mom," Keaton says, slurping his cup of punch. "This is Luke."

She laughs at both of us. "Don't get up. Would you say this is more like lions feeding or...?"

"Hyenas, maybe," Keaton says. "Lions take turns."

"It's nice to meet you, Mrs. Hayworth," I manage to say after swallowing.

"Same," she says, placing a hand on my shoulder as she passes by me. All the Hayworths are touchers, apparently. "I've heard so much about you!"

My face might be permanently red now. And I don't blush. Ever. Then again, I never met my boyfriend's mom before.

"How many weekends of summer are left?" she asks, turning back to consider us. "Now that Keaton is home, I expect to see you boys out here whenever you can be."

"Oh, um, that's very generous," I stammer.

"Six weekends," Keaton says cheerfully. "I'll make sure Luke has the train schedule when he leaves tomorrow."

"Good deal." She yawns. "This summer has been sad. Nobody in that pool unless we throw a party. What a waste, right? I'll just bump up our grocery order." She gives our messy platter a wry look. "There's pancake mix in the cabinet, Keaton, and bacon in the freezer. Night, boys. I need to get out of these shoes."

Her footsteps click away, down the hall. And I'm left wondering what just happened. Does she not *know*? Nobody is that cool about their son's male hookup.

"You should see your face right now." Keaton shovels a giant heap of guacamole into his mouth and smiles at me.

"But..." I don't even know where to start.

"Four things make her happy," he says, ticking them off on his fingers. "My dad, me, spending money in fashionable places, and feeding people. Bonus points if Dad and I aren't fighting and if we put our dishes in the dishwasher."

I eye the platter, hoping it fits in the dishwasher. I'll make it work.

"So you know you have to get on that train every Friday and come out here to stay."

"Um…" I swallow. "Okay. If you're sure."

"Oh, I'm sure." He drops his voice. "My parents go to parties one or two nights each weekend. All over the Hamptons. For *hours*."

"Is that right?"

He grins. "We are going to have so much fun."

After we clean up from our feast (and the platter is safely in the dishwasher) we get ready for bed in Keaton's private bathroom. His parents have their own wing, thank God.

"I'm dating the boss's son," I joke as we climb into his king-sized bed. "Do you think that will be bad for my career in pharmaceuticals?"

Keaton makes an irritable noise and pulls me closer. "I'm dating the frat president. Think that will get me a better lottery number in the room draw?"

"Hey now. I can't play favorites."

"I know that, you stickler." He laughs. "There's something I have to tell you about the room draw, anyway. We're down a resident."

"What? Who?"

He clears his throat. "I got a text from Judd yesterday. He asked why I hadn't invited him to the beach barbecue this year."

I roll over and look at Keaton. It's dark, but I can still see the outline of his smile. "What did you say?"

"I told him it was because I'd invited you, and I didn't think he'd want to come. But I also said, 'Feel free to convince me I'm wrong. We could all hit some gay bars after the barbecue.'"

A bark of laughter escapes my throat. "You didn't."

"I did. Not that I even know where to find the gay bars. But he doesn't get to push me around. I just wanted to make that clear."

"What did he reply?"

"He didn't answer my text at all. And then a half hour later he sent an email to Munsen."

"Our new secretary."

"Yup. And I was CC'd. Judd said to skip him in the housing draw, because he was going to rent an apartment off-campus. He added that he didn't like the vibe of the house anymore."

I make a grumpy noise. "And he made sure you saw this, just to be a dick and make you feel bad."

"Yup!"

"Did it work?" I ask.

Slowly, Keaton shakes his head. "Good riddance. And since he's the worst of the lot, I'm kind of relieved. I don't have to listen to his snarky bullshit in the fall when we go back to school together, and we don't bother hiding our relationship."

I wait for that little flare of panic to hit me, but it doesn't come. "Well, okay then." I put my head down on the pillow. You can hear the ocean from Keaton's bed. How cool is that? "You still can't have a plum number in the room draw." I smile in the dark.

"Don't want one. I was thinking of taking your old room."

"Why?" I yelp. "Nobody wants that room."

"Well, if you took my old one, we could share a floor again."

"Oh," I say slowly. That is a nice idea. Except for one thing. "You keep the bigger one. I don't mind. I already know where all my stuff fits in there. We'll sleep in your room, anyway."

Keaton moves, covering me with his body. "You know I don't care about room sizes, right?"

"Yeah. I got that."

"This year is going to be great either way."

"Sure is," I whisper.

Another wave crashes onto the beach as I tug him closer for a kiss.

———

EPILOGUE

KEATON

"She's cute…" Licking his bottom lip, Luke nods toward the other side of the crowded room. Tonight, Alpha Delta is wall-to-wall bodies, more than a hundred people crammed together as loud music pumps through the frat house. "What do you think?"

The sensual note in his voice makes me narrow my eyes. Is he suggesting what I think he's suggesting? Because in the almost-year we've been together, he hasn't once hinted there was anything missing in the bedroom. Hell, I watched him delete the *Kink* app from his phone.

And now he's telling me he wants to invite some random chick into our bed? Is this what he's been trying to pull me away to discuss for the last hour?

My confusion dies when I lay eyes on the gorgeous blonde at whom Luke is grinning. It's Annika.

"Oh fuck off," I grumble at him, but we're both laughing. My ex-girlfriend catches us staring, and responds with an enthusiastic wave. Then she turns back to the tall, Polo-shirt-wearing guy she's been flirting with all night.

"What?" Luke says innocently. "She's got a great ass."

I roll my eyes. "Not happening."

He brings his mouth close to my ear. A hot shiver rolls up my spine. "Don't worry, the only ass I'll be pounding tonight is yours, Hayworth."

Oh hell yes. Arousal builds in my groin, and my dick goes semi hard.

Bailey clearly knows what his sinful promise has done to my nether region, because he winks and says, "Down, boy. First we've got to talk."

"About this party?" I can't see what there is to talk about.

"Well, sure. We have to smile and nod and pretend Anthony's dance-off isn't the lamest goddamn thing I've ever seen."

I swallow a laugh. I mean, he's not wrong. Anthony Triboli, one of the two Alpha Delt presidential candidates, planned a run-of-the-mill house party. No decorations, no theme, just some kegs and Doritos.

But I guess they can't all be backyard beaches and strippers.

"Nobody will ever top our dance-offs," I whisper in Luke's ear. Then I bite his ear lobe, just because it's right there.

I can't hear his answering groan over the thumping bass line, but I feel it shudder through his muscular body. I'm tempted to slide a hand down his sinewy back and squeeze his ass, but I refrain. You'd think after a year of dating, we'd be past the honeymoon stage, that frantic period where all you want to do is tear each other's clothes off. But we're not.

Not that I'm complaining.

"What do you think Gregg has in store for us tomorrow night? Beer Pong? An exciting game of darts?" Luke mocks.

"Hmmm, no, I think he's got something crazy up his sleeve." I nudge my boyfriend's arm. "Look at his face."

We both focus on Gregg Merkowitz, who's standing in the kitchen doorway, sporting a smug expression as he surveys his competitor's handiwork. Yup, Gregg thinks he's got this in the bag. To be honest, I don't care which one of them wins. They're both solid, intelligent guys, and either one will make a good prez. So I'll probably use a coin toss for my vote.

Luke shifts his gaze back to me, a contemplative glimmer in his eyes. "Do you think we'll miss this place next year?" We're both graduating in May, and we'll be moving out of Alpha Delt shortly after that.

"Honestly? I won't miss it," I admit.

Don't get me wrong, I'll miss a lot of the guys, but I'm looking forward to having some real privacy. Luke and I are planning on finding an apartment together. We're hoping to, anyway. It depends on which graduate program I end up in. And Luke will be working for my dad's company.

"I won't miss it either," he agrees. "But I will miss *you* come June."

"Likewise." A couple weeks after graduation, I'm shipping out on another orca expedition with Doc VanBoerk. "Is that what you wanted to talk about? The Big Willy Remix?" That was Luke's name for the expedition, and the silly name stuck. Even the professor's emails have "BWR" in the subject line these days.

"No, c'mere a second, okay? I want to show you something."

I turn to follow him, but Owen stops us. "Caught you!" he says with a smirk. Then he checks the time on his phone. "Yo! Jako! I win. Everybody owes me twenty bucks!"

"For what?" I'm so confused right now. The weak beer must be going to my head.

"You're sneaking off to your love nest with Bailey at ten o'clock. We have a pool."

"We aren't sneaking anywhere," I insist. "Bailey says he needs to show me something."

"Yeah, his dick." Owen cackles.

"Wait, there's a *pool?*" I ask, suddenly grumpy. "Who bet on midnight?" In truth, I would love to sneak upstairs right now. But now I have something to prove, dammit.

"Nobody has midnight," Jako says. "We're not that stupid. When the third floor is rockin,' don't come a knockin.'"

"If you play 'Love Shack' again, I will cut you," I grumble. Luke and I get a fair amount of teasing. I'm only grumpy because it's well deserved.

"Go easy on these guys," Tanner says, coming up to put an arm around both me and Bailey at the same time. "If it weren't for them, I wouldn't have a big announcement to make."

"Wait, what?" I ask. I'm not aware of any big changes in his life. He already got into the law school of his choice. He's moving to California this summer.

"Cassidy is coming with me in the fall. To Stanford." He grins.

"No fucking way!" I shout. "It's that serious?"

"She's the one." He lets out a happy sigh. "My parents are not amused. They keep saying I'm too young to move cross-country with somebody. What they really mean is that they don't want me shacking up with a stripper. But that's too damn bad. Cassidy is the best there is."

"Oh please," I argue. "Until you've told your parents you're gay and heading for academia, you haven't really tested their love."

Luke clears his throat. "This is a fun chat, kids, but I really need to show Keaton something."

"It's still your dick!" Owen says with chuckle. Because you can't take him anywhere.

Luke is unfazed. "He's seen it already. Go have some more Doritos. My guy and I have to talk."

"Talk all you want," Jako says. "I got ten-thirty in the pool."

Shaking his head, Luke tows me into the front hall, where the mail slots are. "Finally. I'm dying. Here." He grabs an envelope out of my own mail slot and thrusts it at me.

"Wait, is it...?" I gape at the return address, which says Columbia University. This is my first choice school. If I get into Columbia's PhD program, we can live in Manhattan together starting in the fall. I weigh the envelope in my hand. "Would you say this is thin or thick?"

"Are you guys feeling each other up?" yells Owen from the

living room. "If you're making out right now, we'll need a ruling about whether that settles the pool."

We both ignore him. We're staring at each other.

"That envelope has a lot of girth, babe," Luke says quietly. "There's more than one sheet of paper in there. Nobody would say *fuck off* on three or more pages. Open it."

But I don't. Not yet. "There's always Rutgers if I don't get into Columbia. It might not be Miami or LA."

"Open it," he urges. Then he smiles at me. "It's going to work out."

"Are you *trying* to jinx me?" I yelp.

Bailey grabs the envelope, puts the corner between his teeth and actually *bites* it. It's playful and ridiculous. Luke is funnier than he used to be, now that he feels more comfortable with his life. I burst out laughing as he shakes the scrap of paper like a dog and then drops it from his teeth.

For one long moment I still don't take the letter from him. But then I grab it and tear off the end, tugging the pages out. It unfolds in my hands.

Welcome to the graduate program in Arts and Sciences...

"YEAH BABY!" Luke yells. "Guess who's apartment hunting on the Upper West Side this spring?"

And I don't know who moves first. But a moment later I've pushed him up against the mail slots, and his hand is rubbing my ass as we kiss.

"Who's got ten fifteen in the pool?" someone yells.

"Ignore 'em," Luke whispers against my mouth.

And I do. Because the person who matters most is right here in my arms.

THE END

BONUS ROUND

ONE YEAR LATER. IN THEIR FAVORITE APP

KEATON

OMG I love grad school.

LUKE

What's not to love? Every morning when I leave the apartment you are still asleep.

Uh oh. Someone's grumpy. Don't worry, I know a cure for this. But it has to wait a few hours until we're both home…

Sounds promising. I'm just in a very long line for coffee, and I took it out on you. I'm sorry. Why do we love grad school? I'm all ears.

I have to write a paper for my repro class.

Repro?

Animal Reproduction.

So you have to write a paper about…animal sex?

YEAH BABY.

OMG. It's like they know you.

Serious question—shouldn't you just teach this class?

IKR? I chose my topic already. Guess it. Just guess.

Lobster sex? You should pick that for old times sake. Our first app chat. The memories!

This topic I picked is even better.

Um... Flat worms? Cats? Ducks? You've described all their penises to me in great detail.

All fun, but no.

Wait! I got it. You're going to write about animal masturbation.

Nope!

Those female spiders that eat the male after sex?

Nope!

I give up. Please dazzle me with even weirder animal shenanigans. You know you want to.

OK get this—I'm writing about homosexual activity in the animal kingdom.

BOOM!

Dude. Really?

Really.

But if the topic is reproduction, then… Um. I don't know how to break this to you…

I cleared it with the prof. He said "the world needs to know more about queer sex in the animal kingdom." Told you I liked grad school.

Wow. Okay. So you're writing about those penguins at the zoo? The ones that reared a chick together?

They might come up. But the animal world is full of same-sex humping. And I'm just the man to study it.

No arguments here. But don't leave me hanging like this. Which animals are getting it on?

Bonobo monkeys, for starters. They use sex to divert conflict. The females especially. Lots of FF and MM and MF… you get the idea. Bonus: I get to use the phrase "scrotal rubbing" in a paper.

I knew you were a good time.

And then you got your ducks. 19% of all mallard pairs are MM. Also vultures. Pigeons.

Birds are flying the rainbow flag. Got it.

It's not just birds. Dolphins are real sluts. They'll bang anything. And bison have been seen to enjoy full anal penetration. Have you made it to the front of the coffee line? I could go on all day.

Baby I expect to hear more about this tonight.

You don't have a work thing tonight, right? Nothing to do?

Oh I've got something to do all right. A hot biologist.

Oh yeahhhh.

Pick out something for dinner and order, okay? And pick out a movie. I'll be home at six to prevent you from watching it. We'll show those bison who's boss.

You dirty talker.

Can't wait.

Top Secret Around the World

Czech

Dutch

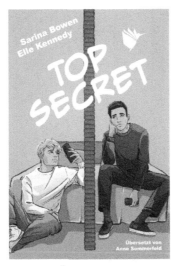

German

Coming soon: French & Taiwanese!

More titles by Sarina Bowen & Elle Kennedy:

Him
Us
Epic
Good Boy
Stay

Thank you for reading our words!

Printed in Great Britain
by Amazon